David Barnett is an author, journalist and comic book writer based in West Yorkshire. He writes in a range of genres for various publishers, works for a wide variety of press outlets including the *Guardian*, *Independent* and BBC, and in comics has written for DC, 2000AD and more.

Also by David Barnett

Withered Hill
Scuttler's Cove

DAVID BARNETT
SCUTTLER'S COVE

CANELO

DK Penguin Random House

First published in the United Kingdom in 2025 by

Canelo, an imprint of
Canelo Digital Publishing Limited,
20 Vauxhall Bridge Road,
London SW1V 2SA
United Kingdom

A Penguin Random House Company
The authorised representative in the EEA is Dorling Kindersley Verlag GmbH.
Arnulfstr. 124, 80636 Munich, Germany

Copyright © David Barnett 2025

The moral right of David Barnett to be identified as the creator of this work has been asserted in accordance with the Copyright, Designs and Patents Act, 1988.
All rights reserved. No part of this publication may be reproduced or transmitted in any form or by any means, electronic or mechanical, including photocopy, recording, or any information storage and retrieval system, without permission in writing from the publisher.
No part of this book may be used or reproduced in any manner for the purpose of training artificial intelligence technologies or systems. In accordance with Article 4(3) of the DSM Directive 2019/790, Canelo expressly reserves this work from the text and data mining exception.

A CIP catalogue record for this book is available from the British Library.

Print ISBN 978 1 80436 753 7
Ebook ISBN 978 1 80436 758 2

This book is a work of fiction. Names, characters, businesses, organizations, places and events are either the product of the author's imagination or are used fictitiously. Any resemblance to actual persons, living or dead, events or locales is entirely coincidental.

Printed and bound in Great Britain by Clays Ltd, Elcograf S.p.A.

Look for more great books at
www.canelo.co | www.dk.com

To Charlie, living by the tides of the sea

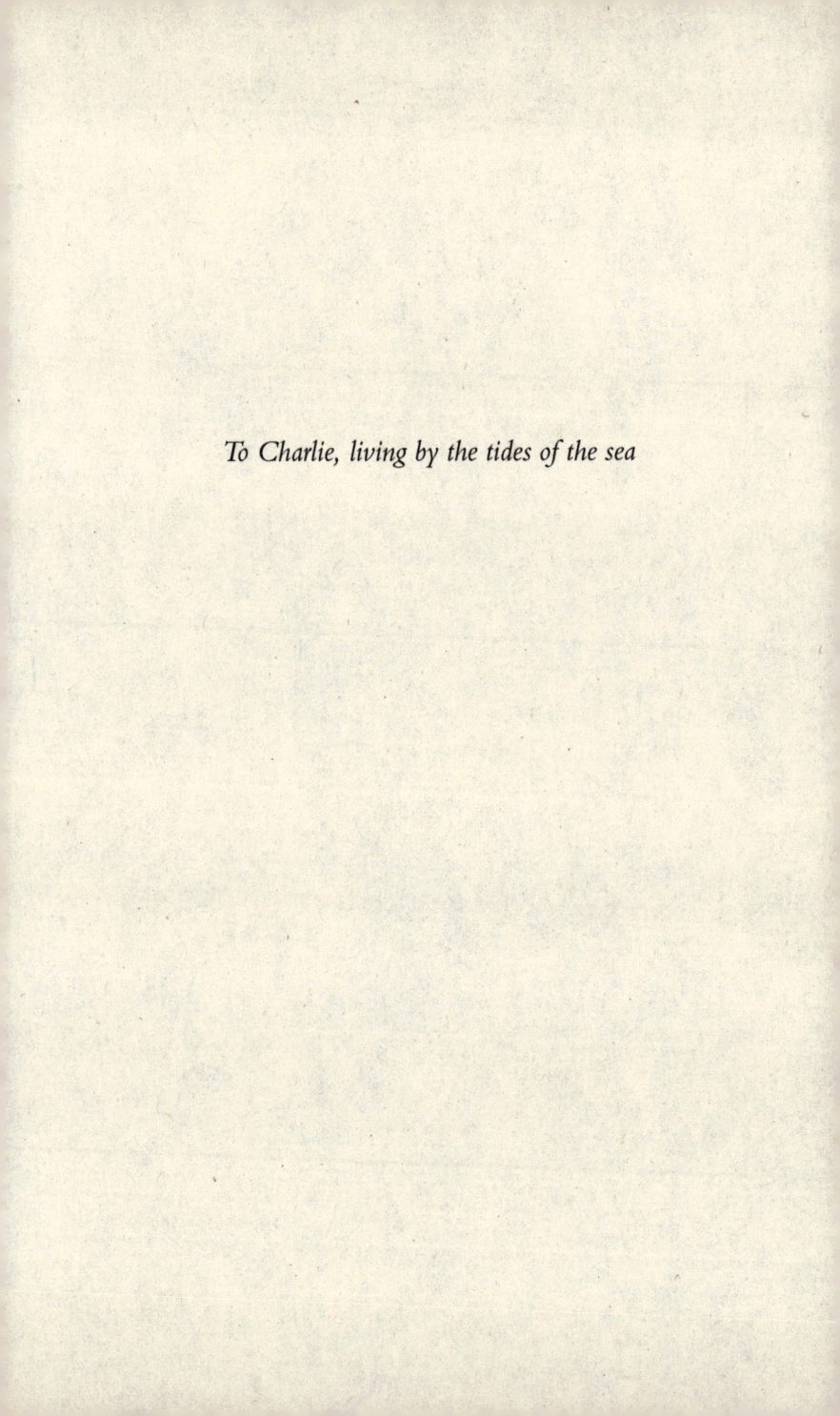

'They are the gods of our wondrous sun-rises and sunsets. The sea; our sea, gives up to us her gods and goddesses ... the gods of our own wild storms; the gods of our bleak moors, of our hills and dales, of our fertile fields; the gods of our bubbling springs, of our babbling brooks and placid rivers; the gods of rowan and the British oak.'

Cornwall: The Land of the Gods, T.F.G. Dexter (1932)

1

MERRIN

Merrin was in the middle of the last blazing row she'd have with Kamal when she got the phone call to say her mother had died. The storm raging inside her blew itself out in an instant, and she just stared at her phone, processing what she'd been told. She was expecting grief to flood in to fill the void left by her anger, but it didn't. She supposed that would come later. What she got was clarity.

'I'm going home,' she said to Kamal when she came out of the tiny kitchen where she'd taken the call.

'What's happened?' he said. There was still an edge to his voice, as though he was just waiting to find out what the call was about before resuming hostilities. Merrin suddenly couldn't even remember what the argument was about.

'Mum's dead.'

'Oh, babes.' He opened his arms to hug her and she shied away.

'I'm going home, Kamal. To Scuttler's Cove.'

'Of course. I'll come with you. Let me call work.'

Merrin was already in the bedroom, pulling her suitcase from under the bed. She began to empty her wardrobe into it, and started to gather up her paints from the easel by the window. Kamal had hung a shirt on the corner, and she tossed it on the floor and picked up the canvas, regarding it critically. Waterloo Bridge in the rain, half finished. Technically very good, but lacking something. Heart. Soul. Passion. She threw it in the corner.

'Babes? Merrin? OK, take a breath. A moment. I'll make tea. You don't need to take all that stuff. The art stuff.'

Merrin looked at him. 'I'm going home.'

'Yeah, of course, I mean—'

'For good.'

Kamal stared at her, running a hand through his black hair. 'You're upset. Of course you are. You're not thinking straight.'

'I am.'

'It was just a silly row. It doesn't mean anything.'

'I'm sick of the rows. I'm going home.'

Anger flashed in Kamal's eyes. 'This is your home! London is your home. You've got a job and friends and…'

He tailed off. Merrin glanced at the discarded canvas. He hadn't said 'and your art'. He thought nothing of her art. Just a place to hang his shirt. She said, 'I hate this flat. And I hate London. I hate my job. And, to be honest, I hate our friends. Because they're your friends, really.'

Kamal glowered at her. 'And you hate me?'

Merrin gave a ragged sigh. 'No, Kamal. I don't hate you. I just don't love you. I'm not sure I ever did.'

She turned back to her suitcase on the bed and emptied her underwear drawer into it. The door to the flat slammed, and she breathed a long sigh. Merrin sat on the case so she could zip it up. Anything else she'd left, Kamal could send on. Or not. She didn't really care. Then she pulled out her phone and booked tickets for the tortuous journey to Cornwall, to Scuttler's Cove, to home.

Merrin had to take a train to Truro, and then get on two buses to take her to the town of Boscanlon, four miles from Scuttler's Cove. At Paddington station she stood amid the moving, shifting mass of humanity and felt suddenly anxious and oddly alone, as though she was already mentally extricating herself from London. She felt suffocated among all the people, assaulted by the air they expelled, the loudness of their voices, their jostling and elbowing and open-mouthed chomping on processed, packaged food. Their faces all blurred and melded into one vast, herd-like mass, and in her yellow T-shirt and blue jeans, her blonde hair tied up with a red neckerchief, Merrin felt like the only splash of life and colour in a sea of the grey and undead. By the time she found her carriage and forced her bulging suitcase into the luggage rack, she was sweating and panting heavily, more from a crawling panic than the exertion. Five hours and she would be in Cornwall. She closed her eyes and forced herself to breathe.

Merrin ordered a coffee and a bacon roll from the buffet car on her phone and watched as the inspector made his way down the carriage, checking tickets and passes. As he approached her the train shuddered with displaced air as it rushed into a tunnel, and the lights flickered on. The conductor was a broad, hairy man with a jolly red face and he squinted at her phone.

'Single to Truro,' he announced unnecessarily. He had a West Country accent. The carriage rocked in the darkness, the lights above her buzzing. 'Holiday, is it?'

'No,' said Merrin. 'I've just been in London too long.'

'Five minutes is too long in London, if you ask me.' He didn't make to move on. 'Still, we all have our sacrifices to make.'

The train sounded a sonorous note and burst out of the tunnel into the bright daylight. The conductor had already moved past her, calling for tickets and passes. Merrin closed her eyes and put her head back on the seat and thought about her mother, and the tears finally came.

At Truro, Merrin hauled her case off the carriage and wheeled it to the exit. It was already late afternoon, and she had at least two hours of bus travel ahead of her. And then she'd have to get a taxi to Scuttler's Cove. But as she dragged her case on to the concourse, there was a man leaning on a silver car, holding a piece of cardboard, felt-tipped on which was her name.

'Miss Moon?' said the man. He was maybe forty, in an off-the-peg brown suit, sweat beading on his forehead from the fierce sun. 'Robert Pengelly. Of Pengelly, Pengelly and Quick. It was me who called you. About your mother.' He held out his hand, thought about it, wiped it on his trousers, and held it out again. 'My sympathies, and the sympathies of my colleagues.'

Merrin stared at Robert Pengelly, and then at the car. 'You came to pick me up? From Scuttler's Cove? How did you know what train I was on?'

'Not quite from Scuttler's Cove. Our offices are in Boscanlon, not too far away. You said you would be travelling this afternoon when I called,' said Robert. A cloud passed over his round face. 'I hope I haven't acted out of turn…?'

'Not at all,' said Merrin. 'Sorry. It's been a weird day. Thank you. I'm very grateful. I'm not sure I could have faced two buses in this heat.'

Robert heaved Merrin's case into the boot of the car. 'Yes, beautiful weather we're having. And so early in the season. I suppose it's global warming. Well, between you and me, I'm all for it.' He opened the passenger door and ushered Merrin in. 'What is it you do in London, out of interest?'

'I work for a company that advises other companies on how to deal with climate change legislation,' said Merrin.

Robert let himself into the driver's seat and turned on the engine, and Merrin felt the cold aircon washing over her. 'Oh. I'm sorry. Spoke out of turn again. It was just a joke, really. I hope I haven't offended.'

'Not in the slightest,' said Merrin as Robert pulled away from Truro station. 'It's deathly dull. In fact, I emailed them on the train to say I'm not going back, and that I'll take my holidays as my notice period.'

'Gosh,' said Robert, following the signs for the A30. 'How brave. What do you plan to do instead?'

Merrin stared out of the window, hoping to catch a glimpse of the sea. She twisted the silver ring on her little finger on her left hand, the soft skin beneath itching. 'Well, I thought that I'd move back into the old place. At least for a bit.'

'Ah,' said Robert. 'About that…'

—

'Explain this to me again,' said Merrin. They had left the A30 and Robert was negotiating country lanes often only as wide as his car, hedgerows teeming with berries and flies and birds rearing up on either side of them, blocking out the westward-sinking sun.

'A year ago, Mrs Moon, your mother entered into an equity release contract. My office handled the paperwork. She was given a sum of money with the agreement that the property would fall to the ownership of the company upon her death.'

'But why?' said Merrin for the umpteenth time. 'What did she need money for?'

'As I said, it wasn't our place to ask that.'

'She's been scammed,' said Merrin angrily. 'You hear about it all the time. People preying on old ladies, ripping them off.'

'Mrs Moon was quite of sound mind,' said Robert quietly. 'We have been your family solicitors for some time. We would not have let harm befall her.'

'How much did she get for it?'

'Considerably less than market value,' conceded Robert, the car scraping tight against a hedgerow as he pulled in to let a camper van squeeze past. 'That's how these companies work, I'm afraid. But it's all above board. Property in Scuttler's Cove is very sought-after at the moment. Lot of second-homers.'

'And the money has all gone? And you don't know what she spent it on?'

Robert hesitated. Merrin glared at him. He said, 'No, it's not all gone. There's perhaps half of it left. Mrs Moon made several large cash withdrawals from her bank over the course of the last year.' Robert looked at her. 'We did perform due diligence, Miss Moon, as did the bank. Your mother assured everyone she was not being pressured or coerced into handing over the money to anyone. She told us, in no uncertain terms, that it was her business and she would thank us to keep our noses out.'

Suddenly the car crested a small hill and the vista opened up, the glittering Atlantic stretching out to infinity. It was a sight that never failed to take Merrin's breath away. Robert paused the car, the sun sinking ahead of them, over the cluster of cottages and buildings nestled between two grass-topped cliffs. The houses fronted a harbour, stone jetties protruding into the water, boats bobbing on the tide. To the right was a wide expanse of sandy beach, a bulwark between the sea and the village.

On the left cliff was something that Merrin hadn't seen before. A small clutch of detached houses, the sun bouncing off the solar panels on their roofs. There were two bulldozers and piles of building materials, the landscaping of the evidently exclusive development still underway on the lower field that sloped down towards the sea.

'Isn't that old Penrose's land?' she said.

'New development,' said Robert. 'Like I said, the village is a very sought-after location these days.' He hesitated and said, 'How long have you been away?'

Merrin had left for university thirteen years ago, and after her degree Cornwall had seemed too small, too restricting. She'd been in London for ten years since finishing university. 'Forever, it feels like.'

'I think you'll find it a very different place to the one you left.' Robert gunned the engine and began to descend on the road that wound through the fields to the village.

To Scuttler's Cove.

Merrin's home.

Or at least, it had been.

2

JEN

Jen felt like a fraud. She didn't belong here. She cast a stricken glance across the bar towards Justin, but he was deep in conversation. With Paul, or Tim. She wasn't quite sure which it was. You'll get to know them all, Justin had assured her as they climbed out of the cab outside the swish Mayfair venue where he had arranged for her to meet all his friends. *But do I want to?* she'd thought as she was introduced to them all one by one. They were rich and London and just not the same as her at all. Still, this was her life now.

'Jen,' said a woman warmly, inserting herself in her eyeline. Jen remembered the name of this one. Tabitha. *Call me Tabby, everyone does!* She was maybe thirty-five, a couple of years older than Jen, but also a world away from her. A universe away. She wore the kind of clothes that if you had to ask the price of, you couldn't afford. Her skin was smooth and her cheekbones and lips plumped with filler. Her hair was layered and blonde and perfect. She was perfect. They all were. Jen wondered what her dad would say about them back in Bradford. *By 'eck, our Jennifer, tha's moving in some swish circles now, girl*. But she hadn't seen him since he left her and her mother when

Jen was ten, so she wasn't quite sure why she cared at all what he might think.

'Tabby,' said Jen, plastering a smile on her face.

Tabby took her arm and steered her towards a table, waving to someone Jen couldn't see. By the time they sat down, a waiter appeared with two glasses of champagne on a silver tray. These were not the sort of people who queued at the bar waving their debit card. They held up a hand and got what they wanted.

'So,' said Tabby, her hand on Jen's knee, 'I must say, we were all rather surprised when Justin broke the news to us. We never thought anyone would make an honest man of him.'

'Why not?'

Tabby laughed. 'Last of the famous international playboys. That was a song, wasn't it?'

That wasn't the Justin that Jen knew. Or at least, thought she knew. She'd met him a year ago, when the finance company she was temping for was dealing with some investments for him. He'd had a meeting with one of the partners and as he walked through the main office he'd stopped, and just stared at her. He was young and good-looking and Jen had reddened and got on with her work. He left and she forgot about him, save for a pleasant, tingly sensation at the memory of how he'd gaped at her. Like he'd just set eyes on the most beautiful woman he'd ever seen in his life. It made her smile inwardly. But whoever he was, she was unlikely to cross paths with him again. Or so she thought.

When she took her lunch break, he was waiting for her outside the office. 'I never do this,' he said, stammering and looking at his feet. It was quite endearing. 'But... can I treat you to lunch?'

His name was Justin Luther, and he ran his own company that invested in funds and businesses all over the world, and reaped the returns. He had a townhouse in Crouch End with a Tesla parked outside. He had brown hair flecked with grey at the temples and a strong jawline. He liked the same books, movies and music as Jen, as they discovered over lunch. Which was a McDonald's in Hyde Park.

'I mean, we could have gone somewhere more posh,' he said, sprawled on the grass on the banks of the Serpentine. 'But, you know... I'm a slave to a Big Mac. Always have been.'

Over the course of the next ten months Justin courted her, which was the only way she could describe it. Flowers, gifts – thoughtful but never too much – dinners, the theatre, gigs, the cinema... Jen was in love with him long before he said, one late spring morning as they lay in his soft white sheets, the sun streaming through his tall sash windows, that he thought Miss Jennifer Forster should perhaps become Mrs Luther.

She'd stared at him. 'Are you serious?'

Justin had chewed thoughtfully on his buttered crumpet. 'Yes. Do you want a big do?'

Jen had always thought that she probably did want a big wedding. But now, the reality of it barrelling down on her, she wasn't too sure. Her dad was gone and her mum was in a nursing home and could barely remember Jen's name on her monthly visits. She had no brothers or sisters and not even any friends to speak of. She'd left Bradford five years earlier after a disastrous relationship ended and she'd run away to London, where she found it almost impossible to make friends.

'No,' she decided. 'I don't want a big do. How about you?'

Justin's mother was dead and he didn't really speak to his father, some big family row going back years which he never really wanted to talk much about. He had no siblings either, but she was sure he must have friends, even if she'd never met them. 'No, I don't,' he said. 'Fuck it. Let's get married.'

Jen had laughed delightedly. 'What? Where? When?'

'Anywhere that will have us!' Justin had kissed her with his buttery lips. 'And as soon as possible!'

'But what about all your friends? Won't they be upset at missing your wedding?'

'We'll tell the gang afterwards,' said Justin, laying a trail of kisses down her neck. 'I just want this for you and me.'

That had been a month ago. One week ago, they'd been married, in a tiny little chapel tucked away in a corner of London that Jen had never even heard of, let alone been to. There were just the two of them, the minister, and two witnesses practically dragged off the street. Then it was time to meet *the gang*.

'I'm not sure I'll ever get to know you all properly,' confided Jen, two glasses of champagne later, to Tabby.

Tabby shrieked in mock affront. 'Of course you will! We're all lovely and we already adore you to bits, Jen.' She took her arm and started to point at people around the bar. 'Take notice, because there will be a test later. That's Paul, the devastatingly handsome chap with the red hair, who also happens to be my husband, talking to Justin and Timothy, the curly-haired tall guy, who is married to

Maggie. She's the brunette in the black Versace, which if I was buying with her arse, I'd have bought a size up. Then there's Simon, who is bearded, overweight, gay and is always parading a procession of the most beautiful young men on his arm, and we have Adaku, who looks like a supermodel and sometimes acts like one. And she is with the perpetually harassed-looking Arthur'—Tabby dropped her voice to a whisper—'who is far too old for her and somehow makes even the most expensive bespoke three-piece suit look like a bin bag on a tramp. She could do much better. I mean, look at her. She's like a goddess. Still, we're all firm friends, so anything rather tart I may have said is best kept between us.'

Jen mentally checked off the names in her head, committing their faces to memory, unable to avoid liking Tabby immensely. Tabby waved for more drinks. 'Anyway, why hasn't that cheap bastard whisked you off for a glorious honeymoon somewhere?'

'We're going in a couple of weeks,' said Jen. 'Justin's got a big contract that needs his attention, and he says he's got a surprise for me this weekend.'

'And I know what that is,' said Tabby in a sing-song voice. 'But I've said too much. The bubbles are here! Now, tell me all about Yorkshire, and growing up there. Did you have electricity?'

—

'Was it dreadful? Were they awful?' said Justin as they got into their Uber.

'No, they were lovely. All of them. Genuinely,' said Jen, and meant it. They had all made her feel welcome, and any awkwardness she felt about her accent and her working-class background she was sure came from her own anxieties, not their treatment of her.

'Good,' said Justin. 'We've an early start tomorrow, so we should turn in.'

'My surprise?' said Jen, draping her arms around him.

'Exactly.'

'Kiss me, Mr Luther.'

'With pleasure, Mrs Luther.'

—

'What, exactly, am I looking at?' Jen was standing on a mud track on top of a cliff overlooking the sea. The sun was beating down with a warm breeze blowing off the ocean. It had taken six hours to drive from London to Cornwall. Jen had never been before. Justin had barrelled along the A30 before turning off on a labyrinth of narrow, hedgerow-lined lanes to here.

Justin pointed at one of five large, detached houses rendered in grey slate. 'That. It's ours.'

Jen stared at him. 'We're moving to Cornwall?'

He laughed. 'Of course not. We're just going to spend summers here. We always spend summers somewhere, usually.'

'We?'

'The gang.' He pointed at each of the houses in turn. 'That's Tabby and Paul's, that's Adaku and Arthur's, Tim and Maggie have that one, and Simon has nabbed the corner plot.'

'You always spend summers together? You didn't last year.'

'That's because I was slavishly obsessed with you.' Justin kissed her. 'Year before that, Provence. Year before, Capri. Always somewhere nice and warm.'

'And this year... Cornwall?'

Justin shrugged. 'Things can be... volatile abroad. The climate. The refugees. The political situation. We all got together and thought, well, summers are hotter and longer in England these days, why not invest in something more permanent?'

Jen swivelled to face a small wooded area at the far side of the plot, and a much smaller, more modest house set away from the others. 'Who is living in that?'

Justin's face darkened. 'Affordable housing. Part of the planning regulations now. We insisted it be built as far as possible from ours. Hopefully whoever it is shouldn't bother us.'

Jen glanced at him sidelong. Justin knew she'd been brought up in a working-class terrace. He said, 'We bought them off-plan two years ago. The houses are finished, more or less, just a bit of landscaping to do. Should all be ready by summer.'

'What's that place?' said Jen, pointing down to the village at the foot of the cliff.

'Scuttler's Cove. Lots of summer homes down there. Old fisherman's cottages, snapped up by people like us. I know a few people who'll be down here for summer. Be like a home from home!'

Jen turned back to the house. Their house. Justin was saying, 'Nice pub down there, couple of shops. We've all been trying to get places in the village but never had enough come on the market at once. Then this place came up. Farmer decided to develop it.' He pointed to a lone tree that stood apart from the woods. 'This place is called *Nans-Avallen*. It means the Vale of the Apple Tree. That's the apple tree in question. Very ancient, apparently.

Hundreds of years old.' Justin paused, biting his lip and looking at her. 'Don't you like it?'

Jen broke out into a smile. 'Oh, Justin, I absolutely love it. Can we look inside?'

He pulled a set of keys from his pocket and jangled them at her. 'Of course. That's why we're here. We need to measure up, decide what furnishings we want in there, and then go shopping.'

She threw her arms around his neck and kissed him all over his face. 'I love it!' she said again. 'This is amazing!'

Jen grabbed the keys from his hand and, laughing, ran towards their new home, her mind bursting with the possibilities of spending summer in such a beautiful place.

Three hours later, Justin would be dead.

3

MERRIN

The equity release company had given Merrin two weeks' grace to empty her mother's house before they took possession of it. They had already sold it, for twice what they paid, to someone from London. On her first day back in Scuttler's Cove, Merrin just sat in the cottage on the harbour, staring at the folded *The People's Friend* magazine on the arm of her mother's chair, at the half-drunk cup of tea on the coffee table. Lizzie Moon had just got up and was preparing her breakfast when she apparently collapsed with a massive stroke that had killed her instantly. There were still two slices of burnt bread sitting in the toaster. An elderly, soft-spoken gentleman in a black suit had visited and informed Merrin that her mother was in the undertaker's premises at the back of the village, and she could be prepared for viewing if Merrin so wished. Merrin did not so wish. He asked if she would like him to make all the necessary arrangements for the funeral. Merrin said yes, please. In the fridge there was some food that was still in date, so Merrin made a tea of chicken breast and broccoli and potatoes. While she ate it, she reflected that in London her evening meals with Kamal had always been called *dinner*. A few hours back home and she was having *tea* again.

She went up to her mother's room, the bed unmade. Merrin's old bedroom had become a storeroom, piled high with boxes of trinkets and clothes. Her bed had long since been removed, but there was still a Death Cab for Cutie poster on the wall. Merrin opened a couple of boxes; her teenage life was neatly packed up inside – CDs and DVDs and shoes and old make-up. In one box she found a little drawstring bag full of rings. Cheap, nothing valuable, but growing in size. She'd worn one since she was little, on the little finger of her left hand, the rings discarded as she grew out of them. Mum had kept them all. Merrin twisted the ring she was wearing now, a pretty silver band with a Celtic design she'd picked up at some market. *Always has to be silver*, a voice said from somewhere, from nowhere. The skin beneath was itching again. She slid the ring off over her knuckle and inspected the intricate tangle of ink that circled the bottom of her finger. It had faded over the years, sometimes was barely visible, stretched and thinned. Now it seemed vibrant, deeper. She scratched the skin until it was red, and slid the ring back on.

Merrin was dog-tired but couldn't face sleeping in her mother's bed, so found a crocheted throw and settled down on the sofa, watching her mother's TV until she fell asleep.

Merrin dreamed. She was on the train again, the carriage rocking through the dark tunnel, the electric lights buzzing and flickering. The conductor was asking for her ticket again, but he was grotesque and animalistic, more pig than man, hunched over her, long tusks protruding from his lower jaw, rasping and spitting on her as he said, 'We all have our sacrifices to make! We all have our sacrifices to make!' over and over and over. Dream

Merrin put her hands over her ears and closed her eyes tight and begged him to stop, and when she opened them again she was in a forest, or a wood. It was night and the moon was shining down, lighting her way as she stepped barefoot through the trees. Then she came to a clearing, in which a lone apple tree stood. There was someone tied to it, draped in a black, hooded cloak, arms outstretched and wrists bound with rope, as though crucified on the ancient trunk. Merrin looked down and realised she was naked, and in her hand she held a long knife with a black, slate blade. Slowly, Merrin walked through the moonlit field to the figure tied to the tree. A woman. Whimpering and begging for mercy. Merrin reached up and grabbed the hood, pulling it back and—

She woke sharply, a crick in her neck from where she'd been lying awkwardly on the sofa. Merrin grasped for her phone; it was a little after three in the morning. She groaned and rearranged the cushions, and lay back. She was already regretting her decision to leave London, to resign from her job, especially now with no house to move into permanently. But she couldn't go back with her tail between her legs. Word would get to Kamal, and he wouldn't be able to resist tracking her down purely to gloat. For better or for worse, she was here now.

Sleep eluding her, Merrin got up and made a coffee. She opened her case and dug out her paints, then went up to her old room. There were some old canvases from her A-level art studies stacked in one of the boxes, awful, twee stuff, views of the sea from her bedroom window, or up on the cliffs. Good enough to get her a top grade and to art college, but nothing worth keeping. Merrin propped one up on her knee and washed over it with white paint, not waiting for it to dry properly before she started layering on the oils, picking out the shape of her mother's chair, the magazine on the arm, the long-cold cup of tea. Then she began to fill in the shape of her mother, or how she remembered her, sitting in the chair. She painted for an hour, putting down layer after layer of oil on oil, the wetness of the paint running and merging until, by the time the sun started to creep in through the kitchen window, Merrin had assembled a muddy, ghostly image of her mother, staring out at her from the canvas.

'Why did you sell the house?' murmured Merrin. 'What did you do with the money?'

But Lizzie Moon kept her own counsel, the colours spreading and running into each other, only the eyes bright and distinct in the hasty portrait.

—

'What the fuck?'

Merrin stood in the harbour street, outside her mother's house, hands on her hips. Scrawled across the door and the stone wall beneath the window was graffiti in angry red paint. It hadn't been there when she went in, that was for sure. Someone had done it overnight.

ANSERGHEK KERNOW said the graffiti, the letters running with still-wet paint.

'Independent Cornwall,' said a voice behind her.

Merrin whirled around to find a man about her age, tanned and weathered, his hair over his collar. He wore a ragged blue shirt, open to his chest, and jeans shoved into boots. She said, 'I know what it means. Did you do this?'

He laughed. 'Not me. Sorry. But this sort of thing happens to a lot of emmets round here. An emmet is—'

'I know what that means, too,' snapped Merrin. 'I'm not an emmet. I'm not a tourist or a second-homer. I was born here. In Scuttler's Cove.' Her eyes narrowed. 'Wait. Taran Tregarth?'

The man's blue eyes widened for a moment. 'Merrin Moon?'

She had been at school with Taran. When she'd gone off to do her A-levels at Boscanlon Community College, he'd joined the family fishing business. He hadn't looked like *that* when she left Scuttler's Cove, for what she thought was for good, when she was eighteen. He'd been a skinny, awkward, bookish teenager who no one thought would have the stamina nor the guts for the fishing life. Evidently, he had.

'I was sorry to hear about your mum,' said Taran. 'She was well thought of in the village.' He appraised her, looking her up and down. 'You went off to London. You talk like a Londoner now. That's why I didn't recognise you.'

'You're fishing, then?' said Merrin.

Taran nodded. 'My dad died ten years ago. I fish on my own, now.'

'Must be tough. I heard the industry's in a bad way.'

He shrugged. 'It was for a long time, but since all these incomers moved in, and the Star and Anchor started doing fancy meals at London prices, I've got a nice little niche. Fishing's always been good off Scuttler's Cove, and I deliver to a few restaurants in Boscanlon as well.' He looked out to the sea. 'Can't complain. Though I should be getting out there.'

Merrin looked back at the graffiti on her wall. Taran said, 'I'll make sure that doesn't happen to you again.'

Merrin glanced at him. 'I thought you said you didn't do it.'

'I didn't.' Taran laughed. 'But I might know someone who did. They'll leave you be now they know you're one of us.'

One of us. Merrin didn't quite know how to feel about that. She was, of course – she'd been born in Scuttler's Cove. But she'd been away for so long. It seemed an alien place to her now. She said, 'To be fair, it doesn't really matter. The house is sold. Not my decision, but it is what it is. I'll let the new owners worry about it.'

Taran nodded. 'So you're not staying, then?'

Did he sound a little disappointed? Merrin said, 'Well, I was planning to, but the situation with the house… What's it like for renting around here?'

Taran laughed. 'Great, if you've got a spare two grand a week for a one-bedroom cottage in high season. Not so great if you're a local wanting somewhere to live.'

'Two grand a week?' said Merrin, silently cursing her mother for selling the house to those equity release cowboys.

'That's for the houses that are owned by letting companies. See these here? The three to the left of your mum's and the four on the right? All second homes. Empty for ten months of the year. Then full of emmets in July and August who think they own the entire village as well as their houses.' He spat on the cobbles. 'Fucking disgrace. My mate – well, you'll remember him, Terry Williams, he was at school with us – had to move to bloody Exeter. Couldn't get a job and couldn't get a house anywhere near here. Can't even rent somewhere, let alone buy.' Taran shook his head, his sun-streaked hair falling over his collar. 'With the prices these houses are fetching, there'll be nobody left in Scuttler's Cove in a generation, apart from emmets.'

The word was a corruption of an old Cornish dialect word for ants. Coined to describe the swarms of tourists that descended on the coastal towns and villages in summer, all burnished red by the sun. These days it covered the growing tide of second-homers, too. That and worse words, thought Merrin.

She said, 'So, I'm stuffed. For somewhere to live.'

Taran rubbed his chin. 'If you're serious about staying, let me make a few enquiries. There might be something, actually. Old Penrose has a thing on the go. I can have a word with him, if you like?'

Did she want that? Shouldn't she just take whatever money her mother had left and give this all up as a bad job? 'Yes,' Merrin found herself saying. 'That would be lovely.'

Taran peered out to sea again. 'Right. I'll be off. You still doing the art, by the way? You were always good at that, weren't you? Is that what you do in London?'

Merrin thought of the canvas of Waterloo Bridge she'd flung in the corner of the old flat. 'Not really. But I might start again. Here.'

'You should. You were brilliant. Right, I'll go see old Penrose later.'

Merrin stood there for a long time, watching Taran walk along the harbour and onto the jetty. Then she blinked as a huge Range Rover squealed to a halt outside the house two doors down from her mother's. She watched as two blond boys tumbled out of the back, followed by a woman in a sundress and designer shades from the passenger door, and a man in a crumpled linen suit from the driver's side.

'All I'm saying, Guy, is that we could be in Sorrento in two and a half hours. It's taken us seven to drive here,' said the woman, her Waitrose tones cutting through the silent morning.

'It's hardly my fault some bloody idiot jack-knifed his caravan, Tessa,' the man said with a sigh. He squinted at the two boys who were fighting on the edge of the harbour. 'Oliver! Archie! For god's sakes can you come here and calm down?' He turned back to his wife. 'Besides, you wanted to buy this place.'

The woman spied Merrin, then saw the graffiti scrawled across the wall. 'Oh. My. God,' she said, walking over on her cork wedges. 'Is that your house?'

Merrin nodded. 'It was done last night.'

Hearing the London accent, the woman pulled down her sunglasses to look at Merrin properly. 'Utter savages, aren't they? What does it say? Something foul, no doubt.'

'Independent Cornwall,' said Merrin.

The man, Guy, joined his wife. 'Bloody idiots,' he said. 'Independent Cornwall. What would they do? Hardly going to get a decent GDP from pasties and the tin mines.' He laughed, then whirled around again. 'Archie! Oliver! For god's sakes!'

'You're new here?' said the woman. Not waiting for Merrin to answer, she said, 'There was an old woman in that place last time we came. Nice to see that it's gone to someone decent. There's a pub over there, the Star and Anchor. You must try the grilled turbot. The landlord's called Clemmo, if you can believe that. Local type, but very accommodating. Tell him that Tessa and Guy sent you.' As Guy ran to break up a fight between the boys, Tessa lowered her voice. 'The fish are caught locally, by a very swoonsome *Poldark* type. Quite rough and ready, if you like that sort of thing. Which I do. But don't tell hubby. Ha ha. Right, we'd better get in and air the place out. Ciao.'

Merrin looked out to sea for a while, watching Taran's boat ploughing out to the deep waters. Then she took a deep breath, steeled herself, and went back into the cottage.

She had a funeral to plan.

4

JEN

Everyone was staring at her, Jen knew, without lifting her eyes from her hands knotted in her lap. The bride of one week. And now a very rich young widow.

She knew what they were all thinking. She'd be thinking the same thing. The northern, working-class woman who no one had ever met until after she'd married Justin in some practically secret ceremony in a dilapidated East End chapel. Now here she was, dressed in black, feeling tiny and insignificant and yet scrutinised and exposed beneath the vaulted ceilings of the church of St Peter-in-Chains, the statues of the saints gazing down on her, no doubt with the same piercing, judgemental glares of the other mourners, if only her neck brace would allow her to look up and see.

Her left leg was in plaster and her head and right eye were bandaged. Her face was criss-crossed with cuts and scabs, despite Tabby's best efforts with her expensive make-up. Perhaps that was Jen's saving grace. The fact that she had almost died as well. She couldn't have planned that, surely.

The gang had taken over the organising of the funeral, the public notices, the contacting of the mourners, and for that Jen would be forever grateful. Even if she hadn't spent a week in hospital after the crash, she wouldn't have had the first idea where to start with organising a funeral, especially for someone who was so important that his death made the newspapers, and his obituary appeared in the *Financial Times*.

She listened to the procession of people reading from the Bible, or poems, the eulogy delivered by Tabby's husband, Paul. She barely recognised Justin from what people were saying about him. It was as though she had limped into the funeral of a stranger. The Justin lying in the ornate wooden coffin on the altar was their Justin, not hers. Her Justin was warm and tender and sweet and thoughtful and beautiful. Their Justin was a success, a leader, a triumph, a businessman.

Either way, he was still dead.

Justin's Tesla sped along the narrow lanes, Jen practically bouncing up and down in the passenger seat. They'd measured every inch of the new house, Justin indulgently following her around with his tablet, putting in orders for beds and sofas and kitchen equipment and soft furnishings.

'We need a TV,' he'd said as they sized up the house. 'What about this 98-inch screen?'

'We won't be watching TV,' said Jen happily. 'We'll be walking along the cliffs and having picnics on the beach and drinking in the Star and Anchor and surfing and—'

'What about when it rains, though?'

'Then we'll sit in front of the log burner and make love and watch storms rolling in from the sea,' said Jen.

'The 98-inch,' Justin had said firmly, hitting the buy button.

Driving back, Justin pulled the Tesla in to let another car past, the driver giving his vehicle an appreciative glance. Jen said, 'Maybe we could turn that downstairs bedroom into a library? I've always wanted a library.'

'A study,' suggested Justin. 'I'll still need to work when we're here.'

'A good compromise,' agreed Jen. 'A study-stroke-library.'

Justin glanced at her. 'Or maybe a playroom?'

'Why, Mr Luther, whatever do you mean? Some kind of sex-dungeon?'

'No,' said Justin, suddenly serious. 'I mean, a playroom. As in, for children.'

Jen stared at him. They'd never mentioned children, either of them. Not that she hadn't thought about it, not that she hadn't weighed up his genes, wondered which one of them a baby would take after, not that she didn't want children – but the last year had been such a whirlwind that she'd never really given it serious thought.

'You want to?' she said, excitement and anxiety wrestling in her gut.

'Do you?'

She thought about it. 'Yes. I do.'

Justin grinned and put his hand on her knee, then slowed to negotiate a tight bend on the lane.

'Justin!' Jen shrieked as the tractor rounded the bend ahead of them. It all happened so fast. Justin stamped on the brakes but the tractor kept coming and ploughed straight into them. Jen was thrown sideways against the side window and momentarily lost consciousness. When she came to, seconds later, cushioned in airbags, the windscreen was shattered, the tractor looming above them. A long spear of metal protruded from the front of the tractor, straight through the windscreen and, she saw when she turned with a stabbing pain in her neck to groggily ask Justin if he was all right, right through her husband of one week's chest.

She later learned it was called a bale spike. She was also told that the farmer had suffered a heart attack and lost control of the tractor. She had broken her femur and ankle on her left leg, had suffered a deep concussion, had almost lost her eye to a shard of glass, and had almost broken her neck.

Everyone said that it was a miracle she was alive.

But Justin was still dead.

—

Jen stood outside St Peter-in-Chains, in the bright sunshine, leaning on her crutch and nodding at the procession of mourners that filed out of the church, each one pausing to murmur some empty sentiment or platitude. They had all known Justin longer than she had, she realised. Even those with just a passing business relationship with him. She was the outsider, the wife of one week. The flash in the pan, whirlwind romance. The gold-digger. There. She'd thought it. What everyone else was thinking.

A tall man stopped in front of her, dressed in a black suit. He stared down at her, his eyes seemingly blazing. Eyes that she somehow recognised.

'Ah. You're the wife.'

Jen just stared at him, her hand held limply out. He didn't take it. 'I'm Justin's father,' he said.

She blinked. All she knew about Justin's father was that he and his son didn't talk, that they'd had a falling out a long time ago. Over business.

'Mr Luther,' she whispered.

He continued to stare at her, then looked over his shoulder at the church. 'This was your idea? St Peter-in-Chains?'

Jen shook her head dumbly. It had been the gang who had organised everything. But to say that sounded weak and pathetic, like she didn't care. Instead she said, 'It was a beautiful service.'

Justin's father snorted. 'My son was a godless heathen. I presume he told you that's why we were estranged? No? I suppose you're cut from the same cloth, like all those fools he runs around with.'

'I loved him,' said Jen, not knowing what else to say, tears pricking her eyes.

'No doubt he loved you, too,' said Mr Luther mildly. 'Almost as much as he loved money.'

'Justin wasn't like that.' Her words were bold, but her voice was cracked and quiet.

His father sneered. 'Then you didn't know him very well. Perhaps when you're sitting in your fancy house opening his bank statements, you might give pause to where it's all come from, and how much love a man must have for money to beget himself so much more of it.'

Someone coughed. There was a line of mourners behind Mr Luther, keen to get through the business of shaking Jen's hand. He glared at the woman behind him and turned back to Jen. 'A beautiful service, yes. A beautiful church. But a dozen camels will leap like spring lambs through the eyes of a hundred needles before that son of mine ascends to the kingdom of Heaven.'

Then he turned and stalked away from Jen, not looking back.

'Sorry,' whispered Tabby later. They had taken over the entire top floor of a restaurant in Soho for Justin's wake. 'I should have warned you about Papa Luther. I'm surprised that Justin didn't.'

'What a heartless prick,' said Jen, sitting on a sofa with her plastered leg sticking out in front of her. 'To talk that way about his own son.'

'He's certainly old school,' said Tim, bringing over a tray of drinks. 'Fire and brimstone, all that.' He looked around. 'Has anyone seen Maggie? I could do with a bump.'

'Timothy,' said Tabby quietly, 'is the funeral of one of your best friends really the time and place to do cocaine?'

'I'd have thought it was entirely the time and place,' said Tim. 'I'm grieving, Tabby.' He lowered his voice. 'Maggie's got a huge bag of it in her Louis Vuitton, if anyone wants to join me.'

Jen stared at the flute of champagne Tim had put in front of her. 'Who's paying for all this? Who do I owe?' she said, helplessly. Her head was beginning to throb as the strong painkillers she was taking four times a day wore off. She wasn't even sure if she should be drinking.

'Don't worry about all that just now,' said Tabby. 'We'll sort it all out with you later. Now you just have to get well, and get over Justin's death.'

She said it as though Jen just had a cold. 'But what am I meant to do now?' pleaded Jen. 'I'm lost without Justin. I don't know anyone.'

'You know us, don't you?' Jen looked up to see the statuesque Adaku looking down at her, cornrow hair piled high on her head. 'We're your friends, aren't we?'

'Are you?' said Jen in a small voice.

'I should bloody well hope so!' said Simon, his gut straining at his black waistcoat, a brandy in his hand. 'You're one of us, Jen. I could tell from the moment Justin introduced you to us. You're one of the gang, and you'll always be one of the gang.'

Slowly, the gang gathered around her. Paul put his arm around Tabby's waist, and Tim sniffed loudly, wiping his nose. Arthur and Adaku sat down beside her, and Maggie brought her over another glass of champagne. Simon tugged at his beard and Adaku said, 'Uh-oh, I feel a speech coming on.'

'Quite right!' boomed Simon. 'Speeches are for the important occasions in life, weddings and funerals chief among them. We have lost one of our number, a lynchpin of our gang. But the gang endures, because together we are stronger than we are as individuals. Just as it takes a village to raise a child, so it takes a gang to look after each other.'

'Steady on,' muttered Arthur. 'You're drifting into the stormy seas of socialism here.'

'Nonsense!' declared Simon. 'I am simply explaining to Jen that as a fully paid-up, card-carrying member of the gang, she has nothing to worry about at all. We're your friends and your family. We'll be here to pick you up when you fall, and to cheer you on when you fly. Because we know you'll do the same for us, one day. That's how it works. That's how it always works.'

Jen suddenly felt better. Just a tiny bit. The yawning chasm of Justin's loss was still all around her, but for the first time since waking up in hospital she thought she just might have spied a path to help her across it, given time and friendship, which she rather unexpectedly seemed to have.

'I thought I'd just be sitting alone in that house in Crouch End with everyone hating me,' she said, wiping her eye.

'Silly thing,' said Arthur. 'Besides, in a few weeks we're all decamping to Cornwall for the summer.'

Jen blinked. 'All of us? Including me?'

'Especially you,' said Arthur. 'How could you even have thought otherwise? And it's pirate country, Jen. If you've still got that eyepatch you'll fit right in! Aaarrr!'

※

He had a hangover that felt like it was just one more thud in his head away from finishing him off completely. He didn't know how long he'd slept, or why he was so filthy, why it burned every nerve in his poor, aching body to even move. But move he did, out of the shadow of the trees, into the pale sunlight, which warmed him sufficiently that he could move his legs, still with some difficulty, and walk into the grass.

There was something over his face, something cold and clammy, which made it hard to see and trapped his foul breath inside. He clawed at it but his fingers wouldn't work properly, felt worn to stubs, so he gave up and just stood by the old apple tree, staring at it, trying to remember.

He needed a drink. His throat felt like it had been cut. He gasped hoarsely and looked at the houses, a thin line of them. Houses? Had there always been houses? There must have been, he supposed. Houses don't grow overnight. And houses meant people, and people meant food, and drink. He was so hungry, so terribly thirsty. Parched. His throat was sandpaper, his voice rasped gutturally when he tried to speak. Stumbling and stiff, he walked towards the nearest house.

It was empty – more – it was unlived in. It was new. There were still crosses of tape on the bare windows, and when he peered through, pressing his face – what was that covering his head? – against the glass, he could see no signs of habitation. No people. Which meant no water. He took a step back and a cloud passed over the sun, and suddenly he could see his reflection in the window.

Ah, so that's what he had on his head. He gave a chuckle, remembering, but it came out as a dry bubble of stale air. He frowned. Something happened later on, didn't it? Something...

On the breeze he smelled something. Or perhaps heard it. Or felt it, maybe. He didn't know. None of those things. Something borne to him by a sense he didn't recognise. A deep knowledge, inside him. A sudden recognition of...

No, surely not. That was impossible, wasn't it? How could that be? He didn't have a...

The sharp bark of a dog from somewhere behind him caused him to turn away from the window, and his reflection. Far across the field there was a man and his animal, walking towards them. He didn't think he'd been seen, so he stole down the side of the new, empty house, and watched the man walking across the land, the sea glittering behind him, then crept back towards the safety and shadows of the trees.

5

MERRIN

Merrin made a start on clearing the house, beginning with all her old stuff her mum had helpfully already boxed up. She spent longer than she intended sorting through it, absorbing the memories that charged like potential energy each book, CD, T-shirt. She'd forgotten so much about her life in Scuttler's Cove. Brushed it away, let London in instead. The village had become just a picture postcard to her, a vague jumble of images. She hadn't been back, not once, since she left at eighteen for university.

It was only then that she started to wonder why that was.

Merrin closed up the boxes. It could all go. All of it. She had no use for the past, whether here or in London. She tackled the bathroom and the kitchen next, sweeping all the toiletries and perishable foods into black bags for the bins, boxing up the tinned and dried goods to take to a food bank somewhere. Her mother's furniture was old and ratty: the same sofa and bed that had been in the house when Merrin left. She supposed she could break it up and burn it in the garden, depending on what this thing was that Taran had mentioned. Perhaps she could live with it for a little while, if he'd found her a flat or something.

Taran Tregarth. She'd barely recognised him. What had happened to the intense, geeky kid he'd been when she left Scuttler's Cove? It was quite the transformation. She supposed that a decade or more of being out on the sea, fishing, would do that. She vaguely remembered that Taran had held a bit of a candle for her when they were at school. She, of course, hadn't given him the time of day. Now look at him. It was like one of those romance novels where the high-flying small-town woman comes home from the big city for Christmas and hooks up with her now-hunky ex. If only mother had left her a bakery or candle shop or something, instead of nowhere to live and lots of unanswered questions.

'Silly cow,' she muttered. 'You've not come home for that.'

Which begged the question, what had she come home for? She didn't really know, other than that, suddenly and clearly, it was what she wanted to do. No, not even what she wanted to do. What she *had* to do.

She was jolted out of her daydreaming by a sharp rapping at the front door. It was Taran. 'Hope you don't mind me just calling round,' he said, looking at her then looking away. He might have suddenly acquired the body of some seaside Adonis, but that awkward kid still looked out from his blue eyes.

'Not in the slightest, come in,' said Merrin.

'It's just, I've got a van,' said Taran, glancing around the living room. 'In case you wanted to move stuff out. Take to the dump, or whatever.'

'Do you want a tea? Coffee? That said, Mum's only got this awful cheap shit. Tastes like dishwater.' Suddenly, Merrin realised she'd not eaten all day. 'God, I'm famished. And I've thrown all her food away.'

'We could go to the pub, if you like?' said Taran, staring at his boots.

Merrin couldn't help but smile at his discomfort. Like when they were sixteen and he'd asked her if she wanted to go to Boscanlon for a coffee. She suddenly cringed inside as she remembered she'd laughed at him.

She didn't laugh this time. 'That would be lovely. I have it on good authority that the turbot is very good. I hear a whisper as well that the fisherman who caught it isn't bad, either.'

Taran's weather-beaten face burned an even darker shade, and Merrin had to tell him she was only joking. 'Let's go and see what's on the menu,' she said, feeling suddenly awkward herself.

The Star and Anchor was run, as it had been when Merrin left Scuttler's Cove, by Clemmo, a tall, broad, bearded man with a roaring laugh. That was the only thing that was the same. What had once been a shabby boozer's joint had undergone a transformation almost as radical as Taran. It was clean and modern inside, with tables set out for dining and a cocktail menu chalked on the wall. The staff – formerly Clemmo's wife and daughter – were now an efficient squadron of young people wearing striped nautical T-shirts. It had become a gastropub.

Taran went to the gents' as soon as they got in, and Merrin went to the bar and asked for two menus. Clemmo looked exactly the same, but evidently didn't recognise Merrin. She ordered a glass of rosé and wondered what Taran would have. There was a selection of craft ales with colourful names on the pumps, and Merrin ordered him a pint of something with a maritime name.

'Find a table and someone will be over to take your order,' said Clemmo, almost looking through her. Merrin looked over the menu, and her breath caught in her throat at the prices.

Suddenly, Taran appeared at her shoulder. 'Not those menus, Clemmo. The local ones.'

Clemmo blinked at him and looked at Merrin again, frowning. Taran laughed, 'Don't you recognise her? You sold her enough snakebite when she wasn't old enough to drink, back in the day. It's Lizzie Moon's daughter. Merrin.'

Clemmo looked at her with fresh eyes. 'Been a while, young Merrin. I was sorry about your mother. The village won't be the same without her.'

Taran guided Merrin into what used to be the snug, off the main lounge, and still seemed to be. There were a couple of locals drinking in there, and when Merrin looked at the menu she saw pretty much the same dishes but at half the price.

'Can't blame Clemmo for cashing in, with all this money swishing about the place now,' said Taran, sipping his beer. He licked his lips and said, 'Good choice, by the way. What I always drink.'

'Did you have a word with old Penrose?' asked Merrin when they'd ordered, a steak and ale pie for Taran and the grilled turbot for her.

Taran seemed to hesitate for a moment, then said, 'Yes, I did. See that development up on the cliff? That's his land.'

'I remember. Nans-Avallen.' For some reason, the name and faint memory of it made her slightly shudder. 'I bet they're not going cheap.'

'Can't blame him for cashing in,' said Taran. 'Emmets are buying up property in Scuttler's Cove as fast as it comes on the market. Penrose thought, if they'll do that, they'll probably buy new, as well. So he got planning permission, and sold them off-plan, and put them up over the past couple of years.' Taran took another drink. 'Thing is, under planning regulations now, any new housing development has to include affordable housing. Local authority guidelines. Designed to stop local people being forced out. So he's got one smaller property on the site.'

'How affordable is it?'

'It's some kind of rent-to-buy scheme. I don't understand the ins and outs totally myself, but basically you pay rent and half of it goes towards building up a deposit, then after five years or so you have the option to try to get a mortgage and buy the property. Something like that, anyway.'

Merrin still hadn't found out how much of her mum's money was left, but this sounded like it would give her the breathing space she needed, while she worked out what to do. 'And it's available?'

'Well, that's the thing. There's a lot of interest as you can imagine. But I mentioned your name to Penrose, and he had a lot of time for your mother, so…'

'I didn't realise Mum was so well thought of,' said Merrin quietly.

Taran shrugged. 'You've been away a long time. And even before you left, you were…' He tailed off.

'Up myself?' said Merrin, suddenly recalling what Taran had said years ago when she had laughed at his suggestion that they went for a coffee.

He reddened again, and looked into his pint. 'You remember that. I'm sorry.'

'It's me who should apologise,' said Merrin. And then the food arrived and saved them both.

The next morning Merrin got up early, to bag up all the things for the dump before Taran came round with his van. Most of her mum's clothes were too ratty and moth-eaten to even consider taking to the charity shop. And there were still wardrobes and a chest of drawers upstairs to tackle.

With a mug of tea, she started with the drawers. They were locked, and Merrin couldn't find a key anywhere, so in the end she jemmied open the top drawer with a kitchen knife. It was filled to the brim with… well, she wasn't quite sure what. Scraps of paper, notebooks, shells, rocks. She picked up one stone, worn smooth and perfectly circular with a hole in the centre, like a donut. Impulsively she held it up and squinted through the hole with one eye.

Merrin flicked through one of the notebooks, filled with her mum's tight, crabbed handwriting. She couldn't make sense of any of it. It seemed to be names of local people in one column, with nonsensical words in the next. Love. Fertility. Infidelity. Revenge. Money. Her eyes lingered on the last word. Was this something to do with what Lizzie Moon had done with the money she got for selling the house? She put the notebook to one side and picked up a corn dolly, so old and desiccated that it crumbled to dust in her fingers, and a small wooden figure, beautifully carved, of what appeared to be a woman in robes, fish jumping at her skirts. Scattered across the bottom of the drawer were lumps of sea-glass, multicoloured and shining in a shaft of sunlight that lanced through her mum's bedroom window.

The next drawer down was filled almost exclusively with curled scrolls of yellowing paper, each one daubed in thick paint with an almost childlike hand, all the same crude design. Merrin couldn't decide whether the image was meant to be the sun, or an eye, or some combination of the two. It put her in mind of the evil eye popular in countries such as Greece, for warding off evil. It was weirdly familiar, though she couldn't quite place it. Absent-mindedly scratching her little finger, Merrin forced open the final drawer.

All it contained was a manila folder, and inside was a stack of paper receipts, each one handwritten on a square of lined foolscap, with the words *For My Lady Endellion, received with thanks*. And then a pound sign and a figure. *£2,000, £5,000, £2,500, £10,000*. Merrin scrabbled in the top drawer until she found a pencil then, on the back of one of the evil eye drawings, she did some rough calculations. Almost £100,000, which was pretty much the half of what Lizzie Moon had received from the equity company, and which had been drawn out of her bank accounts.

—

'Well?' said Merrin, the folder of receipts open on the kitchen table, surrounded by the things she'd found in the drawers.

Robert Pengelly picked up the donut-shaped stone. 'A hagstone,' he said, putting it to his eye and looking at Merrin. 'You're supposed to be able to see witches through it, or something like that.'

She showed him the little notebook, and the evil eye paintings, and the scattered pieces of coloured sea-glass. 'And what's this horrible thing?' She held up a smooth wax candle shaped like a hand, a wick sprouting from each finger.

'A hand of glory,' said Robert. 'They used to make them from the pickled hand of a hanged man. Very powerful witchcraft.'

Merrin stared at him. 'This stuff doesn't freak you out?'

Robert shrugged. 'You've been away a long time. You've forgotten what places like Scuttler's Cove are like, or at least, used to be like. The old ways still cling on, when the tourists aren't looking. It doesn't mean your mother wasn't in her right mind, if that's what you're thinking.'

That was exactly what Merrin was thinking. If her later years had been coloured by these weird... obsessions, then maybe Lizzie wasn't thinking straight when she signed over the house. Merrin grabbed a handful of the receipts. 'These total up to the money she drew out of the bank. Who's Lady Endellion?'

Robert shrugged. 'I wouldn't know. Certainly not a client of Pengelly, Pengelly and Quick, ha ha.' Seeing the anger on Merrin's face, Robert's voice softened. 'Merrin, please be assured that we took all care and attention we could do with your mother's affairs. We are satisfied that nothing untoward took place. What she did with the money... well, that is her business, ultimately. It's perhaps not an ideal situation from your point of view, but it is what is.' He brightened up and added, 'And, I have better news.'

'Oh?' said Merrin. He was right, really. Whatever her mum had done with her money, it wasn't really Merrin's business.

Robert took some papers from his briefcase. 'We've been over the paperwork on the house up at Nans-Avallen. You qualify for the purchase scheme, being born in Scuttler's Cove. There has been a lot of interest in it locally, as you might expect. But Mr Penrose has indicated to us that you are a favoured bidder for the property. And on top of that, he's willing to reduce the payments by fifty per cent for the first six months.'

'He is?' Merrin frowned. 'Why would he do that?'

'Mr Penrose had a lot of respect for your mother,' said Robert. 'And, on top of that, he is also one of our clients. In fact, we handled the work for the sale of all the houses on Nans-Avallen.' He paused, and put his head on one side, and considered Merrin. 'I was born in Scuttler's Cove, too, you know. I was quite a few years ahead of you at school. You wouldn't remember me.'

Merrin shrugged awkwardly. 'I don't really remember much about growing up here, for some reason, and never felt any desire to come back.'

'Perhaps just as well,' Robert said with a nod. 'I'll leave the paperwork with you to look at, and if you're agreeable and wish to sign I can pick it up later this week, and you can be in the new house very soon.'

'I'll sign now,' said Merrin decisively. As he handed her his fountain pen, she said, 'Why did you say that? About it being just as well that I don't really remember much about living here?'

He smiled again. 'Well, it's hardly exciting, is it? Even at the height of the season. I'm sure London was much more thrilling.' He watched Merrin sign the papers and took them from her, along with his pen. 'Anyway,' he said as he closed his briefcase. 'You're back now. That's what counts.'

6

MERRIN

At ten o'clock sharp on the morning of Lizzie Moon's funeral, a drum started beating a lonesome, plaintive sound. As instructed by Mr Bosanko the undertaker, Merrin stood outside the cottage, now empty of all but the most basic requirements for living. The next day she was due to give it up. Today, though, was all about Lizzie Moon.

Merrin didn't know exactly how many people lived in Scuttler's Cove, but they surely must all have been out on the narrow streets and the harbour. It was a warm morning, the sun high in a cloudless sky. Merrin had found a black dress, last worn at some party in London, now her mourning weeds. She stood at the door, staring straight ahead at the sea. Nobody spoke, the radios and TVs had been silenced, no car gunned its engine. There was only the slap of the sea on the hulls of the boats moored in the harbour, and the sound of the drum, getting closer.

Merrin felt the villagers stir, and glanced to her left. Rounding the corner on the cobbled road was the source of the sound, Mr Bosanko himself, a battered old drum hanging from his neck, him striking it rhythmically, the four men behind him marching to his beat. Taran was one of the four, shouldering the coffin, all men from the village, all dressed in black. As they passed through the streets, the people watching fell in behind, forming a solemn procession. That stopped outside the cottage, Mr Bosanko's drum falling silent.

As instructed, Merrin took her place behind the coffin, and the procession marched on, Mr Bosanko sounding his drum, until the entire population of Scuttler's Cove was silently following, up the winding streets and alleys to where the lichen-spattered stone edifice of St Ia's Church sat on its hill, waiting for them.

The service went by in a blur. Reverend Bligh, a wiry man with squinting eyes and a lined face, spoke about Lizzie Moon and the void she had left in the parish, about her life and her achievements and how the villagers had come to rely upon her wisdom and counsel. It was almost as though he was talking about someone Merrin didn't know. Or rather, about someone she had forgotten. She began to wonder to herself why she had stayed away from Scuttler's Cove for so long, why she had never come back. It was as though she had been becalmed by a London fog that had kept her away, and now she was back, the mists were clearing.

Oh god, she thought to herself. My mum is dead. And as they carried the coffin out to the open grave in the churchyard, amid the headstones smoothed by the salty ocean winds, Merrin almost collapsed, the strength deserting her, tears flowing as though ripped out of her.

It was only later, as she had a drink in the Star and Anchor, among the rest of the mourners, that she realised that not once had Reverend Bligh ever mentioned God.

Merrin stayed in the pub until late, drinking wine and eating the buffet that had been laid out. She had no idea who had organised it, or what the cost was, or who she should pay. People she had forgotten from her past, her childhood and teenage years, queued to pay their respects to her, to welcome her home. Somehow during the afternoon she had acquired a packet of cigarettes. She hadn't smoked for five years, but wanted one now so badly. As the mourners thinned in the pub, she went outside to gulp down the clean, sea air, and light herself a cigarette.

She hadn't seen Taran for an hour or so, and then there he was, marching along the harbour, out of his black suit and back in his jeans and shirt. On his shoulder he balanced something huge wrapped in muslin, stained red at the edges. It looked for all the world like a body.

He hailed her and crossed the cobbles to where she was slumped against the pub wall. 'What's that?' she said.

He hefted the load up on his broad shoulder and opened the corner of the wrapping. It was a butchered pig.

'What are you hoping to catch with that? A Great White Shark?' she said, slurring the words and realising she was a little drunk.

Taran laughed too. 'It's not bait. It's more... an offering.'

Before she could ask what he meant, he told her he'd see her tomorrow, and marched off towards the jetty. She watched him load the dead pig into his boat and then the engine thrummed and he nosed it out to sea. Merrin lit another cigarette and watched Taran's boat dwindling into a dot that disappeared around the headland.

—

It was dark when Merrin decided to walk back along the harbour to the cottage. She felt like she should be...

sadder, perhaps. More grief-stricken. She had just buried her mother, after all. But all she felt was dog-tired, and a yawning abyss of nothingness inside her. Merrin felt that people were judging her for going away for so long, that the situation with the house was probably all that she deserved. *Thought you'd just come back after ignoring your mum for so long and take ownership of a bit of prime real estate? How's that working out for you?*

Of course, nobody had said that to her at all. But as she wandered along the harbour, the sea lapping against the wall, she did wonder just why she'd never been back to Scuttler's Cove after leaving for university. It was beautiful, and the people were lovely. She'd forgotten that. How had she forgotten that? Had she been so wrapped up in herself, so intent on forging a life away, that she'd just... blanked everything out? It was natural for a young person to want to spread their wings, and even paradise paled when you'd grown up there all your life. But surely... *surely*... she should have come home at least once or twice?

What had made her stay away from Scuttler's Cove?

She paused by the harbour wall, looking out at the black sea. Was Taran still out there? She hadn't seen his boat come back into the harbour. Night-fishing, perhaps, restocking the fridges at the Star and Anchor and wherever else he sold his catch.

Quite a catch, she found herself thinking, and smiled. Geeky, gawky Taran Tregarth. There was no denying he had grown into himself. Perhaps she might not have missed that if she'd come home now and again.

Merrin pushed herself off the wall and felt her head swim. She really shouldn't have had so much to drink. But everyone kept pushing glasses into her hands, wanting to mark the respect they had for Lizzie Moon, and that was the only way they could show it. By buying her daughter booze and getting her blind drunk.

Merrin turned and was met with a shower of something in her face, something dry and gritty that half-blinded her and speckled into her mouth. She spat it out and rubbed her eyes and jumped as the face loomed at her.

She recognised the woman, old and weather-beaten and smiling, but didn't know her name. She'd been at the funeral, and still wore a black dress and shawl. Merrin wiped away the – dirt? It was dirt! – from her face and stared at her. The woman had thrown dirt in her face.

'Welcome back, Daughter,' she said, her voice dry, her Cornish accent thick.

'Daughter?' said Merrin.

Then she became aware of more figures in the darkness. A man, a little younger than the old woman, but not by much, took off his trilby and gave a half-bow. 'Welcome back to Scuttler's Cove, Daughter.'

'What are you talking about?' said Merrin. Were they crazy people? Should they have carers with them or something? She backed away and started to walk towards the cottage, then stopped dead.

The little road was lined with people on both sides, local people. Young and old. People she recognised. Mr Bosanko, the undertaker. Janet from the Driftwood Gallery. Librarians and shopkeepers and cooks and newsagents and… and everybody from Scuttler's Cove, it felt like. She scanned the silent, smiling faces but could not see Taran, or anyone she really knew by name rather than by faint, fuzzy memory.

Another shower of dirt hit her in the face. 'Welcome back, Daughter.'

'Mr Bosanko?' said Merrin, but the undertaker was smiling at her, with the same kind of blank fervour as the rest of them. She felt soil raining on her, and her heart began to pound. 'What are you doing? What are you all doing?' she said, her voice trembling.

'Welcome back, Daughter.' One voice at first, then another, then another and another until it rose up in a chorus. 'Welcome back, Daughter.'

Panic overtook Merrin, and she began to run, between the line of people, the words thrown at her, soil thrown at her, and everyone smiling and smiling. Merrin moaned and ran to the door of the cottage, looking fearfully over her shoulder, but nobody followed her. They had just gathered in the road, bunched together, watching her. With trembling hands she managed to get the key in the lock and open the door, and she fell inside, gasping for breath, soil falling from her hair and clothes, and slammed the door shut hard, slumping against it and sliding down to her knees, sobbing.

The next morning when Taran came round, Merrin felt almost foolish recounting how scared she was. 'It was weird though, right? I mean, throwing dirt at me? Calling me daughter?'

'You've been away a long time,' said Taran, sipping the coffee she'd made. 'You've forgotten. Scuttler's Cove was always a weird-ass place. You're looking at it through the eyes of an outsider, still. Don't you remember? All the odd little rituals and ceremonies we grew up with? Last night... it's just what people do when an old resident dies. What the old folks do. God knows why. It'll die out with them, no doubt.'

'There were younger people there,' pressed Merrin.

Taran shrugged. 'Every town has its strange little customs. I wouldn't worry about it too much.' He grinned. 'Besides, I saw you with a glass of Clemmo's cider in your hand. You do remember that stuff rots your brain, right? Would make a polar bear trip for an hour.'

Merrin smiled back lopsidedly. 'That is true. And I did shift quite a bit of it. People kept buying me drinks.'

They sat in silence for a moment, then Taran said softly, 'How are you feeling, Merrin? Now that the funeral is done?'

Merrin didn't really know how to answer. Numb, frozen, empty. Not as grief-stricken as she would have expected. Perhaps that would come later. Perhaps it wouldn't come at all. Merrin couldn't really put into words what her relationship was like with her mum. She loved her, had loved her intensely as a child. But then she went away to university and… rarely thought of her. Before she allowed grief in, she would have to deal with the strange guilt of that which was bubbling in her chest.

Instead of trying to put all that into words, Merrin went to get the bag of things she'd found in her mum's chest of drawers, and emptied it on the coffee table. 'What do you make of this?'

Taran shrugged. 'Trinkets. Like people accumulate.' He reached forward and picked up the small carved statuette of the woman. 'My dad did this.'

'Really?' Merrin took it from him, examining it in the morning light streaming through the windows. 'He carved it?'

'From a piece of driftwood.' Taran seemed to hesitate. 'I gave it to Lizzie. To your mum.'

Merrin frowned at him. 'You gave it to her? Why?'

Taran shrugged again. 'She liked it.'

'Is it meant to be her?'

Taran laughed. 'No. It's Endellion.'

'Endellion?'

'The Lady of the Sea,' said Taran. He glanced at the watch on his tanned, strong wrist.

Merrin said, 'You need to be out fishing?'

'No. I pulled a late one last night. After the funeral.'

Merrin giggled. 'Oh, yes. I saw you with that pig. Did you catch the shark?'

Taran smiled tightly. 'I need to get the catch out to the restaurants and pubs, and then there's a meeting later about the Fish Festival.'

Merrin's eyes widened. 'Oh my god. The Fish Festival. I'd almost forgotten about that.' She furrowed her brow. She *had* forgotten about it. Which was weird because—

'You used to love the Fish Festival!' Taran laughed. 'More than Halloween, more than Christmas, more than anything.'

'I did, didn't I?' said Merrin softly. 'And it's coming up again.'

'Couple of weeks,' said Taran. He drained his coffee cup and stood up.

Merrin looked at the little carved figure again. 'The Lady of the Sea. What was her name, again?'

'Endellion.'

'Endellion,' Merrin repeated. She'd never heard of her. Or had she? She seemed to have forgotten so much. The Cornish had a god for everything, though. Stood to reason there'd be one for the sea. There were probably several.

Taran seemed to hover, as though unsure what to do, and Merrin half-stood, thinking to kiss him on the cheek, but faltered, and in the end he smiled and just left. She stood at the window and watched him walk along the harbour and out of sight.

It was only when he'd gone that she remembered something, and picked up the manila folder with those receipts stuffed inside. Each one headed, in careful script, *For My Lady Endellion*.

7

TARAN

After the funeral ceremony, Reverend Bligh had taken Taran to one side as the mourners made their way down the hill to the Star and Anchor. 'You're playing a dangerous game,' he said.

'It's not a game,' said Taran, pulling at the collar of his white shirt. The suit made him hot and itchy in the warm sunshine. 'You know that as well as anyone.'

Reverend Bligh looked out to sea from the churchyard, by the freshly filled grave of Lizzie Moon. 'You are going directly against her wishes, you understand? There was a reason she kept Merrin away from Scuttler's Cove for all these years.'

'It's Merrin's destiny,' said Taran. 'It always has been. You know that. You were a part of it from the beginning. Lizzie let her heart rule her head.'

'Hardly surprising,' the older man said and sniffed. 'Who wouldn't want to protect their child from that kind of responsibility?'

Taran tugged at his collar again. 'Our hand has been forced. The incomers will take up those houses on Penrose's land in a matter of weeks. Things will move quickly.'

Bligh nodded. 'The pieces are on the board, or soon will be.' He turned back to Taran. 'Though it could be said that if there was no queen, then a game of chess could not even begin.'

'You *can* play without a queen,' said Taran. 'It just makes it all a one-sided game. And one we can't afford to lose. Our queen is on the board, for better or for worse.'

'But who moves first?' said Bligh, as Taran began to walk away. 'Black or white?'

'That remains to be seen,' said Taran.

He went to the Star and Anchor to pay his respects, watching Merrin nodding as the villagers spoke to her about her mother, and what a loss she was to Scuttler's Cove. Merrin didn't know the half of it. Lizzie Moon had made sure of that. He had a couple of drinks then went back to his cottage to change out of the hateful suit, then on to Carlyon's butcher's.

Bobby Carlyon was waiting for him, wiping his hands on a cloth. 'Just finished,' he told Taran. 'Need a hand? It's bloody heavy.'

'I'll manage,' said Taran. The pig was wrapped up in muslin. Carlyon lifted the cloth to show the stitching on its stomach. Taran nodded.

'I heard you've been talking to Penrose,' said Carlyon. 'About Merrin taking that house.'

'I have,' said Taran, hefting the pig up onto his shoulder. Carlyon was right. It was heavy.

'Lizzie wouldn't like it.'

'Lizzie's dead,' said Taran. 'Have you got my blade?'

Bobby nodded and from beneath his counter pulled the knife, its curved black blade wiped clean of pig's blood. 'Though it's not yours, by rights, is it?'

'No,' said Taran, as Bobby wrapped it in newspaper and tucked it into Taran's belt. 'It's Merrin's.'

Bobby gestured towards the pig. 'Then what's all this about? If the blade's for her anyway?'

Taran let Bobby open the door for him, then looked at the butcher. 'Because, despite what everyone thinks, if there's another way then I want to try it. I just think, when it comes down to it, there won't be.'

Taran walked along the harbour and spied Merrin standing outside the pub, smoking. She asked him if he was going fishing for a Great White when he showed her the pig. He didn't answer her when she questioned him about saying it wasn't bait, it was an offering. He felt her eyes on him all the way to his boat, where he dumped the pig on the deck then prepared to go out.

As the engine chugged and he nosed the boat out of the harbour, Taran reflected that he'd once been properly in love with Merrin Moon, in the way that only a seventeen-year-old loner can be in love. There'd been something different about her from the off, ever since they were small children. Something wild and free and independent. Nobody they were at school with had any ambitions to leave Scuttler's Cove. Everyone had a mother or father in some kind of business, and it was expected that they would follow them into it. Taran's father was a fisherman, Bobby Carlyon — who had given him the pig — would take over his father's butcher's. They were all, at the age of five, farmers or shopkeepers or labourers in waiting. Not Merrin. She was always like a caged bird, fluttering around, longing to be set free. Later, he'd be given pause to wonder whether that was always in her nature, or it was her mother's doing. Because, just like everyone else,

Merrin was destined to join the family business, whether she knew it or not.

But Lizzie Moon was having none of that, because her business was something dark and secret. And everything might have been all right, had Penrose not decided to develop his land.

They'd gone to see Penrose, when news got out what he was planning. Taran, Reverend Bligh, old Mr Carlyon, and Lizzie Moon. They'd visited him in his farmhouse, and he'd let them into his living room, a fire blazing in the hearth.

Penrose lived alone. His wife had died long ago, and they had never had children. His fields were mainly for grazing, and mostly let out to other farmers. The farmhouse walls bowed out and the roof dipped in the middle. Inside it was dark and dusty, and Taran caught a movement in the shadows from the corner of his eye that could have been a rat.

'You're a motley crew,' said Penrose, settling into a moth-eaten chair.

It was true. The minister, the butcher, the fisherman, and Lizzie Moon. Everyone knew what Lizzie was, but nobody ever said it out loud. It was Lizzie who spoke first, asking Penrose if it was true that he was planning to develop Nans-Avallen.

'It's my land,' he'd said. 'It's been in my family forever. I can do what I like with it. Said with all respect, Lizzie Moon. You know I have a lot of time for you.'

'Nans-Avallen is no more yours than the sea is mine,' said Taran. 'We're merely custodians.'

Penrose had sneered. 'Your daddy would have sold the sea if he could, young Tregarth, so don't come at with me with that.'

Lizzie Moon had leaned forward and stared into Penrose's eyes. 'That's not just any land, though, is it? You have a dozen fields you could develop. Why Nans-Avallen?'

'Why not? It's got good access and views out over the sea.' Penrose leaned forward, smiling, his teeth crooked like the headstones in St Ia's churchyard. 'You should see what they say I can get for the houses on there. I can retire at last.' He looked around. 'Maybe do this place up.'

'Nans-Avallen, though,' said Lizzie. 'The Vale of the Apple Tree. You talk of daddies to young Taran. Even if you don't believe, Penrose, your father did. He treated that place with respect. And, aye, fear. He knew whose land that really was.'

'Pshaw with your fairy stories and piskie tales,' said Penrose. 'I know you helped my dad a lot in his final weeks, Lizzie Moon, and I will always be grateful for that. But it's *my* land and that's an end to it.'

'Don't pretend you don't know what we're talking about,' Bligh said. 'Don't take us for fools, Penrose.'

'And you a man of God,' scoffed the old man.

Bligh had fixed him with a level stare. 'I am a man of many gods, Opie Penrose. You know that. Your father knew that. Don't play dumb with me.'

'I've no idea what you're talking about,' said Penrose, standing stiffly from his shabby chair. 'You can go now.'

At the door, Lizzie had turned to him. 'And you're going to let incomers live on Nans-Avallen? Londoners? Their blood will be on your hands, Penrose.'

'And their money will be in my pockets. Take your stupid threats and piss off,' said Penrose, closing the door on them.

Out to sea, Taran looked back at the cliff, at Nans-Avallen. The sun glinted off the solar panels on the roofs of the houses. The Londoners would be arriving for summer, soon. To their little Cornish paradise, their coastal idyll. They had no idea what they would be coming to. No notion what suffused the land on which their second homes were built. How could they?

He wished that Merrin Moon hadn't come home. Nans-Avallen would still be Nans-Avallen, would still be the Vale of the Apple Tree. It would still be very bad for whoever chose to live there. But with Merrin in the picture...

Lizzie had told him the story, when his daddy had passed on to him not only the fishing boat, but the other family business. The darker one. She'd been thirty-five when she was pregnant with her daughter, and the father had long since disappeared. A casual farm labourer, a drunken liaison at the Fish Festival, Lizzie had said. When her time came, she called them. Reverend Bligh, and Taran's dad, Bobby's father. Others, including the village midwife. None of them wanted to do it, but neither could they not. They'd taken her up to Nans-Avallen and in the light of the moon Lizzie had screamed her agony and birthed her daughter in the shadow of the apple tree.

Lizzie had cursed them all, then wept, and hugged her baby. She hadn't wanted that for Merrin, no mother would. But in the end, she had accepted it. Lizzie Moon was who she was, and now so was Merrin. A Daughter of the Soil, her path set.

On Merrin's first birthday, Lizzie gave her a knife, its blade a piece of slate, and its handle made of tin from the mines that criss-crossed the earth beneath them. A black gift that Lizzie prayed would never have to be wielded.

When he was far enough out, Taran unwrapped the pig and, grunting with effort, strung it up on the boom that was usually used for dragging his catch in. He took a long drink from his water bottle then swung the boom out so that the pig was hanging above the gentle waves of the Atlantic.

Taran took the newspaper off the knife, holding it up so it glinted in the sunlight. A tin handle and a slate blade. Forged from the land. He took a moment to clear his mind, just as his father had taught him. To let the waves of the sea travel through him, to feel the rise and swell, the ebb and flow. He felt the depths within him, fathoms-down, black, cold. But not empty.

Never empty.

Taran put the slate blade to the stitching that Carlyon had done on the pig's torso, and cut. The animal opened like a purse, spilling out glittering pound coins, a flood of them, pouring into the sea. A thousand of them, at least, dropping into the water, sinking down, down, down to the black deeps. Then he cut free the pig's corpse, and watched it follow the sparkling coins to the bottom.

Taran hoped it would be enough. It would have to be.

It was the last of Lizzie Moon's money.

8

MARY

Sergeant Mary Wells had worked the Scuttler's Cove patch for the best part of twenty years, but that didn't mean she was accepted wholeheartedly into the community. Her children would be, her grandchildren almost certainly. But Mary didn't have either and was well past the age of having kids, only three years away from her pension, and divorced to boot. She was only from a couple of miles up the road, but to Scuttler's Cove that might as well have been Timbuktu. They were what you might call a little insular, if you were being polite. Behind closed doors, at least. They were all smiles and rustic Cornish charm when it came to taking the money from the wallets of holidaymakers and second-homers. But there was something about Scuttler's Cove… The reason only she had taken the beat when it came up, and everybody else at Boscanlon police station had breathed a quiet sigh of relief.

She didn't really know why, but Mary understood. There was something in Scuttler's Cove you couldn't quite put your finger on. Even the name sounded a bit… creepy-crawly. Put her in mind of *things* scuttling. Of course, she knew the reason the town was named that, and it was the same reason, probably, that the townsfolk would never really take a copper to their hearts. Like many parts of coastal Cornwall, the community had made part of its living from the cargo of wrecked ships a couple of hundred years back. They'd had quite a neat little operation set up here, though. The reefs and rocks off the coast meant shipping had to gingerly and slowly pass by, especially in stormy weather. The wreckers would put out to sea in small boats and board the ships under cover of darkness and weather, creep into the holds and blow holes in the hull with gunpowder from the inside, scuttling the ships and spilling the cargo out into the sea. They said that some goddess of the ocean which the townsfolk honoured always brought the cargo floating directly to shore, and quite handily always left the ships' crews drowned or dashed on the rocks.

It was a nice story to tell the tourists, and Mr Bosanko, the Scuttler's Cove undertaker, also did a nice trade in the summer months leading ghost walks around the town, telling the lurid tales of the scuttlers and their dark deeds. There was no such excitement for Mary Wells, though; most of the crime in Scuttler's Cove these days was the result of someone drinking too much, especially at the annual Fish Festival. Which was why she was here today.

She parked up by St Ia's Church, the domain of the redoubtable Reverend Bligh, where a meeting was being held in the church hall about the forthcoming festival. The Fish Festival was one of those things you got all over Cornwall, like the 'Obby 'Oss festival in Padstow, its origins lost in the mists of time, something fun but also slightly creepy. There was a procession and an offering to the sea and then everyone got very, very drunk. It attracted a few tourists, but was really something for the locals. During Mary's tenure it had generally gone off without much incident, save for a few fights or one of the farm workers from around the town getting too frisky with a local girl or a holidaymaker. There had been reports of people going missing at the Fish Festival, but not for more than thirty years, and usually some itinerant worker who nobody was exactly sure hadn't just wandered off and never come back. Going back further to the Sixties and beyond there had been a couple of deaths, the reports at the time scant and undetailed and usually putting them down to someone drinking too much and falling in the sea.

Hopefully there'd be none of that this year, thought Mary as she locked the squad car and headed into the church hall. A nice, quiet festival.

Mary's first Fish Festival as a copper had been just a few weeks after she took the beat. After her training she'd worked in Truro for a while, then transferred to Boscanlon, near her home. She'd been to the Fish Festival once or twice before, as a kid, but those who grew up just outside of Scuttler's Cove didn't really go into the town. In summer it was just too busy, and too expensive. Boscanlon was a working town, with proper shops for ordinary people. And there was that generally unspoken sense of disquiet about Scuttler's Cove. As she got older, Mary thought that it was, in some way, jealousy. There were prettier seaside villages just down the coast, but they didn't get much more than a few day trippers. She often wondered what it was that made one town become so popular among tourists and, latterly, second-homers. The number of people buying up old properties in Scuttler's Cove was insane, as were the prices they were willing to pay. Mary couldn't have afforded to live in Scuttler's Cove, even if she wanted to.

It was a double-edged sword. On the one hand, the locals complained about them, especially those who couldn't get on the housing ladder because prices had gone through the roof. On the other hand... they spent money. Lots of money. And it was doubtful Scuttler's Cove would be so successful without that money. Whatever stardust or magic had settled on Scuttler's Cove to make it so desirable, Mary knew that other villages and towns would have killed for it.

Mary's predecessor had been a Scuttler's Cove man, born there, lived there and died there. He retired in his fifties and dropped dead a week later. Some of his colleagues at the Boscanlon nick said they always knew he'd fade away without the life of a copper to sustain him, but they weren't expecting it so quickly. Mary had naively thought that being from just a few miles away would mean Scuttler's Cove would take to her as the replacement. But on her first visit to the town as the official police presence, she'd been stared at as though she'd landed from Mars, talked about in whispered conversations that silenced as she passed. They hadn't exactly been overtly hostile, but not what you'd call friendly, either. She did wonder if Mitchell, the sergeant who had policed Scuttler's Cove for thirty years before, had been on the take, somehow, given the level of suspicion she faced. Or maybe that it was just that he was local, more local than her.

It was quite a thing to see, the Fish Festival. There was a procession, of course, and floats. At the head was the Fish King, who was decked out in finery and for as long as anyone could remember had been one of the Tregarth line, Scuttler's Cove's leading fishing family. Old Jago as long as Mary could remember, and after he died a few years back, his son Taran. The thing that Mary liked least about it all was that everyone wore these cheap plastic fish masks that covered their faces and heads. There was something unsettling about the way you didn't know who anyone was, how all those bulbous synthetic eyes seemed to stare at you when you passed. That first Fish Festival, Mary had stood on the harbour, in her uniform, watching the parade, feeling scrutinised by the dozens of fish masks. Even the children. It was no wonder that the detection rate of crimes at the Fish Festival was shockingly low; nobody ever knew who had committed an infraction. And if they did, they weren't saying.

'Ah, Sergeant Wells,' said Reverend Bligh as Mary walked into the stiflingly hot church hall. The Fish Festival committee was seated around a long table, shuffling notes and agendas. 'We wondered if perhaps you might want to go first…? We presume you have better things to do than sit in here all day. Keeping us safe from crooks and ne'er-do-wells, all that sort of thing.'

Mary went through the standard policing plan for the Fish Festival. The road closures for the duration of the procession, that she would have two constables on duty as well as her, and that there would be a particular focus on keeping young women safe, following a complaint of sexual assault the previous year that had amounted to nothing because, of course, the complainant wasn't able to identify the alleged perpetrator thanks to the proliferation of those bloody fish masks. She said, 'We'll also be keeping a close eye on underage drinking,' directing her comments towards Clemmo, the landlord of the Star and Anchor.

'It's not the pubs the kids get their booze from, it's the supermarkets and corner shops,' he said.

'I'll be speaking to them, too,' said Mary with a nod.

'It all sounds thorough, as ever,' said Reverend Bligh. 'If you wanted to be excused, Sergeant Wells...'

'There was one other thing,' said Mary. 'I heard Lizzie Moon's daughter is back, and someone wrote graffiti on her cottage.'

'Not hers any more,' Bligh answered. 'She's taking up one of Mr Penrose's properties on Nans-Avallen, I believe.'

'Yes, I'd heard. And there are Londoners coming to take up the rest. I know emotions run high about this sort of thing, but criminal damage won't be tolerated, nor will any attempts to terrorise incomers.'

'Oh, the Independent Cornwall group hasn't been active for decades,' said Bligh. 'Since before your time,' he added pointedly to Mary. 'It's just young people, high spirits.'

'Well, have a word with your young people,' said Mary, standing up. 'High spirits is one thing, but harassment is another. Anti-social behaviour won't be tolerated.' She turned to Clemmo. 'I mean, you wouldn't want any kind of orders being imposed on the harbour area, would you? That, say, curtailed opening times? Not with the summer season approaching. And the Fish Festival almost upon us.'

Mary left them with that to chew on and left, sitting in her car for a bit with the aircon blasting. She didn't have the power to impose any such order, they knew as well as her, and it would mean endless local council meetings to even get anywhere close. But it was worth dropping the idea into their little gathering. They'd all be grumbling about her right now, she knew, asking who she thought she was. Mary Wells didn't care. She might never be accepted here, not properly, but she knew Scuttler's Cove. Sometimes they thought they were a law unto themselves.

They weren't. There was only one law in Scuttler's Cove, and it was that upheld by Sergeant Mary Wells.

9

JEN

Jen stood in front of the house, watching the men from the transport company carrying the boxes of her things into it. The sky was a faultless blue, the sun beating down on her bare head. Behind her she could hear, or more like sense, the sea, rolling and whispering. Her leg had healed, aside from some cramps when it got cold, and her eye was fine, though it got blurred quicker than the other one when she spent too long staring at a screen. Her heart, though, was a different matter. As the two men carried in her suitcases of clothes, she saw Justin's ghost weaving among them, measuring up, tapping on his phone, ordering things for the house.

How was she meant to do this? She had done nothing but cry for a month after the funeral, and then felt a kind of numbness settle about her, like a cloud on a hilltop. The gang were as good as their word, embracing her into the fold, enmeshing her in their world, tangling their lives with hers. On the few nights she got to sit alone in the Crouch End townhouse, she tapped at her phone, buying things she neither wanted nor needed, just for the rapidly palling thrill of being able to have whatever she wanted, finally.

Whatever she wanted, except for Justin.

'I do not fucking believe it!'

Jen's head snapped to the left, to where Maggie was standing with her fists on her hips, head on one side, luscious hair falling over her white shirt, while Timothy hopped around her, trying to placate her. Jen followed their points and stares to their property, and then she noticed the angry red letters sprayed right across the front of the house, windows and door and everything.

ANSERGHEK KERNOW.

'What does it mean? What language is it even in?' shrieked Maggie. The others were drifting over, Arthur and Adaku, Tabby and Paul, consoling Maggie with hands on her shoulders and unbelieving stares. Jen glanced right and saw Simon, sitting on a steamer chair outside his corner plot, in a Panama hat and shades. He raised a violently coloured cocktail at Jen. She frantically waved for him to come over.

Jen went over to the others, then walked to the house and ran a finger over the red paint.

'I'm not sure you should touch it, Jen,' called Paul. 'This is probably a crime scene.'

'It's just spray-paint,' said Jen. 'It'll scrub off easily enough.'

'Have you got that fucking farmer on the phone?' yelled Maggie.

'I'm on to him now,' said Timothy, his Adam's apple bobbing, his curly hair hiding his phone. 'Hello? Mr Penrose? Yes, yes, thank you, we're moving in now. But we have a bit of a problem...'

Mr Penrose, the landowner who had sold them the site and their new houses, stood in the sunshine, squinting at Maggie and Timothy's house. He ruminated for a moment then said, 'Independent Cornwall.'

'Yes, we know, we did bloody Google it!' said Maggie. She was very highly strung, Jen had learned, given to explosive bouts of temper and over-passionate pronouncements. Everything Maggie did was *big*. Bigger than it needed to be.

'It's Cornish,' said Mr Penrose. 'And that's a cock and balls, if you'll excuse my crudeness.'

'There's a Cornish language,' said Simon. 'Who knew?'

'The cunt who daubed that on my fucking house, that's who knew,' said Maggie, rounding on him. 'If everyone will excuse *my* fucking crudeness!'

'Calm down, Mags,' said Tabby quietly. 'This isn't Simon's fault. It isn't anyone's fault here.' She turned to Mr Penrose. 'Do you get this sort of thing a lot?'

He shrugged, and pushed back his flat cap, scratching his head. 'A bit, yeah. Second homes, holiday homes, that sort of thing. Pay it no mind. I'll send one of the lads up to scrub it off.'

'Call the police, Timothy,' said Maggie firmly.

Tim started to jab at the phone again and Mr Penrose said, 'Oh, I'd not bother with that. They won't do anything. Look, whoever did it has had their fun now. They'll not worry you again, I'd imagine, now they've made their point.'

'I suggest we all decamp to mine and drink cocktails in the sun,' boomed Simon, in his short-sleeved Hawaiian shirt that his gut was straining to burst out of, and khaki shorts from which his pale, stick-thin legs jutted. 'Let the men move all your stuff in, and Penrose's chap clean the graffiti off.'

'It's not a bad idea,' said Arthur, and Adaku nodded beside him. She was wearing a gold pantsuit, shimmering in the sunlight.

Timothy looked around, his finger poised above his phone. 'Am I calling the police, or what?'

'Oh, forget it,' said Paul. 'Let's do what Simon says and all go for a drink.'

That decided, the men forged ahead while the women fell in with Maggie, who had finally found the resources to start crying. Jen watched them go then Simon waved his cocktail at her. 'Come on, young Jen.' He dropped his voice to a stage whisper. 'Wouldn't be us if we didn't have a drama to kick off the summer season, would it?'

Simon seemed to have an insane amount of garden furniture for a man living on his own. On the grass in front of his house he assembled three more steamer chairs and a big round table with a large canvas parasol, then brought a seemingly unending supply of drinks out from his kitchen. At some point, Paul and Arthur went to pay the men who had brought all their stuff for the summer, and the procession of vans drove away. The sun was at its strongest, and Jen watched a thin figure walk through the field with a bucket, and then start to scrub at the graffiti on Maggie and Timothy's wall. The lad that Mr Penrose had promised.

'It's so hot,' complained Maggie, fanning herself with a glossy brochure that Simon had been reading.

'I agree,' said Adaku, standing up. 'I'm going to change.'

'Anyone fancy nibbles?' said Simon as Maggie followed Adaku. Jen was struggling with the idea that these houses, this land, was *theirs*. It felt as though they were on holiday for a weekend. Not that these were their second homes. Summer stretched out in front of them. Jen felt a stab of working-class guilt. She had never been on holiday for longer than two weeks. She wondered what she would do with herself.

'Not too much food, Simon, darling,' cautioned Tabby as he hefted himself up from his steamer chair.

'That's right,' said Paul. 'We've got a booking for dinner at the Star and Anchor in the village at eight.' He waggled his empty glass. 'Drinks, on the other hand, you can keep coming.'

As the others talked about business and money and investments, Jen watched Adaku walking back from her home. She had changed into a white bikini, so small that the fabric of both top and bottom would barely have been enough to fashion a handkerchief from. Adaku was lithe and toned, not an ounce of fat on her, Amazonian in stature and with the bearing of one who was utterly confident in everything she did in life. Jen saw Mr Penrose's worker pause in his scrubbing to watch the vision stride by. Then Maggie came out of the house, wearing a black bikini, more curvy and rounder than Adaku, but no less utterly confident. Jen saw her speaking to the boy, who must have thought all his birthdays had come at once, Maggie's pneumatic boobs almost in his face.

'That's better,' said Adaku, lying on one of the steamer chairs. Arthur picked up the brochure from the table, one produced by the development company to showcase the wares of the place they now, Jen reminded herself, owned.

'Apple Tree Vale,' said Arthur, reading aloud. 'Known in Cornish as *Nans-Avallen*, taking its name from the tree that grows at the centre of the land, thought to be hundreds of years old.' He squinted in the sun towards the big tree that stood at the beginning of the wooded area at the back of the site.

'Speaking of Cornish, that boy Penrose has sent up has done a good job getting rid of that vandalism,' said Maggie, suddenly casting her shadow over Jen. 'I said you'd give him something for his time, Timothy.'

All gangly arms and legs, Timothy jumped up. 'Right-o. Think I've got a few quid in the house somewhere.'

'I'd imagine that five minutes staring at your tits was payment enough for him,' said Tabby mildly, raising an amused eyebrow at Jen.

'I hope so. They cost enough.' Maggie peered towards the one piece of the land that didn't belong to them, the small house sitting with its back to the woods at the side of the site. 'Do we know who's in there, yet? Some awful yokels, probably. Not sure I like the idea of them staring at us.'

Jen followed Maggie's gaze. 'I'm sure they're just normal people,' she said quietly.

Maggie glared at her. 'Darling, *we're* normal people. And you can guarantee they're nothing like us.' She shook her head, and made a snorting noise. 'Affordable homes,' she said, as though they were words in a language as alien as those scrawled across the front of her house.

'I'm going to look at the apple tree,' declared Arthur. 'Anyone coming?'

'How dreary,' said Maggie.

'I'll come, darling,' said Adaku, sliding off the chair. 'Jen?'

Jen walked with Arthur and Adaku peering at the thick covering of trees at the back of the site.

'The woods are lovely, dark and deep,' intoned Arthur. 'But I have promises to keep. And miles to go before I sleep.' He turned to Jen. 'Do you know that one? *Stopping By Woods on a Snowy Evening.* Robert Frost.'

'How altogether too cold,' said Adaku. She stopped in the shadow of the apple tree. It really was huge close up, Jen couldn't even estimate how tall. She couldn't have encircled the trunk with her arms, and the lowest branches were thicker than her waist. Adaku pulled her phone from the tiny waistband of her bikini bottoms and handed it to Arthur. 'Get some shots for my Instagram.'

Adaku went to stand by the tree, leaning on it with one hand. Jen squinted at the trunk. It was old and weathered and the bark was split and grey. It almost seemed to shimmer in the sunlight, the dappled shadows of the leaves dancing on it in the merest of breezes. Arthur began to shoot pictures as Adaku posed and preened. Jen felt so dumpy and lumpy beside her. She focused instead on the tree. It really did look as if the bark was...

It *was*. It was moving. Undulating. As though...

'Ow!' cried Adaku suddenly, snatching her hand away from the tree trunk as though it was suddenly red hot. She glared at her wrist, then put the inside of it to her lips.

'Darling...?' said Arthur, worry creasing his face.

'Something fucking bit me!' said Adaku, staring at the tree. Then her eyes widened. 'Oh my god.'

Arthur and Jen ran over, and Jen skidded to a halt in the long, cool grasses in the shade of the tree. The trunk was indeed moving, or rather the things on it were.

Spiders. Spiders with long, spindly legs and bulbous bodies the size of five pence coins, in a startling, shimmering yellow. Thousands of them, it felt like, pouring down from the upper trunk and the branches, crawling and skittering across the thick, cracked bark of the apple tree trunk.

Jen began to back away. She hated spiders. Didn't everyone? And she'd never seen anything like these brilliant yellow creatures. They would almost be beautiful, if they weren't so horrible. Arthur was looking at Adaku's wrist. 'I can't see anything. Just a nip. Come on, let's go and get a drink.'

Adaku and Arthur went back to the others, she leaning on him somewhat dramatically. Jen waited a moment, watching the tree, frowning as the spiders began to pour up the trunk, disappearing into the branches, until it was as if they had never been there at all.

※

He watched them come by moonlight, a line of giggling figures climbing up the path from the harbour and on to the darkened field. Boys from town. Full of mischief. He smiled. He was like that, once. He stepped out of the darkness of the trees to get a closer look. He didn't know how long it had been since he woke, desperate for a drink, but he hadn't slept since, though he was sure days had passed. Some bloody hangover. He wasn't sure about much of anything, to be honest. Couldn't even remember his own name. Or what he was doing here. Or why he was here, still, and not gone home.

Home. Where was home? He couldn't remember that, either. This place would have to do for now. Besides, he wasn't even sure he could leave here. Felt like he was tied to this place by some invisible thread. He hadn't even tried to go down to the town, and he wasn't really sure that was his home anyway.

The apple tree was framed against the canopy of stars scattered across the night sky. This felt like home, at least, where he belonged. This field, and those woods, and that apple tree in particular. Or maybe... not that he belonged in this place, but he belonged to it.

Well, it didn't bear thinking about too deeply. He was more interested in what these kids were up to. He walked silently through the grass to hide behind the apple tree, and watch them. They were laughing and standing in front of one of the houses, and one of them had a can of spray-paint in his hand. He watched as the boys drew a big penis on the door.

Before he knew what he was doing, he was walking over to them. Not like that, he was trying to say. Like we did when I was a lad, when these incomers rocked up to take over our places. He tried to stutter the words but only ended up gasping harshly.

The boys turned round and saw him, their eyes widening. They grabbed each other and yelled, and then started to run, back the way they'd come, shrieking as they pelted down towards the path that would lead them back to town.

He felt saddened. They were the first people he'd tried to talk to. He kept out of the way of the farmer and his dog, because something about that man tickled his fogged brain, reminded him of something bad. And nobody had come to live in the houses, not yet.

The kids had dropped their spray-paint. With effort, his bones creaking and his muscles straining, he bent to pick it up, looking at it through the eyeholes of the thing on his head, his stumps of fingers pressing at the top until it gave a satisfying hiss.

Cock and balls. No imagination, kids today. If you really want to put the frighteners on incomers, you have to go back to the old ways. He held out the can and started to spray, straight across the front of the house, windows and all. Then he stepped back to admire his handiwork.

ANSERGHEK KERNOW

That was it. That was what they used to do when he was a lad. He looked at it for a long time, mourning the childhood he could only remember in fits and starts, then lumbered back towards the trees.

10

MERRIN

When Merrin was a child, she and her friends roamed all over the countryside around Scuttler's Cove. Everywhere except Nans-Avallen. Stories abounded of ghosts and monsters and killers lurking in the woods that bordered the clifftop field, but the real reason was old Penrose and his zero-tolerance policy of local children playing on his land.

Standing facing the lone house set back against the trees, all those old stories suddenly came back to Merrin, and she shivered.

Penrose coughed and handed her the keys. 'I'm glad it went to someone local,' he said, shifting his weight from foot to foot. 'And to someone... well. You know. Had a lot of respect for your mother.'

'Thank you,' said Merrin. Everyone had a lot of respect for Lizzie Moon, it seemed. Except her own daughter. That's what she imagined they were thinking. Everyone except her own daughter, who went away for thirteen years and came crawling back from London with her tail between her legs.

'I won't give them any trouble you know,' said Merrin suddenly. 'The rich people. I just want a place to live and to keep myself to myself.'

Penrose coughed again. 'Well. Yes. Of course.' She knew he'd rather have not had to build affordable housing on here, but regulations were regulations. 'They're coming bright and early tomorrow morning,' he said. 'I think they've stayed in a hotel in Boscanlon and all their stuff is arriving early doors.' He paused, and looked around.

'Taran's bringing my things up later in his van,' said Merrin. 'After he's been fishing.'

Penrose nodded. 'Well. Aye. Hope you'll be happy here.' He peered towards the deep woods. 'And if you, you know, at night, if you…'

Merrin frowned at him. 'If I what?'

He shook his head. 'Nothing. The wind coming off the sea can sound funny in the trees, that's all. It's nothing.'

Though the sun was high in the sky, Merrin felt colder than ever, and shivered again.

—

It only took Merrin and Taran a couple of hours to unload his van and arrange what she'd kept of her mother's furniture in the house. The old things looked incongruous in the bright, modern setting of the new place, as though ancient and modern were wrestling to assert their dominance. 'It'll do for now,' said Merrin, catching Taran's bemused frown as he looked around the open-plan kitchen and living space. 'I'll see how the money's going and find out if IKEA will deliver here.'

'I like it,' said Taran, though a tad uncertainly to Merrin's ears. 'It's nice to honour your mum like this, keeping her stuff.'

Merrin looked at him, her head on one side. 'You knew my mum quite well, didn't you? I don't really remember you being so close to her when we were young. In fact, I don't even remember you talking to her.'

Taran shrugged. 'I suppose it was after my dad died, and I took over the fishing. Got a lot more involved in what was going on in Scuttler's Cove.'

'Did you never want to leave?'

Taran thought about it. 'You left. Then you came back.'

'I've not come back forever, Taran.'

He met her eyes. 'Haven't you? Are you sure?'

The question wrong-footed Merrin for a moment. 'Well. Are any of us ever sure about anything?'

Taran sat down heavily on the moth-eaten sofa. 'Once my dad died and I took over the business, that was my future set in stone.' He looked at his feet. 'Sometimes we can't outrun our destiny, Merrin. No matter how far we go.'

She couldn't stop herself laughing. 'Taran Tregarth! You're talking like one of those mystical old sods who tell tall folk tales for the tourists in crystal shops.'

He forced a smile. 'Want to go to the pub?'

She pulled a face and shook her head. 'No, think I'll just settle in here tonight.'

'One sec,' he said, and headed out into the late afternoon. He came back with a carrier bag. 'I brought you some food. Nothing special. Couple of ready meal curries.' He reached into the bag and pulled out a bottle of wine. 'And this. Second cheapest one in the shop.'

Merrin was suddenly touched by his kindness with the food. The wine, though, that was something else. She reached for it, her fingers brushing his as she took the bottle, an electric shock passing between them. Merrin coughed and looked at the wine. 'There are some words in French here, so it must be good.' The unspoken thing hovered between them. He was waiting for her to ask him to stay and drink it with her. She wasn't quite sure she wanted to go there. Not quite yet, at any rate.

'Well, if you've got everything, I'll be off,' said Taran. Merrin was quite impressed by his intuitive reading of the situation, which conversely made her want to actually ask him to stay and drink it with her. But she took a deep breath and stiffened her resolve, and gave him a kiss on the cheek at the door. As he was walking away, she called him back.

'There was something I meant to ask. About my mum's missing money.' Did he stiffen slightly? Or had Merrin imagined it? 'One sec.'

She reappeared at the door holding the manila folder. 'I found these in Mum's things. Receipts. It all adds up to the money she drew out of the bank after selling the house. And look at what's written on top. *For My Lady Endellion*. That was the statue your dad carved, wasn't it? That you gave to Mum?'

Taran looked through the receipts, frowning. 'Hmm. And you have no idea what this means?'

'No. I thought you might. As it says Endellion.'

He gave a smile. 'God, you have forgotten a lot, haven't you? Don't you remember the stories about Endellion when we were kids?'

Merrin shrugged. The name rang vague bells, but nothing she could land upon. 'Not really. Then again, I didn't come from a fishing family like you. So you don't know?'

'Sorry.' Taran handed the folder back. 'I mean, you know your mum... she was into all this stuff, wasn't she? All this folklore and, well, witchy stuff. I'll see you tomorrow, maybe?'

She watched him drive away until his van disappeared down the road, thinking that, no, she didn't really know her own mum at all, not as much as other people seemed to, then she went back in to sit in the shiny silence of her brand-new home.

Merrin slept long and dreamless, awoken only by the sound of engines, slamming doors, and voices. She stirred, momentarily confused as to where she was, the bright sunlight lancing in through the windows she hadn't yet bought blinds for. She'd made her mother's bed her own, with new sheets and a duvet, and slid out from under it, peeking around the edge of the window in her vest and knickers, watching the newcomers arrive.

She saw the angry red words painted on the second house along at about the same time as the loud woman with brown hair did, as she climbed out of the passenger seat of a BMW parked next to a van from which seemingly endless suitcases were being unloaded.

ANSERGHEK KERNOW. The locals had struck again. She wondered if it was some kind of necessary outlet for them, to compensate for having to smile and kow-tow to the emmets and incomers all day, a pressure-release valve to cope with the fact the village had been overrun. She wondered if it was Taran, after all, who was behind it. She'd told him last night that the Londoners were arriving early today. Plenty of opportunity for him to come back in the dead of night with a spray can. Merrin had a foot in both camps, she felt, after thirteen years away from Scuttler's Cove. She sympathised with her countryfolk, of course she did. On the other hand, she thought, the denizens of Scuttler's Cove were more than happy to take the money from tourists and second-homers. For the past couple of weeks while the house on

Nans-Avallen was being finalised, she'd been splitting her time between a Travelodge near Boscanlon and staying in a couple of locally owned holiday homes lent by people who, like old Penrose, had a lot of respect for Lizzie Moon and had wanted to help. She'd studiously avoided Taran's offer of a sofa, for reasons she didn't quite fully understand, or care to admit to herself. But she'd seen Scuttler's Cove getting busier and busier over those weeks, the narrow streets choked with traffic, the harbour and pubs full of tourists, and the season hadn't even properly got going yet. When the schools broke up for summer the place would be almost unbearable. It was no wonder the locals needed to let off a bit of steam now and again.

Merrin luxuriated under the shower for a while, then dressed in shorts and a T-shirt and made breakfast. Taran had put some bacon, bread and butter in the bag he'd thoughtfully dropped off for her, and now her brand spanking new kitchen smelled of bacon butties as well as last night's microwave curry. Starting to feel like home already. She dug out her paints and made a note to try to buy a new easel. She'd left some stuff back at the London flat, and had a terse text from Kamal asking if she wanted to collect it or if he should send it all to the charity shop. She didn't even bother to reply. Merrin walked around the house, gauging where the light was coming in, working out where the best place was to set up to paint.

She wanted to go outside, but felt strangely and unaccountably as though she shouldn't. The Londoners had set up camp in the end house, acting as though they were on holiday. Which, Merrin supposed, they were. At least, come September or so, they'd be off back to London, and she would be blissfully alone on Nans-Avallen. The thought didn't make her feel as comfortable as she'd hoped, and from the downstairs window she spied on the incomers. There was a tall Black woman in a tiny black bikini who had the figure of a 90s supermodel, who she watched posing for photos by the apple tree. Something in Merrin's gut made her want to shout for the woman to get away, but she wasn't quite sure why. Did she feel proprietorial about the ancient tree, for some reason? Or was it anxiety and fear that rumbled in her gut?

There were five houses, and eight people. Merrin worked out that the brash brunette whose house had been graffitied was with a lanky, curly-haired man. The gazelle-like supermodel seemed to be with, incongruously, a rather shabby-looking older man. And there was another couple, a well-groomed man with silver fox good looks and a stylish-looking blonde woman. That left a large, boisterous man in his late fifties who was obviously, effusively and flamboyantly gay, and a younger woman about Merrin's age, who seemed somewhat at odds with the others. More ordinary looking, compared to their expensive grooming and, she was sure, surgical tweaks, but also more... luminous. Naturally beautiful, from what she could see at this distance. Merrin wondered who she was and why she was living alone in that big house. Perhaps her husband or partner was going to arrive later.

After unpacking a few more boxes with her meagre possessions and the things she'd saved from her mum's house, and struggling and cursing for an hour to get a signal on the old TV she'd brought, Merrin opened the fridge and stared into its bright emptiness. She was going to have to do a shop, and unless she was going to suck up getting stung by local store prices forever, she was going to have to get a car. The rent-to-buy scheme on the new house was reasonable enough, and she had what was left of Lizzie's money, but she was going to have to think long term, and get a job. Not for the first time in the past month, she cursed her mother and wondered what the hell she had done with half of the money from the sale of the harbour cottage. Merrin had been into the bank, of course, but they couldn't tell her any more than the solicitor had. Lizzie Moon had made several large cash withdrawals over the course of about a year, not told anyone what it was for, but had seemingly passed all the stringent checks in place to ensure she wasn't being scammed or defrauded. Merrin didn't believe it for a minute. Her mother had somehow got rid of a huge sum of money and had nothing to show for it. And she would find out where it had gone.

For now, though, Merrin needed food, and that meant walking down into Scuttler's Cove and using one of the convenience stores. They were all starting to stay open until late now, as the season began to get underway, so she should be fine to get supplies for the next couple of days, at least. Then perhaps she'd have to prevail on Taran to take her to one of the big supermarkets so she could do a proper, and more economically sensible, big shop.

As if she'd summoned him up, her phone buzzed, and Taran's name appeared, heralding a text message.

Pint? was all it said.

Merrin looked out of the window. A pair of taxis from the local firm had pulled up outside the houses, and the Londoners were all piling in, dressed up to the nines. Merrin suddenly felt like she could breathe again.

On my way. Star and Anchor? she replied.

The sun was already dipping behind the trees, painting the sky a deep, dark blue, shot through with fiery orange, which Merrin's artistic eye appreciated. As she set off to walk to Scuttler's Cove, she glanced at the old apple tree, framed against the chromatic drama the evening sky was staging. Its leaves seemed to catch and hold the falling sunlight, shimmering with the absorbed heat. A breeze suddenly blew off the sea, and whispered through first the apple tree, and then the other trees in the woods behind her home. And that was exactly what it sounded like. Whispering. She remembered what old Penrose had said that morning.

The wind coming off the sea can sound funny in the trees, that's all. It's nothing.

'It's nothing,' said Merrin aloud, hurrying along the Tarmac road that cut through Nans-Avallen, separating her lone home from those of the Londoners, in most of which lights were still brightly burning, though they'd all gone out. 'It's nothing.'

The whispering sounded louder, and didn't sound very much like *nothing* at all, but Merrin just concentrated on the bright lights of Scuttler's Cove ahead of her, and not the murmuring darkness rising at her back.

11

TARAN

There was a meeting in the church hall at 6 p.m. about the plans to transform the dilapidated old nursing home on top of the hill into a budget hotel. Most of Scuttler's Cove was opposed to it, because the traffic around the town was bad enough at high season without a 200-bed hotel adding to it. Taran didn't really care one way or the other, and he suspected most of those making impassioned objections didn't either. More people meant more money, and that was what Scuttler's Cove was all about these days. Something like seventy per cent of the jobs in the town were related to tourism, either directly or adjacently.

The meeting was being chaired by Reverend Bligh, and on a table on the small stage were a couple of parish councillors, someone from the Cornwall Council planning office, and a county councillor from Boscanlon up for re-election next year, who was suddenly taking a rare interest in Scuttler's Cove.

'If nothing else,' Reverend Bligh thundered, as though delivering a fire and brimstone sermon from his Sunday pulpit, 'the bloody thing will be an eyesore! Not at all in keeping with the local architecture. It'll stick out like a barnacle.'

'I think you mean a carbuncle,' said the county councillor, a florid, bald man in a suit.

'I know what I mean!' roared Bligh, banging the table with his hand, making all their paper cups of water wobble alarmingly. 'If I say barnacle I bloody well mean barnacle!'

The woman from the planning office leaned forward, a little trepidatiously given Bligh's contorted red face, and said, 'It should be pointed out that there are no legitimate reasons under the planning regulations as they relate to the structure and design of the building for officers to recommend refusal of planning permission.'

Bligh glowered at her. 'Just because you can do something, it doesn't mean you should.'

And then, across the crowded hall, his eyes seemed to meet Taran's and hold them for a long moment.

Bobby Carlyon, the butcher, nudged Taran and whispered, 'I'm bored. Pint?'

Taran nodded. 'Pint.'

When they got to the Star and Anchor, the little room that used to be the snug, where the locals hid once tourist season began, was closed off behind a pair of velvet curtains draped over the double doors. Taran looked querulously at Clemmo as he ordered drinks for him and Bobby. 'What's happened to the snug?'

'It's not a snug any more,' said Clemmo, pulling the pints. 'It's a private dining room.'

'Since when?' Taran sipped the IPA. It was cold and fresh.

'Since today. New thing for the new season. Got my first booking for tonight.'

'And where are the locals supposed to drink?'

Clemmo shrugged, and Taran could practically see the pound signs in his eyes. 'In here, when all the tables aren't full. Out in the beer garden, now it's coming summer.'

They took their beers outside and found a table at the front of the pub, looking out over the harbour. Give it three or four weeks, once the school holidays started, and you wouldn't be able to move out here. Bobby said, 'I reckon it's going to be a good summer this year, for you and me at least. Fish and meat always do well. And if they open that big hotel on the hill, we'll do even better.'

'They probably get their food shipped in from some central suppliers, a chain like that,' said Taran. Two taxis were negotiating the harbour road and pulled up outside the pub. They watched the eight people get out, dressed up to the nines, sweating money.

'They'll be the Nans-Avallen lot,' murmured Bobby.

'Paid them a visit yet?' said Taran, not taking his eyes off the newcomers. There was a statuesque Black woman, a camp fat guy, and a mousy-looking girl who caught his eye then looked away, and seemed cut from different cloth than the rest. Interesting.

'Our Danny took his mates up last night apparently,' said Bobby. Danny was his cousin's son. 'Nice to see the new generation getting involved.'

'They did a proper job,' said Taran. 'Saw it this morning. *ANSERGHEK KERNOW* right across the house.'

Bobby looked visibly impressed. 'Surprised the little sod can even spell it. He told me they drew a big cock on the house then somebody turned up. They thought it was Penrose and did a runner.'

'Well, somebody left them a little welcome message.' They fell silent as the eight people trooped loudly into the pub. Probably Clemmo's private dining booking. Taran said, 'If Penrose finds out, he'll have your Danny's balls.'

Bobby laughed. 'Oh, they expect it, the incomers. They'd be disappointed if it didn't happen. Something to tell their mates at the dinner parties when they go back to London. It's practically a tourism service now, giving them a bit of the old Cornish nationalism. Adds a little spice to the summer for them. Even if it is just kids.'

'That's one lot who won't be needing any extra spice,' said Taran quietly.

Bobby nodded. 'Which one of them do you think it will be.'

Taran had his ideas, but wasn't yet totally sure. He drained his glass and said, 'Shall we have another? I've texted Merrin, see if she fancies it.'

Bobby grinned. 'You were always sweet on her. Shame she had to come back under present circumstances, though.'

The mood was suddenly serious. It was easy to forget, or at least not think about, what was happening, the gears that had been set into motion, the events that were inevitably going to play out this summer. Well, not inevitably, not in Taran's view. But it was an opinion nobody else shared. As far as everyone else was concerned, there was only one way this was going to go.

And it was not going to be good.

Merrin arrived half an hour later, dressed in T-shirt and shorts with a cardigan over. She was already looking more relaxed, more like a local. When she said hello to Bobby, she'd even started to get a Cornish burr back in her voice, Scuttler's Cove sanding off the London varnish it had acquired over the last dozen or so years.

'That's me,' said Bobby, finishing his pint. 'Early delivery tomorrow. Great to see you again, Merrin. Hope you're settling in up at Nans-Avallen.'

Merrin nodded and smiled. When they'd been kids, they all avoided that place like the plague. Not just because old Penrose was such a grumpy bastard, but because of the old stories, the legends, the folklore. Back then, Taran had been as deliciously scared of the tales as anyone. Most people grew out of that sort of thing though. Except when you learned it was all true.

Merrin sat down in the seat Bobby vacated and shivered a little. It was still early in the season, and once the sun went down there could be a chill in the air. 'Shall we go inside, see if there's a table free?' suggested Taran.

There was, and after Clemmo had warmly greeted Merrin, and supplied them with drinks, they sat in the corner, Taran facing the old snug, now the private dining alcove. Raucous sounds of conversation and laughter were issuing from behind the curtain. Merrin turned round to look in that direction and Taran said, 'Your new neighbours, come to sample the local fare. You met them yet?'

Merrin grinned. '*The Real Housewives of Scuttler's Cove?* I saw them moving in this morning. And one of Penrose's farm lads scrubbing the graffiti off one of their houses.'

Taran couldn't conceal a smirk. Merrin gave him a look. 'It's not funny, you know. It's childish.'

'It wasn't me!' he said, putting up his hands.

Merrin raised an eyebrow at him, but a smile was playing on her lips. 'But you might know who it was?'

'I might,' agreed Taran.

'What time does Scuttler Stores shut these days?' said Merrin, glancing at her smartwatch. 'I've got literally nothing in. Scoffed all that food you brought for me.'

'Ten, now summer's underway,' said Taran. 'But you don't want to go there. Prices are sky high from June to September. If you can hang on without expiring I'll take you to the big Tesco on the ring road at Boscanlon in the afternoon.'

Merrin smiled, and his stomach flipped a little. 'That would be so kind. Aren't you fishing tomorrow?'

Taran shook his head. 'I'll get a couple of hours in early. Got more bloody Fish Festival business at lunchtime. I swear, we do this every year. I've no idea why we need to talk about it so much.'

'I've never really thought about it since I left. How weird,' said Merrin. She began to twist the ring on the little finger on her left hand. 'The Fish Festival.' Then her eyes widened. 'Oh god! That means you're…'

Taran smiled, a little embarrassed. 'Yeah. The Fish King. One of my dad's legacies I could have lived without.'

And not the only one, he thought. Oh to not know anything at all about what was stirring at Nans-Avallen, and how it was all destined to end. Merrin broke him out of his sudden reverie with a delighted laugh.

'The Fish King! Oh my god! You sit on the float and everything? With the… the stick, and the ball?'

'Sceptre and orb, I'll have you know,' said Taran.

'And the crown!' cackled Merrin. 'Now I'm glad I came home just to see this.' She shook her head wonderingly. 'Taran Tregarth. The Fish King.'

'All right, stop taking the piss.' He clinked his empty glass against Merrin's. 'Another?'

'Why not?' she said, shrugging off her cardigan. Taran glanced at her slim body, then forced himself to look away. *You were always sweet on her.* He coughed and said, 'Same again?'

While he was standing at the bar waiting for Clemmo to pull the drinks, one of the staff came out and tied back the curtains to the snug, now the private dining room, so another could walk through laden with plates for the group's first course. Taran got a good look at them for the first time. Which one would it be? He scanned each face surreptitiously. There were four women, and it would be one of them. There was a loud brunette, holding forth loudly with some story about something terribly hilarious that had happened in London. A classy blonde, who even at this distance Taran could see was rolling her eyes at everything the other was saying. The chiselled, tall woman, her hair in cornrows, was talking to the waitress who was putting her plate in front of her. And the fourth was the woman Taran had momentarily locked eyes with outside. Not as *done* as the others, not as tweaked. More natural. And, in Taran's eyes, by far the prettiest among them. Her eyes kept darting from one to the other in her group, listening to the fast-flowing conversation but rarely joining in.

Clemmo put the drinks down in front of Taran, who tapped his card on the machine. He picked them up and took one more glance at the group, before the waitress closed the curtain, and then looked back at Merrin, who was gazing out of the window at the lights of the harbour, now draped fully in night.

The high priestess and the sacrificial victim. Both of them in the same place, probably for the first time. Taran knew, of course, who one was, but not yet the other. And neither of the women concerned had any idea at all. Not yet, at any rate. Taran took a deep breath, plastered on a smile, and took the drinks over to Merrin.

12

JEN

After their main course, the landlord of the pub, Clemmo, came into the little room to ask how their meal had been.

'Absolutely divine!' said Tabby. 'Those seafood sharing platters were incredible.'

Jen had to agree. She'd eaten some amazing, expensive food since meeting Justin, but there was something almost supernaturally good about the seafood here. The landlord smiled broadly and turned, pointing to the bar.

'All caught locally, and there's the man who catches it! Taran Tregarth, Scuttler's Cove's finest fisherman. Taran! Over here!'

Jen could sense the indrawn breaths of Maggie, Tabby, Adaku and Simon as the man Clemmo had beckoned sauntered into the room. He was tall and slim, his dark hair falling in loose curls around his weathered face. He wore jeans and a checked shirt, half-tucked in.

'Compliments to the fisherman,' purred Tabby. He glanced around the table and nodded, his eyes drinking them all in. His gaze landed on Jen's, and she looked away, suddenly blushing, though she had no idea why.

'Just doing my job,' said Taran, a little awkwardly. 'Glad you enjoyed your meal. Hope you enjoy your time in

Scuttler's Cove.' He paused, then said, 'You're up at Nans-Avallen, aren't you?'

'Apple Tree Vale,' said Paul, idly flicking through his phone. 'We bought it.'

'Bought the houses.' Taran nodded.

Jen saw Paul look up finally, his steely stare on Taran. 'Bought everything.'

Taran shrugged, and looked around the table again. 'Well, enjoy your summer.'

When he'd gone, Clemmo handed out the dessert menus and said he'd be back in five minutes. Simon took out his wallet and withdrew a crisp note, placing it on the table and sliding it over to Jen. He said, 'Shall we say twenty?'

Jen frowned and looked at him. 'What?'

'Shall we say twenty. For our wager.'

Tabby groaned, putting her face in her hands. 'Simon.'

'What wager?' said Jen.

'Which of the two of us — as the only single and therefore eligible members of the gang — gets to fuck the fisherman first.'

'Fuck's sake, Simon,' said Paul, shaking his head.

Simon looked around, his face a picture of mock innocence. 'What? The pussy-thrumming around this table when he walked in was louder than the galloping of the horses on the final furlong of the Grand National!'

Jen looked down at her lap as the group broke out in protestations and groans and Arthur said, 'Simon, old boy, don't you think it's a little soon for Jen to be thinking like that…? I mean, it's only been a couple of months since… you know… Justin…'

Simon's hand flew to his mouth, and then he placed it on Jen's. 'My dear. I'm so sorry. Please forgive a tactless old queen who has had too much to drink of this excellent wine. I was only joking. I didn't think.'

'It's fine,' said Jen, forcing a smile. 'It was funny.' But tears were pricking her eyes, and when she looked down at the menu she couldn't see at all for them blurring her vision.

—

Jen was stuffed after the Cornish ice cream smothered in hot espresso. And she couldn't handle another glass of wine, as dry and gorgeous as it was. Everyone had fallen into conversations, mostly about money and business and some big forthcoming opportunity, as far as Jen could tell. Her head was swimming a little. She looked across the table at Adaku, who was scratching the inside of her wrist. She was wearing a plaster exactly matched to her skin colour over the place the spider had bitten her.

'Is that sore?' said Jen.

Adaku looked down, almost in surprise at where she'd been absently scratching. 'A little itchy, is all. It's nothing. Just a little British spider.'

Arthur leaned over. 'Nothing compared to what she had to grow up with in Nigeria, eh, love? Some big buggers over there. Tarantulas!'

Jen shivered. 'Well, I'm sure those on the apple tree aren't poisonous.'

'All spiders are venomous,' said Adaku. 'It's how they subdue their prey. It just depends on whether that venom is poisonous to humans, too.' She scratched at her wrist again and smiled. 'But I think a little thing on an apple tree in Cornwall won't be too much of a problem.' She put her hands in her lap.

'What say back to mine for cocktails?' announced Simon.

Everyone groaned. 'No, dear, it's been a long, busy day for all of us. I think Paul and I will get back and just flop out.'

'We've got all summer, Simon,' said Timothy.

Arthur nodded and pulled out his phone. 'I'll call that cab company. Then we can all get back and spend our first night in Apple Tree Vale.'

Nans-Avallen, thought Jen to herself. The fisherman, Taran, hadn't seemed too impressed at the name change the gang had decided to give the site. She thought she preferred the original Cornish version anyway. It sounded more romantic, more authentic. Clemmo came over with the card machine and Jen dipped into her purse, but Simon put his hand on her arm and said, 'This one's my treat. Your turn will come.'

In the cab back up to Nans-Avallen, sandwiched between Tabby and Paul in the back seat, Jen felt her eyes drooping and her head nodding. Once they were out of the town and wending their way up to the cliff, the darkness ahead seemed thick, absolute. She couldn't wait to get into her bed, close the blinds on the night, and find out what the first full day of her summer in Cornwall would bring.

Jen's first night in the Cornish house was a restless one, punctuated by dreams. In one, she was back in the Tesla with Justin, reliving every slow-motion second of the accident on the lanes not far from Scuttler's Cove. In another, she saw her mother, not in the care home where she had lived for the past few years, not knowing what day it was, not knowing who Jen was when she visited, but in a dank and dark cell in some kind of Victorian asylum, bound in a dirty straitjacket and straining at chains that held her tight to the damp walls, screaming and screaming over and over. Jen woke with a start and stood at her bedroom window, looking out at the ripples of the Atlantic illuminated by the moon. But then the waves started to roll and boil, becoming more and more violent, until they reared up, like a living thing, and came together to form a huge tsunami that bore down on Nans-Avallen, and Jen woke again, realising it was another nightmare.

Finally awake, with the merest sliver of orange to the east, Jen pinching her arms to reassure herself that she was truly not still dreaming, she gazed out of the window at the apple tree in the centre of the vale. Despite the spiders that had bitten Adaku, she felt drawn to it, a pull so strong that she had to stop herself from walking downstairs, in her pants and vest, pulling open the door, and padding across the newly laid Tarmac access roads and the damp grass to the huge, imposing frame of the tree. As the sun began to rise properly, and the birds alighted on the tree and started singing, Jen gave up any hope of more sleep, and went downstairs to make herself a coffee in the machine that Justin had chosen, and watch the news on the TV that he had insisted they buy. As she curled up on the sofa, her eyes grazed to the closed door of the downstairs bedroom, the one that Justin, just before he died, had suggested that they turn into a playroom. She was suddenly strangled by a sob that rose from deep inside her, and her hands went to her stomach. What sort of mother would she have been? She would never find out. Or at least, she could not even consider it right now. She was only thirty-three, but she was a widow. And she was enmeshed in her dead husband's friendship group, whether she liked it or not.

Jen paused. There was a sound coming from somewhere in the house. A kind of... scratching, she thought. She turned off the TV with the remote and listened in the still morning silence. There it was again. Scratching, or something like claws, skittering on a hard surface. Just when she was beginning to think she'd imagined it, she jumped at the very clear and definite sound of a bump.

It came from the downstairs bedroom.

Her scalp crawling, Jen crept off the sofa and to the door, and listened. Could it be rats? Or had something got into the house while she'd been outside with the door open – maybe a fox? Even a dog from the town? Got itself locked into the bedroom?

There was a faint noise from inside, like a moan, or more of a whine. Jen bit her lip and looked around. Maybe she should go and get one of the men. But it was too early, nobody else would be up, and she hated herself for even having the thought. She took a deep breath. The Jen-before-Justin wouldn't have thought twice about dealing with this herself. And now she was thinking she had to get help from one of the *men*?

'What's happened to you?' she murmured to herself. She looked around and spied a long-handled brush propped against the door of the utility room, from where she'd cleaned up after dropping a glass last night. If it was a dog, or a fox, she'd be wise to have something to keep it away from her. Jen grabbed the brush and then opened the front door wide, so whatever was in there could just run straight out. Then she took a deep breath, brandishing the brush, and turned the handle on the bedroom door.

She opened it a crack, and it was dark in there, pitch black. Had the blackout blinds been down when she moved in yesterday? She couldn't remember. She must have pulled them down before they went out to the town. Cautiously, Jen pushed the door a little more. She could sense movement in there, definitely, even if she couldn't quite make out any sounds.

Then the door was seemingly yanked open from within, the handle dragged out of her hand, and she wasn't looking into the bedroom but into a dark cell with wet stone walls, and her mum, straitjacketed and raving like a lunatic, pulling at a chain leash that was around her neck and secured her to the wall.

'Be a mother? Be a mother?' screamed her mum, spittle flying from her thin, cracked lips, her thin white hair matted and tangled. 'You don't even know how to be a daughter!'

Jen fell backwards and screamed, and when she landed on her backside, the room in front of her was empty, normal. She stood up and slammed the door closed, hugging herself and shivering, half expecting to wake up and this all be a nightmare. But she didn't, so she went and made a strong, black coffee, and curled up on the sofa. Was this grief? Guilt? Some combination of both?

Jen sat there until she heard a door slam somewhere, and the unmistakeable voice of Maggie, calling out to Tabby. She sat there until she heard an engine gunning up the hill, and the opening and closing of doors. Feeling exhausted, she went to the window, and saw the gang gathered around an Ocado delivery van. Tabby turned and, shielding her eyes against the glorious sun, peered at Jen and waved her to come out.

Jen went to her bedroom to grab her robe and slipped into it in the window, looking out at the glittering blue sea beyond Nans-Avallen. Her eye was drawn to the apple tree, and she frowned. She was sure that when they had arrived yesterday, when she had gone right up close to the tree, when Adaku had been bitten by that spider, the branches bore nothing but leaves. But now the boughs were heavy and bending with what Jen was sure, even at this distance, was a bountiful crop of shiny red and gold apples.

※

He stood on the edge of the cliff, staring out to sea in the thin light of dawn. The pull of the tides mirrored the pull of something inside him. Blood, though he wasn't sure if it flowed in his veins any longer. The pull of blood. Was that why he had awoken?

He was pretty sure he should not be awake. And yet, there were other things awake that should not be.

The apples, for one. He turned from the sea and beheld the apple tree at the centre of Nans-Avallen. They were early. Too early. It was wrong. Everything was wrong. This place was wrong.

The apple tree made him feel… angry. Sad. Pained. And frightened, as well. Frightened for what power infused this place. The power that meant he was walking across this field on this clifftop, when he had no right to be here.

It was wrong. Everything was wrong.

The people in the houses… it was one of them, he was sure. The reason his blood roared in his head. The pull of blood, like the tides.

Everything was wrong. But it had to be made right.

He walked further towards the houses, heading behind them, where their small gardens backed on to the woods. This house? Or this one? Perhaps this one? He couldn't decide, did not know. The memory eluded him, but his blood continued to pound. The pull of blood. Everything wrong to be made right.

A movement inside one of the houses. A woman standing in the window, filling a kettle with water from the tap.

He watched her for a long time, wondering. Was this the one? Then she saw him, and screamed.

13

JEN

Jen emptied the Ocado bags onto the kitchen work surface and proceeded to put everything away in the cupboards, fridge and freezer. She didn't know who had decided to order for her, and wasn't sure that she shouldn't be feeling a little more put out that someone had just assumed what she would want. They could have asked. But she was too exhausted to even properly be annoyed about it. Besides, they had ordered pretty much what she would have ordered herself. Was she that transparent, easy to read? That obvious?

In one of the bags was something that evidently wasn't Jen's. A bottle of shampoo formulated for black hair. She was still un-showered and not properly dressed, but pulled her robe around her and went over to Adaku and Arthur's place with the bottle. The door was open and she hesitated, wondering if she should knock first, but then saw Maggie sitting at the kitchen island, waving at her.

'I guess this is yours,' said Jen, putting the bottle on the worktop. She paused. Adaku looked upset. 'Is everything all right?' She had been about to tell them about the weird vision of her mother, but Adaku looked in a worse state than Jen felt.

'Adaku had a bit of a shock this morning,' murmured Arthur. 'She says she saw a man in the back garden.'

'I did see a man in the back garden.' Adaku scowled. 'He was standing by the trees. He was there one minute, and I screamed and dropped the kettle, and then when I stood up he'd gone.'

'Oh god,' said Jen. 'What did he look like?'

Adaku shrugged. 'I didn't see him for long enough.'

'I've phoned the police,' added Arthur.

'Arthur, be a love and fix me a latte,' said Maggie, rubbing her temples. 'I was feeling a bit delicate already and this has just made it worse.' She picked up one of the glossy Apple Tree Vale brochures that was sitting on the island and began to waft herself with it. 'Going to be a scorcher today. And so early in the season, too.'

'That'll be climate change for you,' said Arthur, putting a pod in the coffee machine.

'Well, bring it on,' said Maggie. 'I think we should go down to the beach today. Fancy that, Jen?'

Jen just wanted to go back to bed. But a day on the beach would be lovely and relaxing, and might wipe away whatever anxiety had caused her to freak out this morning. She'd been taken shopping by Tabby before they came, and had a case full of swimsuits and bikinis to try out.

'Why are you all talking about the beach?' snapped Adaku. 'There was a man in the garden!'

'I'm sure he didn't mean any harm,' said Jen, as gently as she could. 'Probably some local, walking his dogs or something.'

'Well, they shouldn't, not on our land,' said Arthur. 'I'm sure the police will deal with it.'

Suddenly, Maggie shrieked and slapped the brochure down on the island worktop, hard. Arthur turned round and blinked as Maggie cautiously lifted up the booklet, peering underneath.

'Ewwww,' said Maggie. 'Is that one of those things that bit you?'

Everyone gathered around to peer at the pulpy mess on the worktop. It was indeed one of those yellow-bodied spiders that had been crawling all over the tree yesterday.

'You shouldn't kill spiders,' Jen heard herself muttering. She stopped short of adding what her mum always said. *Or you'll make it rain.* She couldn't help herself glancing out at the clear blue sky to see if dark clouds were suddenly scudding in.

'Jen's right, they eat pests,' said Arthur, putting a coffee in front of Maggie. He scooped the corpse of the spider up in a wad of kitchen tissue.

'They eat your wife as well, or had you forgot?' said Maggie, looking to Adaku for support. 'You're glad I killed it, aren't you? Not like these two new members of the Cornish Spider Preservation Society.'

But Adaku merely looked impassively at Maggie as Arthur threw the scrunched-up paper into the pedal bin. 'No, you shouldn't kill spiders,' she said softly. 'Gizo wouldn't like it.'

Maggie sipped at her latte then said, 'Gizo? Was he the landlord of the pub last night?'

'That was Clemmo,' said Jen. She looked at Adaku. 'Who is Gizo?'

'Trickster spider god,' said Adaku, still staring at the place on the worktop where the spider had been squished. Jen noticed she was scratching idly at her wrist again. Speaking almost absently, Adaku said, 'Once, long ago in my country, there was a very bad drought and a long summer and the worst famine anyone could remember. Everyone was hungry, even the gods. Even Gizo. But Gizo had a plan.'

Maggie opened her mouth to say something but then seemed to think better of it, and listened. Adaku went on, 'Gizo went to the elephant, and said many flattering things to him, that he was the master of all the land. And that the hippopotamus, who was the master of all the waters, deferred to the elephant and wished to give him a gift. He would give a horse to the elephant, but the elephant had to give a gift to the hippopotamus in return.'

Jen could almost see the cogs turning in Maggie's mind, wondering what use an elephant had for a horse, but the other woman kept silent. Adaku said, 'The elephant agreed to give a hundred baskets of grain to the hippopotamus, in thanks for the kind gift that was forthcoming.

'Then Gizo went to the hippopotamus, and said the elephant wished to give a gift of a fine horse in deference to hippopotamus's mastery of the water, but would like a gift of a hundred baskets of fish in return. Of course, neither the grain nor the fish reached their intended recipients. And Gizo's belly was full while everyone else starved.'

'So he scammed them,' said Maggie at last. 'I like this Gizo. He would do well today. What happened when the elephant and the hippo didn't get their horse?'

Adaku shrugged. 'Something about Gizo giving each of them the end of a rope and saying the horse was tied to it, but they were as strong as each other so no matter that they kept pulling on the rope, actually pulling against each other, they never got their horse.'

'I'm sure there's some kind of moral in all that,' said Arthur, putting a latte on the island in front of Jen. He winked at her. 'Never kill a spider or you'll end up pulling on a rope for a non-existent horse. Something like that.'

Jen saw Adaku shoot him a veiled look. 'Don't make fun of the old stories, Arthur,' she said. She grabbed the bottle of shampoo Jen had brought over. 'I'm going for a bath. Put some brunch on. Everyone can come over here for it then we can go to the beach.'

'Aye aye, captain,' said Arthur, saluting.

Maggie slid off her stool. 'Better go and get beach-ready then. See you all back here in, what, an hour?'

Jen sat there, somewhat awkwardly sipping her latte, as Arthur started to get the things for brunch out of the fridge. She said, 'Where did you and Adaku meet, Arthur? I'm not sure you've ever told me.'

He clattered in the pan draw, pulling out a variety of utensils. 'Have I not? You know I used to be a photographer? Yonks and yonks ago. Some fashion, bit of glamour.' He turned round and tapped his nose. 'Bit of sauce, when the opportunity presented itself.'

'And Adaku was a model?' guessed Jen.

'Not at first. I spotted her at Camden Market and thought she was quite the most beautiful creature I had ever seen. I immediately stopped her and asked if she'd pose for a set of shots for me. Of course, she told me to fuck off. She wasn't long in London from Nigeria, and had been warned about men like me. Thankfully she took my card, though. Had a good couple of years doing magazine stuff with her.' He sighed. 'That girl could have been a superstar, you know. Could have made millions.'

'Why didn't she? Didn't she like it?'

Arthur laughed. 'She didn't need to. Her father is an actual prince. He's stinking rich, and so is she. And now, so are we. Another latte?'

'I should be getting on, get ready for brunch,' said Jen. Money came so easily to the gang, and they were so unconcerned how it did so or who it came from, or what had to be done to get it. The only reason Jen had any money was because she met Justin, and he had died.

'Top hole. See you back here in a bit. Then we can check out the beach. See if it comes up to everyone's exacting standards. Tabby used to vacation in the Maldives as a kid and Maggie in Sri Lanka.'

'I'm sure it will for me,' said Jen. 'Furthest I got as a child was Filey.'

Arthur brayed a laugh, as though that was a brilliant joke, and turned back to his pans, whistling.

Jen was heading back to her house, thinking she might get a nap in before brunch, when she saw Simon waving at her from the corner plot. Inwardly sighing, she pulled her robe tighter about her and carried on to where he was sitting at the table under the parasol, the Financial Times spread out, anchored with a cafetière and a coffee cup to stop the warm breeze blowing off the sea lifting it up.

'Jen!' he said. 'I wanted to apologise again for last night. For my insensitive comments.'

Jen waved him away. 'It's fine. Forgotten already.'

Simon dropped his voice to a conspiratorial whisper. 'I don't think it would have been much of a competition, anyway. I saw the way that fisherman looked you up and down. Don't think he goes out to bat for my side at all.'

Jen felt suddenly flustered. 'Really? I mean, I'm sure he wasn't.' She shaded her eyes against the bright sunlight and looked out towards the tree. 'Oh, the apples. I thought I saw them this morning.'

Simon frowned and followed her gaze. 'Apples? Bit early for them, isn't it?'

Jen shrugged. 'I'm not sure. Do apples have a season?'

They walked together over the grass — was it lusher underfoot than it had been yesterday — and stood in the shadow of the tree, looking up. 'Far too early,' said Simon. 'September, mostly. And take it from one who knows; as a callow youth I spent an autumn working on a cider farm in Devon, and had my sexual awakening on a hay bale with a rather rough boy called Trevor who had the most remarkable callused fingers.'

They stared up at the branches, weighed down with the fruit. 'And yet, there they are. How odd.'

What was even odder was that Jen was absolutely sure that the apples hadn't been there yesterday. She said, 'They don't... grow overnight, do they?'

Simon barked a laugh, and didn't bother to answer. 'Must have a word with that Penrose chap. Perhaps he can give some insight into it. But I've never in my life heard of apple trees fruiting so early in summer.'

Jen stepped closer to the tree and inspected the thick, wide trunk. There were no spiders to be seen. She said, 'One of those spiders that bit Adaku on the tree yesterday was in her kitchen this morning.'

'Must have liked the taste of her,' said Simon. 'I looked them up last night.' He delved into the pocket of his shorts and pulled out his phone, and passed it to Jen. 'Does that look like it?'

The page was open on a Wikipedia entry for the yellow sac spider. It did indeed look like the ones that had been crawling all over the tree yesterday, though the text said they were usually much smaller than the ones Jen had seen. Simon said, 'Love apple trees, apparently. Quite common in the UK. Bites aren't dangerous, but can cause a bit of swelling and itching.'

'Mystery solved,' said Jen, handing back the phone.

'And, there, perhaps, is another enigma unwrapped,' said Simon. He was looking off towards the smaller house set apart from theirs, the affordable housing unit. Jen looked too, and saw a woman in shorts and a T-shirt carrying what looked like a bundle of long poles. She walked almost to the cliff edge and set the poles on end, and Jen realised as she opened them out that it was an easel. She placed a large blank canvas on the easel, and stepped back, head on one side.

'Our neighbour,' said Simon. He glanced at his phone. 'I believe brunch was mentioned round at Arthur and Adaku's? I had best go and perform my ablutions. I shall see you there.'

'Did you hear about the man?' said Jen. 'Adaku saw someone by the woods early this morning. Quite shook her up.'

'Some yokel, poaching or some-such,' nodded Simon. 'I'm sure it's nothing to worry about.'

Jen had to laugh. 'Poaching. You make it sound like we're living in *Lady Chatterley's Lover.*'

Simon sighed theatrically. 'I wish.' He headed back to his house, and Jen looked at the woman on the clifftop as she laid a box of what must be paints down on the grass, and picked up a pencil, and began to sketch on the canvas.

14

MERRIN

Merrin had been painting for an hour when she felt a presence at her back. She'd been almost in a trance, putting watercolours on the canvas, her sightline lost somewhere in the middle distance overlooking the calm Atlantic, and hadn't heard anyone approach until the polite cough announced a visitor. Merrin blinked and looked at what she'd painted so far; if it was meant to be a facsimile of her view right now, she hadn't done very well.

'Hiya. Sorry to bother you.'

Merrin turned round to see the young woman from the newcomers, the one who seemingly lived alone. She was wearing a sundress and flip-flops, glancing over Merrin's shoulder at the painting. Merrin smiled and held out her hand. 'That's fine. I'm just daubing. Getting back into practice. I'm Merrin. I live in the…'

They both looked towards Merrin's little house, dwarfed by the huge properties of the London set. 'It looks lovely,' said the woman, quickly. 'Just the right size. I'm rattling round in that place.' She took Merrin's hand and said, 'Merrin is a lovely name, too. I'm Jen.'

'You're northern,' said Merrin. 'Yorkshire?'

Jen nodded. 'Bradford. Are you local? To Scuttler's Cove?'

'I grew up here,' said Merrin, nodding. 'Been away for a long time though. Lived in London for a few years.'

Jen looked out across the sea. 'I can see why you came back. It's beautiful here.'

Merrin glanced over at the new houses. 'It's a nice place to holiday, but not so great if you have to live here. I didn't really plan to come back. My mother died.'

Jen's hand went to her mouth. 'Oh, I'm so sorry.'

Merrin shrugged. 'So, your friends aren't from Bradford, are they?'

'No. London. I've lived in London for a while, too.' Jen bit her lip. 'To be honest, they're not really my friends. Not properly. Well, I suppose they are now. They're my husband's friends.'

'Ah. Is he joining you soon?'

Jen stared at her manicured toes. 'No. Justin died. Three months ago. We were in a crash. Not far from here.'

Merrin's eyes widened. She remembered reading about that. Scuttler's Cove came up so infrequently in news stories that it was very notable when it did. She'd read on one of the local newspaper sites about a crash in the lanes, a car with a tractor. 'God, that's awful. I'm so sorry.'

Jen was blinking away tears. 'We'd just come to see the house for the first time. We were making so many plans. Justin was even talking about…' She coughed, and looked back at the house. 'Anyway. The gang was all coming down here for the summer, and they wouldn't hear of me not coming with them.'

The gang. Merrin watched as the Londoners began to seep out of their big houses, one by one and in pairs. They wore their wealth like an aura, in a way that Jen didn't. Merrin couldn't help but like her. She was staring at the half-done painting, and frowning.

'Oh,' said Jen. 'That's just broken my dream from last night.'

Merrin turned back to the canvas, frowning a little herself. 'You know, I'm not entirely sure where that came from.'

It was the view from where she was sitting, but rather than the placid sea in front of them, the ocean was raging and roaring, rising up like a tidal wave under a dark, stormy sky. An impossibly high tidal wave, one that if it was real would crash down and obliterate Nans-Avallen.

'Does the sea often get like that?' said Jen, sounding a little worried.

Merrin laughed. 'Absolutely never. In fact, I'd go as far as to say it would be an impossibility. I've no idea why I painted that at all, to be honest.'

'Just like my dream,' said Jen softly. She watched Merrin dabbing at the painting, then said, 'What did you do to your hand?'

There was a bright blue plaster around the middle finger of Merrin's right hand. She'd been slicing bread that morning and slipped with the knife, leaving an angry gash on the finger. 'Just clumsy old me, as usual,' she said.

There was a shout from the houses, and they both turned to see the others waving at them.

'We're going to check out the beach,' said Jen.

'Well, have fun,' said Merrin, picking up her brush again. She saw Jen frowning at the painting again. 'And, like I said, don't worry. That absolutely never happens. You'll have a lovely day.'

Jen bit her lip, then said, 'Maybe we could... I don't know... have a drink, or something? It's nice to meet someone who...'

She trailed off. *Someone who is more like me*, Merrin guessed she was going to say. 'That'd be lovely,' she said, and nodded towards her house. 'You know where I am.'

Merrin watched Jen walk back across the grass and the Tarmac roads to *the gang*, who picked up their bags of beach stuff and headed off towards the path that would take them down the cliff to the shore.

Merrin painted into the afternoon, pausing only when she heard Taran's van labouring up the hill and on to Nans-Avallen. She'd forgotten he was taking her to do a shop. She'd also forgotten to eat lunch, and finally noticed her stomach grumbling in protestation.

'Hey, that's brilliant,' he said after pulling up, and seeing her painting. 'I didn't know you were so good.'

She shrugged, suddenly and stupidly coy. 'Just getting back into it, really.'

'You should have a word with Janet. At the gallery.'

'God, is she still alive?' said Merrin, packing up the paints. Taran grabbed the easel, and they walked back to her house. 'She must be a hundred.'

Taran laughed. 'Not quite. But she's no spring chicken, that's for sure. She's always looking for local artists to showcase at the Driftwood.' He cast an eye over the canvas that Merrin held. 'Not sure that's quite the thing the tourists will go for, mind. What made you paint that?'

'I'm not really sure,' admitted Merrin as they walked into the cool of the house. 'Funny thing is, I spoke to one of the Londoners. Except she's actually a northerner. She said she dreamed about the exact same thing last night.'

'Oh? Which one?' said Taran, airily. Almost too casually.

'The only one who doesn't have fake tits and hair extensions and look like she wipes her arse on fifty-pound notes.' Merrin grinned. 'Her name's Jen. She seems quite nice.'

As Merrin propped the canvas up on the kitchen worktop, Taran said, 'Oh, that reminds me, brought you something. One tick.'

He returned with a plastic bag that stunk of fish. 'Couple of turbot. Cost you a fortune in the Star and Anchor.'

'I could eat them raw,' said Merrin. 'I'm famished. Skipped lunch.'

Taran suddenly started opening drawers and clattering utensils on the side. Merrin said, 'What are you doing?'

'You should never shop on an empty stomach,' he said. 'You'll buy all sorts of crap you don't want. Here, this won't take a minute.'

Amused, Merrin sat at the little kitchen table and watched him cook up the turbot in her grill pan with a little butter and a few cloves of crushed garlic from a bulb he, bizarrely, pulled from his jacket pocket.

'Do you always carry garlic in case a damsel in distress needs an emergency meal?' she teased as he put the plate down in front of her. 'Or has Scuttler's Cove become overrun with vampires since I was last here?'

Taran laughed. 'A bit of both.' He put the other fish in her fridge and started to wash the pots as Merrin ate. God, it was gorgeous. She'd never tasted fish like it. She smiled as she watched Taran drying and putting away. Kamal would never have thought to do any of that in a million years.

Stop it, thought Merrin, stealing a glance at him as he bent over to put the grill pan back in the big drawer. *You're not home for that.* And another voice murmured, *Well, what would it hurt?*

'Ready?' said Taran, drying his hands on a tea towel.

As Merrin locked up, she noticed Taran gazing towards the apple tree at the centre of Nans-Avallen. She looked too, then said, 'Oh. The apples are out.'

'Yes.'

Merrin looked at him. 'Aren't they a bit early?' She walked over to the tree, gazing up into its branches, which were heavy with fruit, ripe and golden and red. 'Surely far too early?'

Taran joined her, looking up. 'Far too early, yes.'

Merrin glanced at him. He seemed suddenly... strange. Distant. Lost in thought. Then he turned to her and said, 'Can I have that painting? Of the sea?'

She was a little taken aback. 'What? You like it that much? But it's not even finished...'

'I'll pay you for it,' he said. 'When it's finished.' He smiled, but it seemed a little forced. 'I'm Scuttler's Cove's fisherman, remember. The sea is my thing. Then you can do something more... touristy. For Janet.'

'You really think she'll take my work for the Driftwood Gallery?' she said as they walked to his van.

'I'm sure of it,' nodded Taran, letting her into the passenger side. 'These rich Londoners, they'll pay stupid prices for something local and authentic. Especially as good as yours. You could make a tidy little living off it, over summer.'

Blushing with pride, Merrin clicked her seat belt in and Taran gunned the engine and took them off Nans-Avallen and towards the delights of the big Tesco.

—

When they came back an hour and a half later, the back of the van stuffed with bags, the Londoners were there, all gathered around the front of Jen's house. Taran let the van roll to a halt outside, the engine idling, as Merrin leaned over him to see what they were all looking at. Jen was in the middle of the huddle, crying and being placated by the other women. A tall, gangly man with curly hair hopped over to them, looking the van up and down. 'Are you from the police?'

Taran laughed. 'No. Merrin lives over there. In the other house.'

The man stared at Merrin, then over at her house. 'We called the police,' he said. His eyes screwed up. 'Are you locals?'

'Like he said, I live over there,' said Merrin. 'What's happened?'

The group parted and Merrin saw the two things simultaneously. On the step on the front of the house, the mangled, bloody remains of what had unmistakably once been a fox. And on the front door, evidently daubed in the animal's blood, some kind of shape or symbol. It was like an eye, with lines or lashes radiating out from it like the sun's rays, a round pupil in the middle. It was familiar, but Merrin couldn't quite place it, even though she felt as though she should be able to.

One of the other Londoners, a handsome man with silver hair and a tanned, chiselled face, joined the gangly one and peered into the van. The curly-haired man said, 'She lives in the other house, Paul,' as though Merrin wasn't even there.

The man, Paul, glared at her. 'Did you see anything?'

Merrin glanced at her watch. 'We've been out since about three. There was nothing there when we left to go shopping.'

'You know we had some vandalism on another house when we arrived?'

Merrin shrugged uncomfortably. She felt as though she was being interrogated. Taran said, 'Local youths, probably. High spirits. Pay them no heed.'

Paul looked furious. 'Someone has killed an animal and put some kind of...' He stared back at Jen's door. 'Well, I don't know what it is. Sounds like more than high spirits to me. Sounds like harassment.' He straightened up. 'Anyway, I'm sure the police will want to speak to you about it when they arrive.'

Taran nodded and drove the van to Merrin's house. She said quietly, 'Do you know anything about this?'

'I've been with you all afternoon,' he protested.

'That isn't what I said. It's Bobby Carlyon, isn't it?'

'He might have had something to do with the Independent Cornwall graffiti on your house, and I think he knows the kids who did the one up here,' admitted Taran, turning off the engine. 'But not this.'

'How can you say for sure?'

'Bobby will have been in his shop all day. I'm sure he's got a hundred alibis.'

'Then who did it?' pressed Merrin, climbing out of the van.

'I don't know,' said Taran thoughtfully, opening up the back and grabbing four of the carrier bags, two in each hand. 'But I'm sure we'll find out. Now let's get this stuff in the fridge before it spoils.'

✵

The fox had gone for him while he sat, slumped against a tree, staring into nothingness. He hadn't done anything to it, hadn't threatened it or its cubs. But it just stood there, its teeth bared, its tail puffed up, and then pounced. It bit him on his arm, but he didn't feel anything, just watched its teeth sink in with almost distant curiosity. Maybe the fox knew what he was, even if he didn't. Maybe it could sense that his presence was somehow wrong. That he shouldn't be here. Not on this land.

He grabbed the animal and in one swift move, broke its neck.

He still hadn't eaten, and didn't even know if he wanted to. It was almost like… a memory of hunger, a conditioned response that he should eat, because he hadn't for so long. But he felt no real desire or need. Still, he pushed up the thing on his face and put his teeth on the belly of the animal, where the skin was taut. He pierced the flesh, blood running down his chin, and tore off a hunk. He chewed the warm flesh and fur, and forced himself to swallow. It was not pleasant.

He had liked food, once. A pasty and a pint of beer. He felt nostalgic for it, for whatever life that had been before he found himself… here.

Though he didn't really know for sure, he had a growing, keening sense of whose land this was, and why he was here. And he knew that those people who had come to live in the houses… one of them was important to him. He didn't know which one, or why. But he felt almost… a duty. That was the only way he could describe it. A duty to what or to who, he didn't quite know.

Dragging the fox corpse behind him, he walked to the edge of the trees to look out at the houses. The sun was high, and something about it shining through the branches of the big apple tree stirred something within him. The sun, and the apple tree, and the land on which he stood… they were all connected, entwined. And it was something to do with him, and something to do with the incomers, or one of them, at least.

The people in the houses had all gone out in their cars, so he walked across the field, towards the silent homes. He was drawn to one in particular, though he couldn't have said why. Those connections, that entwining. Whoever lived here was part of it all, he was sure.

He stumbled towards it and dumped the dead fox on the step. Then he bent, with difficulty, and dipped his fingers into the wound on its belly. He straightened and began to trace an outline on the door in the fox's blood. When he'd finished he stepped back to look at it.

The sun, or maybe an eye. He wasn't sure. But it seemed to fit. Seemed to fit this place, this land, the sun shining through the branches of the apple tree.

Yes, it seemed to fit this land, and that which slumbered beneath it.

Slumbered, but stirred.

15

JEN

'Why do they hate us?' said Jen, feeling sick to her stomach. She felt like she actually might throw up at the sight of the mangled fox corpse on her doorstep.

'The locals?' said Maggie. 'Because we're rich and beautiful.' She gave a little laugh, which Jen thought was wholly inappropriate in the circumstances.

'It's the perception of us,' said Arthur. 'That we come in and take the houses and drive local people out. But it's not the case, really. We come down here for summer, spend money in the pubs and shops, use local tradesmen if there's a problem. We're boosting the economy. Without us... well, places like Scuttler's Cove would die, wouldn't they?'

Tabby turned to Paul. 'Can we get rid of that awful dead thing?'

He rubbed his chin. 'Perhaps the police would need to see it... in situ, as it were.'

'Oh, I shouldn't imagine the police will be rushing here with their blue lights on over a dead fox,' boomed Simon. 'We should call Penrose, get him to clean it up. We can take photographs.'

'Good idea,' said Tabby warmly. 'Paul, put it in a bag. We can't leave it out here. God knows what other vermin it'll attract.'

Jen hugged herself, watching them all talking, feeling detached and separate. Why her? Why her house? She... the thought flitted across her mind. She wasn't like the rest of them. Not really. So why single her out?

Paul came back with a bin liner and a pair of gloves, and gingerly picked the fox up by its tail, dropping it inside. 'I'll stick it in our garden until Penrose sorts out a proper disposal.'

Tabby tapped a painted nail on her lip. 'This has been a horrible day, and I know just what we need to make it better.' She broke out into a wide grin. 'Girls' night out.'

It was the last thing Jen wanted, but Tabby wouldn't take no for an answer. Her, Tabby, Adaku and Maggie were going to the Star and Anchor, for drinks. Paul said, 'Poker night for us, then.'

Simon put the back of his hand theatrically across his forehead. 'Ah, and what of me? Girls' night out or poker night in with the boys? This is the dreadful dichotomy of falling between two stools.'

'Poker night for you,' insisted Tabby. 'Strictly girls allowed. Let's set off at... seven, say?'

At six, having showered, and still in her slouchy jumper and joggers, Jen went back outside to stare at the design on the door. She'd tried to do an image search on the Internet but hadn't come up with anything conclusive. Penrose had said he'd send someone over to clean it up this evening, and take away the fox. Jen squatted down, her fingers brushing the grass at the front of her house. Was there a slight indentation there? Like a footprint, perhaps? She stood up and looked at it again. Yes, it did look like a footprint. A boot, maybe. Jen scanned the grass. Was that another one? She took photos with her phone, for when the police finally decided to show up, then turned and scanned the woods. Was someone in there, watching them? Watching her? She felt a shiver at the nape of her neck. Adaku had seen someone behind her house. On a whim, Jen walked to the end of the houses, in the direction the second footprint seemed to have been pointing. She went behind Simon's, at the end, to where the fences separated their gardens from the trees at the beginning of the woods. They were packed closely together, and light struggled to penetrate, making them look dark and foreboding.

Jen walked along the fences, which she could just see over if she stood on her tiptoes. She could see people moving about behind windows, hear voices and snatches of conversations. Simon, Timothy and Maggie, Adaku and Arthur. She walked the length of the fence, then back, and paused at Tabby and Paul's house. The French windows were open into the garden and she could hear the low murmur of voices, and then a giggle.

Cautiously, Jen peered over the fence, then ducked back down again. Tabby and Paul were in the house, her leaning against the kitchen island, Paul standing in front of her. And on the worktop beside Tabby... Jen looked over the fence again, sure her eyes must have deceived her. But no. There it was. The dead fox.

Tabby was talking quietly, and Jen couldn't hear what she was saying. Then her eyes widened as she saw Paul put his hand on the fox, palm down, sinking his fingers into its mauled corpse. What the fuck? Jen couldn't tear her eyes away as Paul lifted his hand, dripping with gore.

And then wiped it down Tabby's face.

Jen's hand flew to her mouth and she felt her bile rise. What weird shit was this? Was Paul... she didn't know. Abusing Tabby, somehow? But then Tabby put her arms around his neck and drew him to her, and he kissed her, hard and savagely, on her lips. Her lips covered with fox blood.

Paul's hands went to Tabby's hips and in one smooth movement he lifted her, sitting her on the kitchen island, next to the fox corpse. She wrapped her legs around him and he started to tug at his belt, at the same time lifting Tabby's summer dress over her waist. His hand was still slick with blood, staining Tabby's dress and thighs.

Jen sank down behind the fence, her hand still over her mouth, more to stop her voicing her disbelief at what she was seeing than anything else. Then, as silently as possible, she stole back along the fence-line and ran into her house.

—

'And so I said to him, "darling, you've more chance of sticking that thing in the Queen of Sheba than you have in me",' said Adaku, and everyone collapsed into gales of laughter.

Jen was pleasantly drunk. They had a table in the Star and Anchor and had been served what seemed an endless succession of cocktails. She kept glancing around at the pub, busy with holidaymakers. Everyone was casting furtive glances in their direction, especially the men. Jen liked it. It made her feel part of something, at last. Part of the gang. She understood, at least a little, what Maggie had meant when she said the locals were jealous of them because they were rich and beautiful. Jen did feel rich and beautiful, there at that table, drinking cocktails and not worrying about the price or who was going to pay for them.

'You never talk about your family,' said Maggie suddenly to Jen.

Jen blinked, unsure what to say. Tabby laughed lightly. 'Oh, who talks about their families, Maggie? They're all generally hideous.'

Jen looked sidelong at Tabby. All she'd thought about all evening was what she'd spied over the fence. Paul wiping the fox blood over Tabby's face, and lifting her up onto the worktop. She gave a little mental shrug. People could be kinky, especially in the privacy of their own homes. It was weird, for sure. But who was Jen to judge? Besides, Tabby had always been kind to her, and she felt she needed that allyship from her.

'I don't mind,' said Jen. 'My dad left when I was little. Never seen him since.'

'Men are cunts,' said Adaku sagely.

'My mum…' Jen swelled. 'My mum is in a care home. Dementia. She doesn't even know who I am. So I don't visit. It just upsets me and confuses her.' She looked down at the dregs of the vibrant blue cocktail, the name of which she'd forgotten. 'I suppose that makes me a bad person.'

'Oh, God, not at all!' said Maggie, braying a laugh. 'I wish my mother would go doolally. Stop her bothering me constantly and trying to visit. Hate the bloody woman.'

Tabby laid a hand on Jen's and smiled at her. She murmured, 'You know, you and me have more in common than you might think.'

Jen was just about to ask her what she meant when Adaku said, 'If she's being cared for, that's all you can do.'

It was meant to be a kindness, Jen knew, but it just made her feel worse. The others, they couldn't understand what it was like. For them, a 'care home' probably meant something like a stately home that came with attentive staff and the best medical care money could buy. For

Jen's mum, up until she married Justin and found herself with money to burn, it had been a social services-run home staffed by young girls on minimum wage, where the patients were locked up most of the day or sat in a dayroom and largely ignored. Jen's mum had never owned her own house, so her care had been paid for by the state, which put her on the bottom rung of the ladder. But now… well, now she had money, things were different. Maybe that was what that weird vision of her mum on the first night, chained in a Victorian cell and shrieking at her, meant. Maybe that was her subconscious guilt, telling her that she could throw money at a problem but that didn't mean it went away. She said slowly, 'I saw her, when we first moved into the houses. Or thought I did. It was horrible.'

'A nightmare,' said Tabby.

Jen shook her head. 'I wasn't asleep. I was sure of it.'

She felt Tabby squeeze her hand again. 'With everything that you've been through, it's no wonder that you've been having nightmares.'

Everyone started to say sympathetic things about Justin. Adaku said, 'I have some pills if you're having trouble sleeping. Remind me and I'll drop some round for you.'

'Talk about bloody nightmares,' chimed in Maggie. 'All I dream about is spiders. Killed three of those little bastards in my kitchen today.'

Jen noticed Adaku scratching her wrist beneath the long, tight top she wore. Tabby said, 'God, I've had them too! Think we should get a pest controller in?'

Jen suddenly needed the toilet, and stood up, too sharply, her head swimming with the alcohol. She made her way to the bathrooms and staggered, banging herself on the door frame as she went through. The cubicles were empty save for one, and she went to the end one, sitting down heavily on the toilet. She was a lot drunker than she thought. As she peed, she stared through one eye at the graffiti on the back of the toilet door. The landlord's evident gentrification of the pub hadn't stretched to refurbishing the bathrooms yet. There were the usual rude words and promises of a good time, and felt-tip drawings of genitalia. Then Jen's gaze was drawn to a shape etched into the wood of the cubicle door, almost hidden by the overlaid scrawl of black ink. She reached out and her finger traced the shape. An eye, with lashes, or perhaps a sun radiating heat.

The symbol that had been drawn on her door in the blood of the mutilated fox.

Jen stood up and flushed, and went to excitedly tell the others. But when she got back to the table, Adaku was having a stand-up row with a chastened-looking middle-aged man who had apparently knocked the table and spilled their fresh drinks. The entire pub was looking until the landlord, Clemmo, came over and made the peace, ordering a fresh round of cocktails for the gang, on the house, and Adaku was mollified. By the time the drinks came, Jen had forgotten completely what she was excited about telling them.

An hour later they were in a taxi back to the clifftop, Jen sitting by the open window, letting the sea air wash over her and sober her up. It wasn't working. Her head was spinning and her stomach was flipping somersaults. Far too much to drink.

She felt the pressure of Tabby's hand on her leg and the other woman murmured, 'Don't you find something about this place makes you feel... excited? Reckless? Maybe even a little crazy? Apple Tree Vale.'

'Nans-Avallen,' slurred Jen.

Tabby's voice dropped to a whisper, and Jen felt her breath on her ear. 'I know you saw us. When Paul smeared that blood on my face. Did you watch him fuck me, too? I wouldn't mind if you did.'

Then the taxi stopped and Jen tugged at the door handle, half-tumbling out just before she copiously threw up on the grass. She wiped her mouth as the others got out of the taxi, Maggie laughing and Tabby making sympathetic noises. 'Straight to bed for you,' said Adaku.

There was a chorus of drunken goodnights and Jen woozily let herself into her house, exhausted and shamed, the front of her top covered in vomit. She couldn't wait to get into bed, but something was making her mind buzz. Something she'd seen at the pub. Something to do with the dead fox, and the graffiti on her door.

Something, she thought suddenly, to do with the apple tree.

Jen went to stand at her window, staring at the apple tree. The apples. It was all to do with the apples. She frowned. What was to do with the apples? What did she mean?

But that was all she knew. It was all to do with the apples. And then she saw a movement, in the darkness, and a figure walking towards the apple tree.

16

MERRIN

As darkness fell over Nans-Avallen, Merrin couldn't stop thinking about apples. She'd eaten dinner, and was full, and had started on a bottle of rosé wine. But she couldn't stop thinking about apples. Specifically, the red and gold apples that hung in their dozens from the boughs of the tree that gave Nans-Avallen its name. Merrin flicked through the TV channels, settling on nothing, then went to her painting, set up on the easel by the window, and added some finishing touches. It was ten p.m. and she felt dog-tired. But she couldn't stop thinking about bloody apples.

Eventually, she pulled on her boots and padded over the grass, dew settling on it, and stood by the apple tree. The night sky was a deep blue and the tree was framed against it when she looked up at its leafy, fruit-laden branches.

Now what?

There was a dull thud by her feet, and when she looked down an apple rolled in the grass. Then another one fell a few feet away. Then another. Suddenly, there was a sound like drumming, or galloping horses, and apples were falling from the tree in rapid succession, as though being fired from a gun. Merrin looked around at them, two dozen at least. Then she pulled up the hem of her summer dress and bent to pick them up, depositing them in the makeshift hammock until she had gathered them all and held them close to her, looking as though she was pregnant. Pregnant with apples.

Now what?

Merrin turned on her heels to face the Londoners' houses. There were lights on in most of them, including Jen's. The symbol in fox's blood had been scrubbed off, the animal's corpse removed. Who had done it? Merrin had taken a surreptitious shot with her phone and searched the Internet for it, but couldn't find anything conclusive, and nothing linking it to Cornish nationalism. But something about it niggled her, something about it was vaguely familiar, but forgotten. As she stared at the houses, Jen's door opened, at first a crack, and then wider, the silhouette of the woman framed in the rectangle of light there. Merrin didn't know why, but she started to walk towards her, carrying her burden of apples. Jen stepped out of her doorway and began to walk to meet her.

They stood in the starlight, on the damp grass, facing each other. Jen said, 'I was thinking about apples.'

'Me, too,' said Merrin softly.

They looked down at the apples gathered up in Merrin's dress skirt. Jen tentatively put her hand down there, and pulled an apple from the pile. She turned it this way and that in the night, and Merrin watched the faint light of the stars shining off its plump skin. Then Jen locked eyes with her, and bit deep into the apple. It made a satisfying crunch, and Merrin could see the juice running down her chin. Jen held out the apple to Merrin.

Something screamed at her inside her head, something forgotten, from childhood. *Don't eat the apples from*

Nans-Avallen. They'll drive you mad, or poison you, or make you jump off a cliff.

Merrin ignored it, opened her mouth, and sank her teeth into the apple.

It tasted good. Better than good. Like no apple she'd ever eaten.

Jen tossed the apple away and reached into Merrin's skirts to take another. She bit deep into it. Merrin let go of her skirt and the apples tumbled to the ground at their feet. She bent to retrieve one, straightened up, and began to eat. The two women kept their eyes on each other, gnawing at apple after apple, almost with a frenzy that Merrin seemed to be watching from afar, like a passenger in her own body. She could hear Jen's breathing, getting heavier and heavier, as she bit into another apple, then threw it to the ground. Merrin felt out of breath, too, as though she'd run a mile. She didn't know how many apples she'd eaten, but her hunger for them didn't seem to be abating. Her desire for them. She looked at Jen, her face slick with apple juice, the front of her T-shirt stained with it. Merrin felt the juice on her own chin, dripping down onto her dress, soaking it.

Merrin wasn't sure who moved first, her or Jen. But suddenly Merrin's hand was held out, palm outwards, and Jen was doing the same. And when their palms touched, it was like an electric shock sizzling through Merrin's body. Her mind was assaulted by images and sounds and even smells she couldn't make sense of. The apple tree, fruiting as though in a sped-up film reel, the sun rising and sinking several times a second as the fruit grew heavy on the boughs. The sea, churning and violent in the darkness, crashing on the cliffs. A dark-bladed knife, a splash of bright blood, and then a scream that pierced her ears, and a hand, a woman's hand, reaching up from the soil and being slowly dragged down, down, down to whatever lay beneath.

And then, as though separated by a bolt of lightning, they both stepped back. Whatever fog had descended in Merrin's mind, it was suddenly lifted, and she could see from the stricken look in Jen's eyes that the same had happened to her.

'I…' began Merrin, but she didn't know where to take it from there.

Jen's face crumpled, and she turned and ran for her house. A heartbeat later, Merrin spun around and did the same.

-

Merrin would have thought it all a dream, except she woke up to another glorious day with her face sticky with apple juice, her pillow stained with it. She spent a long time in the shower, washing away the scent of apples that clung to her like a perfume.

What the fuck?

Merrin was making toast for breakfast – her stomach grumbling as though she'd not eaten apple after apple after apple last night – when there was a sharp rapping at the door.

It was Jen.

'I thought I'd better come to see you,' she said, staring at her feet.

Merrin took a deep breath. 'Yes, we should probably talk. Come in.'

Over coffee at the kitchen table, Jen, who had not met Merrin's eyes, stared into her mug and said, 'Did you… did you… see stuff?'

'Yes,' said Merrin. 'I don't know what it meant. I don't even know why I was out there. Why were you out there?'

Finally, Jen looked up, her eyes red-rimmed, betraying a lack of sleep. 'I was just thinking about apples.'

'Me too.'

'And I couldn't stop.'

'Same.'

'I had to go out. To the apple tree. I didn't even know why.'

'Exactly the same.'

'And when I did, there you were.'

'There I was,' agreed Merrin. 'And there you were.'

They sat in silence for a moment. Merrin broke it eventually, saying, 'I don't understand any of what I saw, or why I saw it.'

'Neither do I,' said Jen. 'So why did it happen?'

Merrin had no answer to that.

'Things feel weird,' said Jen. 'That dead fox and its blood all over my door. The apples coming out when they shouldn't. And then, last night…'

Merrin was turning the ring on her little finger, faster and faster. Jen noticed it and glanced down. Merrin stopped. The skin around the ring was red and inflamed. 'Have you hurt another finger in the kitchen?'

Merrin smiled, looking at the plaster on her other hand. 'That reminds me, I should probably change this.' When she peeled it off with a wince, she stared at her finger for a long moment.

The cut, which had been not really very deep but certainly noticeable, had completely gone. She looked at Jen. 'How weird. A cut shouldn't heal in a day, should it?'

'Miracle plasters,' said Jen. 'That other finger, though, you should put some cream on that.' Jen smiled. It was as though some kind of storm that had been threatening suddenly dissipated. Merrin felt relief wash over her, the tension of Jen's arrival and the awkwardness of whatever had happened last night suddenly gone. She slid the ring off and held up her hand to Jen.

'Oh. You have a tattoo on the finger.' She peered closer at it. 'It's quite faded. And stretched. Have you had it a long time?'

Merrin pulled a face. 'Apparently since before I was one year old.'

—

It was when she started school that Merrin first realised that not everybody had a tattoo on their little finger. She couldn't remember a time without it, had half got the idea that she was somehow born with it. It was a boy who noticed first, on the first day at school, who pointed at it and loudly asked what that scribbling was on her little finger. The teacher had come over to see what all the ruckus was about, and Merrin would remember for a long time the look of distaste on her face as she said, 'Oh. It's a *tattoo*.'

No other five-year-old that Merrin knew had a tattoo on their little finger or anywhere else.

At home time she'd asked her mum, for the first time ever, why she had a tattoo, rolling the unfamiliar yet pleasing-to-say word around her tongue.

'Because you're special,' Lizzie Moon had said. 'Don't think about it.'

That night, before bed, Merrin had scrubbed and scrubbed at the tattoo with the sponge in the bath, hoping it might come off, like the paint she often splattered all over her when she did the pictures she so enjoyed doing at school or at home at weekends. It wouldn't budge. Merrin didn't want the tattoo. She didn't want to be different from the other children. She didn't want to be special.

When she got to big school, the tattoo marked her out as some kind of alternative hippy goth chick, which Merrin quite liked, and for the first time she was proud of her tattoo, liked to show it off. Even by the time she hit her teenage years it had started to fade and stretch as her body grew, and by the time she did her A-levels and started applying to university, it was grey and, if the lines and curves had meant anything at all at some point, it was now illegible and just a faded tangle.

It was then that Lizzie Moon gave her a ring to cover it.

'But I like it!' protested Merrin. 'I don't want to hide it.'

'Always wear a ring, and it always must be silver,' said Lizzie Moon.

'But why?'

'Because I want you to make a life away from Scuttler's Cove,' said her mother.

Merrin didn't understand, and didn't much like it, but she did what her mother had asked. By that time, at the age of eighteen, she knew how much respect people in Scuttler's Cove had for Lizzie Moon. She helped many people, and at the same time was not to be trifled with. So Merrin did as she was told, and for the next thirteen years always wore a ring over the tattoo on the little finger of her left hand, and always made sure it was silver.

'Wow,' said Jen. 'And I thought it was scandalous when Maisy Harding got her ears pierced in year three.' She held Merrin's hand in hers, inspecting the tattoo. 'And your mother never told you why she'd had it done?'

Merrin shrugged, withdrawing her hand. She'd slathered the finger with Sudocrem and it had already stopped itching so much. She forced a smile. 'Just an old hippy, I suppose.'

She looked at her finger. Whether it was the cream she didn't know, but the ink suddenly seemed more vibrant, deeper, than it had for a long time. Jen was looking at it, frowning. She reached out her hand and then faltered, the unspoken incident with the apples last night hanging between them. Then she said, 'Do you mind? Something just struck me.'

Merrin nodded and put her hand out. Jen put her fingers around Merrin's little finger, and pinched the skin tight, drawing it together at the top, making the tattoo contract, come together, look a little more like the tattoo it might have been when it was first done, when Merrin was little more than a baby.

'Oh,' said Jen, staring at the finger. Then she looked up at Merrin, a quizzical look on her face.

Merrin inspected the tattoo, pinched together in Jen's fingers. The design did look more coherent, more together, less faded, less stretched. And there was something almost recognisable there, a distinct shape, right on the top of her finger, close to the knuckle.

It was an eye, with a dot of a pupil and long lashes at the top and the bottom. That's what it looked like, anyway. And Merrin had seen it before. In the paintings that she'd found in her mother's things when she first came back to Scuttler's Cove, and had forgotten all about in the whirlwind of the funeral and moving house. But not only that…

It was the symbol that had been painted in fox blood on Jen's door yesterday.

17

TARAN

Taran sat on his boat, staring at the horizon. The sea swelled gently under him, filling his nets with fish. He wondered if he'd done enough. He wondered if it would even work anyway. Bligh and the others thought not, were of the opinion that he shouldn't even try. It was what it was. Nobody was happy about it, but it wasn't something that could be avoided. And what Taran was doing could only make things worse, they said.

But he had to try.

He'd been twenty-two when his dad fell ill with the cancer and died within two short months. Twenty-two when he took over the family business, and his fate was sealed as Scuttler's Cove's only real full-time working fisherman.

Twenty-two when he found out the world was nothing like he had always thought it to be.

'I need to talk to you, son,' his father had said in the hospital at Boscanlon, pulling the oxygen mask off his face.

Taran gently put it back, but his dad ripped it off again. 'No. I need to talk. The end's coming.'

'Don't talk like that, Dad.' Taran had lost his mum when he was just five. He could see his father withering and shrinking before his eyes, but he didn't want to talk about it. He just wanted their final moments to be as happy as they could be.

Jago Tregarth shook his head. 'The business is yours, son. You always knew that. The boat's yours. You'll make a good fisherman. Make a good living.'

'The sea's always been good to us, Dad,' said Taran gently.

'Aye, and that's no accident.'

Taran frowned. 'What do you mean?'

Jago leaned forward, coughs wracking his frail body. He spat into a tissue, and Taran saw it was flecked with blood. He stood to get a nurse or doctor but Jago stayed him with a hand on his arm.

'The sea is good to us,' he said, once he'd recovered, 'because we are good to the sea. We honour it. In ways that only we can. In ways that only we remember, just as my daddy did, and his daddy, and all the Tregarths who've ever fished the ocean did. And now, so must you.'

'Honour the sea?' Was this some speech about respecting the ocean, staying safe on it, taking due care and attention? Because Taran had all that drummed into him before he could even walk.

'Not so much the sea,' said Jago, lapsing into another coughing fit. 'But that as lives in it.'

'The fish?' Taran was lost.

'No. I'll tell you now, but you won't believe me, not at first. Then you'll have to believe me, if you want to carry on fishing. It's all written down. In a book. It's locked in the drawer on the boat. Read those words, written not by me, nor my daddy, nor even his daddy, and you'll understand. You have to understand. And you have to believe.'

Jago paused, as though gathering his thoughts, then he began to speak, reciting something he'd said or read many times. 'She's named for a saint, so some say, but that's not the case. The saint was named for her, because she's older than the saints, older than the people, older than the land, for did not the seas come first when the world was created…?'

She's named for a saint, so some say, but that's not the case. The saint was named for her, because she's older than the saints, older than the people, older than the land, for did not the seas come first when the world was created…? And when man fails to understand something, or wishes it to not exist, he takes its name and gives that name to some other thing, something he has created, something he can manage and control and which is not as fearsome as the thing whose name he has stolen. But she cannot be managed, nor controlled, she can only be honoured, and that is both the curse and the bounty of the Tregarth line…

Taran closed the weathered cover of the leather-bound book on his lap. He'd read it a hundred times since his daddy died ten years ago. At first, he had thought it a joke, or the work of a madman. But over time, after he'd buried Jago and took his mantle, and began to fish the waters off Scuttler's Cove, he learned that it was true. It was all true. And once he believed, once he had seen for himself that his daddy was not lying, nor raving with illness, he was approached by Reverend Bligh and Lizzie Moon and inducted into the other life of Scuttler's Cove, and the skin of what he had always considered normal life was peeled back, and he was shown the secrets and horrors that swarmed beneath.

More than once in those early years he'd wished he'd got out like Merrin Moon, gone away to university, never had to shoulder the weight of this burden. But it was right there in the book, written by his ancestors. *That is both the curse and the bounty of the Tregarth line.*

Taran hauled in the catch, and sorted it into big plastic bins on the deck. Another good day. He went to the stern of the boat and stood there, gathering his thoughts. Then he spoke the words he had after each successful fishing expedition, the prayer, the salutation, that at first he had haltingly read from the old book, feeling stupid as though the victim of some practical joke, but now knew by heart. Then he reached behind him for the black bin bag, reached inside, and closed his hand around what was within.

'A sign, lady,' he said. The dead fox was stiff and no longer bleeding, and already stunk to high heaven. Maggots were crawling in its wounds. He held it by the scruff of its neck, out over the water. 'The surest sign yet. I hope my tributes have been sufficient, and that you awake from your slumber. For this is a sign.'

He heaved the fox into the water, and it sank almost immediately. He hadn't killed it, or daubed that symbol on the door of the woman on Nans-Avallen. Neither had Bobby Carlyon and his mates. Neither had anyone in Scuttler's Cove. It was exactly what Taran had said. A sign. Penrose had sent a lad up to clean off the graffiti and get rid of the fox, and Taran had slipped the boy a bag of wrasse for his mum's fridge to be told where the animal had been dumped.

The waters that had closed over the fox and carried it to the black depths just ebbed and swelled as normal. Taran had no idea whether his salutation had been heard, or the sign acknowledged. He turned on the engines and pointed the boat back towards the harbour.

Even in the last couple of days, Scuttler's Cove had become busier with tourists. The school holidays were still two weeks away, and at least they'd get the Fish Festival done before the town was utterly swamped. A lot of the second-homers had pitched up, and after sorting and despatching his catch on the harbour, Taran decided to have a drink. Not the Star and Anchor, though; it was already too full and Clemmo was like a Great White Shark in a feeding frenzy, seeing nothing but the colour of the incomers' money. He'd be glad to have the locals back come September though. For now, Scuttler's Cove people would fill out the tiny Kerid's Arms, up the hill towards the church. It was there, on one of the tables set up outside in direct contravention of the local planning regulations, that Taran found Bobby and Reverend Bligh waiting for him, a pint glistening in the late afternoon sun, though the tall buildings and narrow street would soon put them in shade.

'Pew,' said Bobby. 'You stink of fish.'

'And you stink of dead meat,' said Taran, taking a long draft of the beer. 'So there we are.'

'What do I stink of, then?' said Bligh. 'Hypocrisy, no doubt? Wearing this dog collar yet sitting down with you boys to talk of forbidden things.'

Bobby sniggered. Bligh shot him a look. 'The young generation does not take these things as seriously as your fathers did.'

'I just threw a dead fox into the sea,' said Taran mildly. 'Don't tell me I don't take things seriously.'

Bobby raised an eyebrow. 'Dead fox?'

'It was found on the doorstep of one of the Londoners on Nans-Avallen yesterday. Its blood had been used to draw this on the door.'

In the head of Bligh's as-yet untouched pint of Guinness, he drew with his finger the symbol of the eye. He said, 'And the apple tree is in full fruit.'

Bligh sat back, considering. 'Then there's no doubt about it. That which sleeps beneath Nans-Avallen is awake. And it has already chosen. I thought we might have had a little longer.'

'Probably Merrin living up there has moved things along a bit,' said Bobby quietly. 'The high priestess and the sacrifice. Both on Nans-Avallen. Both marked out.'

'Things will move a lot quicker now,' said Bligh. He fixed Taran with his stare. 'You are continuing in your course of action on the sea? Despite all good advice?'

'I think the fact he's sent a dead fox and tens of thousands of pounds of Lizzie Moon's money down to Davy Jones's Locker would suggest he is,' said Bobby.

Bligh shook his head. 'This cannot end well.'

'It wasn't really going to end well anyway, was it?' said Taran, finishing his pint. 'At least not for the Londoners, and not for Merrin Moon.'

'It is what it is,' said Bligh. 'It would be what it would be. But you have opened a can of worms, young Tregarth. None of us know what might happen now. Or if it will even work, if it hasn't been just a colossal waste of time and money.'

'Couldn't we just send Merrin away?' said Bobby. 'If she's not here, then nothing can happen, can it?'

Bligh shook his head. 'But she is here. She is a Daughter of the Soil, she is bound to Scuttler's Cove. Nans-Avallen is awakening, the tree is fruiting. Do you know the last time the apple tree fruited so early in the year?'

Bobby shook his head.

'Well, you should. You should have listened to your dad's stories more closely.' Bligh lifted his Guinness and drunk practically all of it in one go. 'It was the day that Merrin Moon was conceived.'

'Merrin has painted a picture,' said Taran. 'And the woman, Jen, who had the sign on her door… she dreamed the exact same thing the night before.' He opened his phone and found the photo he'd taken of Merrin's painting. The others looked at it.

'Apocalyptic,' said Bligh, forebodingly. 'This is why such things should not be meddled with. We have no idea what might happen.'

'But what does this mean?' said Bobby, pinching the photo to expand it so he could see the detail of the storm-tossed seas.

'I think it means that my salutations, and the offerings, have been heard,' said Taran. 'And accepted.'

'Then God help us all,' said Bligh. 'Another drink?'

'Why not?' said Bobby. 'My shout.'

'Yes,' said Taran absently, staring at the picture of Merrin's painting. 'But which god, Reverend Bligh?'

18

LIZZIE

Denzel Penrose walked with difficulty across the floor of the church hall to the table at which Lizzie Moon sat with Reverend Bligh, Jago Tregarth, and Pasco Carlyon. He leaned heavily on his stick and got his breath back, then he reached into the pocket of his shapeless old coat and put what was in there on the table between them.

'It's started,' he said. 'I'd hoped to God I wouldn't see it in my lifetime.'

They all stared at the red and gold apple, full and ripe and juicy, weeks and weeks before its time.

'None of you remember the last time,' said Denzel, sitting down heavily on the chair waiting for him. 'I was only a boy myself. My father made me watch the ritual. The next one will happen when the apple tree bears fruit early again. Thank God I won't be around to see it. But this is the sign. The conception must happen.' He looked back at the door of the church hall. It was early, but the Fish Festival was already getting started. 'It will happen. Today. And then the whole sorry thing starts again.'

'It's the way of things,' said Bligh slowly. 'I too hoped to not see this. The time before the one you watched, Penrose, when was that? A hundred years?'

Lizzie stared at the apple. 'May you live in interesting times, the Chinese say. I suppose it's just our good fortune.'

She felt Pasco Carlyon's eyes on her. She was thirty-five, and he'd always carried a torch for her. Even if she presented it to him on a platter right now, he would run a mile. He wouldn't touch Lizzie at Fish Festival, not with that apple sitting there on the table between them. He wouldn't touch any woman, nor would any man round that table. Just as she would never so much as look at a man.

They all knew what that would mean. But somebody in Scuttler's Cove would, somebody who didn't know any better. Someone filled with drink and the high spirits of Fish Festival. And everyone here knew what that meant, and what they would have to do.

'Perhaps,' said Lizzie slowly, 'perhaps it doesn't have to happen. Perhaps it could end. Here. Now. With us.'

Bligh looked at her, uncomprehending. 'It has happened for a thousand years, and it will happen for a thousand years more. It's just what happens. It's just what happens in Scuttler's Cove. When the apple tree on Nans-Avallen fruits early.'

'And what if it didn't? What if we took no part in it?' said Lizzie, looking from one to the other, from Bligh to Carlyon to Tregarth to Penrose. 'What if we just made it stop?'

Nobody said anything, because nobody had ever asked that question before. Not in a thousand years, and nobody expected it to be asked for a thousand years more.

'Scuttler's Cove would die,' said Bligh eventually, uncertainly.

It was then that Lizzie Moon's decision was made.

The floats and procession had wound its way through town hours ago; now darkness had fallen it was time for the Fish Festival revelry. The pubs were pumping out Britpop and dance music and everyone was falling down drunk, the tourists ushering their children back to their cars as the festival descended, as it always did, into Bacchanalia.

Jago Tregarth, the Fish King, was holding court in the Star and Anchor. He'd just found out his wife was pregnant, and though she'd begged him not to say anything until she was three months gone, he wasn't going to pass up the opportunity to have drinks bought for him all night. Lizzie smiled as he raised his glass unsteadily and called yet another toast, for the son who would follow in the family tradition. And it would be a son. The Tregarth line was always boys. Just like the Moon women always had girls.

Before going out, Lizzie had concocted a brew of mandrake root and red clover, liquorice and black cohosh, and some other things, made with certain words said over it, words passed down along the line of Moon women. It had tasted foul and even after her third WKD Blue she could still feel it on her tongue. Still, if it did its job…

Lizzie scanned the pub for a likely candidate. The music was getting louder, and faster; what Reverend Bligh distastefully called the devil's music. He was only five years older than Lizzie but he'd been middle aged since he was a teenager. She supposed that was what happened when your course as Scuttler's Cove's vicar was set from the day you were born. Just like hers had been, just like Jago Tregarth's and Pasco Carlyon's and Denzel Penrose's. And their children would be brought into the world with the expectation that they would continue the family business.

Except Lizzie had other ideas about that.

She moved from the Star and Anchor to the Kerid's Arms, which was where most of the casual farm labourers gathered of an evening. The pub was full to bursting, drinkers spilling out into the street. Lizzie smoothed down her summer dress and squeezed inside, waving for a drink. Then she stood at the bar and waited.

Even without the little rituals she'd performed before she went out, she wouldn't have had much trouble. Lizzie Moon was a good-looking woman, she knew that. The man who approached her wasn't good-looking, and he was very drunk. He offered to buy her a drink, pulling a wad of cash-in-hand wages from his combat trousers pocket, and waved a fiver at the barman. He was tall and broad, with a shaved head and a nose that had been broken more than once. While they waited for their drinks, Lizzie got from him that he was an itinerant worker from Exeter who spent his summers travelling between farms in Cornwall and Devon, doing manual labour. No, he didn't have any family. Footloose and fancy free, he was, he said with a crooked grin. When he put his spade of a hand on Lizzie's backside, though her skin crawled, she didn't protest.

He was so drunk that he had to lean on Lizzie as she guided him to her little cottage on the harbour. There was a brew waiting there for him, too, which she poured into a glass of beer and watched him drink, sprawled on her sofa, while she stood before him and slowly unbuttoned the front of her sundress. He pushed his combats down to his boots and she straddled him. It was over mercifully quickly, the brew she'd made for him doing its dual job of making sure the ton of booze he'd shipped didn't affect his performance, and then putting him into a deep, snoring sleep. Lizzie found a pair of old gardening gloves and put them on him, then went round the house with a bottle of antibacterial spray, wiping anywhere he might have touched. She threw the glass he'd drunk from in the bin.

There was no point phoning anyone, as they'd all be in the pubs. So Lizzie buttoned up her dress and put her knickers back on, and went out to find Bligh, who she surmised would be the least drunk of them all. She found him leaning on the harbour wall outside the Star and Anchor, contemplatively drinking a pint.

'It's done,' she said.

Bligh stared at her. 'What is?'

'The Daughter of the Soil is conceived.'

'How do you know?'

Lizzie patted her stomach.

Bligh frowned at her. 'You do know what you've done, Lizzie?'

'I do,' she said. 'I've saved us a heap of bother. Spending the next days and weeks finding someone who fell pregnant tonight, making sure the father wouldn't be missed, and setting the whole thing in motion.'

Bligh rubbed his chin. 'The father?'

'Asleep on my sofa. He won't be missed. Trust me.'

'Then I'd better get the others.'

Bligh drove Jago Tregarth's van up the hill to Nans-Avallen. Jago was almost insensibly drunk, but he had to be there. Pasco Carlyon sat in the back of the van with the still-snoring farm labourer, Lizzie sandwiched between Bligh and Jago in the front. As they got to the top of the rough track, Denzel Penrose was waiting for them, holding a big lamp.

The land was rough and pitted, the grasses high, so they had to leave the van and walk across Nans-Avallen to the apple tree, Pasco and Bligh dragging the labourer between them. He was starting to stir, mumbling and drooling. Penrose led them to the tree where he'd already set up the ropes.

Bligh said, 'You didn't bring Opie? I'd have thought you'd have wanted him to see this.'

Penrose shrugged. 'You know what young people are like. I'm not sure he holds with the old ways the same as us.' He looked around at them. 'I take it one of you has the knife?'

'I do,' said Lizzie, taking it out of the shopping bag. Its blade was black slate, its handle battered and dented tin. None of them had used it before, and only Penrose had seen it used, when he was a very small boy.

'Does it matter who does it?' said Lizzie, staring at the knife.

'I'll do it,' said Bligh. 'My soul is stained enough as it is.'

Briskly, Bligh, Penrose and Carlyon tied the labourer to the tree, while Jago Tregarth watched, swaying unsteadily. The man was starting to wake properly now, looking around him, squinting through one eye. Lizzie looked up at the branches, heavy with fat, juicy apples. The tree seemed to shiver and bristle, as though it knew what was to come.

'You sure you've caught?' said Penrose to her.

'I'm a Moon. I know when I've caught,' she said, rubbing her belly again. She could almost sense the child growing in there, the cells coming together to create what would, in nine months, be her daughter.

'Whasss going on?' said the labourer.

Bligh held his hand out for the knife. 'Are you a godly man, son?'

The labourer peered at Bligh, taking in his dog collar. 'Fuck off. Where am I?'

Bligh looked expectantly at Lizzie, and she stepped forward. She cleared her throat and said the words she'd hoped to never have to utter in her lifetime. 'Avallen, lord of the vale, who dwells beneath the apple tree, we have seen your sign. The seed has been planted and the flower will bloom, just as your fruit grows on the bough. As is the tradition of our people, to ensure the future vitality of our town, we bring to you the offering that you demand.'

'Any final words?' said Bligh to the labourer, who was straining at the ropes that bound him tightly to the tree.

'Fuck off,' said the man again.

Bligh nodded, and lifted the slate blade to his throat. The labourer's eyes widened, and he tried to twist away, but Penrose moved forward to hold his head still. The man started to scream. Lizzie looked away. She saw Jago suddenly convulse and throw up, then the man's cries were silenced. Lizzie looked back to see Bligh swiping the knife away from the labourer's throat and dark blood gushing from his neck. They all stepped back as the blood poured down and pattered onto the soil at the base of the apple tree's vast trunk. The man shuddered, then was still.

'And it is done,' said Bligh, wiping the blade on the long grass.

Carlyon glanced at Tregarth. 'No stomach for it, Jago?'

Jago grinned and wiped his mouth. 'No stomach for fifteen pints.'

'What now?' said Lizzie.

They all looked back at the dead man tied to the tree. Penrose said, 'I'll let him bleed out then I'll get rid of the body. Then we wait.'

'We wait until the child growing in Lizzie's belly reaches adulthood.' Bligh nodded. 'Our Daughter of the Soil. Then we wait again for an incomer, one touched by death.' He looked up at the apple tree. 'Then we wait for another sign.'

'How long?' said Jago.

'Twenty years, thirty, we do not know,' said Bligh. 'But a sacrifice and a high priestess; that is how it works. And the early fruiting of the tree. Perhaps none of us will be here to see it, who knows?'

As they walked back to the van, leaving Penrose with the body of the labourer, Lizzie thought that only one thing was sure. The child growing inside her would be here to see it.

At least, that was what everyone thought. Lizzie Moon had a different destiny in mind for her daughter.

19

JEN

The days bled into each other, each new dawn seemingly more glorious than the one before. Jen had got into a routine of coffee, breakfast, and sitting out in the morning sun until someone decided what they were going to do for the day. The consensus of the gang was everything; they did whatever anyone wanted to do together, it was never in question that Jen wouldn't tag along. So far that had mainly involved going down to the beach, or wandering around Scuttler's Cove, the occasional drive out to another pretty coastal village. Arthur was pressing everyone to go and visit the ruins of a nearby tin mine, but his suggestion had been gently ignored so far.

Jen shielded her eyes from the sun and put down the paperback she had bought from the little bookshop in town. She looked across Nans-Avallen at Merrin's house. They hadn't spoken since that night with the apples, but not because Jen was necessarily avoiding her. It was just that their paths hadn't really crossed.

That night had receded into almost a dream, a blurred memory as though on a drunken night out. Perhaps they had been a bit drunk, Jen rationalised. Maybe there was something wrong with those apples, hence their early fruiting. Perhaps they were sour, or just one step away from being cider. Jen still wasn't entirely sure that it hadn't been Merrin's instigation after all, because she knew it hadn't been hers. But Merrin had seemed almost as aghast at the incident the next morning as she had been.

'Too much sun, maybe,' said Jen to herself, settling back into the steamer chair to get yet more sun, picking up her book. She'd been reading for perhaps half an hour when she heard what sounded like an argument, voices being kept low but also shrill with emotion. Jen turned around and figured they were coming from behind Maggie and Timothy's house, in the rear garden. Despite herself, she strained to listen, and when she couldn't quite make out what was being said, she quietly walked over to the side of the house.

'I just think, enough is enough,' she heard Maggie saying.

'I understand you're upset,' said Timothy in hushed tones.

'I don't think you do, Timothy,' said Maggie. 'In fact, I don't think you've thought any of this through very much at all.'

There was momentary silence, then Timothy said, 'It's just for this summer. We don't even have to come back next year, if we don't want. We could sell the house, if that's what you wanted.'

Jen stepped a little bit closer, and her foot kicked a stone, which ricocheted off the fence. She sensed a sharp intake of breath from inside the garden and winced, standing stock still. Eventually, Maggie said, 'Well, I'm going to get a shower, and get ready for however it's been decided I will spend my day.'

'Don't talk like that,' said Timothy, and Jen heard them both head back into the house. She quickly but silently headed back to her steamer chair.

Jen had just settled down again when she saw a car crest the hill and drive on to the Nans-Avallen site. It was a police car. She sat up, and grabbed her beach throw, putting it over her head. The others had evidently seen it too, because Tabby and Paul emerged from their house, and Adaku from hers. She saw Timothy peering around the blinds, and a moment later he and Maggie came out to greet the approaching car.

'About bloody time,' said Paul as a middle-aged woman in uniform climbed out of the car, and nodded to them. 'We called you days ago.'

'Busy time of year, sir,' said the woman, looking Paul up and down. Arthur had come out of his house now, and Simon was hurrying over from the end plot. 'My name is Sergeant Mary Wells, stationed at Boscanlon, but Scuttler's Cove is my patch.'

'We have been the victims of quite the most horrendous hate campaign,' said Simon, huffing up. 'Not really what we expected when we came to stay here for the summer.'

Sergeant Wells glanced at the houses, then back at Simon. She took out a small notebook. 'We had a report of graffiti. Was it your house, sir?'

'It was Jen's,' said Arthur, pointing at her.

'Actually, it was ours first,' said Maggie. She shot a look at Jen that made her wonder if she'd been seen eavesdropping earlier. 'The day we arrived, actually. Something about an independent Cornwall daubed across our door.'

'That's right,' said Timothy.

Sergeant Wells made notes and then turned to Jen. 'And you?'

'It was a fox,' said Tabby, before Jen could say anything. 'Mutilated. And this was drawn on the door in its blood.' She took out her phone and showed the policewoman photos of the strange eye symbol.

Sergeant Wells nodded and closed her notebook. 'I'll make some enquiries,' she said.

Paul stared at her. 'Is that it? I mean, I hate to say this, but you don't know who we are…'

The policewoman raised an eyebrow. 'To be honest, sir, there's a lot of this as summer gets underway. Some of it's genuinely political, but much of it is just kids messing about. I understand it's an inconvenience and can be worrying—'

'It's criminal damage, is what it is,' said Adaku. 'It starts with graffiti and dead foxes, but where does it end?'

Sergeant Wells smiled tightly. 'Probably ends there, ma'am, to be honest. But, as I said, I'll make enquiries.'

'You could perhaps start there,' said Paul, pointing across Nans-Avallen towards Merrin's house. 'She's local. Affordable housing. They had to build it on the site due to stupid planning regulations. What's her name, Jen? You've spoken to her.'

'Merrin,' said Jen, feeling a strange and sudden sense of betrayal, as though she was getting Merrin in trouble. 'But I don't think—'

'I'll have a word, see if she saw anything,' said Sergeant Wells.

'Did anything, more like,' said Paul. 'I appreciate all this stuff about the locals not being happy about their houses being bought up and things like that, but they're more than happy to take the money. And where would this place be in summer but for people like us?'

Sergeant Wells put her notebook, with some finality Jen thought, into the pocket of her trousers. 'Quite, sir. Where would we be without your money? I'll be back in touch if we find anything out.' She reached into her pocket and handed Jen a business card. 'I'm usually based at Boscanlon, but I also work from a part-time police station in the next village. So I'm never far away. Call me if anything else happens, or anything occurs to you.'

'Why did you give the card to her?' demanded Maggie. Jen felt her face burning.

Sergeant Wells shrugged. 'Mrs Luther seems to have been the victim of the most serious potential offence. Of course, any of you are free to call me, any time.'

They watched the police car execute a three-point turn and drive back towards the road that led down to Scuttler's Cove. Paul shook his head. 'Unbelievable.' He looked at Arthur. 'Did you hear the way she said that? Where would we be without your money? I've a good mind to put in a complaint. She didn't even go to see the affordable housing girl.'

'Oh, leave it, Paul,' said Tabby, pulling on his arm. 'It's such a beautiful day, I don't want us getting all wound up.' Tabby looked around at the others. 'I was thinking the beach again?'

'I've been reading up on that tin mine—' began Arthur, but the others all groaned.

'Beach,' agreed Adaku. 'Let's all meet here in an hour.'

20

MARY

Sergeant Mary Wells walked into the Star and Anchor, negotiating the tables busy with tourists eating lunch. She glanced at the specials board on the wall and whistled at the prices. Still, there seemed to be no shortage of people willing to pay over the odds for pub grub. Stick a few phrases such as locally sourced or line-caught on the menu, and you could bung prices up by a few quid to make people think they were benefitting the local economy.

There was a young local girl behind the bar, and Mary sat on a stool and asked her for an orange juice. 'And not tourist prices,' she warned. 'Where's Clemmo?'

The girl handed her the glass. 'Upstairs in the flat, I think. Do you want me to get him?'

'You do that,' agreed Mary. While she waited she looked around the pub again. Clemmo had certainly capitalised on the tourist market. She blinked as the girl behind the bar reappeared and said something to her.

'Clemmo says to go up.'

Mary climbed the steep stairs off the bar. At the top Clemmo was in a kind of entrance hall to the flat, sitting at a desk with a laptop open. Mary said, 'Cooking the books again?'

'No need,' said Clemmo, turning around on his desk-chair. 'Making money hand over fist, I am. All legit, too. What can I do for you, Sergeant Wells?'

Mary walked over and stood by the desk, looking out of the window over the harbour. 'Getting busy out there,' she mused. 'And not even summer holiday season yet.'

Clemmo nodded. 'Second-homers come down earlier and earlier. We get the weather, see. Always had good weather in Scuttler's Cove.'

'The place is blessed,' agreed Mary. Something about what she'd just said made her pause, though. A voice at the back of her head saying, *is blessed really the right word?* She shook it away. 'Actually, it was the incomers I wanted to talk to you about. You seen that new group up on Penrose's land?'

'Nans-Avallen,' said Clemmo. 'The Londoners. They've been in. Splashing their money about. They can come again.'

'Had a bit of bother up there,' said Mary, still gazing out of the window. You could just see Nans-Avallen over to the far left. 'Bit of graffiti, mutilated fox on the doorstep. Report of someone hanging about, staring into the houses early in the morning.'

Clemmo shrugged. 'Kids, probably.'

'High spirits, yes,' said Mary. 'So everyone keeps saying.' She looked at Clemmo thoughtfully. 'Everyone complains about kids today, says they spend too much time in front of their phones and games consoles and whatnot. Seems to be in Scuttler's Cove they're constantly in high spirits. And harassing the incomers.'

Clemmo sighed. 'Look, Sergeant Wells, you know me. I was landlord of this pub for twenty years before you came to Scuttler's Cove, and God willing I'll be landlord for twenty years more. I don't know what you're insinuating, but if you're suggesting I'd know anything about what's been going on up at Nans-Avallen, then think again. If I did know who'd been doing those things, I'd clip their bloody ears for them. Those people are my livelihood, Sergeant Wells. Why would I try to drive them away?'

There was an apple on Clemmo's desk. She picked it up and looked at its shiny, red and gold skin. 'And the man they saw lurking around? That wasn't a kid.'

'I don't know. Probably old Rowe, poaching rabbits in Penrose's woods again. Why not ask him about it?' Clemmo reached up and carefully took the apple from Mary's hands. 'You don't want a bite of that, trust me.'

'Why wouldn't I?' she said.

Clemmo laughed. 'It's a Nans-Avallen apple. Not for eating. Not for cider. Not any sort you'd want to drink, at any rate.'

Mary frowned. 'Bit early for apples, isn't it?'

'It is. Far too early. Sign that it's going to be a good summer.' Clemmo rubbed his thumb and forefinger together. 'Especially for the Star and Anchor.'

'What do you mean?'

Clemmo sighed. 'You're not from Scuttler's Cove, are you, Sergeant?'

She laughed. 'Clemmo, I grew up ten minutes away.'

'Ten minutes away from Scuttler's Cove is not Scuttler's Cove,' said Clemmo. 'Unless you're from here, really from here, you can't understand it.' Suddenly his eyes were shining, with something Mary could only think of as fervour. 'People are jealous of Scuttler's Cove, Sergeant Wells. Wonder why we get the weather and the tourists and the money. Wonder why we thrive. They say we're lucky, but it's not luck. And if it is, it's luck we make ourselves. Nothing that happens in Scuttler's Cove is by accident. It's because we made it so.' He held up the apple, the sunlight glancing off its skin. 'And this is a sign that our good luck is going to continue for some time yet.'

Mary leaned on the harbour wall, watching the tide creeping in. She hadn't really thought Clemmo had anything to do with what had gone on up on Penrose's land, of course she hadn't. She wasn't so unintuitive as to think the landlord of the pub coining it from tourists and second-homers would be part of any kind of campaign to frighten them. And, really, what had happened up there? The Independent Cornwall graffiti was standard. The dead fox… well, that was unpleasant, but not exactly the crime of the century. And Clemmo was right, people probably did still use those woods, whether the rich Londoners had bought their houses there or not. Poachers, courting couples, kids high on laughing gas. She wasn't even sure why she was giving so much thought and energy to it. This sort of thing happened all the time.

But something niggled at her, nipped at the edges of her understanding, raised those old copper hackles. And she had no idea what it was, which frustrated her no end. The way Clemmo had looked at that apple, his certainty that this was going to be a good year for Scuttler's Cove because of it. That subtle gear shift, an almost unnoticeable change from genial, boisterous landlord to… practically a religious respect for something Mary couldn't quite latch on to.

Mary turned and looked back at the pub, and then a movement caught her eye. Janet, who ran the Driftwood Gallery, was rearranging her window display. Janet was ancient, had been ancient when Mary took over the

Scuttler's Cove beat. On a whim, she decided to go over and talk to her.

Mary stood outside the window for a moment, watching Janet, her grey hair tied up messily, putting a big painting on an easel at the centre of the display. Mary wasn't much of a connoisseur of art, so didn't know what to make of it. Reckless splashes of blue and yellow, which vaguely put her in mind of the sea and the beach. In the sky, an abstract, almost childlike rendition of the sun. Something about that sun made Mary frown. Then Janet saw her and waved her inside.

'Sergeant,' said Janet, going back behind the counter. 'Coffee?'

Mary agreed and Janet went into the back room to make a brew, bringing out two cracked mugs of steaming instant coffee. 'What crime in Scuttler's Cove today? Drug smuggling? Murder most foul?'

Mary smiled. 'Nothing like that. Just doing my rounds. How's business?'

'Fair to middling,' said Janet, sipping her coffee. 'It'll pick up a lot in the next couple of weeks. Get the Fish Festival out of the way and the tourists'll start flocking in.' Behind Janet was a notice tacked on the wall. *We can ship artworks anywhere in the world.*

'What's that one you were putting in the window?' asked Mary.

'Local artist,' said Janet. 'You like it? Yours for eight hundred quid.'

Mary whistled. 'I'll stick with my Jack Vettriano prints, thank you.'

'Philistine,' said Janet. 'That's proper art in the window, that is.'

'Looks like a kid did it,' said Mary, with a laugh. 'That sun…'

Then it hit her. 'Wait a minute. Come with me.'

Mary led Janet outside and they both looked at the painting in the window. She got her phone out and showed Janet the graffiti on the door of Jen Luther up at the new houses. The one that had been daubed in the blood of the dead fox. It was exactly the same design, a cross between an eye and a sun.

'The Eye of Avallen,' said Janet, looking at Mary with a frown. 'You don't know it?'

Back in the shop, Janet dug under the counter and pulled out an old book about Cornish folklore. She flipped through it and turned it around, pointing to the same image on a drawing on the page. 'The Eye of Avallen.'

'Avallen as in Nans-Avallen?'

'The same. Old story. Surprised you've never heard of it.'

'Not really much of a one for folklore and old stories, to be honest,' said Mary.

'It's why we have the Fish Festival, in part,' said Janet. 'The story goes that Avallen was the lord of the orchard, and Endellion the lady of the sea. They were in love, but Avallen spurned her. She was furious and vowed to destroy Scuttler's Cove, which was the domain of Avallen, and which he brought prosperity to. The Fish Festival every year is held to appease Endellion and to thank her for the bounty of the sea. In olden times everyone would have an Eye of Avallen in their window during the Festival, to ward off the vengeance of Endellion.'

'So why paint it on one of the incomer's doors? In blood?' wondered Mary. 'Why try to scare them off with that?'

'Maybe it's not a threat,' said Janet. 'Maybe it's a warning.'

Mary narrowed her eyes at her. 'Do you know something about this?'

Janet laughed. 'You think I'd be dragging these old bones up the hill to Nans-Avallen to splash blood on someone's door? Not me. I'm hoping to sell those Londoners a few choice pieces at a nice, tidy profit. I'm not in the business of scaring off my customers.'

'So why would it be a warning?' pressed Mary. 'A warning against what?'

The bell above the door tinkled and a couple came in, stinking of money and London. They started to browse and Janet straightened up, scenting business. 'It's just kids,' said Janet, as though it was a script they'd all learned.

'The apple tree has fruited early on Nans-Avallen,' said Mary suddenly, remembering the look in Clemmo's eye. What had he said? *And if it is, it's luck we make ourselves. Nothing that happens in Scuttler's Cove is by accident. It's because we made it so.*

Janet looked at her oddly. 'Yes, you're right. The apple tree has fruited early. Just one of those Scuttler's Cove things. Probably best not to worry about it at all, Sergeant.' Then she slipped out from behind the counter, heading towards the customers. She turned one more time to Mary and said, 'It's all just old stories, Sergeant Wells. Nobody really believes in the power of Avallen or the vengeance of Endellion, you know. Not any more.'

21

JEN

The beach was directly below the cliff on which Nans-Avallen perched, an expanse of golden sand that sloped gently into the sea. It was only really accessible from the path that led down from their homes, so mostly they had it to themselves. Today, though, there was a family at the other end, in an encampment of garish windbreaks and beach tents, prams and cool-boxes littered around. Two boys were batting a ball to each other in the shallows.

Paul was glaring at the family. He said, 'I wonder if Penrose owns this beach? We should think about making him an offer for it. Keep it private for us.'

'Or build a pool up there,' said Adaku, rubbing glistening lotion into her long arms. Jen noticed that Adaku now wore a bandage around her wrist. Had the spider bite got worse?

'Or both,' said Tabby, peering over her sunglasses at the sea. 'We'll have enough money soon. Do you think the sea's warm enough to swim in?'

Out back towards the harbour Jen could see a flotilla of paddle-boarders and heads bobbing in the water. She said, 'I think it should be fine.'

Maggie stood up, pulling the seat of her black swimming costume out of her bum. 'I'm going to find out. I'm boiling hot here. Anyone coming? Tabby? Adaku?'

'In a bit,' said Tabby, holding out her empty glass to Paul. 'I think I'll have just one more Aperol Spritz from the cooler.'

'I just put lotion on,' said Adaku, lying back on her towel.

'Arthur?' said Maggie. He looked up from his book on Cornish archaeological digs. 'Maybe later. I'm at a good bit.'

Maggie snorted and walked quickly across the hot sand to the water, washing gently on the shore as the tide went out. 'Be careful!' called Timothy.

'She'll be fine with those flotation devices on her chest,' said Tabby quietly, and sniggered.

Jen watched Maggie gingerly easing herself into the water, and when she got to thigh-height she turned around and gave a thumbs up. Jen would have quite fancied a swim, but Maggie had pointedly not asked her. She wondered what she'd done to upset her. Of all the gang, Maggie had been the least friendly to her since she met them. She wondered if she had secretly held a torch for Justin? She wondered if they'd actually had any history?

'So what was it like, growing up in... Leeds, was it?' said Tabby.

'Bradford,' said Jen. What was there to say? She'd grown up with a single parent in social housing, and had been desperate to get away to university. She'd returned to work there, had a string of awful relationships, then finally decided to decamp to London. Five years later she'd met Justin. And that was all there was to tell. But the further she got from home, the longer she was away, the more defensive of it she got. 'It was great,' she said. 'It's a great city. Fantastic people.'

Tabby had already lost interest and was accepting a drink from Paul. Jen turned back to the sea, where Maggie had finally ducked her shoulders under, and was swimming out on the millpond calm surface. She heard Paul saying, 'I've been talking to Penrose about the best time to act, once things are all in place. About maximising the investment.'

Jen cocked an ear his way. They kept talking about investments and opportunities, but had never brought her in on the conversation. But Penrose was involved, too? The man who had sold them Nans-Avallen?

'Maggie's worried about it,' said Timothy. 'I don't know how on board she is with the whole idea, to be honest.'

'She'd better be,' said Paul, a little vehemently to Jen's ear. 'There's no backing out now. There's a lot of money at stake.'

'Quite,' said Tabby, and Jen saw her glancing in her direction. Fine, she thought. You talk about your big money deals. The working-class outsider will just get out of your way.

She stood up and tugged down her swimming costume at the legs, and padded down the sand to the water's edge. She breathed in sharply as the cold water ran over her feet. West Yorkshire was landlocked, and though she'd been to the seaside plenty of times, the ocean wasn't Jen's natural element. She looked out to where the horizon met the clear sky. There was something about the idea of the whole sea being one big, flowing mass, and so full of life. Life which, if you didn't want to eat it, probably wanted to eat you. Though Jen did concede this idea had mainly come from movies. Maggie was a little way out, moving with strong strokes up and down, parallel to the shore.

She paused to wave, and suddenly, pathetically touched by even the merest show of friendship from Maggie, Jen took a deep breath and waded in further, gasping as the water rose to her thighs and then her waist. Then she ducked under, head and all, gasping and laughing as she came up for air.

Her mum would have loved this. Jen's fondest memories from childhood were at the seaside, train or bus journeys to either Whitby, Scarborough or Filey on the east coast, Blackpool and Southport to the west. Before Mum started to get ill. In fact, it was on one of the last trips, when Jen had become a teenager, that the signs first started to show. Jen remembered sitting on a blanket on the beach at Scarborough, waiting for her mum to come back from the ice cream van with two 99 cones on a sweltering hot day. They ate them in silence, Jen itching to get into the amusement arcades and spend the bag of coins she'd saved for the trip.

'Let's have ice cream first,' said her mum, standing up.

Jen laughed, then stared at her, realising she was deadly serious. 'Mum, we just had ice cream. Like, literally, just now.'

'Don't be stupid,' said her mum. 'Pass me my purse from the bag. The queue's massive.'

'Mum. We both just ate a 99. Like, ten seconds ago.' Jen brandished her hands at her. 'My fingers are still sticky.'

Her mum's face darkened, then her lip wobbled, and she said, 'You're a bad girl, trying to make out your mum is going daft. A bad, spiteful girl.' Then she snatched the purse and stormed off to the ice cream van, bringing back another 99 which Jen forced down with confused tears in her eyes.

Jen ducked under the water again, to wash away the memory. Locked up in that home, her mum had missed so much of Jen's life. Going down to London. Meeting Justin. Getting married. Being widowed. Jen broke the surface with a gasp, turning to look back at the beach. At her friends. At the gang. Above them, Nans-Avallen loomed.

Jen would give it all up for one more day with her mum as she was before the dementia stole her away.

'Ow!' Jen cried out as she stubbed her toe on something hard. A rock. But when she put her foot down again, it hit something smooth and solid. Something smooth and solid that moved quickly from under her, pushing her off balance in the water. Instinctively, Jen recoiled, pulling up her legs and treading water, and peered down into the clear seawater. There was something down there. Something moving. No, several somethings. Flat, dark shapes and—

Suddenly a scream sounded, amplified by the surface of the sea, bouncing off the cliffs. Jen looked around, swishing her arms and legs, still treading water, just in time to see Maggie, further out, suddenly duck under.

Then something brushed against Jen's leg, and she cried out, too, pushing at the water to propel her backwards, back to the shore. She heard shouts from the beach, and as her feet found purchase in the sand she saw Paul and Timothy standing, peering out to sea to where Maggie had resurfaced and let out another high-pitched yell.

Childhood nightmares of *Jaws*, of *Moby Dick*, of octopi and krakens and piranha from films and stories panicked Jen as she staggered in the surf, even as Timothy and Paul splashed past her, Tabby and Arthur following behind. Jen turned to see Maggie waving frantically, and something was hanging from the soft flesh of her upper arm, a dark shape. It dropped away and Maggie seemed to be swept forward suddenly, by the incoming tide, bringing her closer to shore. She was evidently in a place where she could touch the bottom, because she rose up a little suddenly, chest high, and Jen gasped.

Maggie's upper body was covered in the dark shapes, stuck to her like limpets. Her sobs ricocheted round the beach. What on earth were they...?

Then Jen looked down and screamed, leaping backwards. Something scuttled in the shallows, no, several somethings.

Crabs.

Jen stared at them, half in horror, half in fascination, as the ebbing tide lifted them from the sand. Then she heard Timothy cry Maggie's name. He and Paul had reached her and were dragging her into the shallower water, now barely around their waists. Maggie found her footing on the sand beneath the sea and staggered forward, still screaming. As she emerged from the water, Jen saw she was covered in cuts, all over her body, her swimsuit ripped across the stomach, one breast hanging out. She heard Timothy cry out and bat ineffectually at a crab hanging from Maggie's hair.

Tabby ran up with a towel and waded in just as Paul and Timothy brought Maggie, sobbing, to the shore. The cuts criss-crossed her flesh and she seemed to be festooned with crabs dangling from her hair, her swimsuit, her skin. Tabby shrieked and began to slap at them, and one by one they fell off, plopping into the surf.

Jen pulled a face and stepped further backwards onto the sand. She looked down and the shoreline was full of crabs, rolling in the small waves breaking on the sand, their shells glistening in the sun, their claws opening and closing. Tabby wrapped the towel around Maggie and she collapsed, hyperventilating, onto the beach, the cuts all over her oozing blood.

'Do we need to get her to a hospital?' said Timothy, hopping about ineffectually from foot to foot.

'I don't think so,' said Paul quietly. 'I think she's going to be fine.'

'She's bleeding,' said Timothy, imploringly.

'I think Paul's right, old chap,' said Simon, crouching down. 'They're just scratches, really. Nothing a liberal splash of Dettol and a couple of plasters won't fix.'

Maggie was sitting up, wrapped in the towel, rocking backwards and forwards, her eyes wide and wild, scanning the sea. She was muttering silently, her lips moving but nothing coming out, at least, nothing Jen could hear.

In Jen's opinion, Maggie probably should go to the hospital. Yes, the scratches were small, but there were a lot of them. The pincers had drawn blood. But, more than that, Maggie looked traumatised. In shock. She started to shiver in front of Jen's eyes, her eyelids flickering, as though she were going to pass out.

Jen wasn't surprised. Maggie had been attacked. By crabs. She had never heard of anything like that happening before, ever in her life. Jen watched with a growing sense of horror gnawing in her gut as the retreating tide washed the crabs back into the depths of the sea.

22

MERRIN

Janet, her face wrinkled like a piece of the driftwood that gave her gallery its name, looked over the three watercolours Merrin had done in the past couple of days. As Taran had suggested, she'd chosen more tourist-friendly subjects than the storm-tossed nightmare she would drop off for Taran next. A view of Scuttler's Cove from Nans-Avallen, a panorama of the coast, and her personal favourite, the apple tree framed against a glorious blue sky.

Janet ruminated then said, 'You've got talent, Merrin Moon. I'll give you that.'

'Think you can sell them?' asked Merrin. She was close to having to start looking for a job, but if she could make a bit of extra money from painting, it might help.

Janet closed the portfolio and pushed it back across the counter. At the sight of Merrin's crestfallen face, she said, 'I'll take fifty per cent commission. Take these into Boscanlon today and get a dozen professional prints made of each. I'll put the prints on at, say, twenty and the originals at… a hundred?'

Merrin did some swift mental arithmetic. If they all sold, even with Janet's cut, that would be… more than five hundred quid. She said, 'You really think they'll sell for that?'

'If they do, we'll bump up the prices of the next lot. You are working on more?'

Merrin nodded enthusiastically, though she hadn't started anything yet. Janet flipped open the portfolio again and looked critically at the apple tree one. 'More like this. Sea views are ten a penny. This has something... draws you in. Speaks of hidden things.' She nodded, as though having reached a decision. 'The Nans-Avallen Collection. By Merrin Moon. Yes. Good. How soon can you get me more?'

Merrin went out to check when she could get the next bus to Boscanlon, and her eye was drawn to the clifftop, where an ambulance was wending its way down from Nans-Avallen. What had happened now? As she was staring up at the cliff she almost ran straight into Taran on the harbour.

'You went to see Janet?' he said.

'She wants them all,' said Merrin excitedly. 'She wants me to get some prints done, though.' Merrin pulled out the card of the printers in Boscanlon. 'At this place. I was just going to get a bus. Glad I've seen you though, I've got this.'

She opened the portfolio and handed him the finished painting of the stormy seas. He held it in both hands and smiled. 'Perfect. Thank you. What's Janet selling originals for?'

'Hundred quid!'

Taran tucked the canvas under his arm and delved into his jeans pocket, bringing out a clip of folded twenties. 'A fair price,' he said, peeling five off.

'Honestly, after everything you've done, consider it a gift,' said Merrin, holding up her hand.

Taran shook his head. 'You're a professional artist now. A fair price must be paid.' He pressed the notes on her, and Merrin took them, grinning broadly. He said, 'What say I meet you up at yours in an hour and I'll drive you over to this printers in Boscanlon?'

'You don't need to, really. I can get the bus. I've imposed on you enough.'

'Sooner we get them there, sooner you can get them back,' insisted Taran. 'You want them in the Driftwood for Fish Festival weekend. I bet you'll sell right out!'

—

By the time Merrin got back up to Nans-Avallen, she was hot and sweating. She'd just have time for a shower and a bite to eat for lunch before Taran arrived. She paused on her way to the house, staring at the apple tree, sizing it up. Perhaps from the other side, so she could see the ocean as well? She peered deeper into the woods. Maybe even from in there, get more trees in the foreground. As she was gazing up at it, she heard one of the doors of the houses open, and saw Jen walking towards her.

Merrin hadn't seen her since the day after what she'd started referring to in her head as the Apple Incident. To be honest, it almost felt like it had been a dream, though she knew it hadn't. She gave a tight smile as Jen approached, and realised that her standing there staring at the apple tree probably didn't make her look in any way sane after what had happened.

'A gallery is taking some of my paintings,' she said, patting her portfolio. 'One of the tree. They want more.' She was talking too quickly, saying too much.

Jen looked up at the apple tree, then back at Merrin, and said, 'Something really weird happened today.'

Suddenly, Merrin remembered the ambulance. 'Oh god, is someone hurt? Were the paramedics here? What's happened?'

'Maggie went for a swim. The dark-haired one. She was attacked in the sea. By crabs.'

Merrin stared at Jen. 'Crabs?'

Jen nodded. 'They were hanging off her. There were hundreds in the water. Maybe thousands. They ripped her swimsuit and cut her to ribbons.'

Merrin gaped. She had never heard of that in her life. She had spent the first eighteen years of her life in Scuttler's Cove and never heard of anyone being attacked by crabs. The odd tourist getting their toe pinched, sure, but not an attack. 'God. Is she all right?'

Jen nodded. 'They put loads of antiseptic on her and plasters. The cuts weren't that deep, really. Mostly scratches, to be honest. But she's pretty freaked out. She hasn't stopped crying.'

'I'm not surprised,' said Merrin. She shivered. 'Crabs. Never heard anything like that in my life.'

They both stood silently for a moment, then started speaking at the same time.

'Look,' said Merrin. 'About the other night…'

'I just wanted to say,' said Jen. 'That night…'

They both stopped, then laughed. Jen shook her head. 'Look, let's just forget it, is what I was going to say. Obviously this is a weird shit kind of place. Just stay off the apples, all right?'

'Deal,' said Merrin. 'I don't even like them anyway.'

'Bottle of wine one night, though?' said Jen. She dropped her voice. 'Between us, it'd be nice to spend a few hours with someone a bit more… normal.'

Merrin tapped the side of her nose. 'Deal, again. And your secret's safe with me.'

She watched Jen heading back to her house, and then went home to get showered and changed.

—

'Crabs,' said Taran. He didn't seem to think it was as funny as Merrin thought he would, and that made her feel guilty for gossiping so lightly about what had happened.

'I mean, she wasn't really hurt, apparently. Just shaken up. But, yeah. Crabs. Weird, eh?'

'Weird,' agreed Taran. He didn't say any more about it, but seemed lost in thought as he drove her to Boscanlon and waited outside the printers while she put in her order. They were quiet and said they'd have them driven over straight to the Driftwood Gallery the next day.

Taran drove her home mostly in silence, and when he dropped her off he reached out a hand and grabbed her arm. 'Don't you miss London?' he said suddenly. 'Don't you think about going back?'

She frowned at him. 'I've got a house, I've got a gallery taking my work.' She pulled her hand away and looked out to sea. 'Why would I want to go back to London? I'm home. I can't even remember why I stayed away so long.' His eyes met hers and after a moment she said, 'I thought you were pleased I was back.'

'I am,' he said. She waited for him to say more, but he just put the van into gear. She slammed the door and watched him drive away.

There was still plenty of light left in the day, so Merrin took her easel and paints to the far side of the apple tree, where the woods began. She set up and sized up the tree, then moved back a little, then a little more. There was a line of trees between her and the apple tree now, and she liked the way the branches framed the bigger tree, with the blue sky behind it.

She'd been painting for an hour when she felt suddenly cold, the sun having dipped behind the trees. She took the cardigan from around her waist and slipped it on, and considered what she'd painted. Janet said if her work sold, she could charge more for the next batch. Her mum would be so proud, Merrin thought.

And with that thought came a barrage of more. Why had Taran been so weird today, ever since she'd mentioned the crabs? Why had he even suggested she go back to London? And that brought a cascade of more ponderings. Why had Merrin stayed away from Scuttler's Cove for so long? She hadn't been back, not once, since she'd left for university at the age of eighteen. And she'd never thought that odd, or weird. She'd spoken to her mum by phone, but not as often as she should have done.

Why had she never come home?

Suddenly, Merrin was assaulted by a wave of grief. Sobs were wrenched from her body. She had gone away and never come home, and now her mum was dead. And Merrin hadn't even seen her for the past thirteen years.

'What the fuck?' she said, tears mingling with snot. It all seemed so ridiculous, now. So *weird*. As though she'd left Scuttler's Cove and almost forgotten about it. As though something had kept her away, clouded her mind, dulled her senses. Now, it felt as though her life in London was a dream, was something fogged and indistinct. What had she been doing all these years? Merrin took a deep breath, inhaling the scent of the woods, the fresh air, the sea breeze filtering through the trees. It felt like she had been dead and had suddenly come to life. She knew, with unerring certainty, that this was where she was meant to be. This was where she had been born, and grown up.

Why had she left?

Why had Lizzie Moon made her go?

Why had she never asked who her father was? Why had he abandoned them?

Her little finger was itching under the silver ring. The tattoo. The tattoo with the same design on it that had been painted on Jen's door in fox blood. What was *that* all about?

Questions crowded her head, buzzing like bees. Questions she'd forgotten to ask, or never felt the need to. It wasn't normal, was it? Leaving home and never coming back? Not even for a visit? Not even to see your mother? She had never fallen out with Lizzie Moon. In fact, she remembered crying on the day she departed for university, promising to be home soon, saying she would be back at Christmas and then Easter and summer and…

And Merrin Moon never came home.

She took a ragged breath, and then started. Throughout all that she had continued to paint, though she hadn't realised it. She took a step back from the canvas. This was not something that was going to sell to tourists in the Driftwood Gallery.

The apple tree was there, framed by the trees in front of her, the last thing that Merrin remembered painting. But now there was a figure, standing against the tree. No, not standing against it. Tied to it. A man. And an angry red stream flowed from his neck, down his body, to the packed ground at the foot of the tree. A man, his head lolling, his throat cut.

Merrin put her hand over her mouth, shaking her head. Why had she painted that? Where had it come from? It was horrible. What did it mean?

And across the canvas crawled a spindly-legged spider with a bulbous yellow body, trailing from the bottom left corner up to the right, and disappearing over the top edge.

23

LIZZIE

Lizzie stood on the apron of the bus station at Boscanlon on a dull September day and watched as Merrin climbed up the steps of the coach and took her seat near the window. Her heart was breaking. Her beautiful, smart, wild, intelligent daughter was off to university.

And she would never come home. Never come back to Scuttler's Cove. At least, not while there was breath left in Lizzie's body. And the Moon women lived a long time.

Tears were streaming down Merrin's cheeks as the bus started to pull away, and she waved frantically and blew kisses. Lizzie caught them in the air, as she'd done since her daughter was a baby, and waved and waved until the bus turned off the station and was lost to sight in the streets of the town.

By the time the coach got onto the A30, Merrin would have almost forgotten her, forgotten Scuttler's Cove, forgotten everyone in the village. At least, if Lizzie's plan worked. And why wouldn't it? She was Lizzie Moon.

Lizzie waited for the bus that would take her back to Scuttler's Cove, and for the half-hour ride back watched the countryside unfolding and giving way to the glittering sea. They passed Nans-Avallen and wound down to the harbour, and Lizzie let herself into her suddenly empty-feeling cottage on the front, and waited. Because she knew they would come.

Bligh came first, then Tregarth and Carlyon together. Denzel Penrose had died the year before, and his son, Opie, according to the old man's predictions, seemed to want nothing to do with what they did. Not that he had much choice. Not now he was the custodian of Nans-Avallen. He'd come round, he'd have to. Eventually. But today was not about Opie Penrose. It was about Lizzie Moon and her daughter, Merrin.

'It won't work, you know,' said Bligh, pacing the small living room of the cottage.

'How do you know?' said Lizzie, pouring tea. 'Nobody has ever tried before.'

'It's the way of things,' said Jago Tregarth, though a little doubtfully. 'It's the way things have always been.'

'You can rearrange those words into a different order all you like,' said Lizzie gently. 'But it doesn't change the fact that I've done it.'

'But what will it mean?' said Pasco Carlyon, looking up at Bligh. 'Perhaps Lizzie is right. Nobody has ever done this before, but that doesn't mean it won't work.'

'It can't work!' Bligh said, seethingly slapping the back of his hand into his other palm. 'The Daughter of the Soil is born, and when the incomer who has known death comes to us, then the sign will be made, and the ritual takes place. It's how it's always been. How it always will be.' He glared at Lizzie. 'Does she not bear the sun-eye mark on her very flesh of that which dwells beneath the apple tree? Did you not bring her to me when she was not yet a year old? Did I not tattoo the binding sigils on her finger myself, while you held her in your arms? You were the one who decided to mother the Daughter of the Soil. This is on you.'

Lizzie calmly put down the teapot and stood to face Bligh, some two feet smaller than her. 'Do not think to talk to me like that, Reverend Bligh,' she said, her voice shaking with barely contained fury. 'Yes, I took it upon myself to mother the Daughter of the Soil, and for this very purpose. The poor bastard who fathered her has already died at our hands. I was not having my daughter grow up in this godforsaken town to fulfil a destiny handed down to her by men and women long turned to dust.'

'You cannot break the cycle,' said Bligh.

'You only say that because nobody has ever tried before,' spat Lizzie. 'Times are changing, Bligh. Not all the old ways are good and right. Perhaps it's time to try something new.'

'But what happens when Merrin comes back?' said Jago. 'University is only three years. She'll be home for Christmas, and summer. The incomer could arrive any time, we could get the sign in six months, or a year.'

'She won't come back,' said Lizzie quietly, sitting down again. 'I've made sure of that.'

Bligh glared at her. 'What have you done?'

Lizzie blinked away tears. 'I have used all the skills and talents passed down through the Moon line since time immemorial to make sure that once Merrin is away from here, she will never even think about coming back. I have sent my little girl away from me forever. To save her from that horrible destiny, and to save this cursed place from the tyranny of tradition that we have been yoked to for millennia.'

'It was always said that Scuttler's Cove would die if the prophecy wasn't honoured,' said Carlyon quietly.

Lizzie forced a humourless laugh. 'Die? Scuttler's Cove? Look around you, Pasco. The place is awash with money. You think that's going to dry up because we few old fools don't hove to some nonsensical old ritual? Because we don't spill blood?' She shook her head. 'You should thank me. You, Pasco, and you, Jago. I've made a better world for your boys, for Taran and Bobby. Do what I've done. Send them off into the world. Let them make their own way, instead of being hamstrung by tradition, hogtied to old prophecies.'

They sat there in silence. Bligh broke it eventually, saying, 'It won't work, Lizzie. As much as I wish it would, it won't work. What dwells beneath Nans-Avallen is too strong. Too old. And if it does work, if you somehow succeed in denying it... well. I fear for us all, in that case. I fear for us all.'

The first time Lizzie saw Merrin again, her resolve wavered and she almost ran to hug her. But she didn't. She had travelled to the far town where Merrin was studying at university, and it was a simple matter to make herself unnoticeable, even to her own daughter. She spent an afternoon trailing around after her, watching her lie in the sunshine in a grand park, listening to music and reading books, then shadowed her around the grounds of the college, and then watched from the street as Merrin went with a gaggle of young people into a pub booming with music. Her daughter seemed happy, so Lizzie was happy, even though her heart trembled with the missing of her. She took the last train back to Cornwall and sat at Boscanlon bus station watching the sun come up, waiting for a bus to take her back to Scuttler's Cove.

Lizzie did that twice a year while Merrin was at university. Then her daughter moved to London, to work and live and love. Lizzie visited once a year then, tracking her down as she moved from flat to flat, watching her go to work, standing right behind her on the Tube as it rattled through the dark tunnels. She watched Merrin paint on the bridges over the Thames, saw her fall in and out of love, and in it again. And each time, when she was close enough, she almost put out a hand to touch her, to turn her around, to dispel the fog she had put in her mind that made her not think of her mother and her home at all. But each time, she didn't, because she knew what that would mean.

There were times when Lizzie cursed herself, wished she had just let tradition run its course, let some other woman mother the Daughter of the Soil. Perhaps it would all be over by now, the ritual, and might never take place again in Lizzie's lifetime. She would have Merrin with her at home, and her heart would be healed. But what future would she be forging for Merrin even if she wasn't the Daughter of the Soil? She would be Merrin Moon, latest in the line of Moon women, and at some point in the future it would be her up at Nans-Avallen, handing the slate-bladed knife with the tin handle to Taran Tregarth or Bobby Carlyon, or wielding it herself, cutting the throat of some poor innocent whose only crime was to get drunk in the wrong place on the wrong weekend. And years after that, to oversee the ritual, to bring together the high priestess and the sacrifice, to spill more blood, or watch it spilled.

No. Lizzie was convinced she had done the right thing. She had given Merrin a life, and she had freed Scuttler's Cove from the ties that bound it. They should be celebrating the name of Lizzie Moon, not glowering at her from the shadows for daring to put a stop to something that no one else had ever dreamed could be ended.

By degrees they all forgave her, even Bligh, and there was plenty to be done in Scuttler's Cove that had nothing to do with Nans-Avallen, but still employed the old ways, plenty of good that Lizzie Moon could do. Jago Tregarth died, and then Pasco Carlyon, and their sons took over the family businesses, and also the darker, more secret trade their fathers had plied. Lizzie had wished they hadn't, wished their dads had sent them off to university, or to work in other towns, or merely let the secrets die with them. But the old ways were strong in Scuttler's Cove, and while what Lizzie had done had eventually been grudgingly accepted, they were not all ready for more sweeping changes quite just yet.

Lizzie had begun to allow herself to believe that it had worked. That Scuttler's Cove was no longer in thrall to that which lived beneath the apple tree on Nans-Avallen. That finally, they were free. And the only price they'd paid was the banishment of Lizzie Moon's daughter.

Until, that is, one day a dozen years after Merrin Moon had left for university, they came to see Lizzie in her cottage. Bligh, Taran Tregarth and Bobby Carlyon. And they had news.

'It's Opie Penrose,' said Taran.

'What's he gone and done now?' said Lizzie.

'He's selling Nans-Avallen,' growled Bligh.

She stared at them all in turn. 'Selling Nans-Avallen? I mean… how? Why? Who to?'

'To Londoners, by all accounts,' said Bobby. 'Rich ones. He's going to build big posh houses up there and sell the whole lot to them. He'll make millions.'

'Is he insane?' said Lizzie. 'He can't sell Nans-Avallen. Does he not know what lives in the earth there?'

'Oh, he knows, but he doesn't believe,' said Bligh, almost triumphantly. 'And that's your fault, Lizzie Moon. You and your meddling. Breaking the cycle, you said. We don't need the old ways, the old traditions, you said. Come summer, Nans-Avallen is going to be home to incomers. And how do you think that is going to work out?'

After a long, thoughtful silence, Lizzie said, 'I think we should pay Opie Penrose a visit.'

24

JEN

The next morning, Jen called round to see how Maggie was doing after her ordeal on the beach. The door to her house was ajar, and she could hear voices inside. Jen pushed the door a little, and called, 'Hello?'

She could hear Timothy and Paul talking, but couldn't see them. Jen dithered on the doorstep, unsure about whether she should go in or just leave, but the shrillness of Timothy's voice gave her pause. The two men were evidently in the kitchen diner, and Jen could hear every word.

'She can't go home,' said Paul evenly.

'Paul, you don't know her like I do. When her mind's made up...'

'Oh, I think I know her as well as you do. Better than you do, Timothy.'

There was a heavy pause, then Timothy said, 'What does that mean.'

Jen heard the clanking of cups and the hiss of the coffee machine. She stepped in a little further to listen over the sound.

'I know, for instance, that you and Maggie haven't had sex for two years.'

'She told you that?' said Timothy, aghast.

'She didn't need to. She's like an alley cat in heat. You know half of London has fucked her, presumably?'

'Including you, Paul?'

Paul laughed. 'Why would I go out for burgers when I have fillet steak at home? Get real, Timothy. She's with you because of your money. And you'd better tell her that there's a lot more money on the way, enough to pay for a brand-new pair of tits and a new arse for her, and plenty more besides. But she has to stay focused, and with the programme.'

There was a long silence. Jen bit her lip, wishing she could creep out, but she was too scared to move a muscle in case they heard.

Finally, Timothy said, 'I'll speak to her.'

'You do that,' said Paul. A tap started running. 'Nobody leaves, Timothy. Do you understand?'

Jen turned quickly, thinking she could just get out under cover of the tap, and screamed. Maggie was standing there, at the bottom of the stairs, staring at her with heavy-lidded eyes. She was wearing a robe, hanging open, and was naked underneath, her smooth, tweaked body covered in plasters covering the crab claw-marks, almost on every expanse of toned, tanned flesh.

'Maggie,' said Jen, plastering on a smile. 'I just thought I'd call in and see how you were this morning.'

Hearing voices, Timothy and Paul emerged from the kitchen. Jen smiled broadly at them. 'I just walked in to see if Maggie was all right.'

Maggie, as though in a trance, walked roughly past Jen, knocking her with her shoulder. She said something in a low voice, which Jen couldn't catch, but sounded like *this is all your fault*.

'For god's sake, cover yourself up,' muttered Timothy.

'Well!' said Jen brightly. 'If there's anything I can do…' Then she beat a swift retreat back to her house.

In light of the incident at the beach – Jen couldn't shake the horror of seeing those crabs clinging to Maggie's bleeding body in the surf – nobody had seemed to plan anything for today, and Jen felt at a loose end, as though without the gang to tell her what to do she didn't know how to entertain herself. She read a bit of her book, but couldn't seem to focus on it, and pottered about the huge kitchen, making herself a salad for lunch. She brooded on what Maggie had said, or what Jen had thought she'd said. *This is all your fault.* How could Jen be blamed for what had happened to Maggie at the beach? And her mind was still reeling with what she'd overheard in the house. Paul had sounded vicious and vindictive, accusing Maggie of sleeping with other men. Maybe this was the world she lived in now. She wondered if Justin had slept with other women while they were together, or if he would have done eventually? Maybe he was one of the men who had fucked Maggie. Perhaps that was why she had always been cool towards Jen.

She made a coffee and sat in front of the TV, letting it wash over her. Something caught her eye on the floor, scuttling along the edge of the wall. Jen pulled a face and went to get a glass, trapping the spider under it and looking around for a card or letter she could slide beneath it. It was the third or fourth one she'd seen in the house, since that day Adaku had been bitten. Grimacing, she took it out of the back door and let it go at the bottom of the garden. Perhaps they should have a word with that Penrose about it. Maybe he could get some pest controllers in.

You're thinking like the rest of them, she thought. *The gang. If there's a problem, throw money at someone to sort it out.*

Restless, Jen decided to go for a walk. Perhaps she could go into Scuttler's Cove? It felt almost scandalous to do something without the gang, but she couldn't just sit around here all day. She went to find a sundress and some strappy sandals and considered her reflection in the full-length mirror. Even covered in plasters and scratches, Maggie had looked perfect. A goddess. Jen was so… ordinary. Tabby had already dropped hints about introducing her to a couple of doctors they knew. Tabby was obviously done as well, but far more discreetly than Maggie.

When Jen let herself out of the house, she saw Simon sitting at his table with Arthur and Adaku. Adaku was wearing tiny shorts and a tight-fitting long-sleeved top that plunged at the neckline to show off her cleavage. Jen could never decide whether Adaku had gone under the knife too, or just naturally looked like an Amazon warrior.

'Jen!' shouted Simon, waving her over.

'I was just going to go for a wander into town,' she said, shading her eyes from the sun and standing over them. She glanced down and saw what looked like a vein standing proud on Adaku's thigh, just below the hem of her shorts. It was yellow-ish and raised. For some reason, it gave Jen a little stab of satisfaction. *Not so perfect after all, then.*

'We are staying here and drinking cocktails in the sun,' declared Simon. 'You absolutely must join us.'

'I will, after my walk,' promised Jen.

'And this weekend we all go into Scuttler's Cove,' said Simon. 'There's apparently some kind of hilarious parade on, called the Fish Festival, if you can believe that. Floats and Morris Dancers and all kinds of strangeness. And then afterwards, everyone gets terribly drunk and fucks like rabbits.'

'You made that last bit up,' said Arthur.

Simon boomed a laugh. 'I may have. But you can imagine, can't you? I bet that lot down there are positively bacchanalian once they've got a few jugs of scrumpy inside them.'

'You wish,' said Adaku, gazing off towards the sea. She was pulling her shorts down over the vein that Jen had seen, self-consciously. It reminded Jen of the varicose veins that marbled her mother's pale, thin legs, except yellow, not blue. Jen almost asked if Adaku wanted her to get something from the chemists in town for it, then shut her mouth. She was sure Adaku wouldn't take too kindly to her pointing it out. Jen had already made an enemy of Maggie, it seemed, and she didn't want to make another one.

'Did you know you can walk through the woods?' said Arthur. 'Was looking at an Ordnance Survey map earlier.'

'It's a wonder I don't die from the excitement,' said Adaku quietly.

Arthur twisted and pointed to the woods. 'It starts there, more or less, and winds through the woods and comes out a little way up the access road we normally use to get here. Perhaps you want to try it out?'

'She's not bloody Bear Grylls, Arthur, old chap.' Simon laughed. 'Or the other one. Who's the other one?'

'David Attenborough,' said Adaku.

'No!' scoffed Simon. 'The other one like Bear Grylls. Does those shows about how to make a bivouac from a used condom and light a fire with a stone and a crow's beak.'

'Ray Mears,' said Arthur.

'That's the fellow,' said Simon. 'Anyway, our dear Jen is neither Bear Grylls nor Ray Mears and doesn't want to walk through the woods to test out some old map you found in your glove compartment.'

Jen squinted at the woods. 'Actually,' she said, 'I might want to, after all.'

Jen had always loved walking in the woods, ever since being a child. Bradford was a dense, ramshackle, urban bowl of humanity surrounded by nature and open countryside. One minute you could be in a warren of terraced streets, and the next on the moors, looking down on the soot-blackened stone. Woods were like a magnet to Jen, and she always found them, unerringly, their hushed canopies providing some kind of escape from her home life with a mentally disintegrating mother and no father. In the woods, Jen could be a princess, or an adventurer, or an explorer, anything separate from the mundane world she inhabited.

She walked across Nans-Avallen, passing the tree and glancing at the trunk. There were no spiders. As she walked on, there was a double thump, and she turned to see two apples rolling in the grass, just behind her. Without knowing why, she bent to pick one up, and carried on to where the trees opened and a clear path led into the woods.

The woods were peaceful, the trees packed tightly enough to not see far beyond them, but not so close together that they were oppressive. The sun pierced the canopy of trees, casting dappled shadows on the path in front of her, sunbeams picking out her way like a trail of breadcrumbs. The apple weighed heavy in her hand, and she allowed herself to think of that strange night with

Merrin. She was having trouble putting a name to. Some kind of... rapture. Ecstasy. Connection.

Connection. That was it. Connection to this place, this land. Jen strode on through the trees, the birds singing above her. A squirrel scampered along the path ahead of her then shot up the trunk of a tree, disappearing into shaking branches. Without even realising it, she took a bite of the apple in her hand.

As she chewed the pulp of the fruit and swallowed its juices, there it was again. A sense that tendrils were growing out of the ground, reaching for her, entangling in her legs. But when she looked down there was, of course, nothing there. Then she felt as though with each step forward she was sinking, descending into the soil, becoming one with the land. She took another bite of the apple.

Dust motes danced in the lancing sunbeams, and became flies, then butterflies, A fox ran across the path ahead of her. It stopped, in a crouch, to stare at her, then skittered off into the undergrowth. Above her in the tall trees she could hear the caw-caw-caw of crows. The path wound deeper into the woods, and when she looked back she couldn't see where it had begun, nor when she faced forward could she see where it would end.

It ends with blood, the trees whispered to her.

It ends with a knife made of the land, spilling blood on the earth, the butterflies sang.

It ends with a high priestess and a sacrifice. As it has always done. A Daughter of the Soil and an incomer, touched by death. It always ends that way, cawed the crows.

With crystal clarity Jen saw the tractor coming towards them, the fearful spear she later learned was a bale spike looming in the view from the windscreen. She was screaming again, calling Justin's name, as the tractor kept coming and the spike pierced the window, and then Justin, pinning him through his chest to the seat of the car.

She saw the face of the man driving the tractor. She had later been told he had suffered a heart attack, which caused him to lose control of the vehicle.

He was laughing. He was laughing and laughing and laughing and laughing and—

With a start, Jen realised she was at the edge of the woods, the path leading out on to the road that passed Nans-Avallen and wound down to Scuttler's Cove. She looked down at the apple in her hand; she had eaten it down to the core, which was turning dry and brown in her fingers. She cast it away from her.

As she stepped onto the Tarmac road, the sense of connection to the land, to Nans-Avallen, seemed to evaporate. Her walk through the woods was fading, as though a dream. All she could remember was the laughing face of the man who had killed Justin, and the cawing of the crows high in the trees. Talking of priestesses and sacrifices and—

A Daughter of the Soil and an incomer, touched by death.

An incomer touched by death. It didn't take a genius to work out who *that* meant.

And Daughter of the Soil? As Jen stood there, staring out over the glittering sea, she remembered that tattoo on Merrin's finger, the symbol that was the same as the one daubed on her door in fox blood.

The connection.

'What the fuck is in those apples?' she said aloud. Were they some kind of weird hallucinogen, like magic mushrooms? She shook the thoughts away, which was easier to do now she was out of the woods, and set off down the hill towards Scuttler's Cove.

And tried to ignore the hunger that gnawed in her belly, the craving for just one more of those Nans-Avallen apples.

25

MERRIN

There was a package waiting on Merrin's doorstep when she finally opened the door mid-morning to take her easel and paints out on to the clifftop. But not one left by the postman.

It was loosely wrapped in newspaper – the *Cornishman*, dated the week before – and tied with twine, and inside that was another layer, tightly wrapped black cloth. And inside that...

Was a knife. Not any kind of knife that Merrin had ever seen before. The handle was made of tin and the blade... the blade was formed from curved slate. And sharper than Merrin could have guessed. She ran her thumb along the edge and almost drew blood.

Merrin sat for a long time at her kitchen table, pondering the knife. She didn't know what to think, to feel. Scared? Confused? Was it some kind of threat? A warning? She looked at her thumb, the thin line where the blade had almost cut the skin. Then she examined her finger which she *had* cut, while slicing bread. The one that was now clear of any blemishes or wounds. Ever since...

An idea popped into Merrin's head, and before she could think too deeply on it, or talk herself out of it, she picked up the knife in her right hand, testing its weight, its balance. Then she held out her left hand, and drew the point of the blade across her palm, effortlessly raising a red line of oozing, bright blood.

Around four o'clock, there was a knock at the door. Merrin opened it to Jen, who held up a plastic bag from Scuttler Stores. 'I thought two bottles of wine?' she said. She looked at the bandage on Merrin's left hand. 'Clumsy in the kitchen again?'

'Something like that.'

They sat at the kitchen table, and Merrin poured two large glasses of red. Jen grabbed one and gulped half of it down in one go. Merrin said, 'I'm guessing you needed that.'

Jen fixed her with a stare. 'Has this place always been weird?'

Merrin shrugged neutrally, sipping the wine. 'How do you mean?'

Jen let out a long sigh. 'I barely know where to start. Spiders. Crabs. Symbols in blood on my door.' She dropped her voice. 'Those apples. I had another one. I walked through the woods and ate an apple and it was like...'

Merrin leaned forward. 'Yes?'

'Like I was tripping. I was hearing voices. Seeing things.' She shook her head. 'Maybe this sort of thing is normal for Scuttler's Cove.'

Merrin hesitated a moment, then said, 'Do you want to see something really weird?' Without waiting for an answer, she went to retrieve the knife from the kitchen worktop, carefully unwrapping the black cloth. 'This was left on my doorstep this morning.'

'The Independent Cornwall people?'

Merrin shook her head. 'Why would they? I'm Cornish.' She pulled out her phone. 'Anyway, when I got it I cut my hand.'

'Oh god! Are you OK?'

'I don't mean by accident. I mean, on purpose.'

Jen's eyes widened. 'On purpose? Why?'

With her good hand, Merrin pulled out her phone. She opened her photo gallery and showed Jen a picture of her hand, bleeding, where she had drawn the knife across it. 'I took this so you'd believe me.'

Jen was looking wary, even a little scared. Merrin could hardly blame her. She said, 'Why wouldn't I believe you?'

In response, Merrin unwrapped the bandage around her hand, and showed it palm-up to Jen. There wasn't a mark on it.

'You could be lying,' said Jen slowly. 'That could be an old photo, or faked, or AI or something.'

'I could be lying,' agreed Merrin. 'But I'm not.'

Jen shook her head. 'So... why did you do it? And how has it healed?'

'I did it because I realised that the cut I did on my finger – the accidental one – had disappeared after we ate those apples. So I thought...'

'You thought that the apples healed it?'

'Yes. So I cut my hand and went and ate two apples and...'

She waved her palm at Jen again.

Jen was silent for a long time. 'I mean, apples that can do that... fucking hell. They'd be worth a fortune. Priceless.' She tapped her finger on her chin. 'They should look into that instead of whatever big investment opportunity everyone keeps talking about.'

'Your friends?' said Merrin.

'Not friends enough to bring me in on whatever it is,' said Jen. 'I just keep hearing them whispering about it.'

'Was your husband involved in it?'

Jen shrugged. 'Possibly. He didn't talk to me much about his business dealings.' She leaned forward. 'And that's the other thing. When I was in the woods, after eating the apple, I… sort of relived the accident. And I saw things I hadn't seen before. The man who drove the tractor that crashed into us, he was laughing all through it. It was horrible.'

'Who was he?' said Merrin.

'I never knew. Some local farmer, apparently. I was told he'd had a heart attack at the wheel.'

'Told by who?' said Merrin, retrieving her phone and tapping at it. She was looking for news reports of the accident. There were a dozen from the time, all mainly culled from the official police press release about it.

'By Tabby, I think. Or one of the others. I was in a bit of a state at the time.'

Merrin read through the reports. 'It just says that the tractor driver was believed to be a local man. No name given. Was there an inquest into Justin's death?'

'I think so,' said Jen, sounding a bit wretched. 'Those weeks after he died… the gang looked after me. A doctor came to see me. Private. One they all used. He gave me some… medication. To calm me down. I don't remember a great deal of what happened after the funeral, to be honest.'

'What sort of medication?' said Merrin, frowning.

'I can't remember. He prescribed it and it just appeared.' She stared at her hands. 'Doctor Heygate. That was his name. That's all I remember.'

Merrin poured them both another glass of wine. 'I mean, this vision in the woods, the man laughing. It could just have been fatigue, or grief, or—'

'Or the apples. Or something else.'

Merrin said, 'What sort of something else?'

'I don't know,' said Jen, hitting her leg with her fist in frustration. 'It just feels all… I don't know! Weird. The woods. This whole place. There's something going on that I don't understand.' She pointed at the knife on the table. 'And that. What the fuck is that all about?'

Merrin said slowly, 'If we were in a horror film, what would we do?'

Jen shook her head.

'We'd go and investigate ourselves, in the woods. Probably get killed,' said Merrin.

'But we're not in a horror film. We're in real life. So what should we do?' said Jen.

'I think we should call the police,' said Merrin.

Jen reached into the pocket of her jeans and pulled out a business card. 'Luckily enough, I have their number here.'

—

Sergeant Mary Wells arrived at five o'clock. She said, 'You're lucky I've been having a quiet day. I was going to come and see you anyway, Merrin Moon.'

'What for?' said Merrin. She went to put the kettle on. 'Tea? We're having wine but I suppose you can't.'

'I've officially clocked off,' said Wells. 'So wine would be great.'

She was a little over fifty, Merrin estimated. A world-weary, no-nonsense air about her. She said, 'I was coming to see you to talk about the dead fox and the blood daubed on the door of Mrs Luther here. But it seems you two are quite cosy anyway.' She pulled out her notebook. 'You can still tell me what your movements were on that day, though. For the record.'

When Merrin had recounted her recollections of the day, which wasn't much of substance, Wells nodded and said, 'So. Why did you want to see me? You said there's strange stuff happening.'

They had agreed to not talk about the apples to Wells, not yet at any rate. They didn't want her to think they were mad, or drunk, or both. Merrin unwrapped the knife and showed it to her. 'This was left outside my door overnight.'

Wells pulled out a pair of thin rubber gloves and gingerly picked it up by the handle. 'Who's touched this?'

'Just me,' said Merrin.

Wells squinted at it. 'There's some staining on the blade.'

'I cut myself with it,' said Merrin. Jen glanced at her. 'By accident. I didn't realise how sharp it was.'

'There's older staining,' said Wells thoughtfully. 'I think I'll take this away for forensic testing.' She pulled from her pocket a transparent plastic ziploc bag and popped the knife in. 'I'll give you a receipt for it. Anything else?'

'Do you think this could be linked to the dead fox and the symbol on my door?' said Jen.

Wells pulled a face. 'I'd have said that what happened to you was just an extension of the graffiti on the other house. The locals getting a bit creative.' She looked down at the evidence bag. 'This sort of puts a new light on it. I doubt that, or this, is the work of Bobby Carlyon and his mates.'

Merrin stared at her. 'You know it's Bobby?'

'The Independent Cornwall stuff? Of course I do. Just can't pin it on him. It's all a big laugh to that lot. They don't mean anything by it. They don't even want an independent Cornwall. Bobby Carlyon's butcher's shop would be closed in a month if it wasn't for the tourists. This, though…' Wells rubbed her chin. 'This feels different.'

The police officer looked at Jen. 'You're northern. Don't seem to fit in with the other lot. I wonder why you were targeted? You've no links to Scuttler's Cove, have you?'

'I'd never been before I came to look at the house,' said Jen. 'I wish I'd never come at all.'

'Her husband died,' said Merrin. 'There was a crash on the lanes. Tractor.'

Wells's eyes widened. 'That was you? I was on leave that week. Heard about it when I got back. Well, I'm sorry for your loss. Not the best introduction to Scuttler's Cove.'

'I was trying to find out what happened to the man in the tractor,' said Merrin. 'There was nothing in the papers after it happened. Jen was told he'd had a heart attack.'

'Mainly because the papers are run on a shoestring and barely have any staff these days,' said Wells. She narrowed her eyes. 'Is it important?'

Merrin hesitated. She didn't want Wells to think they were hippy dippy or overwrought or anything like that. She said, 'Jen was hurt in the accident as well. She's only just starting to get some memories back. She was walking in the woods today and she remembered the man laughing as he drove into them.'

'And you think that is somehow linked to the knife, and the dead fox?' Wells frowned.

'No,' said Merrin. 'Well. It just feels…'

'Connected,' said Jen. 'Everything feels connected. I can't explain it. The knife and the tractor and the fox and the spiders and the apples and the crabs…'

'Apples? Spiders? Crabs?' Wells was frowning even more deeply.

Merrin shot Jen a look. They'd agreed to keep this at least marginally sane sounding. She said to Wells, 'One of her friends was bitten by a spider. Another was attacked in the sea by crabs. I'm sure it's nothing, but you can see how it all might be too much for Jen, who's lost her husband so recently.'

Wells nodded and finished her wine, and stood up. 'Right. I'll get the lab to look at this knife tomorrow. And I'll see what I can turn up on the tractor driver. For a bit of closure for you, Mrs Luther, if nothing else. If I don't get back to you before the weekend, I might see you at the Fish Festival.'

They watched Wells drive away in her police car, and Merrin poured the last of the wine into their glasses. Jen let out a long, ragged sigh. 'I should have got three bottles.'

26

MARY

Three years, and Mary Wells could take her pension. She knew she wasn't going to, even as she knew she wasn't going home after visiting Merrin Moon. That was why Mark had left her five years ago, and divorced her a year later, and why she'd never bothered to try to find anyone to replace him. It was a terrible old cliche, but Mary Wells was married to the force. They'd have to carry her out in a box, everyone said behind her back, and sometimes to her face, at Boscanlon nick.

Bobby Carlyon's butcher's shop would be closed now, but she could hazard a guess where she'd find him. She struck out at the Star and Anchor, which was filled with holidaymakers and second-homers, but found him sitting outside the Kerid's Arms with an empty pint glass, still in his red and white striped apron. As she walked up the hill, she saw Taran Tregarth emerge from the pub with two fresh ones.

'Bobby, Taran,' she said, sitting down at the table with them. They both looked at her with wariness. Since they'd been kids Mary Wells had been pulling them up for all kinds of infractions. Hot-headedness, mostly. The usual bored kids' stuff you'd find in any rural or coastal village.

'Sergeant Wells,' said Taran. 'To what do we owe the pleasure?' He'd grown into a fine-looking man, Taran Tregarth. Like his daddy had been. Mary'd had a bit of a crush on Jago Tregarth thirty-odd years ago, when she was a rookie PC who'd just been assigned Scuttler's Cove as part of her beat.

'Just passing,' said Mary. She looked at Bobby. 'Just been up to Nans-Avallen. Had a chat with Merrin Moon, and one of the incomers. You been up there at all?'

Bobby could have won an Oscar for the look of surprise he put on his face. 'Me, Sergeant Wells? Why would I go up there?'

She shrugged. 'Oh, I don't know. Bit of graffiti, perhaps?'

'I don't know what you're talking about,' said Bobby, staring into his pint.

'Of course you don't.' She glanced down the street, at the tourists thronging the harbour. 'Not that I've got time to waste on Independent Cornwall. There was something else, though.'

Taran and Bobby waited for her to go on. 'Dead fox. Blood all over one of the incomers' doors.' They both shrugged. 'And this morning, someone left a knife on Merrin Moon's doorstep.'

Mary had been in the job long enough to notice those little physical cues, which most people wouldn't even register at all. A flaring of the nostrils, a glancing away of the eyes, a slightly sharper intake of breath. You'd have to be watching closely to see them. You'd have to know what you were looking for. Mary knew what she was looking for, and saw it all in both Bobby and Taran too.

'Knife?' said Bobby. 'And you've come here because I'm a butcher?'

Mary helped herself to a mouthful of Taran's beer. 'Not that sort of knife, Bobby. Odd looking thing. Slate blade. Very sharp. Tin handle. Mean anything to either of you?'

They both shook their heads. Mary said, 'Well, it's off to forensics tomorrow.' She stood up. 'So if either of you have your memory jogged by anything, before the lab gets hold of it, you know where to find me.'

Mary almost drove home, but at the last minute carried on to the little part-time station. She was generally the only one that used it, preferring the solitude of the old building to the bustle of Boscanlon nick. Every year they made rumblings about closing it for good and selling it off, and she'd be surprised if it lasted much longer. There'd been no desk staff, no direct telephone, no coppers other than her using it for the past five years. But it had her files, and a terminal linked to the Police National Computer, and a kettle and stock of teabags. Mary parked up outside and let herself in, and made a brew before settling down at the terminal.

She put the evidence bag with the knife in it on the desk, and did some Googling, but couldn't turn up anything that remotely offered any clues. It looked old and well used. Taran and Bobby knew more than they were letting on, she was sure. She'd drive it up to Boscanlon in the morning. Why leave it on Merrin Moon's doorstep? Everyone had known Merrin's mother, Lizzie. Four hundred years ago she'd have been called a witch, and probably hanged as one. In the years before her death, she was Scuttler's Cove's equivalent of a national treasure. Everyone respected Lizzie Moon, even if few talked about why. A decade ago, Mary had consulted her over a missing child case. Not officially, and she'd never written it up, but she knew that girl would never have been found alive but for Lizzie's information. Which was why Mary felt inclined to help Merrin out, even if she didn't truly understand why and what good it would do.

She called up all the files about the death of Justin Luther. It had, on the face of it, seemed straightforwardly tragic. Londoners in a Tesla going a little too fast along the lanes, tractor with a bale spike attached coming the other way, heart attack suffered by the driver. There had indeed been an inquest at Truro a month ago, a fairly quick affair given the nature of the accident. The coroner recorded a narrative verdict, saying that nobody was seemingly at fault, and the incident could not have been avoided by any action on the part of anyone involved. The tractor was being driven by an itinerant farm worker named Calvin Draper, aged fifty-nine, of no fixed abode. He did not attend the inquest, having no address for any summons to be issued to, but his statement to the police was read out, stating that he had suffered chest pains and lost control of the vehicle. A medical report said that Mr Draper suffered from a previously undetected heart condition that had given him no trouble or indication of its existence previously. Jen Luther did not attend, nor any other members of Justin Luther's family, if indeed they existed.

Mary did a quick search for Calvin Draper, but he had no previous form, and there was no mention of him again. After the accident he had seemingly just disappeared into thin air, which wasn't uncommon with casual farm labourers. He'd been treated at the scene for minor injuries but had not been admitted to hospital. There was no mention from the paramedic statement of a heart attack, though given Justin had died and Jen was severely injured, and the paramedics would have been busy with them, that might not be surprising.

Mary flicked back to the medical report on Draper that had been submitted to the inquest. It had been written by a doctor from London. A private GP. Odd. Mary made a note of his name, Heygate, and resolved to look him up in the morning. Not that she knew why; this all seemed to be fairly standard and above board.

She rubbed her eyes and looked at her watch. It was almost nine. She really should call it a day. She was going to call Merrin to tell her what she'd got on Justin Luther's death, but thought it might be too late. She bashed out a quick email and sent that instead, saying she'd be in touch the next couple of days.

Just then, there was a hammering on the locked door of the police station. Probably someone had lost their cat, or wallet, or way home. The station was in a little hamlet midway between Scuttler's Cove and Boscanlon that had not yet succumbed to the second-homer invasion, but it was only a matter of time. There'd be some local out there whose car had been scraped on the lanes by an SUV or something.

Mary was surprised when she opened the door to Bobby Carlyon, still in his butcher's apron. 'I need to talk to you,' he said, looking around as though he was afraid he'd been followed. 'Privately.'

She made Bobby a cup of tea and sat down with him at the desk. He looked pale and hollow-eyed. After a moment, Mary said, 'If this is you confessing about the graffiti—'

'It's not about bloody graffiti,' said Bobby, looking at her at last. 'It's bigger than that. Much bigger.'

'Is it about the knife?'

He nodded, staring at his feet. She felt as though she was going to lose him, he was going to take fright and bolt.

'Go on,' said Mary softly.

He covered his mouth with his hand, shaking his head. 'I could get in so much trouble for talking to you.' Bobby took a deep breath. 'There's something going on in Scuttler's Cove. Has been for years. Decades. It's bad.'

Mary sipped at her tea. 'How bad?'

'People have died,' said Bobby in a whisper. 'More people are going to die.'

'Tell me.'

'You wouldn't believe me,' said Bobby. 'I think it's better if I show you.'

They went downstairs and Mary flicked her key fob at the car, but he shook his head. 'I'm not going in that. Someone will see me and then that's me done for. Let's go in my van.'

His knackered old Transit with *Carlyon & Son, Family Butchers, Scuttler's Cove* painted on the side in faded red lettering was parked on the street. Mary shrugged. She should call this in, if it was as serious as Bobby was saying, but she didn't want to scare him off. Something about his manner told her that he was telling the truth. Whatever this was, it was big. And bad. She could feel it in her copper's senses honed over decades. Big and bad. Big and bad.

Bobby drove in silence back towards Scuttler's Cove, along the dark lanes. He pulled up by the side of the road where the woods that bordered the back of Nans-Avallen opened out onto the lane that led down to the town. He took a deep breath and turned off the engine. 'It's in there.'

Mary turned on her torch and stood at the entrance to the woods, shining the beam on the path. 'How far?' she said. 'Bobby, what are you showing me?'

'Not far,' he said. 'Five minutes. Follow the path.'

She walked forward cautiously, the torch picking out the path between the trees. 'Who's involved in this?' she said.

'I need my name kept out of it,' said Bobby behind her. 'Or it'll be very bad for me. Very bad.'

'You know I can't promise that,' said Mary. 'Not if this is as big as you say and it comes to court. Who's involved?'

'Taran,' he said eventually. 'Penrose. Reverend Bligh. More.'

Her phone buzzed in her pocket. She took it out and read the email that had come in. Approving her three-week leave of absence on compassionate grounds. It was from her boss, who said he was very sorry for her loss.

Mary hadn't requested a leave of absence. As she puzzled over it, she shone the torch around. They had been walking for more than five minutes now, and the trees loomed dense and oppressive over them. 'What are we looking for, Bobby?' said Mary.

I didn't request a leave of absence, she thought. *What loss?*

'Nothing you could ever understand,' said Bobby behind her. His voice sounded odd. It took her a second to understand why. It was her voice. Bobby Carlyon was speaking to her with her own voice. Mary turned round, shining the torch at him, every hair on her body standing on end.

The first thing she saw were his eyes, shining with something like fervour. Something like madness. No, not shining. Blazing. Blazing red and gold.

The next thing she saw was the meat cleaver in his hand, held high.

The last thing Mary Wells saw was Bobby's arm coming down, biting the cleaver into her neck with an awful, wet *chokkk* sound.

27

TARAN

At the municipal yard on the far west side of Scuttler's Cove, the finishing touches were being put on the floats and costumes for tomorrow's Fish Festival parade. Taran strode around, distracted. The ritual knife would be on its way to the forensics lab at Boscanlon police station by now. His fingerprints would be all over it, and God knows how many people's blood, going back centuries. Even if they couldn't match the DNA to anyone, the mere presence of it would be ringing alarm bells. Taran took a deep breath. Don't panic, he told himself. Don't panic. There'll be a way out of this, somehow. It was just that he couldn't quite see what it was at the moment, and the clock was ticking.

He stopped by the Fish King's float, watching the team of villagers putting the final strokes of blue paint on the canvas skirt around the flatbed lorry, freshening up the jaunty waves. On the back of it was the throne, spray-painted gold with a navy-blue cushion, on which Taran would sit tomorrow and lead the festivities. The Fish Festival had been a fixture of Scuttler's Cove's early summer calendar for centuries, to honour the bounty of the sea that had always been part of the village's prosperity.

Something a lot of people seemed to have forgotten, lately, thought Taran. And here was one of them, Bobby

Carlyon, stalking across the yard, his red and white striped butcher's apron flashing. He had a plastic bag under his arm.

'Bobby,' said Taran as he approached, but without a smile. He knew that Bobby would be as worried as he was about the police, and more to the point, how to get the knife back.

As if reading his mind, Bobby pushed the plastic bag hard into Taran's hands. 'I've sorted your mess out for you.'

Taran started to open it, but Bobby took his arm and steered him to the far side of the yard, where it was quieter. 'Not here.'

Hidden from everyone else by a jutting outbuilding, Taran peered into the bag. It was the knife, still in a police evidence bag. Taran gaped at Bobby. 'How did you get this?'

Bobby seemed antsy, anxious, shifting his weight from foot to foot and glancing around furtively. 'Sorted it, like I said.'

Taran put a hand on his arm. 'Bobby. How?'

Bobby fixed him with a hard stare. There was something different about him, about his eyes. They were shining, subtly shining with red and gold. Bobby said, 'I paid Sergeant Wells a little visit last night.' He looked around again and hissed, 'Why the fuck did you leave that knife on Merrin's doorstep?'

'You know as well as I do that she has to take possession of it before the ritual,' Taran whispered fiercely back. 'How was I to know that she was going to go to the fucking cops?'

'Because she's not one of us any more,' said Bobby. 'Look, the knife's back. We just need to get through the ritual and everything will be fine. Provided you haven't fucked things up with your meddling.'

Taran said slowly, 'One of the Londoners was attacked in the sea. By crabs.'

Bobby frowned. 'Crabs? And you think that's a sign?'

Taran shrugged. 'How many crab attacks have you heard of in Scuttler's Cove? In any place?'

Bobby rubbed his hand over his mouth, hopping from foot to foot again. 'Fuck. I swear, Taran, if you've fucked this up after all I went through to get the knife back…'

Taran looked down into the plastic bag again. 'How did you get it, Bobby? Why did Sergeant Wells give it to you? What did you say to her?'

'She didn't give it to me,' said Bobby, suddenly grinning. It was horrible.

'Bobby, what did you do?' said Taran slowly, narrowing his eyes.

'I took care of her,' spat Bobby. 'She won't be bothering us again.'

'You *killed* her? Tell me you're joking.' Taran felt his bile rise. 'Oh my god. You fucking idiot.' He dropped his voice to a whisper. 'You killed a copper. We're done for.'

Bobby laughed. 'No, mate. I fixed it so they think she's on leave for three weeks. Should be plenty of time for us to get this finished.'

'Fixed it? How?'

'I'm really sorry, boss, but I need some time off,' said Bobby. Taran stared at him. It was exactly the voice of Sergeant Wells. 'My mother's died. I'll need two or three weeks.'

Taran stared at him. 'What the fuck?'

'Those apples are amazing,' said Bobby casually. 'The things they can let you do.'

Taran felt his legs turn to jelly. 'Nans-Avallen apples? You've been eating them? Bobby. No. You're lying.'

Bobby flexed his bicep. 'I feel incredible. Why has nobody ever eaten them before?'

'Because they're *his* apples, you fucking idiot,' hissed Taran. 'They contain *his* essence. And now, so do you. Jesus fucking Christ. I can't believe you've been so stupid.'

Bobby suddenly grabbed the front of Taran's shirt, slamming him back against the brick wall. 'Don't call me a fucking idiot, Taran,' he said, his face contorted in rage. 'I'm cleaning up your mess. Do you want the ritual to fail? Do you want Scuttler's Cove to die? Because I'll tell you one thing, I don't. And if that sacrifice doesn't go ahead, then we can both kiss goodbye to our businesses.'

Taran put both hands on Bobby's chest and pushed him roughly away. They squared up to each other, the blood pounding in Taran's ears. But Bobby just shook his head. 'It'll be done, soon. You can thank me later.' Then he turned on his heel and stalked towards the yard gates.

—

One fine September evening when they were both thirteen years old, Bobby came calling for Taran. 'Where are we going?' said Taran as they walked along the harbour front, past the stragglers of the holiday season enjoying ice creams and chips in the last gasp of the warm weather.

'Scrumping,' said Bobby.

There were half a dozen farms with orchards around Scuttler's Cove, half of them with their own cider breweries on site. It was something of a Scuttler's Cove rite of passage for teenagers to attempt to make their own homebrew to keep them entertained in the autumn months, and the town's airing cupboards were full of white buckets of pulped apples and yeast and sugar, which within a couple of weeks produced cloudy, foul-tasting brews that had a ridiculously high alcohol content.

Bobby had come armed with a pocketful of plastic carrier bags, and they crept into one of the orchards on the east side of town, silently gathering up the windfalls. When they had four bags' worth, Taran whispered, 'That's enough.'

'One more stop,' said Bobby as they climbed back over the fence on to the lane. Then he led them up the cliff path. To Nans-Avallen.

'You're fucking kidding me,' said Taran as they hid behind a bush, staring at the lone apple tree in the centre of the site.

'Are you scared?' said Bobby.

'I'm scared of Penrose catching us and sending his rabid dog to bite our balls off,' said Taran, trying to tough it out. But he knew that Bobby knew. Knew that he was actually scared, no, terrified, of even being so close to Nans-Avallen.

No kids played on the clifftop. None of them would go near the apple tree, never mind the woods that surrounded the big field. Nobody talked about why; they just avoided it. It was never even a consideration to go up there, especially not after dark. Nobody questioned it. Except Bobby.

'Why is everyone so scared of Nans-Avallen?' he said, shifting his weight as they crouched down behind the bushes. Penrose's farm was a couple of fields away; he was unlikely to be up here, Taran knew with a sinking feeling in the pit of his stomach.

'It's just boring,' said Taran, with affected nonchalance. 'Let's go to Ramsey's orchard if you want more apples.'

'I want those apples,' said Bobby, pointing in the darkness towards the Nans-Avallen tree.

Taran stared at him. Nobody played at Nans-Avallen, and nobody would even think of eating the apples from that tree. They talked about it, sometimes, when they were camping out on the beach in winter, huddled around driftwood fires. 'You're mad, you,' someone would say in response to a ridiculous suggestion, like skinny-dipping in December. 'Have you been on the Nans-Avallen apples?'

Those apples were poisonous. They made you insane. They made you want to kill yourself, and one time some kid ate one and jumped, laughing, off the clifftop. So everyone said, anyway. Not in their time. Or their parents' time. Their grandparents' time, probably. But it definitely happened. You ate a Nans-Avallen apple, you'd die a horrible death, choking on your own intestines that tried to crawl out of your mouth. You ate a Nans-Avallen apple, it would make your dick drop off. If a girl ate a Nans-Avallen apple, she would be pregnant the next morning. Only she wouldn't have a baby. She'd give birth to a giant spider.

Taran didn't know where the stories came from. The kids had always known them, and probably their mums and dads used to tell them to each other, too. All anyone knew for sure was you didn't go up to Nans-Avallen if you could avoid it, and you certainly never, ever, ever ate those apples from that tree.

'I bet they'd make the best cider you ever tasted,' said Bobby, his eyes on the tree. 'I bet they'd make the best cider in the world.'

'You're fucking mad,' said Taran, his voice wobbling. He abandoned all pretence of off-hand toughness. 'Bobby. Mate. Let's go. I don't like it.'

'Fucking pussy,' said Bobby, standing up straight. 'You go if you want. I'm getting those apples.'

And then a dog barked, just at the other side of the field, and a torch-beam flashed and danced. 'Penrose!' said Taran, dragging Bobby back down. They crouched there for a minute, watching the light come closer, the dog barking and barking, and then they turned and ran back down the cliff road and to the lights of Scuttler's Cove.

—

Taran walked through the town, the harbour already packed with tourists and day trippers. He paused at the Driftwood Gallery. Janet had put Merrin's paintings in the window. Janet appeared behind the glass and gave him a little wave, then plucked one of the original artworks, a view of the Nans-Avallen apple tree at dusk, from its little stand. Taran peered through the window and watched Janet wrapping it for a well-heeled-looking couple. That would be hanging in their holiday home by evening, adding what they no doubt thought was some local authenticity to their coastal bolthole. Taran smiled, despite everything. He was glad to see Merrin doing well. If only it would last. The knife weighed heavy in the bag dangling from his hand. Somehow he was going to have to get it back to her. In time for the ritual. His insides turned to water at the thought of it. The high priestess and the sacrifice. And the knife was for Merrin.

He decided to take the boat out, not to fish but to clear his head, and ponder, and commune. As he steered it out of the harbour, past the pleasure boats and paddle-boarders, he glanced at the painting hanging in the wheelhouse, the one that he'd bought from Merrin, showing the apocalyptic storm-lashed sea. As he looked ahead, the ocean was millpond calm, the sun glittering on it. But the painting suited his mood a lot better.

There was, indeed, a storm coming.

28

MERRIN

Jen came over in the morning, dressed in shorts and a T-shirt and sandals, carrying a bag over her shoulder. 'We're going on a drive,' she told Merrin. 'Maggie still won't go down to the beach, after the crabs. Arthur's persuaded us all to go and look at some tin mine and get a pub lunch somewhere.'

'Sounds lovely,' said Merrin, though in truth she couldn't think of anything worse than spending a day with that lot. She didn't know how Jen put up with them. She beckoned her over to her laptop on the kitchen table. 'I got an email from Sergeant Wells last night.'

'About the knife?' said Jen, shucking the bag off her back and standing over Merrin as she logged into the laptop.

'No, but... something about the crash.' Merrin twisted and looked up at Jen. 'You OK with this?'

Jen nodded tightly, and Merrin called up the email, and they both read it silently. Merrin said, 'Doctor Heygate. London-based. Wasn't that the guy you mentioned who treated you after the accident?'

Jen nodded, frowning. 'Why would he be writing a medical report for an itinerant farm labourer involved in a crash in Cornwall?'

'That's what I was wondering. I mean, it might be a different person, but... it's not a common name. I did some Googling and there is a private practice in Mayfair where one works.' Merrin called up the page, with a photograph of Doctor Heygate. 'Is this him?'

Jen nodded again. 'That's weird. I mean, if the gang use him, presumably he knew Justin as well... Is that why he was involved?'

Merrin shrugged and turned around in her chair to Jen. 'Maybe. Seems weird, though, that he's filed a report for the tractor driver too.'

'Should we call Sergeant Wells and tell her?'

Merrin stood up and put the kettle on. 'I tried. Her phone is going to voicemail. I called the Boscanlon police station direct and I was told that she's on compassionate leave for three weeks due to a sudden family bereavement. As of yesterday.'

Jen's frown deepened. 'But she didn't mention that in her email. In fact, she said—'

'That she'd probably see us at the Fish Festival. And if not, would call in on Monday. That email was sent just before nine o'clock last night. Surely she'd have known by then about this bereavement and taking time off?'

Jen sighed. 'Maybe we're looking for mysteries where there aren't any.' Merrin waggled a cup at her and she shook her head. 'I'd best get back. We're setting off in five minutes.'

'Enjoy the tin mine,' said Merrin. Jen let herself out and Merrin made a coffee, and stood leaning against the fridge, pondering. Was Jen right? Were they looking too hard for weird things? Maybe Sergeant Wells thought her personal life was none of Merrin and Jen's damn business, which was why she'd not mentioned it in her email.

Besides, things were plenty odd enough without seeking out strangeness. Take last night.

She'd woken in her bed, the moon shining down on Nans-Avallen. Merrin had walked silently down the stairs and let herself out of the door, standing naked, the warm sea breeze playing over her, the grass damp beneath her feet. She saw clouds scudding across the moon and the white crests of waves out on the dark sea. Somewhere in the far-off distance a whale sang, and night-birds chattered, and the trees whispered. It was to the apple tree that she was drawn, walking across the field towards it. The tree seemed to be glowing from within, a pale, diffuse, yellow light that seeped through the bark glittered on the extremities of the branches like stardust.

The whispering of the trees grew louder, and it was only when they sighed her name that she dragged her eyes from the tree and walked towards the dark woods. A bird took flight from the ground, clattering through the branches, and a fox cried like a baby. A dog barked a long way off.

Merrin, whispered the breeze in the trees. *Merrin*.

She stepped forward, her feet hitting the dry floor of the woods, twigs crunching underneath her bare soles. There was a movement ahead of her, something lumbering between the trees, coming closer.

Merrin, said the trees again, more clearly, more loudly. The shape of the figure in front of her stepped into the moonlight.

No, it stepped into the living room of the cottage she still lived in on the harbour front of Scuttler's Cove with her mother and her father.

Her father. Her dad. He was carrying a birthday cake, with ten candles in it. Merrin looked down at herself and she was small, in a pretty white dress and sandals. Her mother appeared behind her father, and her mum started to sing *Happy Birthday*.

Her father bent down towards her with the cake and Merrin closed her eyes and made a wish and blew out all the candles with one breath.

'What did you wish for?' said her mother. 'No, don't tell us or it won't come true!'

Merrin told them anyway. 'I wished that you had a face, Dad,' she said.

Her father did not smile, did not even look at her. He couldn't, because he had no face. Just an expanse of smooth flesh, and suddenly Merrin was scared, terrified, and she screwed her eyes up tight and when she opened them again she was standing on the edge of the woods in Nans-Avallen in the moonlight, and the figure had emerged from the trees and was standing in front of her, a man, broad, tall, holding out his arms. And he had no face. No face, but a cruel, violent gash in his throat, from which blood poured, red and angry in the silver light of the moon and stars. Merrin closed her eyes again, and screamed, and woke up.

On a whim she picked up her phone and called Taran. He answered straight away, speaking loudly over what sounded like a strong wind.

'Where are you?' she said.

'Out on the boat.'

Merrin ran outside and to the cliff edge and spied his boat out on the ocean. She jumped up and down and waved with both arms. She put the phone back to her ear and heard Taran laugh.

'I can see you, jumping about like a mad thing.'

'Taran,' she said suddenly. 'Do you know who my dad was?'

He seemed to take a long time before answering, then said, 'Merrin, I was born a month before you. I've no more idea than you have.'

'It's just… you said you'd got close to my mum before she died. I just wondered if she'd said anything about him.'

'No more than you already know,' she heard Taran say. The wind seemed higher, and he sounded more distant. 'She got drunk at the Fish Festival and slept with some bloke, a farm labourer, and never saw him again.'

Merrin said nothing, and Taran went on, 'Why are you asking, all of a sudden?'

'No reason,' said Merrin. 'Sometimes I just wonder, that's all.'

'You didn't need a dad,' said Taran. 'Not with Lizzie Moon for a mother. Anyway, speaking of the Fish Festival, am I going to see you tomorrow?'

'Wouldn't miss it for the world, idiot,' said Merrin, laughing.

'That's Fish King to you, Merrin Moon.'

'Of course, oh exalted and most-high Fish King,' said Merrin. 'Please accept the humble apologies of your most faithful subject.'

She heard Taran say something, but it was buried in a squall of static, and then the connection was lost. She stood on the clifftop for a long time, waving and waving at him, and watching his little boat nose back towards the harbour.

Merrin painted on the clifftop for the rest of the afternoon. Janet at the Driftwood Gallery had called her yesterday to say the prints were selling like hot cakes and two of the originals had gone, and she had some money for her the next time she called in, and could Merrin do some more work at her earliest opportunity? She added that she was going to bump the prices up. For the first time, Merrin allowed herself to believe that she could actually make some money out of this. If Janet could keep selling her stuff at this rate, then by the end of summer she might have a decent sum put away to live off over winter. Merrin squinted into the sun. Things were finally looking up.

She was feeling so positive that she decided to head into Scuttler's Cove and get her money from Janet before the gallery closed. And she might even treat herself to dinner in the Star and Anchor, provided Clemmo was still doing locals' rates and hadn't got too greedy. Merrin was just about to walk down the cliff path when the Londoners came back in their fleet of cars. She waved at Jen, sitting in the back of Tabby and Paul's car, who waved back. The others all turned to look at her as they drove quietly past. Merrin was slightly unnerved by the weight of their stares.

'Fuck you,' she cheerily said aloud, as she started to descend the path. She'd done London and it was shit, and they were welcome to it. Merrin Moon was a professional artist now and she wasn't going to let anything spoil her mood. She turned one more time to look at Nans-Avallen, and was so struck by the beauty of the apple tree against the blue sky that she took out her phone and photographed it. The tourists seemed to like the ones of the tree, Janet had said.

Merrin stood there for a long moment after taking the photo, and realised she was thinking about the apples. Her mouth was positively watering. She told herself not to be stupid, she was about to go and spend a small fortune in the Star and Anchor on food. But the more she tried not to think about the apples, the more her stomach grumbled and her mouth watered.

Well, one couldn't hurt, could it? She set off back across the field, waving at Jen again as she stood watching her, and walked to the apple tree, plucking one of the low-hanging apples from a branch.

Feeling eyes on her, Merrin turned to see that Jen had disappeared but had been replaced by the couple who had driven her on their day out, Paul and Tabby. They were watching her with impassive interest as she stood there, holding the apple.

My apple, she thought, and wondered where that had come from. But the more they stared, the more proprietorial Merrin felt. You've bought the houses, she thought furiously. Not the apple tree. Never the apple tree.

She thought of all the old stories again that they'd told as kids. How the apples from Nans-Avallen would drive you mad, or make you ill, or kill you. If only they'd known. If only they'd known then how sweet and tender they were.

Merrin took a bite from the apple, savouring its taste, feeling its juice run down her chin. Paul and Tabby continued to stare at her. Merrin took another, exaggerated bite, and sighed. So, so good.

Then she started back the way she'd come, back to the cliff road, back towards the town. Every nerve seemed on fire as she bit into the last of the apple's flesh. Every sense heightened. Merrin felt powerful. Unstoppable. Superhuman.

She was glowing, she was quite sure of it, as she descended to Scuttler's Cove.

29

MERRIN

Among the many things Merrin had forgotten about Scuttler's Cove while living in London was the unalloyed joy of the Fish Festival. She awoke early, like a child on Christmas morning, and sat outside her house with a pot of coffee, watching the town come alive in the distance. At ten o'clock, after showering and doing her face as though she was off to a big night out in London, she departed for the town. She thought about asking Jen if she wanted to come with her, but decided she should leave her to her friends. No doubt they'd all have heard about the Fish Festival, and would be curious to see it.

As she walked down the cliff path, Merrin could see the floats gathered at the top of the hill, near the church. The procession would wend its way down to the harbour, then along the front, and finally to the beach below the cliff on which Nans-Avallen stood. Then there would be games and fun on the harbour for the kids, and the adults would get rip-roaring drunk. The latent memories of her first eighteen years in Scuttler's Cove bobbed excitedly to the surface, the remembrances of Fish Festivals past.

The streets were festooned with blue and white bunting, and most of the shops had dressed up their windows in fishy or oceanic themes. There was a roaring trade on eBay every year for rubber over-the-head fish masks, and Merrin laughed delightedly as she dodged a group of fish-headed men, evidently early starters on the beer, dancing along the harbour road. The more dedicated Scuttler's Cove denizens went all out on elaborate costumes, Poseidons and mermaids and sea horses. A man was outside the Driftwood Gallery, playing sea shanties on a fiddle, wearing an all-over bodysuit that had every inch covered with glued-on shells, leaving space only for his eyes and mouth. People pushed carts selling plastic fish dangling from fishing rods, or gaudy hats with shark jaws on them, that clashed together when you pulled two wires that met under your chin. Other local craftspeople sold shell bracelets and sea-glass pendants and jewellery in the shape of crustaceans, friendship bands made from dried channelled wrack or gutweed. And dotted along the harbour were stalls and vans selling fish; fried, grilled, baked fish, fish of all kinds, dressed crab and grilled pomfret and battered cod and more. All around there was music, dancing, laughter.

Merrin checked her watch. It was almost time for the procession to start. She hurried up the hill towards St Ia's Church, where the floats were shuttling themselves into place and order like a game of larger-than-life Jenga. And at the front of it all, leading the charge, was the Fish King.

Merrin simultaneously stifled a giggle, and felt a twinge between her legs. Taran had got so handsome, and there he was, sitting on the back of a flatbed truck on his gold spray-painted throne, dressed in long, blue and white tie-dyed robes, a wooden, golden crown on his head inlaid with barnacles and shells instead of jewels. In one hand he held an orb studded with sea-glass, in the other a weathered sceptre made from driftwood. Around him cavorted teenage mermaids in long felt tails and scallop-shell bikini tops, green lipstick and eyeshadow and seaweed wigs. He saw her and rolled his eyes. To her delight, he was blushing.

Merrin pushed through the milling crowds to the side of the truck. Taran looked down at her, grinning. 'I hate this,' he mouthed.

'You love it, you mean,' said Merrin, laughing. She cocked her head towards the nearest mermaid. 'Digging your harem, Fish King.'

'Buy me a drink after?' he said. The engines were starting up on the floats, Taran's followed by one from the school, and the Scouts and Guides group, the various pubs and clubs and organisations.

'You'll need it,' she said, stepping back. She blew him a kiss and he smiled at her.

Maybe it wouldn't be so bad, you and Taran, said a voice in her head. *Maybe you're ready. Maybe this is always what was meant to be.*

Then she was surrounded by a crowd in fish masks, and Clemmo from the Star and Anchor, the 'Obby-Sea-'Oss costume slung from his shoulders on braces, took his position at the front of Taran's truck. Merrin spied Reverend Bligh marching down the street, and he went to stand in front of Clemmo. Either side of them villagers carrying a range of instruments, drums and fiddles and ukuleles and trumpets, arranged themselves, and the crowd fell silent.

Reverend Bligh lowered his head and muttered what appeared to be a prayer to himself. Then he put a shining whistle to his lips, blew a long note, and started striding forward. The motley band struck up an out-of-tune, out-of-time shanty, made even more discordant by the PA systems on the other floats that burst into life.

Clemmo clacked the jaws of the 'Obby-Sea-'Oss with hidden strings, and began to prance after Bligh. The trucks rumbled forward. The Fish Festival was underway.

Merrin walked alongside the procession, grinning at Taran's growing discomfort as people they were at school with pointed at him and threw handfuls of slimy wet seaweed at him, as was tradition. By the time they had crawled along the harbour front, the road packed with tourists and locals, Merrin wouldn't have cared if she never heard 'Under the Sea' from *The Little Mermaid* or 'Yellow Submarine' ever again in her life. She knew she'd hear them a lot more before the night was out, though.

Towards the end of the harbour Merrin spied Jen and her London friends, watching the parade. She pushed through the crowds to say hello.

'This is Merrin,' said Jen to her friends. 'She lives—'

'Affordable housing,' said the one she knew was Paul, looking down his nose at her.

Jen coughed and said, 'You won't remember all their names straight away, but I'm sure you will soon, as we're neighbours. This is Paul and Tabby, Adaku and Arthur, Simon, and Timothy and Maggie.'

Maggie looked at her through heavy eyes, her exposed skin covered with plasters from the crab attack. She looked uncomfortable, as though the blemishes on her face and body from those crabs were somehow shameful to her. Merrin supposed that was what happened when looks were everything to you.

'Pleased to meet you, dear,' said Simon, taking Merrin's hand. 'Hope we haven't been too vile and loud. You must come over for cocktails with us one evening.'

The tall Black woman, Adaku, gave a little snort and looked away. She was by far the most striking of the group, a head taller than the other women. She was wearing a high roll-neck jumper, black leggings that accentuated the length of her legs, and, most bizarrely given the sun beating down from above, black silk gloves.

'We'd love to have you, of course,' said Tabby, smiling warmly. Though, thought Merrin, a little like a shark might, just before it took your leg off.

'Merrin's got work in that gallery on the front,' said Jen, and Merrin was touched by how proud she sounded of her.

'We'll have to get some,' said Arthur. 'Support the local talent, and all that.'

There was a moment's awkward silence, then Merrin plastered on a smile. 'Right, I'd better catch up with Taran. He's my old school friend. He's the Fish King.'

Simon nudged Jen. 'It looks like neither of us will claim that twenty, sadly.'

Merrin frowned at him, but Jen said quickly, 'You go. We'll see you later, probably in one of the pubs?'

'Definitely,' said Merrin, squeezing Jen's hand, and pushing back through the crowds to the front of the procession.

At the end of the harbour the road became little more than a track, too big for the lorries to negotiate, which led to the beach below Nans-Avallen. Most tourists went to the town beach at the other end of the harbour, but this was where the Fish Festival procession traditionally ended up. Taran was helped down from the truck, and he led the way down the path, followed by the 'Obby-Sea-'Oss, and the mermaids, and the villagers in their fish masks. The band had fallen silent, the onlookers hushed.

Merrin followed them down and stood with them as they fanned out behind Taran, who stood at the shoreline, gazing out to sea. He turned to look at Bobby Carlyon, who had a pig carcass hefted on to one shoulder, huffing along the path to stand with Taran. Taran looked at the pig, and then at Bobby. There was an apple in the pig's mouth. Bobby raised an eyebrow and grinned at Taran, but it didn't seem to Merrin to be a particularly friendly smile. What had gone on between those two?

And she was pretty sure that apple in the pig's mouth was a Nans-Avallen apple. She could almost sense it.

One of the musicians struck up on his drum a sombre, sonorous beat. The few people still whispering or murmuring fell silent. There was a momentary pause, then Taran began to speak.

'Lady of the Sea, we thank you for your bounty and the prosperity you bring to Scuttler's Cove,' said Taran loudly and clearly. The surf washed over his boots. 'Since time beyond memory you have herded the shoals into our nets, fed our bellies, filled our coffers. We thank you and pay tribute to you.' Taran seemed to turn and stare pointedly at Bobby, then behind him at Reverend Bligh, Merrin was sure of it. Then he said, 'For generations, since time immemorial, the Tregarth line has honoured you, even when others turned away. My Lady of the Sea, you have never been more needed than you are today.' Then Taran turned to the assembled townsfolk and tourists, and cried out, 'Turn your backs!'

Merrin was shocked at first by the ferocity and venom in his voice, and then she began to remember, as though a sea-fret had been clouding her mind while she had been away from Scuttler's Cove. She remembered the ritual of the Fish Festival.

All the Scuttler's Cove people watching began to silently turn and look away from Taran and the sea. They turned, as one, to face the cliff, and Nans-Avallen. The tourists murmured, some laughed, others took photographs. But then they fell silent, too, as though they knew they were witnessing something that wasn't just a show for them. Merrin could see in their suddenly troubled eyes that many of them were realising they should perhaps not be here at all, should be far from here.

'What a bloody odd to-do,' she heard Simon say, and as Merrin turned she saw Adaku nudge him in the stomach and shush him. Merrin turned, because she was from Scuttler's Cove, and she remembered. She turned, away from the sea, and to face Nans-Avallen up on the cliff.

It was as though Scuttler's Cove was under a spell, a cone of silence. Not a dog barked, not a gull cried. Not a single holidaying child spoke; they simply held their parents' hands tighter, and would have troubled dreams that night. Only the lapping of the sea on the shore, and the breeze whispering, made even the slightest sound at all.

It was Taran who broke the silence. 'Turn your backs on Endellion, as your forefathers did. Look to Avallen, as your ancestors did. Leave it to the Fish King, the Tregarth line, to maintain the fragile compact with the Lady of the Sea. To whom we give this gift, to appease her for our betrayal.'

Then Bobby staggered forward under the weight of the pig, and hefted it on his shoulder. Taran stepped forward and plucked the apple from the pig's mouth. Merrin was pretty sure she heard him say to Bobby 'Dick'.

The spell was broken. The townsfolk turned back to the sea, and a murmur of muted conversation rose up again. The tourists glanced at each other, then smiled, nodding at the fascinating slice of local folk custom they had just witnessed.

Then Bobby heaved the pig into the sea in an impressive throw. Taran surreptitiously dropped the apple to the pebbles and ground it under his boot-heel. Then he turned to the crowd and said, 'I am the Fish King and this is my decree. Let the revelry commence!'

A loud cheer went up, and from somewhere close by fireworks were lit, rockets screaming into the sky, and everyone started to head back to the town, the band dancing along beside them. Merrin let the people flow past her until only Taran was left on the beach. She walked over to him as he took off his crown with a loud sigh.

'That was, um...' she said.

He looked at her. 'You'd forgotten, hadn't you?'

'I'd forgotten,' Merrin conceded. 'What's up with you and Bobby, anyway? Lover's tiff?'

'Is it that obvious?' said Taran, dragging the robes off and balling them up. He looked more like his normal self in jeans and a checked shirt. 'It's nothing. It's just that he's a dick.'

'Yeah, I heard you call him that. So did most of the kids standing behind you.'

Taran gave her a lopsided grin. 'It's Fish Festival. If you don't want to be shocked, then stay at home. Now, I believe you were going to buy me a drink?'

'The Fish King never goes without drinks at festival time,' said Merrin. After a nanosecond's hesitation she linked her arm through his. He didn't seem to mind, and certainly didn't protest. 'I'm just going to ride on your coat-tails and hoover up your dregs.'

'I am the Fish King and this is my decree,' said Taran loftily. 'You and I, Merrin Moon, are going to go into yonder tavern and get absolutely mortal drunk.'

'Yes, your highness,' said Merrin, grinning, and her heart sang as they walked back towards the harbour and the music and the crowds.

✷

From Nans-Avallen, he watched the revelry below, and as the sun sank and the lights flickered on, he wished beyond anything he had wished before that he could stumble down the path and join the party in Scuttler's Cove.

But he could not. He was tied to Nans-Avallen, and could not leave its bounds. He was tied by blood, and the one who slept beneath the apple tree owned him. He should not be walking, he knew that. It angered he who slept beneath the tree. It angered he for who Nans-Avallen was named. The slumbering rage rippled through the grass, waved the branches on the trees, swelled the apples, because he had dared to defy the master of this place and stood up, and walked, and peered through the windows of the incomers, searching, always searching.

Searching for who, and why, he didn't yet know. But he did know he was close. So close. Blood roared in his ears like the tides. He was close.

They were down there, all the people who lived in the houses on Nans-Avallen. What foolish hubris would lead someone to make their home here, on this land, on this earth that was his domain?

Aye, the hubris he might have once proudly worn himself, like a badge of honour. Back when he believed he could do anything, and nobody could stop him. Back in the days when, if he saw something he wanted, he took it, and the devil take anyone who tried to stop him.

The devil take anyone who tried to stop him, he thought, as he stood as near to the edge of Nans-Avallen as he dared, gazing down on the town below, lit up with life. That was him, once, abandoned and free and raising a glass to anyone and everyone. But then that night happened, and it was, in fact, him who the devil took.

30

JEN

The town was still heaving as night descended, and they stood outside the Star and Anchor, drinking from plastic cups, which Paul in particular seemed to find highly distasteful. He'd been disgruntled at not being able to get a table inside for food, and Jen could see the *don't you know who I am?* frown still clouding his fine features. Jen considered that she *didn't* know who he was, not really. Didn't know who any of them were. But in the circles in which they moved, they were players. Movers and shakers. If you had money, she thought, you probably knew them. Jen had money, but deep in her gut she knew she'd never really be one of them.

'Why don't we get some street food?' suggested Jen brightly. The stalls and vans were selling a cornucopia of delicious-smelling seafood.

Maggie gave her a condescending look. 'And just stand here in the road eating fish and chips? How very northern.'

Timothy took Maggie's arm and steered her away, and they had a hushed but heated conversation. Adaku was standing to one side, seemingly very distracted. She must be boiling in those clothes, Jen thought. Adaku idly scratched at her throat beneath the polo neck sweater.

Only Simon seemed to be thoroughly enjoying himself. He was wearing a cheap sailor's cap and dancing in the street with a group wearing rubber fish masks, laughing uproariously. Jen smiled and turned to glance through the pub window. She could see Merrin standing at the packed bar with Taran, and some other people their age, who she must have grown up in Scuttler's Cove with. They were doing shots. They looked so happy. Jen felt a pang of envy. She wished she was with them and not the gang.

Jen felt a nudge as someone took her elbow, and turned to see Tabby smiling at her. 'We should go out, tomorrow. Just me and you.'

'Just us?' said Jen. 'Where?'

Tabby glanced around and lowered her voice to almost a whisper. 'You don't have to say anything, I can see it in your eyes. They're a boring old bunch, aren't they? I know what it's like for you, Jen, truly I do. I didn't know any of them before I met Paul. It took them ages to accept me. I didn't come from money, like most of them. But I've worked damn hard for what I have. I'm not just a trophy wife, you know.'

Jen felt simultaneously a little better, and a bit more despondent. 'That's all I am, isn't it? Well, a trophy widow. I do want to do something. I want to be involved more. I'm not some stupid bimbo, if that's what everyone thinks. I went to university. I could be a part of...'

'Part of?' said Tabby.

'I hear you talking about some opportunity. Investments. Something lucrative. I haven't asked because it's not my business, but, you know... I have a head on my shoulders. I could work for it, just like you did.'

Tabby gave a little laugh. 'Darling Jen. Of course you're going to be a part of it. A big part. I'll make sure of that. We'll talk more about it soon. In the meantime... what say you and I skip off somewhere tomorrow and do a bit of shopping? There must be a town nearby with some decent stores that aren't Primark or Next.'

'That would be lovely,' said Jen, feeling genuinely touched. She didn't tell Tabby that she rather liked Next and, despite her newfound riches, still shopped there.

'Oh, great, just great,' they heard Paul say, and a second later Jen realised why. It was starting to rain. The moon and stars had become obscured by thick, low cloud, and they were spitting fat gobbets of rain down on them, getting faster and heavier.

'We'll never get taxis with this festival going on,' muttered Paul. Arthur was already on his phone, talking to a cab firm, and gave Paul the thumbs up.

Then the heavens opened and a huge cheer went up from the locals in the street, and the dancing seemed to reach fresh levels of energy.

Simon puffed over, his face red, his sailor cap on at a jaunty angle. Adaku gave him a withering look and Timothy said, 'Aye aye, Captain Birdseye.' Timothy glanced at Maggie, who just scowled at his attempt at levity.

'Why are they bloody cheering the rain?' said Paul, pushing himself back against the wall of the pub in an attempt at shelter.

'That's what I wondered,' said Simon. 'Apparently it's a good omen, rain after the Fish Festival. A good storm gets the seas all perky, and the fishing will be good tomorrow.'

'Taxis,' announced Arthur, waving at two cars parked at the end of the harbour. 'Let's go before someone hijacks them.'

'Let them bloody try,' said Paul, leading the way.

—

Timothy insisted everyone go to his and Maggie's, which Jen suspected was some lame attempt to compensate for Maggie's increasingly long-lasting foul mood. She was still covered in plasters, though had removed some on her face and touched the scratches up with foundation.

'I think I'll make some food!' announced Timothy. Maggie said she was going to get changed.

'Timothy's a whizz in the kitchen,' said Tabby to Jen.

'Cocktails!' declared Simon, rolling up the sleeves of his shirt and inspecting the bottles arranged in the drinks cabinet.

'And can we have some music that isn't connected in any way to the sea or fish,' pleaded Adaku, sitting on the sofa. Jen was inclined to agree. The Star and Anchor seemed to have had 'Orinoco Flow' on repeat all evening. Even now *sail away sail away sail away* threaded through her mind like a tree root.

Music came first, followed by cocktails, then half an hour later Timothy brought tray after tray of incredible food through, blinis and prawns and lamb chops and chunky potato wedges. 'Told you, Timothy's a magician,' said Tabby. Jen didn't say the spread looked like the frozen party food they sold in Lidl at Christmas. None of them would have the faintest idea what she was talking about.

The rain had turned into a full-on storm, wind howling around the house. Out across the sea lightning snaked through the thick, low cloud, and barely two seconds later there was a loud, prolonged rumble of thunder.

'Right above us,' said Simon.

Jen went to the big French windows to watch the storm. A jagged fork of lightning pierced the sea, which was thrashing and violent, waves rising up. She thought of her dream, and Merrin's painting, and felt a sudden cold stab of fear.

'Very dramatic show,' said Arthur, joining Jen at the window. Everyone looked up as the lights flickered in the room.

'We should tell ghost stories,' said Simon. 'Anybody know any?'

'Haven't we had enough of ghost stories?' said Maggie. She had changed into her pyjamas and a fluffy dressing gown, and sat on the sofa, a plate of food untouched beside her.

Jen turned, and frowned. 'I haven't heard any ghost stories!'

'Yes, Maggie,' said Paul pointedly. 'What *are* you talking about?'

'Here's a good story,' said Timothy, carrying a tray from the kitchen. No, not a tray. A mirror, reflective side up. He placed it on the coffee table. On it were several very neatly cut lines of coke. 'Once upon a time there was a magic mirror, and it made everyone very happy. The end.'

Maggie tutted audibly. Adaku shrugged and said, 'When in Rome. Arthur, get me a fifty.'

Jen watched them, one by one, vacuum up the lines. Tabby, rubbing her nose with her thumb and sniffing loudly, handed the rolled-up fifty-pound note to Jen. She shook her head, and was about to make some excuse, when there was an almost apocalyptic flash of lightning right outside, and a crack of thunder almost immediately that sounded as though someone had cleaved the sky in two.

There were shrieks and yells and then sudden, relieved laughter.

'Fucking hell!' shouted Simon. 'I thought my heart was going to give out.'

Then the lights went out.

Everyone got out their phones and switched on their flashlights, shining them in each other's faces. The music had stopped. Timothy was fiddling with the TV remote control, but the big screen stayed black and dead. 'I think all the electrics are out,' he said.

'Is it just us?' said Tabby.

Jen went to the French windows. 'I'm sure Merrin had left a light on across the field,' she said. 'Her house is in darkness as well.'

'What has Penrose got us hooked up to, anyway?' she heard Arthur saying. 'National grid?'

'Supposedly,' said Paul. 'Are the lights on in town?'

Jen cupped her hands over her eyes to dispel her own reflection in the rain-sluiced glass and put her face up against it. She could see some of Scuttler's Cove down the hill, and the lights burned as brightly as they ever had.

'Looks like it,' said Jen. 'I think it must just be—'

She screamed and fell backwards. Simon rushed to her side in the darkness. 'Jen? Jen? What happened? You weren't struck by lightning?'

She felt her mouth working but nothing was coming out. She pointed at the glass with a shaking hand, swallowed, and managed to say, 'Someone's outside! They came right up to the window!'

Jen felt the flashlights of the others all falling on her. Paul said, 'Are you sure it wasn't your own reflection?'

And then there was another flash of lightning, long and sustained, and they all turned to the French windows, and what stood illuminated outside.

It was a man, broad and tall, wearing sodden clothing, a checked shirt and trousers. And on his head, one of those fish masks they had seen so many of at the festival. He just stood there, stock still, five feet from the windows, the empty, glassy eyes of the fish mask staring at them.

Jen heard Tabby scream, and one or more of the men swear. Then there was a baleful roll of thunder. Jen skittered backwards on her bum, coming up hard against someone's legs. The phone flashlights were dancing around in confusion.

'What. The. Fuck. Was. That?' demanded Adaku.

Lightning flashed again, and Jen tensed, expecting the fish-faced man to be right up against the window, smashing the glass with murderous intent. But the spot where he'd been standing was empty. She didn't know if that was a relief or even more terrifying.

Suddenly, everyone was babbling at once, rushing around the room pointlessly and without focus. Paul's voice cut through the melee, demanding that everyone calm down.

'It's just some drunk from the village,' he said, though a little uncertainly to Jen. 'I'm sure it's nothing to worry about.'

'It's not,' said Maggie quietly, and everyone turned their torches on her. 'It's something bad. I just know it is. Something very, very bad.'

'Well, if there's a serial killer on the loose, nobody leave Adaku and I alone,' said Simon.

Jen saw Adaku's phone swivel towards Simon. 'What do you mean by that?' she said.

'Only that in horror films it's always the gay and Black characters who die first,' said Simon, and he barked a laugh that sounded hollow in the room.

Timothy swore and Simon muttered an apology for his attempt at levity that had crashed like the thunder cracking above them. 'We need weapons,' said Arthur. 'Knives, that sort of thing. From the kitchen.'

Then everyone jumped as the lights flickered back on. Jen took a deep breath. Paul and Timothy rushed to the window, cupping their hands round their faces as Jen had done. 'No sign of him,' said Timothy.

Paul straightened up and started jabbing at his phone. 'Well, I'm calling the police anyway. Even if it is just some drunk from Scuttler's Cove, this is private land.' He looked around at all of them as he put the phone to his ear. 'This is our land,' he said.

31

JEN

The storm began to abate, or at least move, because lightning still flashed in the clouds out to sea, and the thunder still rumbled, but more distantly. They all sat in silence until the flashing blue lights of the police car pulled onto Nans-Avallen, just before midnight.

'For fuck's sake, Timothy, get rid of that coke!' hissed Paul as he went to open the door.

A young police officer in his mid-twenties, in a waterproof black coat, stepped inside. He was eating a pie. 'Excuse me,' he said, his mouth full. 'Pork pie from the Fish Festival. Not sure what Bobby Carlyon has put in these but they're delicious.' He finished and wiped his hands on his rain-drenched trousers. 'PC Davis, from Boscanlon. Been working at the festival this evening, so you're lucky I was so close. What seems to be the trouble?' He pulled out his notebook. 'I believe you had a visit from my colleague Sergeant Wells recently?'

'Where is she?' said Jen.

PC Davis glanced at her. 'Compassionate leave. Why?'

Jen shrugged. For some reason she felt it best not to tell the others she'd been talking to Sergeant Wells. Paul said testily, 'The whereabouts of your colleague isn't really the issue here, is it?'

'Why don't you tell me what is, sir?'

'There's a fucking madman outside!' said Simon shrilly.

PC Davis wrote in his notebook 'MADMAN'. He looked up and said, 'Can you elaborate, please?'

They all started talking at once, and PC Davis held up his hand. 'One at a time, please.'

Paul glared at everyone else and took a deep breath. 'There was a man, right outside our window. Staring in at us. In a very threatening manner. And it's not the first time we've seen him. He's been hanging around since we got here.'

PC Davis made more notes. 'Can you describe him?'

'He was wearing a mask,' said Paul. 'One of those fish masks they all had on in the town earlier. Other than that… checked shirt, trousers. Possibly cargo pants. Boots. We only saw him for a brief moment.'

'He could be anywhere,' said Arthur.

PC Davis nodded and said, 'I'll conduct a search of the area. Bear with me.'

He went outside and they all crowded at the French windows, watching the beam from his torch slicing through the darkness. He walked up and down in front of all their houses, then disappeared.

They waited in silence, Jen looking at them all in turn. 'Maybe I overreacted when I saw him first,' she said. 'Frightened everyone.'

Tabby put a hand on her arm. 'Nobody overreacted. It was terrifying!'

'Where's that damn copper?' said Arthur.

'Probably hanging from the tree by now,' moaned Simon. Paul shot him a look.

The door opened and they all shrank back, but it was PC Davis. Of course. He wiped the rain from his face.

'I've conducted a thorough search of your houses both front and back and can't see anything,' he said.

'Perhaps you should get more officers up here,' said Paul. 'What about the woods?'

PC Davis pulled a face. 'The thing is, sir, it's my feeling it's just someone from town, wandering around. There's been a lot of drinking all day.'

'You know we've had vandalism?' said Timothy.

'I saw Sergeant Wells's report, yes. There doesn't appear to have been any damage on this occasion. And the thing is, there's not actually been a crime committed.'

'What about trespass!' said Paul. 'He was right there, outside the window.'

PC Davis wrinkled his nose. 'At a push, sir, yes. But he isn't there now. And he's not been in any of the houses, or even the rear gardens, as far as I can ascertain.'

'He's on our land,' said Paul evenly.

'He was, briefly,' countered PC Davis. 'I mean, you own the houses, yes, but—'

'We own it all,' cut in Paul. 'The whole site. Apart from that affordable housing over there.'

'So you're just going to leave?' said Simon.

'I'm satisfied there isn't any immediate danger or threat,' said PC Davis. 'Please do give us a call if there are any further incidents or problems though.' He walked to the door and turned, smiling. 'I'm sure it'll all look better in daylight. Tomorrow's set to be a lovely day again, once this storm blows itself out.'

—

'Get me some blankets,' said Simon. 'There's no way I'm going back to my house alone. I'll kip on your sofa.'

'You're all welcome to stay here,' said Timothy. He looked around as Maggie walked sluggishly to the stairs. 'Are you getting Simon some bedding?'

'I'm going to bed,' she said.

'Don't be ridiculous,' said Tabby. 'I'm sure we'll all be safe. Like that policeman said, things will look better in the morning.'

'If we survive until then,' muttered Simon.

'For god's sake,' breathed Paul. 'Tabby, come on. I'm shattered by all this. Let's go home and get to bed.'

Tabby turned to Jen. 'You're welcome to stay at ours if you don't want to be alone.'

Jen shook her head. 'Thank you, but I'm fine. I'll walk with you, though.'

'We'll come too,' said Adaku. She gave a loud sigh. 'Here's to absolutely nothing happening tomorrow.'

Paul and Tabby walked Jen to her house, and she let herself in. After the initial shock had worn off, she didn't feel scared at all. She also didn't believe that the figure they'd seen outside was just a drunk who'd wandered up from Scuttler's Cove.

What she hadn't told the others was that she'd felt some kind of connection to him. Something to do with the apples, or the apple tree. She couldn't explain it, even to herself. But it was as though that man, whoever he was… somehow he was of Nans-Avallen. This was his home. She was sure of it, but she had no idea why.

Jen got herself a big glass of water and went up to bed. She got out of her clothes and into her vest and shorts, and stood at the window, sipping her water.

The clouds were thinning, the rain had stopped. Moonlight was once again painting Nans-Avallen in a silver wash. She stood there for a long moment, gazing at the moon and the apple tree, until she heard a car labouring up the hill. It was a taxi, that stopped in front of Merrin's house. Jen watched her get unsteadily out of the cab, which executed a turn and sped away, and spend a long minute trying to get her key into the door lock. Jen smiled. She was glad Merrin had evidently had a good night.

When she looked back to the tree, her breath caught in her throat. There was a figure there, standing in the moonlight in front of the tree. It was him.

She reached for her phone, then paused. What would happen if she called the police? He'd be gone by the time they got up here. And what was he doing wrong anyway? He was just standing there, staring at the tree. Jen had the deepest conviction, right in her bones, that he didn't mean them any harm. Despite Paul's repeated assertions, they didn't own Nans-Avallen. They owned the houses. That's all.

What if he was just a villager who had liked to come up to Nans-Avallen before the houses were built, before they came from London and staked their claim to it? What if, she thought, he was ill, or had mental health issues? What if Nans-Avallen made him happy?

She thought of her mother. Jen's money had allowed her to buy a place in the very best care home she could find back in West Yorkshire, with home comforts and round-the-clock care and bright, well-appointed rooms. Activities designed to stimulate the mind, to try to stave off the final ravages of dementia. She knew her mum was too far gone, now, that Jen would never get her back, but she was able to make her feel comfortable, and safe, and for that, at least, she was grateful.

Perhaps that man, whoever he was, felt safe and comfortable here on Nans-Avallen. Perhaps that tree held memories for him, and brought him some kind of solace. Should they deny him that because he didn't fit into their idea of how the world worked, or at least worked for them?

Jen blinked, and the man had gone. Had he even been there at all? Was he just shadow and moonlight? She stood at the window for a few more minutes, scanning Nans-Avallen and the woods, but nothing moved. Eventually she climbed gratefully into her bed, and fell into a long, dreamless sleep until morning.

The next day was, as predicted, glorious once again. Jen felt rested and calm as she stretched in the window, looking out over Nans-Avallen. The sea beyond was calm, the sky was blue, and the order of summer in Scuttler's Cove was restored. It was as if the storm had never happened, save for a clearing of the pressure that Jen hadn't even noticed had been building in her head. She was going shopping with Tabby today, and there had been the suggestion that she was going to be brought in on this big new project everyone kept dropping hints about. Jen was being accepted, at last, into her circle of friends.

She went downstairs and made breakfast, suddenly ravenous. She sat at the table, looking out through the window, and saw Timothy pacing up and down on the grass outside, rubbing his face, shaking his head.

'Are you all right?' said Jen, standing at her door. 'Is everything OK with Maggie?'

Timothy looked at her with red-rimmed eyes. He looked like he'd not slept all night. 'She's gone,' he said.

'Gone?' Jen frowned. 'Gone where?'

'Back to London.' Timothy saw Jen looking at their car, still sitting on their drive. 'Penrose offered to drive her to the station this morning. Damned decent of him.'

'But why?' said Jen.

'Why did Penrose take her? Because she's fallen out with me. It's fine. She'll come round. She always cools off after a bit.'

'I mean, why has she left?'

Timothy sighed raggedly. 'It was that man last night. It was the last straw for her. After the crabs and everything. You've seen, I'm sure, that she's been struggling.'

Jen heard a door opening further down and saw Tabby and Paul emerge and walk over to them. 'Lovely day again,' said Paul, squinting at the sky.

'Maggie's gone home,' said Jen.

'Yes.' Tabby smiled. 'I heard. Perhaps it's for the best.'

'She's not been having the best of times, has she?' said Paul. It was somewhat at odds with his attitude several days ago when Jen had overheard him talking to Timothy in the kitchen. *She can't go home. There's a lot at stake. She has to stay focused, and with the programme.* What had made him change his mind?

Timothy looked upset. Jen was mildly surprised by that. The way Maggie talked to him, as though he was a piece of dirt on her shoe, and the things Paul had been saying about her sleeping with other men. She'd have thought he'd welcome a little break from his overbearing wife.

'Anyway, Jen and I are going shopping today,' said Tabby. 'Shall we say an hour? Is that enough time for you to get ready?'

Jen nodded, and went back into her house. She had to confess she was secretly relieved that Maggie had left. The woman had never liked her, and Jen felt almost a weight lifted off the site now she'd gone. And with the chance to do a bit of shopping, and get to know Tabby a bit more... well. Things definitely seemed to be looking up.

32

MERRIN

Merrin woke with a mouth dry and shrivelled and a head that banged a violent tattoo as soon as she lifted it off the pillow. So she put it back there, and closed her eyes, and waited for the hammering to subside. She needed the loo and she needed water and she needed coffee and she needed to not have drunk her own bodyweight in alcohol last night.

Still, she thought. Fish Festival came but once a year, and it had been more than a decade since she'd attended her last one. What a homecoming. Speaking of which, how had she got home? She couldn't remember anything. She lay there and tried to put her fractured memories in some kind of order until she got a vague sense that Taran had poured her into a taxi a little before midnight. She groaned suddenly as another memory slotted into place.

'Or...' she had said as he tried to put the seat belt on her. 'Or I could stay at yours tonight. Or you could come home with me.'

'Ask me again when you're not so drunk,' Taran had said, kissing the top of her head.

'I'm not drunk!' she said. 'I resent that.'

Then she'd bent forward and thrown up. Out of the taxi door, fortunately, but all over Taran's boots.

'Take her home,' Merrin remembered Taran saying to the taxi driver. 'Here's another twenty just in case she does that again.'

'Oh god,' she groaned, putting her hands over her face. She would have lain there stewing in her own mortification forever if it had been up to her, but thirst and her bladder finally drove her to slide out of bed like a slinky spring that had lost its bounce.

She was halfway through her second glass of water when she noticed the front door was slightly ajar. Christ. She must have been far gone if she'd not even closed the door, never mind locked it. Though it wasn't like she had dodgy neighbours. Merrin went to push the door closed and then noticed the black marks on the carpet. She must have trodden in a load of mud last night, following all that rain from the storm. Merrin found her keys on the little table by the door, and also her shoes, which she'd evidently kicked off as soon as she got in. So how had she trod earth all over the carpet? She looked at it, and frowned. It seemed to be leading into the room where she had her easel and paints set up, the window that had views of the apple tree.

In the room, she saw the last three paintings she'd done on the table, where she'd placed them to dry. And on the easel was the piece she'd done the other day, while sitting in the woods. The weird, horrible one with the man tied to the tree, his throat cut. She was pretty sure she'd propped that up against the wall, intending to whitewash the canvas and re-use it. But it wasn't just its presence on the easel that caused her to stop and stare at it, almost losing her grip on the glass of water.

Merrin's paints were out and open, and a brush was on the floor, its bristles stained with scarlet. And on the painting itself was daubed one short word in angry red capitals.

RUN.

—

Mid-afternoon, Merrin saw Jen getting out of Tabby's car, the pair of them laden with shopping bags. Lucky bitches, thought Merrin. She could do with a wardrobe refresh for summer. She went to her door and called Jen's name and waved. Jen waved back then pulled out her phone. Merrin's phone pinged with a text. *Ten mins. Something to tell you.*

'Can I go first?' said Merrin when Jen came over. She led her to the art room and showed her the easel. Jen stared at it and said, 'Wow. Did you paint that?'

'The painting, yes, which is weird enough. But not the letters.' She cupped her mug of tea. 'At least, I don't think so. I was pretty blasted when I got back from the Fish Festival last night. I mean, I could have done?' She looked at Merrin for support. 'But why would I?'

'Run,' said Jen thoughtfully. She cocked her head to one side. 'That's... not your usual style. The painting.'

'I know. It's horrible,' said Merrin miserably. 'I was sitting in the woods and I kind of just went into a trance, and when I came to I had that thing. It was just meant to be a nice view of the apple tree.'

'Why would you paint RUN on it?' said Jen.

'I've no idea. Like I said, I was drunk. I can't even remember doing the original painting properly, so maybe I slipped into a trance again. Except...' She looked back through the door. 'When I woke up this morning I'd not locked the door properly. And there were footprints. Leading here.'

'I don't think you painted that word on it,' said Jen, decisively.

'Then who did?'

Jen turned to look at her. 'The police were here last night, Merrin. There was an intruder on Nans-Avallen.'

Two cups of tea later, Merrin had mostly forgotten about her hangover. 'A fish mask,' she said slowly, when Jen had told her the story. 'You must have all been terrified. With the power cut as well, and the storm.'

'It was like something out of a slasher movie,' agreed Jen. 'The policeman didn't really take it seriously. He just thought it was some drunk from the Fish Festival.'

'I mean, that would seem to be the likeliest explanation,' said Merrin. 'The rational one. Except... you said you saw him again?'

'Just staring at the apple tree. In fact, it was right when you came home. I saw you get out of the taxi.'

They both looked at the painting again. 'Why is someone telling me to run?' wondered Merrin, for the dozenth time.

'If that was in my house, or one of the others', I'd just think it was another Independent Cornwall prank,' said Jen. 'But why would someone want you out?'

'Perhaps it's not a threat,' said Merrin slowly. 'Maybe it's a warning.'

'A warning about what, though?'

Merrin shrugged, and looked at Jen. 'Why would someone want me to leave? Me in particular?'

Jen swallowed, and paled visibly. 'Perhaps because something's going to happen to us,' she said. 'To the gang.' She fell silent for a moment, then said, 'Do you think we should call the police back? Try to get Sergeant Wells again?'

'This all feels too weird for the police. I think I'll start with Taran, see what he knows.'

When Jen had gone back to her house, Merrin called Taran. He sounded shockingly bright and breezy. Merrin's headache was coming back.

'Still alive, Moon? I thought it might be touch and go for a while, state you were in.'

'Someone broke into my house last night,' she said. She listened carefully for any tell-tale signs that might suggest Taran knew something about it. She was mildly disappointed but also very touched that he just sounded incredibly concerned.

'What? While you were out with me? Are you all right?'

'I... can't be sure. I only noticed it this morning. And yes, I'm fine. Thank you.'

'Did they take anything?'

'No. But they left something. Hang on, let's switch to video call. It's easier to show you.'

Taran's face suddenly filled the screen. He was at his cottage, on his sofa, shirt half open. Merrin felt a sudden urge to grab him and kiss his face. She saw her own image in the little box in the corner. 'Christ,' she muttered. 'I look like I just crawled out of the grave.'

She switched the camera around so she could walk into the art room and show him the painting. He peered into the screen of his phone for a moment, then sat back. 'Someone broke into your house and wrote RUN on your picture? Also, what even is that painting?'

Merrin switched the camera back and told him about the painting. She said, 'I'm not even sure they broke in. I might have left the door unlocked when I got home last night. I can't really remember.' She paused for a moment, then said, 'Taran, do you think this could be Bobby? Is it something to do with Independent Cornwall?'

He shook his head. 'I don't think this is Independent Cornwall. It's not their style. Anyway, why would they? You're one of us.'

'Jen's not one of us. Nor the rest of them. What if someone wants me out of the way to... I don't know. Do something to them?'

Taran frowned. 'Like what?'

'I don't know,' said Merrin, frustrated. She took a deep breath, and changed tack. 'Bobby though. I could see he was a bit off with you yesterday. And you him. Maybe he's pissed off because you've been spending so much time with me?'

She waited for him to laugh it off, to say Bobby wouldn't do anything stupid like that, but Taran just looked thoughtful. 'I'll ask some questions, speak to a few people,' he said finally. 'I'll give you a call later. Are you sure you're OK? Do you want to come and stay with me for a bit?'

She remembered what he'd said last night, when she asked him if she could stay. *Ask me again when you're not so drunk.* She smiled crookedly, and said, 'Ask me again when you're not so serious.'

—

By early evening, Merrin was starting to feel moderately human, and ready for something to eat. And that immediately made her think of apples, and her mouth started watering.

'No,' she said firmly to herself. Whatever was going on, it wouldn't be made any better by her eating Nans-Avallen apples like there was no tomorrow. Even as she made the decision, she felt a pang in her gut, a pull towards the tree, a hunger for the taste of the pulp in her mouth, a thirst for the sweet juice. 'Christ,' she said. 'It's like being addicted.'

She went to make a big bowl of pasta to fill her up, and afterwards ate most of a chocolate trifle that the packet claimed, in an outrageous lie, contained five to six servings. 'For piskies, maybe,' she muttered. The nights were staying lighter, later, but in the deep blue sky above the moon was already visible, picked out in white relief, marching towards fulness, three or four days hence. As she gazed up at it from her window, she remembered something she'd read years and years ago, that if you slept with the moon shining on you it was a sure way to go mad. Maybe this had all started because she'd not bothered to buy curtains for the bedroom.

A movement caught her eye, off towards the woods. She peered closer, but there was nothing, save for the gentle swaying of the branches. But then there it was again, a dark shape a little way into the trees. Too tall to be a fox, not long enough for a deer. Just about the right shape and size for a man.

Merrin continued to stare at the spot where she thought she'd seen the movement, but there was nothing, and eventually her eyes started to itch, and she turned away, as the sun began to cool and dip and the moon started to shine a little brighter.

✵

The Fish Festival had awakened something in him, brought fractured memories pouring into his fogged mind.

Anniversary.

He didn't know what he meant by that. But it was something to do with the Fish Festival, and this place, and the tree. The apple tree.

He stood beneath it, looking up through the holes in the thing that covered his head, at the apples. And then one fell, as though an invitation. He stooped with effort, and clutched at the fallen fruit, and brought it up to his eyeline.

He pushed up his face covering and sank his teeth into it. It had been so long. So long since he'd tasted anything. But this was sweet and vibrant and... and it almost made him feel alive.

And when he had tasted the apple, he knew. He knew who it was that he was looking for. What was more, he thought he knew why.

He turned to the smaller house, away from the others, and staggered towards it. The door was unlocked and he pushed down the handle and stepped inside.

It was so long since he'd been inside a house. He closed his eyes and revelled in the warmth, the security, the scent of it. The scent of her.

And then he knew, for certain. He went from room to room, touching things, marvelling as his memories came back. Until he found the room with the painting propped up on the easel. He stared at the image for a long time, and a sob wracked his body.

This was the place. This was the woman. He knew what he had to do. At the base of the easel were paints, a palette blobbed with colours, colours that seemed suddenly bright and fresh to him. He dipped one stub of a finger into the red paint, breaking the crust that had formed over it, and lifted it to the painting.

He knew time was of the essence. He had eaten the fruit of the apple tree, and that brought him to the attention of he who slept fitfully below, who would now know that he should not be here, and that he interfered with the plans, the design.

Time was running out. He had to warn her. He had to make it all right.

Across the image he began to daub one word.
RUN.

33

JEN

The mood was lighter with Maggie back in London, though Timothy still seemed morose and distracted. Jen guessed that he didn't really know what to do with himself without his wife to tell him what to do. It was decided they would go down to the beach again. As they gathered outside, Arthur shambled out of his house and said, 'I think we're going to sit this one out.'

'Is everything all right?' said Jen. 'Is Adaku OK?'

'Yes, yes, all fine,' said Arthur.

Timothy also declined, saying he wanted to catch up on a bit of work. 'Just us, then,' said Tabby.

'The most fun people in the gang, to be honest,' said Simon, tapping the side of his nose.

Jen, Tabby, Paul and Simon wended their way down the cliff path in the sunshine. When they set up camp on the beach, Simon gazed out over the sea. 'It looks very inviting, but I might give it a miss today, after the crabs and that butcher fellow throwing the pig carcass in here after the festival procession.'

Paul was tapping on his phone. 'Yes, we might perhaps have to find a different beach.'

'Nonsense,' said Tabby, digging into the cooler for a drink. 'I'm sure that dead pig was removed properly after the festival, and as for the crabs…' She lowered her voice. 'Well. There was a lot to grab on to with Maggie.' She gave Jen a little wink.

Their shopping trip had been lovely. They had driven into St Ives, which Jen had never visited before, and found it a pleasing mix of bucket-and-spade holidaymakers and some gorgeous independent shops. After spending what Jen still considered an outrageous amount of money in the stores, they'd found a nice little restaurant tucked away just off the harbour. 'I'm a bit up to here with seafood,' said Tabby. 'I'm going to go for a nice, juicy steak.'

Jen found Tabby easy to talk to, especially as she found out more of her upbringing, surprisingly not a million miles from Jen's own. 'The thing is,' said Tabby through a mouthful of rare rib-eye, 'once you get in with this sort of crowd you have to style it out. Act like you're as good as them, if not better. They're like sharks, really. They can sense blood. And weakness. If you're going to swim with sharks, you have to be prepared to bite back.'

'You don't make them sound like very nice people, really,' said Jen, cutting into her steak.

Tabby laughed. 'They're not nice people at all! The second lesson in all this is, good things happen to bad people, Jen. It's the way of the world. Everyone thinks it should be good things happening to good people, but that's bullshit.'

'So I have to be a shark *and* a bad person?'

Tabby laughed. 'You just have to be yourself. But make sure that *self* takes no shit from anyone. Men especially. They have to be reminded sometimes that they're fucking with the wrong bitches.' She laughed. 'To use language that only you and I in the gang would appreciate.'

Over dessert, Jen had hesitated a moment then said, 'Tabby, do you remember that doctor you got in to see me after Justin died? Heygate?'

Tabby nodded. 'Yes, do you need anything? Trouble sleeping? Something to lift you up a bit? He's got the works. Like the Willy Wonka of Harley Street, dear old Clarence Heygate.'

'No, it's just… I was reading some reports of Justin's death. The inquest and what have you… stuff I haven't brought myself to be able to look up until now. And I noticed that the medical report on the tractor driver who crashed into us was written by Doctor Heygate.'

Tabby carried on perusing the menu. 'Really? What a coincidence.'

'Don't you think that's a bit odd?' pressed Jen.

Tabby looked at her over her sunglasses. 'Not really. People like Heygate, they've got fingers in many pies. It's how they get so rich. Probably on a paid retainer from Cornwall police force or something.' Tabby put down the menu and took off her sunglasses. 'Jen, I understand how hard this has been for you. I realise the temptation is there to pore over everything, to try to find answers, to torture yourself with wondering if things could have played out differently. It's natural to look for connections that aren't there, or blow the ones that are out of proportion.' She reached over and put her hand on Jen's, and squeezed. 'It'll take time, but you'll get there. We all miss Justin. But now we have you. And we're here for you.'

'You know,' said Paul as Tabby handed him a cold beer from the cooler, 'I've been looking into the planning regulations. I think Penrose might have been railroaded a bit by the council over that affordable housing business.'

Simon squinted at him. 'How do you mean?'

'I think it should only apply to new builds that are put on general sale to the public,' said Paul. 'Apple Tree Vale is essentially a wholly private development, bespoke for us. I think there's a very good argument for appealing the need for the affordable housing element.'

'But Merrin lives there,' pointed out Jen. Paul looked at her as though he had no idea what she had just said, or thought it utterly irrelevant.

'I think Paul's just thinking longer term,' said Tabby, stirring her Aperol Spritz with her straw. 'I mean, Merrin is obviously fine, but what about when she leaves? What if we get some absolutely awful people moving in there?'

'I don't think she's planning to leave,' said Jen.

'I suppose with that house gone, we could make it more of a gated site,' mused Simon.

'Exactly!' said Paul. 'Then we wouldn't have any bother like we did last night, with drunk yokels wandering up to our home and terrorising us.'

Tabby settled back on to her towel. 'Well, it's something to think about for further down the line. I mean, with that house gone, perhaps it would be a lovely spot for a swimming pool…?'

—

Jen felt furious about what they had been saying down at the beach. Talking about Merrin's house as though it was an inconvenience for them. And they'd only be here until September, at the latest. She wondered if she should go over and tell Merrin what they were talking about, but decided against it. She knew what Tabby would say. *You've only known her for five minutes. We're your friends. Remember that.* Jen clattered about in the kitchen, making herself some dinner.

When did you start calling it dinner? she thought angrily to herself. *It always used to be tea.*

Everyone seemed to be staying in tonight, which suited Jen's mood. She watched some Netflix and drank tea until her eyes started to droop. She wished she missed Justin more. But they'd been married two weeks, and she'd known him for a year before that. Her heart was healing faster than she'd ever supposed. And that made her feel terrible.

Jen switched the lights off and locked up and went upstairs to gaze out of her bedroom window. The moon was almost full. She gazed at the apple tree, the ground around the trunk filled with fallen apples. Then she caught a movement from the corner of her eye.

Her first thought was that it was the man in the fish mask, back skulking around Nans-Avallen. But it wasn't. Striding across the grass was the unmistakeable figure of Adaku. But there was something wrong with her.

She was naked, and her body seemed to glow with tiny golden filaments, a network of pulsing lines, branching off like the boughs of a tree. Jen stared for a moment, then ran downstairs.

When she got outside Adaku was standing in front of the apple tree, her arms held high. She was stock still, just staring at the tree. Jen squinted, and rubbed her eyes. It was almost like the tree was glowing from within, that same yellow-gold colour that criss-crossed Adaku's skin, which seemed to pulse almost in reply. As though Adaku and the tree were somehow communicating.

Then the glow, if it had been there at all, faded from the tree and Adaku turned around and started to walk back to her house. Jen crossed the grass to intercept her, gaping at what she could now see were raised veins all over Adaku's naked body, yellow and raised and throbbing.

'Adaku...' she said.

The other woman looked at her with heavy-lidded eyes, unfocused, almost as if she was sleep-walking.

'Avallen doesn't want me,' said Adaku, her voice thick. 'He wants you.'

And then she collapsed on to the grass.

'Some kind of infection,' said Paul, examining the raised, pulsing, yellow veins on Adaku's arm. She had been laid on the sofa in her and Arthur's house, her nakedness covered with a blanket. Paul turned the inside of her left wrist, where a suppurating wound oozed yellow pus. 'That bloody spider bite.'

'Didn't you notice this?' said Tabby in exasperation to Arthur. 'I wondered why she had started to cover up all the time.'

'I saw it at first, but she said it was fine, it would go away,' said Arthur in anguish. He pulled out his phone. 'I'm calling an ambulance.'

'Wait,' said Paul. He put his hand on Adaku's forehead. 'She's burning up.'

'Then what am I waiting for?' said Arthur shrilly.

'Maybe we should get Doctor Heygate,' murmured Tabby.

'Even if he set off now, it would take him hours to get from London.' He dropped his voice low. 'We might not have hours.'

'That settles it,' said Arthur, punching his finger at his phone.

'Wait!' said Paul more forcefully. Arthur frowned at him. Paul said, 'Let's just think about this a moment. Is the local NHS hospital the best place for Adaku?'

Jen watched them all wordlessly. She couldn't understand why they were even debating this. When Adaku had collapsed unconscious in front of her she'd screamed, and they'd all come running out. Timothy was in the corner on his phone, apparently Googling spider bites. Simon was in the kitchen, making a pot of tea. Only she was standing there like a spare part, doing nothing useful at all. Tabby turned to her and said, 'Tell me again what she was doing.'

'I was just looking out of the window and I saw her walking over to the apple tree and...' Jen's voice trailed off. 'Of course! The apples!'

Without another word she ran out of the house and over to the apple tree. The grass was studded with fallen fruit. Hadn't these apples healed Merrin's hand after she drove a knife through it? Couldn't they do the same for Adaku? She picked one up and recoiled as her thumb went through the soft, rotten flesh. It had spoiled on the ground. So had the one next to it, and the next. Cursing, Jen fell to her knees and searched through the fallen apples, eventually finding one, then two, then half a dozen, that had not tipped over into rot. She gathered them in her arms then ran back to the house.

—

'Here, darling, drink this,' said Arthur, lifting the head of the half-conscious Adaku and putting the glass of cloudy liquid to her lips. To Jen's surprise, when she had run back in with the apples, nobody had told her to not be ridiculous, nobody had asked her what on earth she was thinking, nobody had told her to go away with her stupid ideas. Simon had taken them off her, quickly peeled and cored them, and pulsed them to liquid in the kitchen blender. Adaku's eyes fluttered as Arthur coaxed her to drink, and she nodded and swallowed.

Half of the liquid ran down her chin, making Jen want to leap on her and lick it off, the apple craving growing within her. But enough went down her throat. Almost immediately, the raised veins on her body began to subside, and fade, and shrink. Within twenty minutes, Adaku looked absolutely normal, sleeping peacefully. Everyone let out a simultaneous sigh.

'Thank you, Jen,' said Arthur, tears in his eyes. He gave her a big hug.

'Yes, well done,' said Paul with a nod. 'Let's give Arthur and Adaku a bit of space.'

It was only when she'd got back to her house that Jen finally had time to process what Adaku had said to her. *He doesn't want me. He wants you*, and to wonder why nobody had questioned what she had done with the apples, or how she knew they would work.

34

TARAN

They sat on the deck of Taran's boat moored in the harbour, him, Bobby and Bligh. Bobby looked at his watch. 'Where is the old fart? I've got a business to run.'

'He said he'd be here, and he will be,' said Bligh.

'That's him now,' said Taran. They all looked to see Opie Penrose walking along the harbour front towards them. He crossed the gangplank and took a seat on the deck.

'You wanted to speak to us?' said Bligh.

Penrose nodded and reached into the pocket of the thick coat he wore, despite the sunshine and heat. He pulled out an apple and put it on the small table between them. They all looked at it, the flesh brown and cracked, a maggot writhing in a softened patch of the skin. 'The apples are rotting on the bough,' he said. 'It's time.'

Taran felt his insides turn to water. They'd all been waiting most of their adult lives for this, but he still hoped the day would never come.

'They're all rotted?' said Bobby, and Taran noted a flash of anguish in his eyes, a tremble to his voice. The mark of an addict. He hoped this would mean that now Bobby could get back to normal. If any of them could feel normal again, after what was going to come.

'Most.' Penrose sniffed. 'And we won't see early-fruiting Nans-Avallen apples again in my lifetime, I hope to God.'

'Well,' said Bligh eventually. 'The die is cast. The pieces are all on the board. The only question is, when do we make our move?'

'Sooner rather than later,' said Bobby. 'Get this fucking thing out of the way.'

'Full moon tomorrow,' said Penrose.

Bobby looked at him. 'Is that a requirement?'

Penrose shrugged. 'No. But feels appropriate.'

'We've got the small matter of the Londoners,' said Taran. 'I'm not entirely sure this thing should happen with an audience.'

'It's a good point,' said Bligh. 'Who would not be there at all but for your greed in developing that site, Penrose.'

Penrose sneered at him. 'But for me developing that site you wouldn't have your Daughter of the Soil living up there, and the incomer touched by death just across the way from her. You should be thanking me for making this easy for you.'

Easy, thought Taran, looking from Penrose to Bligh to Bobby. Did any of them really think this was going to be easy?

'Anyway, I've thought of that, too,' said Penrose. 'The Londoners are coming to the farmhouse tomorrow night. For dinner.'

Bobby laughed. 'At your wreck of a place?'

Penrose bared his teeth. 'I've got money in my pocket since the last time you were there, Bobby Carlyon. Done the place up a treat. They like that sort of thing, the Londoners. Dining with the natives. They think it's authentic, or something. I reckon I'll be doing more of it.

You should see what they're paying me for a bit of stargazy pie and a few pasties.'

'So that's it, then,' said Taran.

Bobby said, 'I take it your big plan has fallen on its arse? And all Lizzie Moon's money at the bottom of the sea?' He shook his head. 'You're a fucking idiot, Taran. You should have just let things take their course as they were meant to.'

'I had to try,' said Taran softly. 'There is another way, I'm sure of it. A way to avoid all this.'

Bobby stood up, swaying as the boat rocked. 'Couple of days it'll be all over. Things will carry on as they should do.' He looked out over the sea at the flawless blue sky. 'Good summer ahead for Scuttler's Cove, I think.'

When Bobby had gone, Bligh said gently, 'You tried, Taran. Nobody can fault you for that. But sometimes the old ways cannot be deviated from. Bobby's right. In a couple of days it will be all over.'

'Bobby's out of control,' said Taran. 'He's been eating the apples.' He started to tell them about Sergeant Wells, then shook his head. What was the point? Like everyone kept telling him, it would all be over soon.

'Bobby Carlyon has always been hot-headed,' said Bligh, standing up. 'Tomorrow night, then. You have the knife?'

Taran nodded, and Bligh held out his hand. Taran said, 'What, you don't trust me?'

'I don't trust anyone until this is over,' said Bligh. 'Except myself. The knife, Taran.'

Taran got it from inside the wheelhouse and handed it over. Bligh walked along the gangplank, and Penrose joined him on the harbour side. Taran watched them go.

He sat for a moment alone, then began to unmoor the boat, and head out to sea.

Taran stood on the deck, gazing into the sea. Had he been reading too much into the signs? The crab attack on the beach? Merrin's painting – and Jen's dream – of the apocalyptic storm? Was the former just a freak incident, the latter just Nans-Avallen working on the minds of the two women who would be at the heart of the ritual tomorrow night?

'Lady of the Sea,' he said. 'Have I not given the offerings? The money. The dead fox, that was the sign from Avallen himself? Have the Tregarths not served you for longer than anyone can remember?'

The sea swelled and the waves peaked, and Taran looked towards Nans-Avallen on the clifftop. 'Tomorrow night,' he murmured. 'The ritual. Blood will be spilled and Avallen will take a new handmaiden. And the moment will be lost, the chance gone again, for how long? A generation? Longer?'

The waves lapped at the hull of Taran's boat, but only as they always did. 'Endellion!' he suddenly roared. 'Endellion! Wake up! And if you *are* awake, then act! Give me a sign!'

His words travelled out over the waves, and were lost. And no sign came.

Taran slumped down in the chair on the deck, and brooded.

He sat, brooding, until sunset. His stomach was rumbling and there was nothing to be done, nothing more he could do. He began to turn the boat back to shore, watching the glittering waves hitting the beach below Nans-Avallen glowing with the setting sun.

He thought about when they had all gone to see Lizzie Moon, not long after they had been to see Penrose after the news that he was selling off Nans-Avallen.

'It's now inevitable,' Bligh had said. 'The ritual will be called soon. Merrin must come home.'

'Not while there is breath in my body,' said Lizzie.

When Bobby and Bligh had gone, Taran hung on. 'There's another way,' he'd said. 'I'm sure of it.'

'A Tregarth way?' said Lizzie, curious.

Taran had nodded. 'I've been reading the books my dad left me. The notes written by the Tregarth men going back years. Centuries. There's another way. A way things should be, not as we've made them.'

'Tell me more,' said Lizzie, so Taran did, outlining his plan, the knowledge he had gleaned from the old books. She looked at him for a long time. 'And you think that will work?'

Taran shrugged. 'It might. But we need a couple of things. One, lots and lots of money.'

Lizzie had stood, pacing the living room of her little cottage. She looked around at its thick walls. 'That could be arranged. I could sell this place. What's the other thing?'

Taran bit his lip. 'The ritual will have to go ahead, at least nominally. Merrin will have to come home.'

'Not while there's breath in my body,' said Lizzie Moon again.

At the last moment, Taran turned his boat away from the harbour and towards the beach below Nans-Avallen. There was something about the way the setting sun caught the ebbing sea at the shoreline, the way it glittered and twinkled. Like stars. As he bobbed closer, he saw that it wasn't just the sea, it was the beach, too. And the cliff path that led up to Nans-Avallen. He cast about for his dad's old binoculars and focused them on the sand. Then he swore, and let them drop, and gunned the engine to get his boat to the harbour.

Taran ran all along the harbour and along the track to the beach. It was properly dark now, and the tourists had long gone from the sands. He pulled out the torch that he'd brought from the boat and skimmed the beam over the beach.

It looked like the sand was undulating, moving, heaving and falling like it was trying to ape the ocean tide. But it wasn't the earth that was moving. It was—

Crabs. Hundreds of them. Thousands. Creeping sideways out of the surf, marching in a silent procession towards the cliff path. Coming together in a bony, crawling flow, endless crabs pouring out of the sea, jostling together on the narrow cliff path, making their unerring way up to Nans-Avallen.

And each crab gripped in one claw held aloft a shiny one-pound coin.

Taran felt his heart thump and his stomach turn somersaults. He scrambled up the grass beside the path until he was ahead of the marching procession of crabs, and ran up to Nans-Avallen. She had heard him. Endellion had heard his pleas, listened to his prayers, accepted his offerings. She had sent a sign.

There were lights on in all the houses, but nobody outside. Where would the crabs go? To the apple tree, guessed Taran. He silently ran across the site, beyond the tree and into the woods close by Merrin's house. He prayed that she wouldn't come out, that nobody would come out. Nobody should see this. Nobody but him.

Ensconced behind a bush, Taran peered into the darkness, his eyes adjusting, until he saw the first of the crabs begin to flow up the cliff path and over on to Nans-Avallen. They came towards him, a silent, skittering army, their coins held aloft.

The coins that he had poured into the sea, the coins that Lizzie Moon had provided from the sale of her little cottage.

It hadn't all been in vain, he dared to hope. It hadn't all been a waste of time.

The crabs spread out on the grass, marching forward like an army, filling the site from end to end, a carpet of crustaceans advancing on him. A hundred thousand of them, with a hundred thousand of Lizzie Moon's coins. Taran held his breath as they approached, then stopped, as though at some unheard signal, ten feet away from the apple tree.

At first nothing happened, and Taran started to get cramp in his legs, crouched in the woods. But then the apple tree seemed to shiver, and a diffuse yellow glow, hardly noticeable unless you were watching it, emanated from within. And then the branches rustled and the tree seemed to shiver and pulse.

And the spiders came.

They poured down the tree like a wave, their yellow bodies sparkling in the light from Taran's torch. Thousands upon thousands of them, an endless flood, spreading out like a yellow oil slick from the base of the tree until they faced the crabs in the moonlit night.

Taran held his breath.

The breeze fell to nothing.

Nans-Avallen was silent.

Then the first row of crabs simply let go of their coins. There was a faint clattering sound, as the crabs behind them did the same, and the crabs behind them, until all the crabs had released their burdens and they hit the crab in front and rolled into the grass. Then they turned, almost as one living mass, and began to crawl back to the cliff path, and descend to the sea.

As the crabs moved, so did the spiders. In twos and threes they gathered around the fallen coins, and in their small groups hefted them up high, just as the crabs had carried them, with their forelegs. Then they began to scuttle back towards the apple tree.

Taran switched off his torch, better to see the deepening golden glow that emanated from the base of the tree's vast trunk. The spiders were pouring into it and disappearing from sight, carrying the coins with them. He watched, and waited, until the glow from the tree faded, and the spiders had all gone, and Nans-Avallen was dark again.

His entreaties had been heard.

His offerings had been accepted.

The dowry had been paid.

35

MERRIN

The morning dawned cloudy, a warm breeze whipping off the sea over Nans-Avallen. Merrin was grateful for the cooler day after the unbroken sunshine of the past couple of weeks, save for the Fish Festival storm. Blue skies were nice to paint, but a little variation was good as well.

That said, she had a weird feeling in her stomach, a sense of anticipation, of something about to happen. She couldn't quite figure out what it was, though. Not that there was any shortage of strangeness. The fish mask intruder, her painting being disfigured, the odd, dreamlike effect the apples had on both her and Jen. She looked out across Nans-Avallen. The houses of the Londoners were quiet. She wondered if they were getting bored with Scuttler's Cove yet, wouldn't rather be in Capri or St Tropez or wherever those sorts of people normally summered. She'd miss Jen if they upped and left, she supposed. Merrin seemed to have clicked with her, made some kind of connection. Perhaps she should ask her to go into town to get drinks with Taran and the others. If *the gang* will allow it, of course.

Mid-morning she got a call from Janet at the Driftwood Gallery to say the new batch of prints had just been delivered from the printers in Boscanlon, and two of the latest original canvases had already been sold. Merrin was now making what amounted to a fairly healthy income from her art. She mentally stuck two fingers up at Kamal, wherever he was and whatever he was doing in London. That life seemed so long ago to her now, so alien. She couldn't imagine living in the suffocating confines of a city ever again. Not when she had such beautiful landscapes and dramatic scenery and so much fresh air right here.

Summer wouldn't last, though, and Merrin had to think about what would happen beyond September. If she continued to sell at the Driftwood, she could get a nice little amount of savings salted away, but she'd probably need to earn some money over winter. She wondered if Clemmo might consider taking her on behind the bar at the Star and Anchor.

Pulling on a cardigan, Merrin decided to go for a walk. Not into town though, and not down to the beach. Instead she wandered along the clifftop, looking down at the beach. The tide was coming in, the waves crashing against the cliff face. She did a full circuit of Nans-Avallen, passing the houses and feeling the Londoners' eyes on her. Then she paused at the apple tree, kicking with her trainers the rotting fruit that lay in the grass. There were hardly any apples left on the branches now. Her hunger for them – her desire for them – seemed to have abated, for which she was glad. She'd had her fill of apples.

The breeze started to blow harder, and a little colder. Merrin pulled her cardigan tighter around her, and walked on a little way to the woods. They were quiet, almost unnaturally so. No birds chattering, no squirrels skittering up the tree trunks. Not even flies hovering in clouds or bees buzzing lazily. It was as though Nans-Avallen were holding its breath.

Stop being an idiot, she mentally reprimanded herself. The events of the last few days had got her on edge. She rationalised her fears one by one. The man in the fish mask was just some drunk from the festival. The word painted on her picture had probably been done by her, pissed out of her brain. The apples... well, they always said never eat Nans-Avallen apples. Maybe there was something in them, something hallucinogenic. Everything could be explained, if you bothered hard enough to try.

The snapping of a twig brought Merrin out of her reverie, and she realised she'd wandered deeper into the woods than she was planning to. With the sun hidden behind thick clouds, it was dark in here, and cold. She heard the sound again, twigs snapping, undergrowth being trampled on, and felt the hairs on the back of her neck stand up. There was a movement off to her right, and she whirled around. All was still. Then there was a sound behind her, and she pivoted, just as a wood pigeon clattered up from the leafy mulch of the ground and barrelled noisily into the treetops. A russet flash caught her eye, and a fox darted between the trees. Merrin breathed a nervous laugh, and turned to head back out of the woods.

And there he was.

He was tall and broad, his red and blue check shirt filthy, his combat trousers tucked into boots. He wore what looked like thick gardening gloves.

And his head was covered by a rubber fish mask, its colours faded and dirty.

Merrin tensed, and stared at him, unnerved by not being able to see his face, those moulded fish eyes seeming to stare blindly at her. Maybe he was a maniac after all, a killer or a rapist or an escaped convict. She stuck her hand in her pocket and pulled out her key fob, the keys protruding from between her fingers curled into a fist, like claws.

'Can you get out of my way, please?' said Merrin, trying to keep her voice calm, though it cracked as she spoke. She thought it best to not show anger, or fear, or seem as though she was in any way threatening him. She sized him up; he was big enough to crush her with his arms. He took a lumbering step forward, and Merrin backed up, glancing around for the best route to run. He seemed heavy on his feet; if she could evade those bear-like arms she was sure she could out-pace him through the woods.

He held up his hands, showing his gloved palms to her, as if to say he meant no harm. Merrin was not convinced, adrenaline pounding through her, revving up her muscles to fight, or run. She crouched slowly down and her hand closed around a fallen tree branch.

'I'm warning you, back off,' she said more confidently, holding out the stick. He didn't do anything. Why didn't he speak? It was unnerving Merrin even more.

Then he reached into the side pocket of his combat trousers. Merrin backed up a step, brandishing the stick higher. Maybe she could get a good smack in around his head and then start running. She was sure he was about to bring out a knife.

It was an apple. A Nans-Avallen apple. He held it out to her.

Merrin suddenly felt... calm. Unafraid. Something in that act had slowed her galloping heart, quelled her terror. She frowned as he took a step forward, the apple held out.

'For me?' she said.

The fish mask nodded.

Merrin reached out and closed her hand around the apple, waiting for him to grab her wrist, but he didn't. In fact, once she'd taken the apple, he took a step backwards, and waited.

'You want me to… eat?'

Another nod from the fish mask.

This is insane, thought Merrin, but nevertheless she took a bite from the apple.

As she chewed, the man held out his gloved hand again. Merrin shrugged and put the half-eaten apple into it. Then he slid it under the bottom of his fish mask and she heard a smothered crunch as he also took a bite.

Was that all he wanted? To share an apple? Merrin suddenly felt sure he was harmless, perhaps someone who had wandered out of a hospital somewhere. She would get home and call someone, the police or social services. He shouldn't be out here alone, sleeping in the woods. 'What's your name?' she said gently.

And then, suddenly, she knew his name. Her eyes widened, her mouth fell open, the stick dropped from her hand to the ground. She knew his name and why he was here and what he wanted. She knew everything.

She was in his head.

✵

The last thing Kenan Angove really remembered was being in the pub. He'd been drinking all day at the Fish Festival, his first time in Scuttler's Cove. He was from near Exeter, though his family were from near Land's End originally, and spent summers moving from farm to farm in Devon and Cornwall, taking work, moving on when he got bored. He'd very much liked the Scuttler's Cove Fish Festival, especially when the good-looking woman in the Kerid's Arms had agreed to let him buy her a drink. Fit birds like that didn't usually give Kenan the time of day, so when this Lizzie touched her hip against his thigh at the bar, he thought, what the hell. In for a penny, in for a pound. So he put his hand down and grabbed her arse, to see how the land lay.

He'd put some ale away, and the fresh air outside knocked him sideways for a minute. He had to lean on her as she guided him to a little terraced cottage right on the harbour. Kenan couldn't believe his luck, and hoped he stayed awake long enough to take full advantage of it.

She gave him a glass of beer, which tasted a bit funny. After that, things got a bit hazy. He remembered pushing his trousers down to his ankles, and her straddling him right there on the sofa. Next thing he knew he was in the back of a van, rocking along a rough road. It stank of fish.

Then things got properly weird. The cool air woke him up a bit, and somehow he was no longer in the van but against a tree, bound tight with ropes. There was a funny taste in his mouth. There were a few people there, mostly men, and one of them said, 'I take it one of you has the knife?'

He started to panic a bit then, especially when, through his hazy sight, he saw the bird, Lizzie, holding a weird old knife with a slate blade. Then there was a vicar looming in front of him. An actual vicar. At that point Kenan began to wonder if that Lizzie had slipped him some acid or ecstasy.

'You sure you've caught?' said the old man who'd asked about the knife.

Caught what? wondered Kenan.

'I'm a Moon. I know when I've caught,' said that Lizzie.

Kenan finally found his tongue. 'Whasss going on?' he managed to say.

'Are you a godly man, son?' said the vicar.

Kenan had had enough. 'Fuck off. Where am I?'

Then the vicar started off with some mumbo jumbo. It was only much later Kenan would realise what was being said. It was a prayer. A prayer for the dying.

'Avallen, lord of the vale, who dwells beneath the apple tree, we have seen your sign. The seed has been planted and the flower will bloom, just as your fruit grows on the bough. As is the tradition of our people, to ensure the future vitality of our town, we bring to you the offering that you demand.'

Kenan started to strain at the ropes that bound him. The vicar said, 'Any final words?'

'Fuck off,' said Kenan again, panic thrumming through his body. Surely they weren't going to…

The old man held his head tight and before Kenan even knew what was going on, the vicar stepped forward and cut his throat.

As Kenan's life ebbed away with the blood that gushed from his neck, everyone seemed to leave, apart from the old man. Through his failing sight, Kenan could see the man glaring at him. 'Don't stare at me like that,' he said. 'We're just doing what needs to be done.'

Then the old man pulled from his pocket a fish mask, like they'd all been wearing down at the festival. 'Can't stand you looking at me like that while you bloody die,' he said, then put the mask over Kenan's head, and everything went dark.

For a while. He slept in the earth, beneath the trees, where he'd been stuck. but the spark in him never truly went out. Not there, not on Nans-Avallen. Because something else slumbered in the land, beneath the apple tree. Something that infused the earth, that gave off an unnatural energy.

And then the thing that slumbered began to awake, and Kenan did not know how much time had passed, but he somehow found he could crawl out of the pit they had put him in. And he knew why he had awakened, because the seed that he had planted in that Lizzie's belly all that time ago had sprouted, and grown, and blossomed, and was here. Here on Nans-Avallen.

And Kenan Angove had not been a good man in his life, he'd be the first to admit that. But time spent sleeping in the cold earth gives a mind time to reflect, and know what is right and is wrong, and what should and shouldn't happen, and one thing he knew for sure, in that tiny spark of life and awareness that remained inside him, was that his daughter was here, and she was in danger.

☼

Merrin gasped, the connection suddenly severed, and she fell backwards. Sitting in the undergrowth she looked up at the man in the fish mask, staring down at her.

'Dad?' she said.

'*I wished that you had a face, Dad,*' said Merrin in her dream.

Then Kenan Angove reached up with his clumsy hands and pulled the fish mask from his head, a head blackened and wizened by time and rot, the dead flesh leathery and desiccated. His sightless, milky eyes fixed on his daughter and from somewhere deep inside of him he employed the final gasp of his tiny firefly spark of life and opened his mouth.

'Run,' he breathed.

Merrin shrank back as his jaw dropped open and tiny yellow-bodied spiders flowed out of his mouth, spilling down his ragged shirt stained with thirty-odd-year-old blood, endless, countless spiders that Kenan Angove vomited out. Then he shuddered, and crumpled, and fell to the ground in front of her, bones and flesh nothing but dust, finally gone.

Merrin clambered to her feet, and ran.

36

JEN

Adaku was up and about as though nothing had happened, standing in front of her house in a long beach wrap and looking up at the clouds gathering in the sky. Jen saw her through the window and went out.

'I owe you my thanks,' said Adaku, without looking at her. The infection that had caused those veins to swell and discolour all over her body seemed to have completely gone. 'I believe you were instrumental in helping me.'

Jen paused and said, 'You said something to me before you collapsed. Something about *him* wanting me.'

Adaku shrugged. 'The fever was making me rave. I'm sorry if I scared you.'

Tabby called to them, waving from her doorway. 'Don't forget this evening! We thought we'd meet early for a few pre-drinks round at Simon's.'

Jen frowned. 'What's this evening?'

Tabby laughed as she came over. 'The old chap who sold us the site. Penrose. We're going to his farmhouse for dinner. I'm sure it'll be awful but tremendous fun nonetheless. He's going to do something called stargazy pie. Apparently it's got fish sticking out of it.'

Adaku pulled a face. 'Sounds gross.'

Jen said, 'Did I know about this?'

Tabby laughed again. 'Yes, you did.' Then her brow crinkled, or as close as it could get to it with the Botox. 'Or maybe I didn't mention it? Anyway, cocktails at four, then we'll get ready and head off to Chez Penrose.'

—

'I'm not sure I'm enamoured with this lack of sun,' said Adaku, sipping her drink outside Simon's house.

'That's because you're not fifty and overweight,' said Simon. 'I find the respite quite welcome.'

Arthur had found a photograph of stargazy pie online and was sharing his phone around, everyone making 'Ewwww' noises.

'Is that literally raw fish heads?' frowned Paul.

'Just think of it as Cornish sushi,' said Tabby, laughing.

'I don't think they're raw,' said Arthur. 'Baked pilchards. You don't have to eat the heads.'

They drank for a couple of hours then Tabby said they all really must go and change for their dinner. Simon said, 'What does one wear to a farmhouse in the wilds of nowhere? I was thinking my tweed suit.'

'You'll boil,' said Arthur. 'It's still bloody warm, even if it's not sunny.'

Jen nodded. She was feeling somewhat out of sorts, a little... distant. She wasn't sure how much fun she'd be at the dinner. But then she thought, how much fun are you ever? She went back into her house to decide what to wear, and decided to have a quick coffee. All the cocktails had made her a little woozy. She sat down on the sofa, and closed her eyes against a mild headache she felt washing in.

It was dusk when she woke up. Jen frowned, disorientated. What had happened? Why had she slept? Where were the others? She went to the door to find a note on the mat. It was from Tabby. *Darling, we called for you but you were sound asleep on the sofa. I decided to leave you be, you looked so peaceful. I'm sure you won't miss anything with this dreadful dinner. Hope you're not coming down with something. T xxx*

They'd gone without her. Jen went to the window. All the cars were still there. Had they walked? How far was this Penrose's farm anyway? Or called cabs? She didn't quite know whether to feel put out that they'd left her, or relieved that she didn't have to go to the dinner.

Then a movement across Nans-Avallen caught her eye. It was Merrin, running out of the woods as though her life depended on it, heading for her little house.

When Jen knocked on Merrin's door it swung open. She let herself in cautiously, and called, 'Merrin? Merrin? It's Jen.'

'Up here,' called Merrin from up the stairs. Her voice sounded trembly. Jen climbed the stairs to see Merrin in her bedroom, stuffing clothes into a small rucksack.

'Thank fuck you're here,' said Merrin. 'We need to get away from here. Now.'

'What?' said Jen. 'Merrin, what's happened?'

'I just met my dad,' said Merrin, walking around the bed to her table and pulling her phone charger out of the wall.

'Oh. What? I thought you never knew him.'

'I didn't. He just introduced himself to me.' Merrin looked at her, eyes wild. 'Which was nice, as he's been dead since the day I was conceived.'

Jen took a step back, then said, 'Merrin. Just sit down for a moment. Tell me what's going on.'

Merrin took a ragged breath, closed her eyes, and nodded. 'You know you said this place is weird? You don't know the half of it. I need to get out of here. And I suggest you come with me.' She sat down heavily on the bed. 'The man you saw, in the fish mask. He's my father. But he was killed the night he slept with my mother.'

'How do you know all this?'

Merrin shook her head. 'I saw his memories. We shared an apple. It was like I was there, looking out of his eyes.' She looked up tearfully at Jen. 'My mother was involved. So was Reverend Bligh. Taran's dad. And Bobby Carlyon's. Penrose. God, the entire town of Scuttler's Cove might be involved for all I know.'

Jen still wasn't getting it. 'They killed him? What... had he assaulted your mother or something?'

'More like she assaulted him,' said Merrin with a mirthless laugh. 'Just so she could get pregnant with me. Then they brought him up here, tied him to the apple tree, and slit his throat. With that knife we gave to Sergeant Wells.'

'Like your painting...' said Jen.

Merrin nodded. 'It was him who wrote RUN on it. Because that's exactly what he said to me before spiders poured out of his mouth and he crumbled to dust.'

Jen sat down too. 'This is a lot to take in. I mean...'

'I know,' said Merrin, standing and shoving more clothes into her bag. 'But there's something big happening. Something that involves me.'

'A Daughter of the Soil,' said Jen slowly.

Merrin stared at her. 'What did you say?'

'Daughter of the Soil. When I was walking in the woods, when I ate the apple, I heard things.' She closed her eyes, tried to remember, tried to recall the exact words. '*It ends with a high priestess and a sacrifice. As it has always done. A Daughter of the Soil and an incomer, touched by death. It always ends that way.'*

'A Daughter of the Soil and an incomer touched by death,' repeated Merrin. 'A high priestess and a sacrifice.' She put her fist to her mouth. 'Fuck. Fuck fuck fuck. That's you and me, isn't it?'

Jen waited a heartbeat, and said, 'Let's get the fuck out of here.'

'What about the others?' said Merrin as they descended the stairs. 'We should warn them. We should all leave together. In their cars.'

'They went for dinner at Penrose's farmhouse,' said Jen, pulling her phone from her pocket. 'Shall I call them, get them here?' She tapped at her phone. There was no service at all.

'Penrose's?' said Merrin. 'Why didn't you go?'

'I fell asleep,' Jen frowned. 'I don't know why. I just closed my eyes and when I opened them again they'd all gone.' She grabbed Merrin's arm as they got to the bottom of the stairs. 'Do you think they're in trouble? You said Penrose was in this vision of your father. Do you think he's going to do something to them? Shit.' She checked her phone again but there was still no service at all.

Merrin opened the front door. 'Maybe we just get the hell off Nans-Avallen first and call them later. From Boscanlon. We could go to the police. Don't suppose your friends leave their houses unlocked? Might there be some car keys we could borrow?'

Jen stepped out as Merrin pulled the door closed behind them. She stared across Nans-Avallen, in the direction of Scuttler's Cove. 'I don't think the cars will be much use, Merrin,' she said softly.

Merrin joined her and followed her gaze. 'How is that even possible?' she said.

They couldn't see Scuttler's Cove. All that side of Nans-Avallen was now ringed by trees, impenetrably dark. The woodland behind them now stretched in one semi-circle around the field, save for the cliff edge and the view over the sea. Jen frowned and sniffed the air.

'There's something not right. Smell that? Like burning wood. And the air…'

'So fresh,' agreed Merrin. She looked up. 'The stars are so shiny and bright. And the full moon. I've never seen the sky so clear.'

'Like there's no pollution, or anything,' said Jen. Even in Cornwall, even in the wilds, there was always a tell-tale orange glow from distant towns. Beyond the trees they could see nothing but blackness. The sea was dark and quiet, no fishing boats bobbing in the night, no container ships chugging along the horizon.

'It's like how I imagine Nans-Avallen to be a thousand years ago,' said Merrin softly. They both looked back at the houses, sitting almost incongruously in the field, ensconced by the thick woods. Jen rubbed her eyes. 'How can those trees just appear?'

'Let's worry about it later,' said Merrin, pulling her arm. 'Let's walk through the trees. Scuttler's Cove must be beyond there somewhere. We can get help there.'

They ran across Nans-Avallen to the new trees that blocked the lanes and the cliff path. New, but ancient. Jen couldn't see through them. 'There's no path.'

'We keep going in a straight line, we'll get out,' said Merrin. 'From here to the cliff path's got to be, what, thirty metres? Just keep moving.'

Merrin went first and Jen followed, pushing through the tightly packed undergrowth and the branches of the trees. The impossible trees. They crashed through the foliage for what felt like minutes and minutes and minutes. Surely they should be—

'Sssh!' hissed Merrin, holding up her hand and stopping dead so that Jen ran right into her. 'Listen.'

At first it sounded like the wind in the trees. But it seemed to coalesce into words. Or names.

'*Merrin. Merrin. Merrin.*'

'*Jen. Jen. Jen.*'

'Fuck this,' said Merrin, forging on. 'Fuck this and fuck them and fuck everything. We're getting out. Jen, I can see the end. We're getting out. Then we'll get help. I promise we'll get—'

Merrin tumbled forward and Jen fell with her, onto long grass. Jen looked up, expectantly, to see how close they were to the lanes that would take them down to Scuttler's Cove. But they weren't close at all. In fact, they were staring straight at their own houses. 'We got turned round,' moaned Jen. 'We're back on Nans-Avallen.'

'Then we try again,' said Merrin, standing up.

'Wait, what's that?' Jen jumped to her feet. There was a loud noise, as if something was crashing through the trees.

Both women backed up, putting ten, fifteen metres between them and the trees. Jen looked at her phone again. Still nothing. A figure emerged from the treeline, and stopped.

'It's Taran,' said Merrin quietly.

Jen looked at her. 'Do you think he's involved in this?'

'His father was one of those that killed my dad,' said Merrin. She reached down and squeezed Jen's hand, and murmured, 'Go back to my house. Let me work out what's going on here. If it all goes wrong then you can try to go get away through the other side of the woods and raise the alarm.'

Jen nodded and started to run to the house. Merrin called after her. 'Jen? Get knives. Just in case.'

37

MERRIN

'Taran!' screamed Merrin as he approached, hands held up in front of him. 'I swear to fucking god if you're involved in this, I'll kill you.' The world was tilting on its axis. She felt as though her mind was barely holding on to sanity, and consciousness. Oh, how sweet it would be just to switch off, fall down, and sink into infinite blackness.

'Merrin,' he said softly, stopping in front of her. 'I'll tell you everything. But first we need to get away from here.'

'That's what we've been trying to do,' said Merrin, her voice cracking. 'Except somehow Nans-Avallen is now surrounded by fucking trees.'

'We?' said Taran. 'Jen's with you?'

Merrin nodded. 'What's going on, Taran?' she said, trying to keep the fear from her voice.

Taran glanced back at the trees he had just pushed through. He looked around, and up. He muttered, 'It's different here.'

Merrin weighed him up. He was on his own. If Jen had done what she'd been told, they could overpower him together, if it turned out he was one of them. 'In the house. Now,' she said decidedly.

Merrin pushed Taran through the door and Jen was waiting on the other side, holding a long kitchen knife out with both shaking hands. 'I'll cut your fucking heart out if you make one false move,' she yelled.

Taran put his hands up, and looked at both of them. He took a deep breath. 'I do know what's going on, and I am involved in it, but I'm here to help you. I promise.'

Merrin pushed him towards the kitchen. 'In there. Sit down. Hands on the table where I can see them at all times.' She looked at Jen. 'Any luck with the phones?'

Jen shook her head, moving to stand behind Taran, the knife still held out. 'Nothing. Can't even connect to a network. It's like there's just nothing there.'

'In a way, there isn't,' said Taran, walking into the kitchen, his hands still up. 'I can't explain it properly myself, but I think Nans-Avallen is... somewhere else now. Somewhen else, even.'

'What the fuck is he talking about?' said Jen as Taran sat down at the table and put his palms flat on top of it as he had been told.

Merrin went to grab another kitchen knife and held it out to him. 'He's going to tell us, aren't you, Taran?'

Taran shrugged. 'I don't know for sure. But Avallen is awakening, and this place is his. He's pushed the modern world away, for a while. Until the ritual is over.'

Merrin looked at Jen. 'Ritual?'

Jen said, 'Avallen?'

'Avallen is the god of the orchard, the spirit of the land,' said Taran. 'He sleeps beneath the apple tree, and every generation or so he awakens. And then we must serve him, and in return he brings prosperity to Scuttler's Cove.'

'Taran, you're frightening me,' said Merrin softly.

He looked at her. 'You should be frightened. This is what you were born for, Merrin. You're the Daughter of the Soil. Each ritual needs two people. The high priestess and the sacrifice. The Daughter of the Soil and—'

'And the incomer touched by death,' said Jen. 'Which would be me.'

'Who's involved in this madness?' said Merrin. 'Bobby? Bligh? Penrose? Everybody in town?'

Taran shrugged. 'Everyone is complicit, that's for sure, even if they don't know they are. Everyone reaps the benefit of Avallen's grace, even if they take no direct part in the ritual. They all knew, once, long ago. Many have forgotten, or chosen not to remember. Except the faithful few who carried the torch. My family. The Carlyons. Bligh. Penrose.' He looked at Merrin. 'The Moons.'

Merrin felt faint. 'My mum… she raised me just for this?'

Taran smiled gently. 'Merrin, did you ever wonder why you went away from Scuttler's Cove and never came back?'

'I have wondered that a lot, since I came back. When I was away, I never thought about it much.'

'That was Lizzie's doing. She played a very long game. From before you were born. She thought if she mothered the Daughter of the Soil and sent her away, it would break the cycle. It would free Scuttler's Cove from its servitude to Avallen.'

'She sent me away…?' said Merrin slowly. Memories of leaving for university crowded her mind, crying and waving to Mum from the coach. And after that… after that… 'And she made sure I stayed away?'

Taran nodded. 'By doing what only Lizzie Moon can do. And it might have worked, too, if she hadn't died, and then all the knots she'd tied became undone, and you returned.'

'Fuck.' Merrin let the knife clatter to the worktop. She put her head in her hands. 'Fucking hell. What exactly happens at this ritual anyway?'

'I've never seen it, of course,' said Taran. 'Penrose's daddy did, when he was a little boy. Long story short, the high priestess drives the knife of slate and tin into the heart of the sacrifice.'

'I'll not be doing *that*,' asserted Merrin.

'Well, the thing is...' said Taran.

'And the high priestess just goes off and... what?' said Jen, looking at Merrin.

'I said, I'm not doing it,' said Merrin.

'The high priestess becomes the handmaiden of Avallen,' said Taran. 'She is taken down with him to where he lives beneath the apple tree, and they slumber together until she has faded into nothing and Avallen begins to wake, and the whole process begins again.'

'Doesn't sound like this ends well for either of us,' muttered Jen. She looked at Taran. 'You said Merrin's mum tried to stop it by sending her away. What happens if the ritual *doesn't* happen?'

'It's never not happened,' said Taran. 'If it did, once Avallen was awake...' He shook his head. 'It's never not happened.'

'I mean, how bad could it be?' said Merrin tremulously.

Taran looked at her. 'Avallen would be a god denied. How bad can you imagine it would be?'

Jen moaned. 'A god. I can't... I just can't wrap my head around any of this. It's got to be a big practical joke, right?'

'Wait,' said Merrin, her mind spinning. 'You said you were here to take us away. Was that a lie? To get us in here?'

Taran shook his head. 'I have come to get you both away. To stop the ritual happening.'

Merrin shook her head. 'But why? If you're balls deep in the whole sordid conspiracy? And if stopping the ritual would be so terrible and apocalyptic?'

'Because I don't believe it would be so bad,' said Taran. 'Just like your mum wanted to end this curse Scuttler's Cove is under, so did I. And I worked with Lizzie. Because we had a plan. It needed you to come home, and Avallen awaken, and the ritual almost go ahead, but we had a plan.'

Merrin allowed herself a glimmer of hope. 'A plan?'

Taran took a deep breath. 'I think I should tell you what my daddy told me on his deathbed.'

—

'Long ago, men respected the land and the sea in equal measure, and it was a more harmonious time. The world was full of gods, the gods of wild rivers and bleak moors, and in the land dwelt the god of the orchard, Avallen, who lived beneath a lone apple tree on a wood-ringed hill that came to bear his name, Nans-Avallen. On the beach below Nans-Avallen the waves crashed onto the shore, ebbing and flowing when called by the moon, and in those waves lived Endellion, the lady of the sea. Men paid fealty to both Avallen and Endellion, and she filled their nets with fish while he caused their crops to grow and their livestock to become fat. More and more men came to this land, attracted by its prosperity, and the town of Scuttler's Cove was born.

'The land and the sea are opposites, and yet the two halves of which the world is made, and so it was for Avallen and Endellion. When the thunder and lightning rumbled around the bay men would nod sagely and say that Avallen and Endellion were a-bed, their love ferocious and pure. When the rains fed the crops in the field, they would say that Endellion sent the gift of water to her love, and when the fish rose from the depths to be hypnotised by the full moon, and fall easily into fishermen's nets, they would say that Avallen had coaxed her to provide.

'But one year, the crops failed, and the fishing was poor, and the men wondered why Endellion and Avallen had abandoned them. They began to mutter that the capricious lady of the sea had done wrong to the stout-hearted god of the orchards, and he sulked because of her behaviour. So they set about to make things right.

'Being men, of course, they got it all wrong. They decided a sacrifice was required, to appease Avallen. A knife was fashioned, from the tin and the slate for which the area was famous, and an offering was made to Avallen. Because men cannot help but meddle, and make things more complicated than they should be, they consigned the high priestess who they had crowned to make the sacrifice to be Avallen's handmaiden, to comfort him in the absence of his lady's love.

'With blood spilled, and a handmaiden serving sleeping Avallen's needs, the crops returned the following year. But, of course, the men had got it all wrong. Avallen and Endellion had not abandoned Scuttler's Cove, they had merely let their gifts fall fallow, for a year, so that they could be renewed afresh. The crops had not failed, not really, nor had the fishing been poor. They had just not been as bountiful as previous years. But the men had become greedy, and used to prosperity, and anything less to them seemed that it must be a personal affront.

'Avallen had been lured away from Endellion by the rituals of the men, and in her heartbreak she slumbered in the depths. Only the Tregarth line continued to honour her, and in her sleep she continued to fill their nets, grateful for their loyalty.

'Many years passed, and one early summer the Nans-Avallen apple tree fruited well before its time. The men knew this was a sign that Avallen was awake, and the handmaiden they had consigned to him was crumbled to dust, so they set about repeating the ritual. And before long the apples fruited early every generation or two, and Avallen had to be honoured with a new sacrifice and a new handmaiden, and the love between the god of the orchard and the sleeping lady of the sea became forgotten, save for the Tregarth line, which keeps the flame of faith alive.'

—

'And once again, greedy men fuck everything up,' said Merrin. 'So your plan is what, exactly?'

'Reconcile Endellion and Avallen,' said Taran. 'The lord of the land and the lady of the sea. As it should always have been, before man interfered. Restore the balance. End the cycle of sacrifice.'

'And how's that working out?' said Jen.

Taran nodded. 'Well, I think. Better than I could have hoped. Endellion is awake. The dowry has been paid. Thanks to Lizzie.' He nodded at Merrin. 'She sold her house so that we could make the offering to Endellion. To wake her from her heartbroken sleep. To allow her to reclaim Avallen's love.'

Merrin stared at him. 'All Mum's money... you did take it. Those receipts... *For My Lady Endellion*. She gave the money to you.'

'I'm sorry. I couldn't tell you. For obvious reasons.'

'You fucking liar!' screamed Merrin suddenly. 'I asked you directly and you said you knew nothing about it!'

'Merrin,' said Jen quietly. 'We can work through that later. For now… Do you believe all this? What happens next?'

Merrin went to stare out of the window at the black night. 'It all sounds like quite a lovely little fairy story, but for all the sacrificing and heart-stabbing. Do I believe it? I think I do. I think we all have to.' She turned to Taran and Jen. 'As for what happens next… are we going to get the fuck out of Dodge, or what?'

38

MERRIN

'How do you propose we get through the woods?' said Merrin as they stood outside her house. The site was eerily quiet and dark. 'Jen and I tried and there's some weird shit going on in there. We ended up right back here.'

'Avallen doesn't want you to leave,' said Taran. 'He doesn't know any better. He's become so used to the ritual and the sacrifice that it's all he can remember.'

'What exactly are we talking about, here?' said Jen. 'You speak about Avallen as though he's a man. What does he look like?'

Taran shrugged, peering at the trees. 'I think that's just, you know, what's the word? When people give something a human aspect, or something? I don't think he looks like anything. Not anything we would recognise. He's a god.' Taran pointed at the cliff edge. 'I wonder, if we go along there, and try to get through the woods with the sea on our left… maybe Endellion's influence…'

Jen groaned. 'This *Lord of the Rings* shit is blowing my mind. And I think the word you're looking for is anthropomorphism.'

Merrin turned to her as Taran walked over to the cliff, peering along it at where the woods met the edge. She took Jen's hands and said, 'I know this is weird. Fucking batshit crazy. But I believe him. Growing up in Scuttler's Cove… you get used to a lot of the old stories. The folklore. People… believe. And for good reason.'

'OK,' called Taran. 'I think we should give it a— ow!'

Merrin turned to see him slapping his thigh, hard. 'Are you OK?' she said, walking towards him, feeling the welcome freshness of the breeze blowing off the dark sea. The moon was high and full and painted Taran in silver. A thought rose unbidden in her mind. *Get us off here and I'm going to kiss you so hard…*

'Ouch!' said Taran again, slapping his stomach. 'There's something biting me.'

'Oh, no,' breathed Merrin, and began to run towards him. He was hopping from foot to foot, and hitting his arm, his legs, his chest.

And then she was close enough to see them. The spiders. Flowing from the ground, over his feet, up the inside of his jeans. Thousands and thousands of tiny, yellow spiders, glowing in the moonlight. 'Taran!' she yelled.

He doubled over, as though in agony, and screamed. Merrin saw the spiders flowing out of the neck of his shirt, saw his clothes bulging and expanding as they filled them from within. Spiders were all over his face, biting, crawling, covering him.

'The apples,' said Jen, horrified. 'They cured Adaku. Those bites get infected pretty quickly.'

'Go,' said Merrin decisively. 'Run.'

She turned to watch Jen racing towards the apple tree, then looked back at Taran, his face contorted in pain.

'Merrin,' he gasped. 'Go. Go. Get out of here.'

Then he staggered back, almost every inch of his exposed flesh covered by spiders. He screamed, and it was horrible, and still the spiders came, pouring up from the grass, the earth, flowing into him, biting every millimetre of his flesh.

'Avallen, no!' he called, and when he opened his mouth the spiders flooded in. He gargled something else, something unintelligible, but Merrin could guess what.

'He's trying to help you!' she shouted to the darkness. 'He's trying to end this!'

But Avallen didn't answer, merely sent his creatures relentlessly at Taran, who began to jerk and shudder, the venom pumping through his blood, poisoning his organs, overloading his system.

'Taran!' she called, lunging forward to grab him, though her mind screamed at her to do what he'd said, and run, run, run away from the sight of him being consumed.

But it was too late. He pivoted and staggered, and then plunged over the cliff edge.

Merrin ran to the edge of the cliff and threw herself on the grass, inching forward so she could look down. The tide was fully in, the waves crashing against the cliff wall. 'Taran!' she yelled. 'Taran!'

She thought she heard something and listened, head cocked on one side. There it was again. A voice, distant.

'Merrin. Merrin, I'm here.'

Taran. Thank God. He must have hit a ledge, or maybe grabbed an exposed tree root or—

'Merrin. Merrin. I love you,' said Taran, except this time close up, from behind her.

And then he giggled, and it was horrible.

Merrin spun around on to her back. It wasn't Taran at all. It was Bobby Carlyon, standing over her, flanked by Reverend Bligh and Opie Penrose, who had his shotgun cocked in the crook of his arm.

'Merrin, run away with me,' said Bobby, in a perfect imitation of Taran's voice, giggling again. He took a bite from a Nans-Avallen apple and tossed it away from him. Merrin glanced over to the apple tree but it was in darkness, and she couldn't see any sign of Jen. She sent a silent message to her. *Go. Run. Get the fuck away from here.*

'Enough games,' said Bligh, tightly. He stared down at Merrin. 'Get up. It's time.'

She got to her feet, looking at the black void over the cliff edge. Bobby said, 'He loved the sea, did our Taran. Now he's gone to it forever.'

Merrin peered down into the darkness. And there he was, illuminated by the full moon, floating face-down in the surf, his clothes ballooned by seawater. The waves carried him forward, then back, and then he sank under the surface.

The enormity of it hit Merrin like the waves crashing against the cliff. Taran had fallen. Taran was dead. They were going to get off Nans-Avallen. He was going to lead them through the woods. They would run to Scuttler's Cove and get in his van and drive, drive, drive as far away from the town and all this shit as they could. Taran and Merrin and Jen. And now he was dead, battered to pulp as he bounced down the cliff face, blood boiling with spider venom, and if by some miracle he was still alive when he hit the water, drowned within minutes. Taran had gone. Jen had run. Merrin was on her own.

Bligh peered into the darkness. 'That was the incomer. Where did she go?'

'She won't get far,' said Penrose. 'She won't get off Nans-Avallen. Not tonight.'

'What about the Londoners?' said Bobby. 'You said you were dealing with them.'

'I have dealt with them.' Penrose sniffed.

'Why are you doing this?' screamed Merrin.

'You don't understand, child,' said Bligh, almost gently. 'It's the way of things. I wouldn't want this for you, of course I wouldn't. But you walk the path your mother set you on. Now there's no turning back.'

'You don't have to do this,' said Merrin, backing away, trying to sound as reasonable as possible. 'It doesn't have to happen.'

'It does,' said Bligh. 'The Daughter of the Soil and the incomer touched by death. It is as it's always been.'

'We can't risk not doing it,' said Bobby. 'We can't let Scuttler's Cove die. It's our livelihoods. You don't know, Merrin. You went away. You got out. We have to maintain the prosperity of the town.'

'I didn't go on purpose,' said Merrin quietly.

'And neither did you come back because you wanted to,' said Bobby. 'You came back because Lizzie died, and all the woo-woo shit she'd cast to make you forget us just… fell apart.'

They advanced on her, and Merrin took a step back. 'What would you have done if my mum hadn't died? What would you have done if I hadn't come back?'

Bobby grinned. 'We went to see Lizzie, told her that it was time, that she had to bring you back. You know what she said? Not while I have breath left in my body.'

Bobby's smile stretched. He looked quite mad. He said, 'So I made sure she didn't.'

Merrin's eyes widened, and she could see from the stares that Bligh and Penrose were giving Bobby that this was news to them too.

'You killed my mum,' she said.

'You'd be surprised what herbs and potions and lotions Lizzie had in her cupboard. I did a bit of reading up on it all. Borrowed a book from her. She was quite pleased I was showing an interest. Then one day I went to see her. Made her a cup of coffee. With a bit extra in it.' He mimed clutching his heart and rolling his eyes. 'Looked just like a stroke. Left her on the floor. It was quick, Merrin. She didn't suffer. And the spell keeping you away...' He put his fists together then opened them, fingers splayed. 'Poof.'

'You cunt,' said Merrin, and launched herself at Bobby.

Bobby swiped her hard across the face with the back of his hand and she fell backwards, her cheek stinging. She started to get up for another go at him but Bligh stepped forward. 'Enough. Let's get this done.' He reached down and grabbed Merrin's wrist and hauled her up. Then he pressed something into her hand, something cold and hard, and stepped back.

It was the knife. The knife that had been left on her doorstep and she'd given to the police. 'I handed this to Sergeant Wells,' she said. 'How did you get it? Is she one of you?'

'It's a shame for you she had to die,' said Bobby. 'She was on your side.'

Merrin's face fell. 'You murdered her?'

Bobby giggled. Bligh said softly, 'Bobby, you and I are going to have to talk after this. Nobody told you to kill Lizzie Moon, nor Mary Wells.'

Bobby turned to him, his face contorted in a sneer. 'Nobody has to tell me to do anything, *Reverend*. I do what needs to be done, because nobody else has the stomach for it. But everyone wants to reap the rewards, don't they? That's the butcher's lot in life, Bligh. Everyone wants a nice, juicy, succulent chop, but they don't want to cut the throat of a cute little baa-lamb. That's why it takes people like me, and my dad, to stand up and do what needs doing. For Scuttler's Cove.'

Merrin looked down at the knife in her hand. Then she looked at Bobby Carlyon. At Bligh and Penrose. Between them all, they had robbed her of both a mother and a father. She held the knife up.

'You made a mistake giving me this. Come one step closer, I dare you.'

Penrose lifted his shotgun and pulled back the safety with his thumb. 'Don't be daft, girl.'

Merrin waved the knife. 'I mean it, come near me and I'll cut you. You're not going to kill your precious high priestess, are you? Where would your ritual be then?'

Penrose lowered the barrel of the shotgun, but only by a few inches. 'One, I don't have to kill you outright if I shoot you. I can just blow your foot off. We can get this finished before you bleed out. And two…'

'Two,' cut in Bobby, 'you're being a bit presumptuous there. Always knew you were totally up your own arse.'

She frowned and Bligh said, 'You're not the high priestess, Merrin. You're the Daughter of the Soil. You're the sacrifice.'

39

JEN

The apples were rotten. All of them. Jen crouched down beneath the apple tree, sorting through and discarding them. All of them, turned to mush. She looked back at Merrin and gasped. First she saw Taran, writhing and jerking on the clifftop, and then falling straight off into the blackness. Then she saw the three figures approaching Merrin. Jen ran behind the wide trunk of the apple tree and peered around it.

One of them had a shotgun. She bit her lip, wondering what to do. Had they come to help, or…?

Jen's stomach flipped as she heard screaming, but couldn't tell what Merrin was saying as the wind whipping off the sea took her words away. Then Merrin flew at one of the men, who slapped her with the back of his hand, knocking her to the ground.

Not here to help, then.

Should she stay, and go to Merrin, or try to get help? Jen looked behind her, at the dark, uninviting woods. Then she made her decision and ran towards the cover of the trees.

The woods seemed thicker than the last time she had gone this way, and she skirted around the edges, trying to find the path she had followed last time. Focus, she told herself. Whatever is going on here, there's a path. Arthur found it on an Ordnance Survey map. A map made by people. Focus on that. People have stamped their mark on this place.

Just as she was beginning to panic she found the beginning of the path, and leaned on a tree, getting back her breath. She couldn't see across the site now, had no idea what was going on back on the cliff edge. She felt bad for abandoning Merrin, but what could she do against three men, one with a gun? Other than get herself caught too. At least this way, she had a chance of getting outside and raising the alarm.

The thick canopy of the trees hid the bright light of the full moon, and Jen blundered almost blindly forward, holding out her hands against the branches and bushes. Once she was a little way in she risked getting out her phone for the flashlight. There was still no service at all. What had Taran said? Nans-Avallen was somewhere else now. Or somewhen else. She imagined it as two photographs superimposed over one another, the images taken at different times but occupying the same space. Perhaps when she got closer to the road, to the end of the woods, her phone would work again.

As she followed the path, it all began to sink in. A sacrifice. She felt her insides turn to water. Suddenly she stopped, leaning on a tree, and threw up noisily. Panic was rising in her gut as well. She had to get out of here.

A noise ahead of her caused Jen to stop and crouch, eyes wide. She switched off the phone torch and waited, her eyes gradually acclimatising to the darkness. There was a shape, low to the ground some way off the path, snuffling and scratching. Should she run? How far would she get? She took a deep breath and turned on her torch. In the beam, a pair of yellow eyes turned to her. It was a fox, scratching and digging in the dirt. It considered her for a moment, then carried on.

Jen let out a breath, and started along the path again, then she heard another sound behind her, snapping twigs and heavy footfalls on the path. Shit. They'd found her. She started to run when a voice sounded in a loud whisper. 'Jen! Jen! Wait! It's me.'

She stopped and turned, shining the torch behind her. 'Tabby?'

Tabby's hair was mussed, her face streaked with earth, her eyes wide and swivelling. 'Jen,' she said. 'What the fuck is going on?'

Tabby came up to her and grabbed her arm, glancing around. 'I mean, seriously, what the fuck is happening?'

Jen barely knew where to start. 'Where are the others? What are you doing here?'

Tabby put her hand over her mouth, shaking her head. 'They're back at the farmhouse. I don't know what's going on.' She gripped Jen's arms with both hands and said in a breaking voice, 'I think they might be dead.'

'Shit,' said Jen. '*Dead?* How?'

Tabby just stared at her. She looked like she was on the verge of her mind just snapping. 'I called for you but you were fast asleep. I left you a note. We took cabs to Penrose's farmhouse. It was funny at first. Very rustic. The others were all enjoying it. But I wasn't feeling too well. Had a bit of a stomach ache all day.'

'Let's carry on walking,' said Jen. 'This path leads out to the road.'

'Maybe we should go back and get one of the cars,' said Tabby. She was staring at her phone. 'Do you have any signal? My phone's dead.'

Jen shook her head. 'No. And we can't drive off Nans-Avallen. There are trees all at the road-end of the site.'

Tabby frowned. 'What? Trees? How can there be trees?'

'Tabby,' said Jen gently. 'Tell me what happened at the farmhouse.'

She took a deep, ragged breath and said, 'Penrose served up all this food. Local fare. Cornish pasties and this stargazy pie, with fish sticking out of it. Everyone thought it was delicious. They couldn't get enough of it. Then he brought out this apple pie.'

'Nans-Avallen apples?' said Jen.

'Possibly. I don't know. But I didn't touch any of it. My stomach was in knots.' She gave quite a desperate smile. 'You become adept at pretending to clear your plate when you've had a couple of eating disorders.'

'Was there something in the food?' said Jen.

Tabby nodded, her eyes welling up with tears. 'I think so. Simon fell asleep at the table, but that's not a rare occurrence. We were all laughing. And then, Adaku dozed off. And Paul and Arthur and Timothy. I was sitting there, staring at them, wondering what was going on. I heard Penrose in his kitchen, whistling and singing. I got a very bad feeling. I knew then that he'd done something to us. So when he came in, I pretended to be asleep as well.'

'What did he do?'

'Just laughed, and then put his coat on and went out,' said Tabby. 'As soon as he'd gone I went to wake the others.' She put her hand to her face, tears falling down her cheeks. 'Jen, I couldn't. I couldn't wake Paul. Or any of them. They didn't have pulses. Oh god, Jen. I didn't know what to do. So I just got out and ran, ran back in the direction I thought was this way. I couldn't get a signal, then my phone fucking died. Eventually I crashed into these woods, and I saw the light from your phone.' Suddenly she was sobbing. 'Paul's dead, Jen. I know it. They're all dead.'

Jen put a hand on her shoulder. 'Maybe not, Tabby. Maybe they were just really heavily drugged. The quicker we get out, the quicker we can get help.'

Tabby nodded, and said in a small voice, 'OK.' Jen took her hand and they began to run down the path, the branches of the trees whipping into their faces, their feet stumbling on roots. Suddenly Tabby stopped. 'What's that?'

They fell silent, listening. A scratching, digging sound. Jen frowned and shone her torch into the undergrowth. The fox stared at her, then resumed its burrowing.

'Fuck,' said Jen. 'The woods. They've turned us around again. Fuck.'

Perhaps getting out of here was not going to be all that easy. But Jen didn't tell Tabby that.

'Wait,' said Tabby. 'Shine your light over there again. I'm sure I saw something.'

Jen did, and Tabby was right. The fox looked at them again, then slunk off into the undergrowth. Jen stepped off the path and pushed through to where it was digging, Tabby holding on to her arm. She shone her torch down on the ground and yelped, jumping back.

'Oh my fucking god,' breathed Tabby.

Staring up at them were the dead, sightless eyes of Maggie. Buried in a shallow grave, the front of her top stained with dark blood, dirty plasters all over her face and exposed arms. Tabby sank to her knees. 'Oh my god.' Then she threw up noisily into the dirt.

'Penrose took her to the station,' said Jen, remembering. 'Or rather he didn't.' She looked at Tabby and grabbed her by the shoulder. 'We need to move. Get up. Tabby, get on your feet.'

'Why is Penrose doing this?' moaned Tabby as Jen dragged her along the path. *Keep focused*, she told herself. *Stay alert. Stay on the path and don't get turned around.*

'He wants you all out of the way,' said Jen through gritted teeth. 'There's some major shit going down, Tabby, and I don't even know where to properly start with it. But all I know for sure is that if we don't get out of these woods and get help, then there are going to be a lot more dead people on Nans-Avallen, you, me and Merrin among them.'

They blundered on through the trees, Tabby sobbing behind Jen. She was starting to feel sorry for her. Tabby had always been the nicest one of the gang. Always the one who took Jen under her wing. Now she had been plucked from her safe, cosseted world where she was one of the top dogs, and was running through dark woods with her husband and friends probably murdered by a homicidal farmer, and she was not coping with the change in status very well at all.

'Fuck!' yelled Jen. She stopped and Tabby barrelled into the back of her. Jen shone her torch into the undergrowth, its beam picking out Maggie's half-buried corpse.

'How is this happening?' said Tabby uncomprehendingly. 'We've been running in a straight line on the path. How are we back here?' She sank to her knees on the path and began to sob.

Jen took a deep breath and turned to face her. 'Right. Just so you understand how serious this is. You're not going to like it and you're not going to believe it. But under that apple tree lives a god, and every generation or so he requires a sacrifice to bring prosperity to Scuttler's Cove. There has to be a high priestess to deliver the fatal blow, who is born in Scuttler's Cove, and a sacrifice whose blood is spilled, an incomer who has been touched by death. Guess which one I am? So I know this is all very difficult at the moment Tabby, but I really do need you to get your shit together just for the next ten minutes and help me get us the fuck out of this situation.'

Tabby took a deep breath and nodded, then Jen helped her get to her feet. They started to walk briskly along the path, Jen keeping her eyes directly ahead. The path must lead out to the road. She knew it did. She'd walked it before.

And then the trees started thinning ahead of them, and Jen dared to let herself feel a glimmer of hope. She took hold of Tabby's hand. 'Come on,' she said. 'I think we're nearly there.'

Tabby just moaned.

'Lights!' Jen said, spying orange dots through the trees. They must be the lights of Scuttler's Cove, or streetlamps on the lanes. She picked up the pace. 'Come on, Tabby,' she said encouragingly. 'Come on. We're nearly out!'

They burst through the trees.

Straight on to Nans-Avallen.

Jen stared. The apple tree was festooned with little lanterns. The lights she had seen from the woods. And standing in front of her was Merrin, flanked by Bobby Carlyon and Reverend Bligh. Penrose was holding his shotgun at Jen and Tabby. She felt the strength ebb out of her body.

'Ah,' said Penrose. 'Just in time. Our high priestess has arrived.'

Jen stared at him, and then at Merrin, who raised her eyebrows, defeated, and looked away.

'High priestess?' said Jen. 'I thought I was your *sacrifice*.'

Penrose laughed. 'That's Merrin. The Daughter of the Soil. No offence to you, but there's no point in a sacrifice if it's not something of value. You play the role of our high priestess. And Avallen's handmaiden.'

'Handmaiden?' said Jen with horror.

Penrose grinned horribly. 'It's purely a ceremonial term these days. We don't really believe you sink beneath the earth to serve Avallen. It just means we kill you at the end, as well.'

'Can we just get on with this?' said Reverend Bligh testily, looking up at the bright full moon.

Penrose nodded, indicating with the gun that Jen should move towards the tree. 'We can. We're just waiting for the others to arrive.'

Bobby scowled at Penrose. 'Others? What the fuck are you talking about? What others? There are no others.'

And then five figures, dressed in long, deep-scarlet robes, hoods hiding their faces in shadow, stepped out from behind the apple tree.

Jen looked around at Tabby. The fear and panic seemed to have gone from her eyes. In fact, she returned Jen's gaze with a cold, hard look, and smiled.

'I should win a fucking Oscar for that performance,' she said, and left Jen's side, walking towards the five figures flanking the apple tree. The nearest one threw back his hood and embraced Tabby. It was Paul. The others pushed back their hoods. Timothy, Simon, Adaku, Arthur. All of them. All definitely not slumped dead in Penrose's kitchen. Simon handed a robe to Tabby and she shuffled into it. She said, 'Right, shall we get on with this, or what?'

40

TABBY

The first time Lisa Jones saw another person murdered, she threw up violently all down herself. Except by that point she wasn't Lisa Jones; she had already adopted the name Tabby, borrowed from her great-grandmother Tabitha, and she had just a month before swapped Jones for Grey, when she married Paul. It was on their honeymoon in Dubai that Paul had hinted that it was time to bring Tabby more into the business side of things once they got back to London.

That suited Tabby Grey, Lisa Jones as was, absolutely fine. She had grown up the fourth of five children in a council house near Birmingham, to a father who never worked and a mother who was in an alcoholic stupor for most of her waking hours. Two of her older sisters had got pregnant by the time they were eighteen, and her younger brother was, everyone agreed, destined for jail if he carried on the way he was going. Lisa had never felt part of the family, too intelligent by half, though at school she was written off as just the latest of the Jones brood to pass through the halls of the shabby comprehensive, and like the rest of them would probably amount to nothing.

When she was younger she found solace only with her great-grandma Tabitha, the mother of her mum's mum, who lived in a large but ramshackle house in the countryside. Tabitha had nothing to do with the rest of the family, and in school holidays – sometimes even on schooldays – Lisa would take the three buses and two-hour journey to visit her.

'You're different,' Tabitha would say, stroking the girl's black hair. 'You're different, like me. It jumped two generations.'

'What did, great-grandma?'

'Oh, pay me no heed. Just a silly old woman.'

When Tabitha died, Lisa was devastated. She was fourteen. After the funeral, her mum and her siblings fought over the house and the little money Tabitha had left. Lisa didn't care. Great-grandma Tabitha had left her a book. A leather-bound book filled with writings and drawings and symbols, in the old lady's own hand. Lisa read it from cover to cover three times, and thought she was beginning to understand what Tabitha had meant when she said Lisa was different. That she was like her great-grandma.

When Lisa was sixteen, her father left for another woman, fed up of her mum's drinking. Her mum took up with another fella almost instantly, a vile, rat-faced man with foul breath and an unnerving stare, especially in Lisa's direction. One time she caught him going through the washing basket, touching her knickers.

When he eventually came into her room one night when her mum was in an alcoholic stupor, she drove a pen-knife she kept under her pillow into his hand as he tried to slide it under her duvet. He screamed blue murder and took himself off to the hospital, vowing that when he got back he would *sort her out*.

She packed a bag with a few things, including her grandmother's book, and went out without saying a word to anyone, in the middle of the night, with a wad of notes stolen from the jar her mother kept behind the cereal boxes in the cupboard. Lisa caught the first bus to London, reading the book all the way. She knew it off by heart, by now, but for the first time it started to make sense to her. It spoke of old things, older even than her great-grandma. Much older. But things which Lisa knew, in her heart and her gut, that she had some connection to. And she knew instinctively how she could make these old things work for her.

When she got to London, she knew what she had to do. Find somewhere to live, and a job. And the book would help her. She knew that now. All she had to do was believe. Believe in the book, and believe in herself. The first few days and nights were rough, and it would have been easy for Lisa's belief to falter, living on the streets, gazed at with predatory eyes. But she trusted in the book, and in her great-grandma. She followed her instincts, and her heart, and the instructions written quite clearly in the book. She caught a rat and killed it, and then a pigeon, and a rabbit in Hyde Park. And within a week of arriving in London, she had a job, working in a pizza takeaway, and a damp, tiny room in a shared house. But it was only the start. Lisa had gone. Tabby Jones was here. And she might be at the bottom, but she was going to work her way up.

Ten years later she met Paul Grey. By then Tabby was working at a public relations company, her ability to secure clients and contracts deemed almost supernatural by her jealous colleagues. Paul owned several companies, and Tabby had set her sights on them. It was only when he finally agreed to meet her that she realised she had been aiming at the wrong target. Just as her great-grandma had spotted what was special about her, so she spotted what was special about him. The things she did, the little rituals and sacrifices to slowly, painstakingly further herself, improve her life, they were nothing to the aura that Paul Grey wore. And he saw it in her, too.

That night they slept together in his Mayfair home. A year later they were married. And a month after that she watched him murder a man for the first time.

It was a tramp, a homeless man, enticed to Paul and Tabby's home with the promise of food, and warmth, and a bed to sleep in. They were Christians, you see, bleeding heart liberal Christians. They had to give something back. They had to help, even if it was just one person.

Chained to the stone altar in the basement, the man whimpered and soiled himself. Paul stood by his head, naked, the ritual dagger aloft. The rest of them stood around the altar, Timothy and Maggie, Arthur and Adaku, Simon, Justin. Tabby. All naked, all chanting.

You want to see how real money is made? Paul had said to Tabby. *You want to see where real power comes from? We're not talking about sacrificing pigeons here, you know.*

Tabby could feel it as the chanting grew louder. The power. Rising. Seeping in from somewhere. A presence, from elsewhere. Old, like the knowledge in her great-grandma's book. Paul had been right. This had been nothing like what she had ever done. She had been begging crumbs from the table. This was a banquet with the damned. She felt excited and terrified all at once.

And then Paul, as their chanting reached a crescendo, drove the dagger deep into the heart of the whimpering tramp. And she felt it. Felt the power. Knew the exchange had been made, the contract signed. She was sick, violently and copiously, all down herself. Paul didn't care. He approached her, his hand slick with gore from the wound of the dying man on the altar. He was hard and erect. He wiped his bloody hand roughly across her face, then dragged her to him, kissed her hard, and turned her round, bending her over the altar, where he took her brutally and quickly, as the sacrificial victim shuddered his last and the others, the gang, howled like wolves all around them.

After that, it was easy. Once she'd seen the results of what they did, how everything suddenly went their way in their various business dealings, how money fell into their laps, Tabby understood. Her and Paul, the rest of the gang, they were better. Their lives were more important. Those people on the altar, the sacrifices... they were nothing. Nobodies. They existed merely to die, and to gift their superiors power and money. Nothing died without having lived, and life – the life she craved, deserved – could only come after death.

At last, Tabby understood the way of the world.

Contrary to popular belief, male sacrifices were better than female ones. They killed women when they had to, when time or circumstances dictated, but a man always gave a stronger rush of power, a more long-lasting spell of good fortune. Tabby understood why. Those agencies that they sacrificed their victims to, they tasted those tortured souls like fine wine. Women were flat and sour. They gave up too easily. Deep down inside of them, they always knew, or suspected, that eventually they would be murdered by a man. It was ingrained in them. So when it happened, they accepted it with dull, terrible finality. With men, it was different. They refused to believe it was happening to them, that it could happen to them. They were the apex predators, top of the tree. They tried to fight or lie or buy their way out of their fate. They pleaded and begged, and when they finally died, the seeping presences they were sacrificed to rejoiced and the rewards for the gang were all the more sweet.

It was empowering, and addictive, and Tabby could never get enough. Even when their business interests were booming, even when they were getting more money than they could ever spend, she wanted more. Needed more. They all did. Which was when Paul gathered them all together with a proposal.

'This is Robert Pengelly,' he said to the gang when the man walked into the study. 'Of Pengelly, Pengelly and Quick, solicitors of Boscanlon, Cornwall.'

'Not divorcing me, darling, are you?' said Tabby, and they all laughed.

Mr Pengelly laid his briefcase down on the table and brought out a sheaf of papers. Paul said, 'Mr Pengelly represents a party in a town called Scuttler's Cove.'

'Sounds ghastly,' said Adaku.

'On the contrary, it's highly sought-after,' said Mr Pengelly. 'And a plot of land has come up for sale, owned by one of my firm's long-standing clients.'

'And what's special about this land?' said Simon, leafing through the photographs in the brochure Mr Pengelly had prepared. 'It looks like a field on a clifftop.'

'It is,' agreed Mr Pengelly. 'But it comes with planning permission, subject to one or two conditions, for a small development of executive homes.'

'I'm thinking a summer bolthole,' said Paul.

Maggie glanced at the brochure. 'Couldn't we just buy something ready-built? Maybe a nice fisherman's cottage? Why this godforsaken plot?'

'Because it comes with something else.' Paul smiled. He looked at Mr Pengelly.

'You might say a sitting tenant,' said the solicitor. He coughed. 'Not a human one.'

They all fell silent, and then started to talk at once until Paul held up his hands. 'I'll tell you more later, but for now… isn't it time we stopped just getting scraps from these rituals we have to perform every month or so?'

'Fairly considerable scraps, darling,' pointed out Tabby.

'Yes, but nothing compared to what we'd get,' said Paul, his eyes shining, 'if we owned our very own god.'

'God?' said Adaku.

'It's called Avallen,' said Mr Pengelly. 'But that's just the name the locals gave it. It's older than them. Older than anything. It sleeps beneath the site. And it gives prosperity to Scuttler's Cove. But that comes at a price.'

'I'm not enjoying the sound of this,' said Timothy meekly.

'Shut up,' said Maggie. 'What price?'

'A sacrifice,' said Mr Pengelly. 'With fairly specific terms. And not very often; once a generation, perhaps. To renew the compact between Avallen and the people. And the pieces are in place for that to happen again.'

'Which means,' said Paul, sitting back, 'that we can step in. Stage a takeover. Buy the land, and assume control of the contract. And the prosperity Avallen gives to Scuttler's Cove, he will give instead to us.'

Tabby leaned forward. 'What are these… specific terms, Mr Pengelly?'

'It involves two people. A Daughter of the Soil, conceived and born according to the rituals. She is identified, and moves are afoot to bring her back to Scuttler's Cove. And a second party… an incomer touched by death.'

'And that,' said Paul, a self-satisfied smile on his face, 'is where you are going to come in, Justin. How are things going with that common northern girl you've taken up with?'

41

JEN

Bobby Carlyon stepped forward and said, 'Somebody needs to tell me what the fuck is going on here.' He turned to Penrose, his face furious. 'This isn't a spectator sport, Penrose. It's a sacrifice. Have you been selling fucking tickets down at the Star and Anchor? And what's with the bloody robes?'

Penrose shrugged. 'They like a bit of theatre, the Londoners.'

'You said you'd dealt with them!'

'I did. And very lucrative dealings we had too.' Penrose allowed himself a thin smile.

Paul stepped forward. 'We're not spectators. We've not come to watch. We've come to take ownership of what's rightfully ours. Nans-Avallen, and he who dwells beneath it.'

Bligh scoffed. 'You cannot own a god, little man.'

Paul returned his stare. 'You can own anything, if you have enough money. Even a god. Your kind has taught us that, priest.'

Jen met Merrin's gaze. The two stared impassively at each other. Jen tried to send a message through thought alone. *What the actual fuck is going on here?* Merrin gave the minutest of shrugs. She turned to Tabby, and the others.

'You planned this all along? This is the big investment opportunity you've been talking about?'

Tabby smiled. 'Yes, darling, it is. And we did plan it all along. Everything has been moving towards this moment. From before you even knew us.'

'You must have considered yourself quite lucky that Justin died in that accident,' said Jen, her voice cracking. 'Your incomer touched by death, landing right in your laps.'

Simon boomed a laugh. 'That was no accident, Jen.'

She felt the world spin too fast. 'What?'

'Oh, it wasn't meant to be like that,' said Arthur. 'The plan was to draw you in, then Justin would go and visit your dear old mum in that godawful fleapit you'd locked her away in, slip some minimum-wage flunky a wad of cash and some pills cooked up by Doctor Heygate, and she'd have gone peacefully in her sleep, and you would have been indeed the incomer touched by death.'

'Unfortunately,' said Adaku, 'the idiot went and fell in love with you properly. Said he wasn't going to do it. That we'd have to find someone else.'

Jen was reeling. She couldn't process all this. Tabby said, 'And then it got worse. He wanted out. So you and him could go and play mummies and daddies somewhere.' She shook her head sadly. 'So we arranged a little accident. Used our… influence to have some yokel drive straight into you with his big tractor spike thing. Dear Doctor Heygate wrote up his medical report. Then we whispered in the man's dreams until he did the decent thing and offed himself.'

'Nobody leaves,' said Paul. 'Justin found that out. So did Maggie.'

Jen stared at Timothy, who at least had the good grace to look away. She said, 'You killed Maggie too. And you were OK with that, Timothy?'

He stared at his feet. 'Nobody leaves.'

Jen looked back at Tabby. 'What do you mean, you used your influence? Whispered to that man in his dreams?'

She laughed lightly. 'Darling, this isn't our first rodeo. We have been using the… *numinous*, let's say, to further our fortunes for quite some time now.'

'It is, though, our biggest rodeo.' Simon smiled.

'And our most ambitious acquisition,' agreed Paul. 'Speaking of which…' He looked to Penrose.

Bobby stepped in between them. 'I have heard enough of this shit. Avallen is not for sale. We have served him for generations and we will carry on doing that, and he will bring prosperity to Scuttler's Cove. He's not a fucking investment opportunity.'

'I very much think he is,' said Paul evenly. 'You're right, he's brought prosperity to Scuttler's Cove for a long time. Now he will bring prosperity to us. Lots and lots of lovely prosperity. Avallen is going to make us all very, very rich indeed.'

'You're already rich,' said Jen.

Tabby laughed. 'One can never be too rich or too thin, Jen.'

Bobby squeezed the bridge of his nose and turned to Penrose. 'You double-crossed us, Penrose. You double-crossed Avallen. You lied to us.'

Penrose laughed. 'You know what the biggest lie of all is, Bobby Carlyon? That you lot, and your forefathers, serve Avallen. Honour him. Pay tribute to him. You don't. You enslaved him. And then you conveniently forgot that and dressed it up in folklore and myth and sacrifice. You enslaved Avallen, and now he's changing ownership, like slaves do.'

'I won't fucking allow it,' growled Bobby. 'I'm not having it. We're doing this ritual, and we're doing it as it's always been done. For the benefit of Scuttler's Cove.'

He lunged, and grabbed the knife from Merrin's hand. Then he stalked towards Paul. 'You first, big man. I'll cut your fucking throat and then kill the rest of you and then we'll do what needs to be done.'

'Bobby!' warned Penrose.

'Fuck off, Penrose, or you'll be next,' spat Bobby.

'Bobby! Turn and face me!'

Jen gasped as Penrose lifted his shotgun. Bobby turned and sneered at him. 'You wouldn't dare, old man.'

Then Penrose blew Bobby's head off.

There was silence on Nans-Avallen as the shot ricocheted around the trees. Bobby lay spread-eagled on his back on the grass, a mangled mess of blood, bone and brains where his head used to be. A cold wind suddenly whipped up off the sea, shaking the lanterns in the apple tree, rippling the fabric of the Londoners' robes. Merrin locked eyes with Jen. She knew exactly what she was thinking.

They set off at a run together, heading for Merrin's house. If they could get inside they could at least try to lock themselves in a room, arm themselves with knives, anything to escape this insanity. What if they could hold out until morning? What then? Would it be too late to perform the ritual?

Jen's mind was whirling. It had all been a lie. Everything. She'd been marked out from the beginning. Justin was in on it.

The idiot went and fell in love with you properly.

They were going to kill her mum. Justin was going to kill her mum. So Jen was touched by death.

And then it got worse. He wanted out.

None of them had ever liked her. It was all an act. To bring her here. To bring her here and take part in this ritual, so the rich could get richer.

So you and him could go and play mummies and daddies somewhere.

They'd killed Justin. And now they wanted to kill her. Or make her the handmaiden of Avallen. Which sounded far, far worse than death.

They were halfway to the house when Merrin seemed to trip and fall. Jen slowed to help her, then felt something writhing around her ankle, and she went over too. She tugged at her leg, but it was held fast. A root, sinuously snaking out of the ground, wrapped around her foot. Merrin had the same. More roots and vines poked through, wrapping themselves around their legs, their arms, tightening around Jen's waist.

Avallen was not going to let his sacrifice go so easily.

Nor his handmaiden.

Merrin looked at her, anguish in her eyes. 'I'm sorry,' she said.

'It's not your fault,' whispered Jen. She pushed her hand, held fast by the roots, towards Merrin as far as she could. Merrin did the same, and their little fingers just managed to touch.

And then a light seemed to go on in Merrin's eyes.

'What?' said Jen urgently. The others were walking towards them. 'What?'

But Merrin didn't get the chance to tell her. They were both grabbed and the roots and vines started to release them, and they were pulled to their feet, surrounded by the Londoners and Bligh, and Penrose, with his shotgun held up.

'Shall we finally get this thing done?' said Penrose. 'Unless you, Reverend Bligh, have anything to say? Bearing in mind what became of Bobby Carlyon?'

'There's a new church roof in it for you, Bligh,' said Arthur. 'I mean, we do like to give back, when and where we can.'

Jen saw Bligh consider for a moment, then he said, 'Yes. Let's get this thing done.'

They took Merrin and tied her to the apple tree, crucifixion-style, the ropes wrapped around her middle and her wrists. The Londoners put their hoods up, and stood three either side in a circle. Reverend Bligh went to pick up the slate and tin knife from Bobby Carlyon's hand and Penrose pushed Jen forward until she was standing in front of Merrin.

She stared into Merrin's eyes, willing her to try to tell her what she had thought of. She had a plan, Jen was sure of it. Merrin just looked back, her face impassive, giving nothing away. The little lanterns swayed in the branches of the apple tree. The boughs were empty of fruit now, the apples rotting on the ground around them.

Jen felt sick, sick to her stomach. It felt as though there was a weight in her gut, dragging her downwards, altering her centre of gravity. Making her feel unbalanced, different.

She thought of Justin, and a sob escaped her lips. He had really loved her. He had really loved her. He wanted to get them both away from all this. She thought of the last time she had seen him, three months ago, when they came here, to Nans-Avallen, to see the house. The house she thought was going to be their coastal idyll, the two of them. She thought of the last time they'd made love.

'Or maybe a playroom?'

'Why, Mr Luther, whatever do you mean? Some kind of sex-dungeon?'

'No,' said Justin, suddenly serious. 'I mean, a playroom. As in, for children.'

She'd kissed him then, tenderly at first, but with increasing passion. And they'd made love, right there, on the carpet in that room, before driving back to London, a journey that they never completed. Because of them. Because of Tabby and Paul and all of them.

Three months ago.

She felt the heaviness in her stomach, the strangeness, the otherness.

So you and him could go and play mummies and daddies somewhere.

'Oh my god,' Jen breathed.

Bligh forced the cold handle of the knife into her hand.

'It's time,' he said.

42

MERRIN

There was a storm coming in. The wind was getting higher, whipping Merrin's hair across her face, violently swaying the lanterns in the tree branches above her. Jen faced her, looking into her eyes, almost pleadingly. She wanted there to be a plan. An escape. A last-minute rescue. Merrin couldn't promise any of that. All she had was a feeling, the vaguest of inklings, the germ of an idea. She wished she knew what it was.

Jen mouthed something to her.

I'm pregnant.

And then it all fell into place.

Bligh stepped forward, holding both hands high, looking up into the branches above them. 'My maister Avallen, *neb a les dhe'n aval dy ha diwetda genevys dh'y gila*! Lord Avallen, who sleeps beneath the apple tree, it is time for you to awaken!'

Merrin felt the ground tremble beneath her feet, as though with a hum of machinery. The tree felt warm against her back. She looked down and saw the faintest of glows emanating from the base of the trunk.

The Londoners, heads bowed in their robes, began to whisper in Cornish, their learned lines sounding clumsy and unnatural in their mouths. Penrose had been right, though. They liked a bit of theatre. So Merrin decided to give them a little more.

Bligh walked to her and grabbed her left wrist, and pulled the silver ring from her little finger. The tattoo there was almost shining with the same yellow glow that was getting brighter at the base of the tree, the symbols clear and defined on her flesh.

'We bring to you a Daughter of the Soil,' said Bligh, raising his voice over the growing wind. 'Whose sire was killed on this very tree, who was birthed in the sacred vale of Nans-Avallen. Look! She bears your mark, Avallen!'

The Londoners began to chant louder, saying the same thing over and over again. Merrin didn't know much Cornish, but it was probably something Penrose had dreamed up for them, to make it all a bit more thrilling. To make it seem more than what it was.

One woman being forced to kill another.

Bligh turned to Jen, grabbed the wrist of her hand holding the knife, and held her arm up high. 'We bring you an incomer, touched by death. She bears your knife, Avallen! Your knife forged from the tin and the slate on which the land is built. We bring you your handmaiden!'

The tree was getting warmer, and more... tactile. Merrin felt herself sinking into the bark a little. The glow seemed all around her now, leaking from the cracks and fissures in the tree trunk.

Penrose beckoned to Paul, who walked forward, standing alongside Bligh. He pulled back his hood and the Reverend said, 'Avallen, we bring you those who would be your servants, who would honour you and pay fealty to you, and in return beg your indulgence and your prosperity!'

There was a low rumble of thunder overhead. Merrin saw Jen look up, then lock eyes with her. Bligh threw his arms up again. 'So has it always been, so will it always be! Lord Avallen, spirit of the apple tree, god of the orchard! We bring you these offerings!'

Bligh turned and grabbed Jen's arm, roughly dragging her closer to Merrin. He forced her hand forward, his bony fingers clamped around her fist to stop her dropping the knife. 'Sacrifice!' bellowed Bligh. 'Blood! A handmaiden!'

Jen was crying, shaking her head. Bligh forced her to press harder, and Merrin felt the sharp point of the blade prick through her top, into the flesh between her breasts.

'I won't do it,' sobbed Jen.

'Oh, but you will,' said Bligh. He gripped Jen's hand harder, his knuckles turning white. 'One push. That is all. I'll help you. And then it will be over.'

'Wait!' called Merrin. She felt the first spots of salty rain on her face.

'There is no waiting!' said Bligh. 'The hour is at hand!'

'She'll do it herself,' said Merrin, keeping her eyes on Jen's.

'I won't,' said Jen, her face crumpled, tears rolling down her cheeks.

'Is this what you want, Avallen?' roared Merrin suddenly. 'A sacrifice forced by the hand of a man? Does that fulfil the terms of this ritual?'

The tree seemed to pulse against Merrin, the glow abating slightly.

Paul turned to the others, then Penrose, and hissed, 'What is she doing?'

'Delaying the inevitable,' said Bligh. 'It won't save her. She is the Daughter of the Soil. She is the sacrifice. It is as—'

'It is as it's always been,' said Merrin. 'So you keep telling us. So men keep telling us.' She threw back her head and yelled into the night sky. 'Men who enslaved Avallen! Who took him away from his love!'

'What are you doing?' whispered Jen.

The ground trembled again, causing Penrose to stagger slightly.

'You are the Daughter of the Soil,' shouted Bligh. 'It is your place to die here! You carry the mark of Avallen, which I tattooed upon you myself! You are bound to Nans-Avallen, you always have been. By your own mother! Now, enough! High priestess! Drive the blade in by your own hand, or with the help of mine, I don't care.'

'I can't,' said Jen, shaking her head, as Bligh took tight hold of her and prepared to thrust the point deep into Merrin's chest.

'You must,' said Merrin gently. 'Avallen will not fully awaken until the sacrifice is made.'

'That is the way of things,' agreed Bligh. 'I am glad you have come round to this, Merrin. It is what Lizzie would have wanted.'

Merrin fixed him with a dark stare. 'You know, for a long time, I've been wrestling with the fact that my mother birthed me purely so that I could be a sacrifice on this night. I had begun to hate her for what she had done to me.' She looked at Jen. 'But every mother who births a child does so into a world that is dangerous, and fearful, and filled with sadness and terror. Every single mother. Lizzie Moon was no different, it's just that she knew exactly what danger and fear and sadness and terror were my destiny. And like any mother, she took steps to protect me. Until she couldn't, any longer. Like your mother, Jen. She protected you until she couldn't. And those of us who become mothers ourselves, we take on that mantle. We bring children into a world that is filled with horror. And yet we do it. And we try to protect them, until we no longer can, and we try to make a better world for them.'

She stared at Bligh. 'Lizzie Moon had more goodness in her little finger than any of you men have in your whole bodies.' Then she turned to Jen. 'So yes, do it, Jen. Let us awaken Avallen, bring him forth. And hope that the world we usher in will be a better one. Spill my blood, Jen. Use the knife. Spill the blood of one that is connected to this land, the Daughter of the Soil. Sever that connection.'

'I must say, this is awfully good value for money,' she heard Simon whispering loudly.

Merrin met Jen's eyes one more time. She raised her eyebrow. Then waggled her little finger.

Jen's eyes widened. She understood. She shrugged Bligh off. 'I'll do it,' she said. 'Like Merrin said, I'll do it. It's men who have caused all this. Men who have ruined it all. Let it be the women who finish the job.'

Then Jen held the knife high. The ground shuddered again. The tree felt to Merrin as though it was on fire at her back. The light that was coming through was almost blinding. Avallen was almost here.

Jen grabbed Merrin's wrist, and turned to Bligh. She said calmly, 'It was Tabby who told me that this needs saying sometimes. You really are fucking with the wrong bitches.'

And cut off Merrin's tattooed little finger.

Merrin screamed with the agony of it. She felt blood gouting from the wound, and Jen stepped back, looking around wildly. Overhead, lightning flashed, and thunder followed but a second later. The wind that had been blowing over Nans-Avallen suddenly intensified, blowing the lanterns from the trees, lifting the robes of the Londoners. Rain started to fall. And from the tree, the light that shone from within brightened until it was almost too much to look at.

'What. Is. Going. On?' shouted Paul, trying to hold on to his hood. 'What is happening?'

'Avallen comes through!' cried Bligh. 'Avallen is awake and coming through! Prepare yourself to bear witness to a god!'

'But there's been no sacrifice!' Paul shouted. 'Has it worked? Is Avallen ours? What happens when he comes through?'

Bligh turned to Penrose, almost blown off his feet by the wind. 'Opie! Your daddy saw this before! What did he tell you? Is this supposed to happen?'

Penrose shook his head, horror on his face. 'There has been no sacrifice, not a proper one. And yet Avallen comes. This is not how the ritual should be, Bligh. He's been cheated. That which binds the Daughter of the Soil to him has been severed. But not in the proper way. There's no telling what he'll do.' Then Penrose turned, and started to run into the darkness.

Jen stepped forward and cut the ropes binding Merrin to the tree. The pain in her hand was excruciating, almost blackout bad. With the knife Jen cut a strip from her T-shirt and began to wrap Merrin's hand. She whispered, 'What happens now? Have we stopped it?'

Merrin shook her head. 'No. I don't know what we've done. We've freed Avallen. But without the binding ritual.' She looked at Jen. 'It could be the fucking end of the world for all I know.'

Suddenly, Jen was knocked off her feet. Behind her was Paul, his face seething. He bent down to pick up the slate blade. 'No,' he said, shaking his head. 'We won't be robbed now. Not after all the work we've put into this. If Avallen requires a sacrifice to bind him to us, then he's bloody well going to get it.' He turned round. 'Tabby. Here.'

She ran over, bent double against the wind. Paul pushed the knife into her hands.

'Do it.'

She stared at him. 'Why me?'

'Because it needs a woman!' he yelled. 'I don't know why! An incomer! Touched by death!'

'I'm not touched by death!' screamed Tabby.

'Yes you are!' shrieked Paul hysterically. 'The fucking cat got run over last year. You cried for days! Now take that knife and kill this bitch and let's get this over with.'

Tabby held the knife high as Paul took hold of one of Merrin's arms, pushing her back against the hot tree trunk. It felt spongy, elastic, as though she could sink right into it. She saw Jen stirring on the ground. Adaku took Merrin's other arm, blood still pumping from her hand where her finger had been severed.

'Do it,' said Paul through gritted teeth. The wind was howling around the tree. The light was getting brighter and brighter. 'Drive that knife into her heart! Jesus Christ, why has this gone so bloody tits up? Could things get any worse?'

'Oh, you have no idea,' said a voice behind them.

43

ENDELLION

Long ago, men respected the land and the sea in equal measure, and it was a more harmonious time.

This is not that time. I have slept for long, so long, slept like a catfish, one eye half open, keeping a weather watch on my world, without engaging with it fully. And what a world it has become. The land is despoiled and the oceans befouled. The air is choked and the waters ruined.

I have slept for too long.

Yet who can blame me? For what other cure is there for a broken heart than to withdraw from the world? In that way, gods are no different from men. But my ages-long slumber has not cured me, no, not at all. It has deepened the fissures in my soul like the trenches in the deepest seas, hardened my heart like the carapaces of the crabs that do my bidding, sharpened the pain to a fine point like the teeth of the fiercest predator.

And now I am awake, and my fury is unbound.

They took my love away from me, because we dared to not give them the bounty they had become used to. They did not understand, or chose not to understand, that to keep giving, the land and the sea must be allowed to renew, to lie fallow for a time, to replenish. They just wanted more and more, and gave no thought to where it might come from, or what effect their hungers might have.

One year. That is all we asked, my love and I. One year to rest, to recuperate, to replenish, renew. No, said the men. The gods have deserted us. So we must get them back. And they manufactured what they thought would be a way to appease us. Death and blood and sex. Do men think of anything else?

It was to my sweet Avallen, lord of the land, god of the orchard, that they directed their offerings. Because he was a man, in their eyes, and that meant they could understand his hungers, and lusts, and they could give him what they believed he desired. They remade him in their image, which is what men do with their gods. All the better to understand them, and thus own and control them.

Me, they did not care to appease, for the oceans are vast, and teeming with life, and they never considered there would ever be an end to that. As I awake from my chamber on the bed of the sea, I see that while I have slept they have been proved wrong. The silence in the oceans is almost deafening. Some life, that was once so abundant, almost gone forever now, hunted to the brink of extinction for profit.

While I slept, they fed my love with blood and death and sex and turned him into a corpulent, lazy, mirror-image of themselves who had forgotten his own purpose, his own joy in his mere existence. Who had forgotten his boundless capacity for love, and that his love was meant for me.

They named him a god then turned him into a monster.

And me? Endellion, they turned their backs upon.

All, save for one line of blood that drizzles through time, honouring me, worshipping me, and in my slumber I rewarded them, the Tregarth men, with the bounty of the sea. And now I am awake, and it is thanks to the Tregarth man, the one who never forgot Endellion, who never gave up hope, who sought to reconcile Avallen and I.

Who now floats, lifeless and bloated, in the blackness of the sea. Of my sea. My domain. Where my power is absolute.

Because no, not lifeless, not quite. A tiny light flickers within, like the glow of an anglerfish in the sunless depths. Did you know only the female anglerfish has this bioluminescence? It is woman who brings light, always. Men bring only darkness.

And here, in my darkness, Taran Tregarth sinks, and dies, but dies slowly, because he is in my domain and he is loyal to me. And it is time I repaid that loyalty. Because it is in my power to do so.

Rise, Taran Tregarth. Rise through the depths, rise to the surface and the air. Let the sea knit your broken bones, let the sea purge the poison from your body, let the sea buoy you up so you can rise, gasping, and fill your lungs with air.

For I am the Lady of the Sea, and you are my acolyte, and you have awakened me. Now you have a new purpose, to be my envoy, my ambassador, my herald.

Rise, Taran Tregarth. Live. Crawl from the sea, as the first living things did at the dawn of time, and climb the land, and tell them. Tell them that Endellion is awake, and she comes to reclaim her lost love.

Tell them that her fury is unbound.

44

MERRIN

Merrin almost forgot the excruciating agony in her left hand as she stared at Taran, standing there, soaked to the skin. But alive. Definitely alive. And holding Penrose's shotgun, the old man lying prone on the ground behind him.

'How?' was all she could say.

'The Lady of the Sea has returned me,' said Taran. The Londoners had fallen back at the sight of the gun, slowly raising their hands. 'There will be no sacrifice today. Nor any other day. It's over.'

Bligh was staring at him. He said slowly, 'We saw you fall. Saw you drown, if you weren't dead already. This is impossible.'

Taran smiled serenely. 'I am the resurrection and the life, Reverend Bligh. Surely it doesn't come as that much of a shock to you? When you dare to deal with gods, expect the impossible.'

But despite what Taran had said, despite the fact there was no sacrifice, it wasn't over. Merrin could feel it. The apple tree was trembling and throbbing, and she heard it creak and groan. Almost as if it was growing. The light had not abated, and the heat from the tree was almost unbearable.

'Avallen still comes,' said one of the Londoners. 'Should we be here?'

'Avallen comes,' said Taran with a nod, 'because you have awakened him and brought him through.'

Merrin stared down at her severed finger in the grass, the tattoo on it glowing with fierce golden light. Taran smiled at her. 'You've been very clever. You have freed Avallen without death. Only women could have broken this cycle.'

Bligh was backing away, and stumbled over Penrose's unconscious body. 'You don't know what you've done. Things have always been done correctly, according to the proper rituals and rules. This… We don't know what will happen now. Avallen free. Without the succour of a sacrifice. You've let him loose into the world.'

'That's always been the trouble,' said Merrin. 'You've been doing things so long, adhering to the old ways so much, that you never once thought to stop and say, is this right? Can there be another way?'

'And there is another way,' said Taran. 'And this is it.'

'But the old ways…' said Bligh.

Taran smiled. 'This is an *older* way. A way that things once were, and should always have been.'

There was a flash of lightning and a long rumble of thunder. The rain started coming in hard, driving down, the wind tearing across Nans-Avallen. Paul shouted, 'We should get out of here!'

'Nobody gets out of here,' called Taran. 'We are all honoured and invited guests.'

Jen ran to Merrin's side. Merrin held her tight as the gale buffeted them, the rains drenched them. 'Are we going to die after all?' she whispered.

Merrin didn't know.

'Invited to what?' said Bligh.

'Avallen is free,' cried Taran, holding up his arms. 'Endellion is awake. The dowry has been paid. It is time for gods to be reconciled. It is time for their wedding night.'

The ground shook, so violently that Merrin heard a crash from the direction of the houses, and then one of the car alarms sounded, shrill and intrusive. The apple tree seemed to shudder, and Merrin was knocked off her feet by a branch that whipped into her. She looked up and the tree seemed to be growing, getting bigger, taller, the branches stretching and thickening, the light from within it intensifying to a blinding white.

Jen screamed, and dragged Merrin to her feet. Everyone was running, blindly, in all directions. Everyone except Taran, who stood stock still, hands raised to the sky. A bolt of lightning forked through the night, and illuminated him, and it was as though he was calling down the storm, calling down the wind and the rain.

'Oh, God preserve us,' Merrin heard Bligh say.

He was standing, staring out to sea. Merrin looked too, and gasped, as the ground shuddered again.

At first she didn't understand what she was seeing. The rain-drenched sky just seemed... blacker, somehow. Out to sea. As though someone had carved a hole in the blackness, peeling back the night to reveal an even darker layer beneath. There was a thundering sound, as though something impossibly vast was galloping towards them. Merrin felt a gentle pull on her, as if the air was being sucked out of Nans-Avallen, out towards the sea. The wind turned cold and wet, the rain saltier than it had ever tasted before on her lips.

And then, as it roared closer, Merrin finally understood. Out to sea there was a wall of water, growing as it thundered towards them. A tidal wave. Huge. She couldn't even estimate how big it was. But it was growing, swelling, moving towards them, crested with foaming white, bigger than anything she had ever seen, or believed was possible.

—

When Merrin was six years old, her mother took her up the path to Nans-Avallen on a bright, spring day, when the trees were coming back to leaf and the sea was crested with white, a cool breeze whipping across the field. Even at that age, Merrin knew that you didn't play up at Nans-Avallen. But it was different, walking with her mum. Lizzie Moon was scared of nothing, and therefore Merrin was scared of nothing while she was with her.

'Mummy,' she said. 'What will I be when I'm grown up?'

Lizzie smiled. 'Whatever you want to be, Merrin Moon.'

'An astronaut? A train driver? A spy?'

'You can be all those things, if you want to be and you work hard enough.'

Merrin thought about it, looking out to sea. 'Maybe I'll help people like you do. In Scuttler's Cove.'

'You could do that,' agreed Lizzie. 'But I think you are bound for bigger things than living in Scuttler's Cove.'

Merrin gaped up at her. 'There's nowhere better in the world than Scuttler's Cove!' she said, aghast. 'I'm never going to leave! I'm going to stay with you here forever.'

Lizzie squatted down, pushing the hair from Merrin's eyes. 'Ah, you say that, darling, but that's because you've never seen anywhere else. There's a huge world out there, Merrin. And you are going to go out there and see everything and be anything.'

Merrin pushed out her bottom lip. 'Why don't you want me to stay with you in Scuttler's Cove forever and ever and ever?'

Lizzie gave her a big hug. 'Oh, that's what every mummy wants for her daughter. For them to be together forever. The thing is…' She paused, and stood up, and took Merrin's hand. 'Come with me.'

Lizzie walked her away from the cliff edge, towards the apple tree that stood in the centre of the field. Merrin pulled back at her mummy's hand. The children at school said the apple tree was haunted and if you went there at night you would be gobbled up by a monster.

'It's fine, little one,' murmured Lizzie. 'Nothing can hurt you while I'm here.'

They stood in the shadow of the tree, looking up. Merrin said, 'There are no apples.'

'No. They don't come until later in the year. August, maybe.' She squatted down again, holding both Merrin's hands, and looked at her. 'But sometimes, every now and again, the apples come early.'

'I'd like to see the apples come early,' said Merrin.

'No, you wouldn't. And you won't. Because I won't let that happen.' She pointed up at the tree. 'When the apples do come, what happens to them?'

'They fall off the tree,' said Merrin. She wasn't stupid. She was six years old. She knew what happened to apples.

'Exactly.' Lizzie nodded. 'Don't you think the apples would rather stay up on the branches, where they feel safe, and are surrounded by all the other apples they know, and protected by the tree?'

'Yes,' said Merrin, feeling suddenly sad for the apples.

'But they don't. They fall. And sometimes they don't fall very far, but sometimes they hit the ground and roll away, and keep rolling, and go to places a long way away from the tree, and see and do things they would never have seen or done had they stayed hanging from the branches forever.'

Merrin thought she understood. 'So I should roll away, like an apple? And go and find adventure?' She frowned. 'But other people don't leave Scuttler's Cove. Everybody does what their mummy and daddy does, when they grow up. Taran will be a fisherman and Bobby will be a butcher. Like their daddies. Why can't I stay and do what you do?'

Lizzie said thoughtfully, almost to herself, 'When you're young, Merrin, and especially when you're a girl, other people think they know best about what you should do and what should happen to you. They think that because things have always happened a certain way, then they should continue to happen that way all the time. But that way, nothing ever changes for the better. And I have a feeling that you, Merrin Moon'—she playfully poked Merrin in the nose—'will be one of those people who does something different with her life, not just what everyone expects or predicts.'

Merrin looked at the apple tree, then back towards the sea. 'When do I have to go?'

Lizzie laughed. 'Not for ages, years and years and years and years. You don't have to think about it at all. Now, what do you say to an ice cream...?'

—

The sea roared and the light from the tree was blinding, and Merrin felt blindly for Jen, her fingers brushing her hair and grabbing hold, drawing Jen to her. The two women hugged as chaos reigned all around them.

'We're going to die,' sobbed Jen. 'Can you see that? That wave? What is that? How is that even possible? It's the end of the world.'

'Yes, I think you're right,' said Merrin, closing her eyes and burying her face in Jen's neck. They pushed themselves back against the tree, and whatever shelter it might afford. 'The end of one world, anyway. The end of one way of doing things.'

'I still don't understand,' wept Jen. She said again, 'We're going to die.'

'This was Taran's plan all along,' whispered Merrin in her ear. 'I get it now. Taran and my mother. They worked together to do this. To break the cycle. They trusted us to not do what was expected of us. And we did it. We did it, Jen. We changed everything.'

Then Merrin wept herself, for the loss of Lizzie, and all those wasted years, but she understood. She got it. 'They set it all in motion,' she said to Jen. 'But it would never have worked without us. Without you and me.'

A squall of seawater drenched them, the herald of what was coming, what was bearing down on them, gathering force and power as it tore from the sea and closed in on them. Merrin held Jen tighter, and closed her eyes. It was time.

'Endellion comes to reclaim her love,' Taran cried. It was the last thing she heard before the raging sea crashed down onto Nans-Avallen with apocalyptic fury.

45

ONE YEAR LATER

'Yes, and we're here in Scuttler's Cove on the Cornish coast, one year after the devastating tsunami that caused a tremendous loss of life and destroyed an exclusive housing development on that cliff you can see behind me.

'This was only the third confirmed tsunami to hit the British Isles, and the first one in almost three hundred years. The previous one was also in Cornwall, in 1755, and before that you have to go back to the Mesolithic period, some six thousand years BC, when a huge wave is thought to have hit the West Coast of Scotland. The Scuttler's Cove tsunami dwarfed either of those, making it the worst such event in British history.

'People are coming together here today to remember those who were killed that night, and a memorial service is being held in London for those who had bought holiday homes up on that cliff, which they thought were going to be their Cornish paradise getaway. For Paul and Tabitha Grey, Arthur and Adaku Hepton, Timothy and Margaret Gomm, and Simon Furlish, that exclusive development turned out to be their final resting place.

'Here in Scuttler's Cove, the townsfolk are remembering the local people who lost their lives, including the vicar of St Ia's Church, Reverend Colin Bligh, landowner

Opie Penrose, and local butcher Bobby Carlyon. All their bodies were recovered in the aftermath of the tsunami, and one man is also believed dead, though his remains were never found, fisherman Taran Tregarth.

'It's a sombre mood in Scuttler's Cove today, which for the past year has had the effects of that terrible night literally looming over them – you can see behind me that the cliff, known locally as Nans-Avallen, suffered a huge landslide after being hit by the tidal wave, and half of it crashed into the sea below. The houses built there are all gone, and the whole site is off-limits for safety reasons, and is likely to remain that way. Only a lone apple tree still stands on the site, which has become something of a symbol of resilience and hope to the local people here. Back to you in the studio.'

Merrin watched the TV reporter making his live broadcast, then turned to leave. A young woman stepped in front of her. 'Sorry to bother you. I know this is a difficult time for everyone. But I wondered, are you local? Might you want to go on camera to talk about what happened that night?'

Merrin pulled an apologetic face. 'I'm sorry. I don't really remember that much about it.'

'Not sure how you could forget that,' the researcher muttered.

Janet would be cursing her, saying that she'd just passed up a great opportunity for free publicity. But Janet didn't own the gallery any more. Merrin did. She walked over to where the workmen were just finishing fitting the new sign above the window. *The Moon Gallery*. Her painting of the apple tree, framed by a full moon, formed the new business's logo.

Merrin did remember what had happened that night, but she couldn't explain it. As the water bore down on them, she felt herself sink back into the trunk of the apple tree. Her and Jen. It was as though they were enfolded by the tree itself, taken inside it. Everything was a blinding white light, and they had no idea how long it lasted, holding on to each other and screaming. And then suddenly they were falling, onto the grass, the ground awash with seawater, fish flipping in the mud, seaweed hanging from the apple tree's branches. And Nans-Avallen was half-gone, the houses flattened, and everyone dead. And Taran had disappeared.

They had been spared. The high priestess and the sacrifice. As a thank you, she thought, for freeing Avallen and breaking the cycle of the ritual. As dawn broke and the sound of sirens sounded in the distance, Merrin and Jen had fled Nans-Avallen, nothing to stop them now, and never looked back.

Bligh and Bobby had been right, in a way. Not carrying out the ritual had killed Scuttler's Cove. After a fashion. The second-homers had fled, because nobody wanted to live on a harbour that might be swamped by a tsunami at any moment, though the tidal wave had been put down to a freak earthquake that had occurred in the sea just beyond the town, and was unlikely to ever happen again. The tourists stopped coming. All the houses bought up by Londoners were put back on the market for a song, and the local people who had never been able to buy in their own town suddenly found they could. Merrin bought back her mother's cottage.

The Star and Anchor became a drinker's pub again, and a lot of the boutique shops and cafes closed down. But they were replaced by other things, because Scuttler's

Cove might have died, but it had been reborn. After the tsunami, the fishing off the coast became incredible. There was no Tregarth to fish the waters now, but plenty more who were prepared to take the sea's bounty. Scuttler's Cove became a working town again, famous for its fish that went to restaurants and hotels all across the country, and beyond. Even now, standing by the gallery, Merrin could see the fishing boats crowding the harbour, bringing back the morning's catch.

The tourists would come back, eventually. Scuttler's Cove was too beautiful for it to be ignored for long. But it was as though the tsunami had washed away more than the houses on Nans-Avallen; it had washed away the greed. Now that the people of Scuttler's Cove owned their town again, they would not let it go so easily.

Every day, Merrin scanned the sea for some sign of Taran. She had searched the land around Nans-Avallen, looking for the tiniest clue. But he had gone, and she had no idea where. She still hoped that, just as Avallen had looked after Merrin and Jen that night, so Endellion had done the same for Taran.

Merrin left the workmen with instructions to lock up, and she waited outside her cottage for the taxi to take her to Boscanlon, where she would take the train to London. She looked down at her left hand, at the missing little finger. No, she wouldn't forget that night. Not for the rest of her life.

—

It was the first time Merrin had been to London since she had left to go back to Scuttler's Cove after her mother died. Or, she now knew, was killed by Bobby Carlyon.

After more than a year in Cornwall, London felt big and dirty and overwhelming. When she got off the train at Paddington there was a big screen showing the news report that she had seen being filmed that morning. She stood and watched it again. At least Tabby and Paul and the rest of them would have been happy that they got top billing over the local people who had died that night. Then she went to find a cab to take her to the address on the card she had received in the post the week before.

The taxi deposited her outside an anonymous-looking office block in the east of the city. And there was someone else standing outside. She turned and smiled as Merrin climbed out of the taxi and they embraced on the street.

'Jen,' said Merrin. 'God. It's so good to see you.' She stepped back and held her at arm's length. 'You're looking fabulous. Where's Teddy?'

'With the nanny,' said Jen. 'Of course.' She gave a lopsided smile.

'Well, you've got all that money. Shame not to enjoy it. He's what, six months?'

'And teething.' Jen looked down the litter-blown street. 'How's my investment going?'

'Sign went up this morning,' said Merrin. After that night, Jen had gone back to London, and wondered what to do with herself. The gang had gone, but she still had everything she had before. The house and the money. And a baby on the way. Jen had decided to make the money work, not just for her, but for others. She'd started a fund to help people in Scuttler's Cove set up in business, or buy homes. It was Jen who had convinced Merrin to buy the Driftwood Gallery when Janet decided she wanted to retire, and became the main and only investor. 'You should come down and see it.'

'I will, this summer,' said Jen. 'Be nice for Teddy to visit the seaside.'

They both looked down at the cards in their hands. Identical, black on one side with just the word GEMINI in white. On the back, written in cursive script, the words, 'We know what happened on Nans-Avallen. We need to talk to you about it.' And a date, a time, and this address.

'Any more idea what this is about?' said Merrin.

Jen shook her head. 'Couldn't turn up anything on them. Even paid some people to try to get information. Nothing substantial at all. A few guarded mentions on frankly wacko Dark Web pages, real weird conspiracy theory stuff. Mentioned places called Withered Hill and Scratch Moss, but couldn't turn anything substantial up on them either. Whatever this is, it's going to be weird shit.'

Merrin took a deep breath. 'Well, if there's one thing we know a lot about, it's weird shit. Shall we go and find out what they want, then…?'

ACKNOWLEDGEMENTS

It's a few days before Halloween 2024 as I write this. The book you have just read – unless you're one of those odd people who jump to the acknowledgements first, in which case… the butler did it. That'll teach you – is just short of four months from publication and its predecessor, *Withered Hill*, has been out for four weeks.

Withered Hill was my first real foray into horror fiction, and I've been blown away by the response to it. Canelo did an absolutely amazing job on turning my words into a darkly beautiful package, and the same has to be said about *Scuttler's Cove*. I hope anyone who enjoyed *Withered Hill* feels the same about this book, and if you've read this one first, I hope you'll check out *Withered Hill* as well.

I've found in the writing of these two books that horror in general has a lot to tell us about the world we live in, and folk horror in particular. There has been a huge rise in interest in folklore in the last couple of years, and folk horror is also surfing that wave. I think what we like about folk horror is the moral ambiguity of the genre; there are often no easily identifiable heroes and villains. Just people trying to get on with their lives, some in a different way to others. The horror comes when different worlds – usually the modern and the older ways – clash, and are found incompatible. But which one is 'right' is a matter of personal choice and belief.

That *Withered Hill* was a success – and hopefully this book will be too – is down to a huge number of people, not just me, the bloke with his name on the cover. Kit, my editor at Canelo, has been a champion of both books and ensured they are the best they can be, Kate has been supreme in publicising the book and spreading the word. Sarah Whittaker's eerie and gorgeous cover designs are sublime. And special mention must go to Tom Abba, who created *Roads to Withered Hill*, an interactive, immersive audio accompaniment to my first book. If you haven't checked it out, go do so immediately. It'll unsettle you and keep you fit. What more could you want?

My agent Laura Williams, as ever gets my undying gratitude. And thank you to all those wonderful authors who read the books before they were published and said fine words about them, and to all the reviewers and bloggers who talked up the book. I'm truly grateful.

Finally, thank you to my wife, Claire, and children Charlie and Alice, and all my family and friends, who have been behind me all the way.

David Barnett, West Yorkshire, October 2024